FAMILY SURVIVAL

SUSAN THAYER KELLEY

ISBN: 979-8-89031-300-3 (sc)
ISBN: 979-8-89031-301-0 (hc)
ISBN: 979-8-89031-302-7 (e)

One Galleria Blvd., Suite 1900, Metairie, LA 70001
1-888-421-2397

The reason I wrote this book, *Family Survival,* was, because when COVID hit, I saw the different situations it put families in, how it changed lives forever, and how many died from the virus. I saw how hospitals were full of COVID and couldn't take in any more patients. So I decided to write about what could happen to three teens who's mother died of the virus and the predicament it put the teens in because their mother had been a single mom just trying to keep her children safe from an abusive husband., keep a roof over their head, and food in their bellies. I reasoned that the most important thing to the youngsters when their mother died, would be to not let anyone separate them into different foster homes, where they might never see one another again. And thinking like a teenager, I could understand how they might come up with a plan as they did in my book so they could keep their family together.

My book is purely fictional. I have no knowledge of any similar situation in my book. I just wondered what would three children feel like, and what might they do if such a situation as depicted in my book were real.

1

"What's going on, mom?" Aiden asked. "Why wouldn't they admit you to the hospital?"

"I know, honey. But they don't have any beds. The hospital is doing the best they can with so many people with COVID. But they said to call in the morning to see if they have one then. Or they said I could try another hospital, but the closest one is two hours away and I don't want to do that. So, let's try tomorrow."

"Well, they could have put a bed in the hallway, and you could have stayed there if they didn't have a room. This just doesn't seem right. You need to be in the hospital. You're just as sick as those other people. After all, you have COVID too." He paused before continuing, "So they just send you home to gasp for air?" Aiden was very upset with the system, but there was nothing he, nor his mother, could do. He felt helpless. He had become the man of the family since his mother had moved away from his father, and he took his responsibility seriously.

Their mother had contracted COVID-19 from a workmate who had tested positive for the virus, and even though she felt certain she would be alright, she insisted her kids were to stay away from her. She certainly didn't want any of them to get sick.

She had been a beautiful woman when she was younger. However, with the hard life she had lived both with her husband and afterward, and now with COVID, her beauty had faded into a skeletal shriveled woman.

"It's not that they don't have a room, they don't have a bed," she corrected Aiden. "They called the other hospitals around and they are full too. It will be alright, honey. We'll just have to wait a little longer."

He helped his mother out of the car and into bed after arriving home. "Can I get you anything?" he asked after getting her settled in.

"Just some water and a couple of pain pills."

He did as he was asked, wearing his mask for protection each time he was around his mother. He went to wash his hands to begin fixing supper for his two sisters, using hand sanitizer after washing. He asked Lottie to help prepare food, and Izzy to set the table. They ate in silence, each contemplating their mother's illness and inability to be admitted into the hospital. Aiden had insisted neither one of the girls were to go near her, that he would take care of their mother alone. He fixed a plate of food for his mother, but when he took it to her, she shook her head. She was too sick to eat.

After cleaning up the table and kitchen the three siblings settled down to do their homework and soon it was time for showers before bed. They put their masks on, went to their mother's bedroom door, gently opening it to say goodnight to her from the doorway. They each said they would say a prayer for her to get into the hospital tomorrow and that they loved her. She could only gently wave her hand, but just barely. After Aiden made sure she had everything she needed, all three children went to bed very worried about her.

The next morning, the girls got ready for school. Lottie took after her mother in looks, the patrician nose, full lips, long blonde hair that laid in waves down past her shoulders, and ice blue eyes that would make any man's heart melt. She took one last look in the mirror, approving of what she saw. Izzy was a nice mixture of both her mother and father. She had the ice blue eyes like her mother, but had the dark curly hair like her father, and dark skin tones. Aiden looked just like his father, which he hated because he had no love left for his father, and each time he looked in the mirror, he vowed he would not be like his father, no matter how hard he had to try. He was dark complected, had large brown eyes, and wavy black hair.

Aiden let the girls know he was not going to school because he wanted to try to get their mother into the hospital as soon as possible in case they had an opening for her. The girls put their masks on, went to their mother's room to say goodbye, but because they noticed she was sleeping, they left to catch the bus without saying goodbye.

After the girls left, Aiden went to his mother's room to see if she felt like eating, but because she was still sleeping, he crept back out of the room. He phoned the hospital only to be told to call back later in the afternoon because nothing had opened yet.

Again, at noon Aiden went to his mother but again she seemed to be sleeping. He stood staring down at her for what seemed like forever. Then he reached down, put his fingers on her wrists to feel for a pulse. When he didn't feel any, panicking, he moved to her neck to feel for a pulse, but once again he felt nothing. He was frantic and in shock. This couldn't be happening. Surely, he just missed feeling a heartbeat. He tried again, but again felt nothing. Then he put his fingers under her nose to detect breathing but felt nothing. "Oh, no! Mom, no, please, no! Wake up, mom, please wake up!" He gently shook her, but she didn't respond. Then he yelled at the top of his voice, "Noooooo!"

He jammed his fingers through his hair wondering what to do. He just sat in the living room staring off into space, questions and thoughts swirling around in his head. What would happen now, to him, to his sisters? What should he do? For the first time in several years, he hung his head and asked God for help.

When the girls arrived from school, he was still sitting in the living room. He looked and felt lost. When the girls saw him, they knew immediately he had not gotten their mother into the hospital. He sat the girls down to tell them about their mother's death. Both girls burst into tears. He was quiet, kneeling in front of them, he wrapped his arms around both girls as they cried until they were all cried out. He was unable to hold back his tears as well although he tried not to cry. Lottie was the first to speak. "Is she……is she here?"

"I didn't move her," Aiden replied, wiping tears from his cheeks.

"Should we call the police or something?"

"I've thought all afternoon about what to do and I've come up with a plan. We're going to bury her and leave here."

"What?!" both girls asked incredulously in unison obviously in shock.

"Bury her!" Lottie declared. "Why? And why leave?"

"I don't want to leave!" declared Izzy. "This is home!"

He tried to explain. "Look, mom didn't think she would die, she just knew she'd get over this, but that didn't happen. She didn't tell me what to do if she should die. So, we have to figure this out on our own."

Lottie jumped up and ran to her mother's room with Izzy right behind her. They didn't want to believe their mother was dead. When they looked down at their mother their crying got more intense and louder. The girls hugged each other for a long time.

When they went back into the living room, Izzy said, "Why Aiden? Why did she have to die? I think the hospital killed her! She should have been in the hospital, and I don't see why we need to leave home. My friends are here. We could call dad and he could come and live here with us." She was talking fast, almost incoherently, without thinking.

Aiden answered, "And you want to go back to that?! He's a drunk, Izzy! He can't keep a job. He drinks up any money he makes, and he beat mom and us. Do you remember that?! Do you really want to go back to that?!"

"No, but ..." then she began to cry again even harder.

Aiden put his arm around her, "I'm sorry, Izzy, I didn't mean to make you cry, but you need to understand what you are suggesting is not a good idea. And I know you're upset about leaving your friends. Charlotte has friends she's leaving too, and I'll have to leave my friends and my girlfriend. This isn't going to be easy for any of us. Believe me, I understand."

Lottie then asked, "OK, we don't want dad coming to live with us, so why do we need to leave?"

"Well, think what would happen if we do call the police. They'll contact Child Family Services since we're still young. I'm 17, you're what, Charlotte, 15? And Izzy, you're only 12. They'll come and take us away, and put us in foster homes, and we'll probably never see one another again. I want to keep us together. I'm pretty sure you both want the same thing," he looked deeply into their eyes.

"So, what do we do then, just leave mom here and leave?"

"Yes, but we don't leave her in her bed. We need to bury her so people won't come looking for us. We can make it look like we've all left together, including mom."

"*WE* have to bury her?!" Lottie cried out in disbelief.

"I know. It's a terrible thing to think about. But it's the only way. If we leave mom in her bed, eventually someone will find her and know we've taken off, and they'll come looking for us. We can bury her in one of the horse stalls, cover it with straw and maybe no one will ever find her. We can wrap her in a blanket so we don't have to look at her, and we can have our own funeral over her grave."

"I can't!" declared Lottie, "I just don't think I can." She began to cry again.

"Come on, Charlotte, you can do this. Don't you remember when old Rex died? You were able to bury him." Rex had been their dog of many years and it was hard to see him dead when he grew old and just gave up on life one day.

"This isn't the same thing, and you know it. This is Mom," she replied angrily.

She just sat there staring at him, wiping at tears running down her face, while Izzy blurted out, "Well, I won't do it! I refuse to do it! I didn't help bury Rex, and I'm not going to bury mom!"

"Ok," Aiden stated, "You two don't have to help, but I just can't go off and leave mom laying in her bed. That just doesn't seem right and think how it would be if someone eventually came and saw her like that. I don't think mom would want that.

"Look, you two fix something to eat, I'll go out and start digging in one of the horse stalls." He rose to go outside, leaving both girls stunned and crying. However, eventually Lottie showed up in the barn with a sandwich and chips for him to eat. They sat together on a bale of hay, Aiden eating but being plied with questions from her.

"So where do we go? And why won't they be looking for us? How do you think we won't get caught and still sent to foster homes?"

"Well, I think I've got it all figured out. But I'm just asking you to trust me on this." He looked into her eyes and added, "Please." She could only nod and hope he was right.

Soon the grave was dug, and Lottie told him he didn't have to do it alone, she had decided to help. So, after Aiden had their mother wrapped in a blanket and with him at her head and Lottie at her feet, they carried her to the barn. Aiden found a board they laid her on, and with ropes, they lowered her into the ground carefully. After Aiden filled the hole with dirt, he asked Lottie to go get Izzy and bring her to the barn.

When she went inside to get Izzy, she found her slumped on the couch crying. Lottie went to her, put her arms around her, and gently rocked her back and forth. "I'm so sorry, Izzy. I know how hard this is, but let's go to the barn. Don't you want to go say goodbye to mama?"

Izzy swiped at her tears with her sleeve, rose, and slowly followed Lottie to the barn. Aiden tried his best to talk about the nicest things he could think of; about what a good and loving mother she had been to them. He talked about good memories they had shared with her. Then he said a short prayer and wrapped his arms around both girls as all three cried. Eventually he began covering the grave with dirt and straw.

Walking back to the house, he said, "No homework tonight. I want to be ready to leave day after tomorrow, so tomorrow I want both of you girls to pack everything you think you'll need; clothes, toiletries, hygiene things, sleeping bags, blankets and pillows. Things like that. Both of you start making your lists tonight and tomorrow you can get busy gathering things up. Bring everything into the living room, and I'll inspect what things you've got.

"Tomorrow morning, I will call her boss and let him know mom isn't getting any better and will not be in to work for quite some time. I'll also call our schools to let them know we're going away to our grandmother's house to take care of her because she is very sick and we don't know how long we'll be gone. Then I'm going to take mom's car a long way away, leave it, and bring a bus back home. I've got her bank card, so I'm going to withdraw money we might need. And when I get back home tomorrow, I'll begin gathering more things to take.

"And one more thing, don't call any of your friends about any of this. If even one person knows what we're doing, they could tell someone, and then they'll start searching for us, and you know what that could lead to. Promise me, no phone calls."

They both promised, and then Lottie asked, "But wait! Why are you taking mom's car somewhere and leaving it? And our grandmother is already dead, so how are we supposedly going to her house?"

"I know that but everyone else doesn't know that. And about the car, if our car is gone, people will think we've just gone somewhere. That way they won't be looking for any of us, at least not for quite some time. Besides, if we use the car to leave in, if anyone should be looking for us, we could be spotted by the police on the road and then we'd be caught."

Izzy then asked, "So without the car, how are we supposed to leave?"

"Well, we have our horses. I'm planning on making a rack like the Indians used to make that we can pull behind a horse to carry all our things. Besides, I want to stay away from the roads, and horses are the best way to do that."

Izzy then said, "I'm scared."

Aiden replied, "I know, Izzy, me too. But I'm trying to keep us together. I know you want that too, right?"

"Yeah, I do. I'm just so… so sad about all of this. I don't see why mama had to die when so many others have had COVID and got over it."

Lottie then put in, "We're all sad about this, but there's nothing we can do about it now, so let's try to be strong. Let's get some paper and begin making lists of things to take."

"At least," Aiden added, "it's almost May so the weather will be warm to sleep outside. It could be worse. It could be winter."

As the girls got busy writing their lists, Aiden went back to the barn to pick out some tools they might need, along with his camping gear, and bring it all into the living room. Then he went to his mother's bedroom closet and retrieved his father's rifle and ammunition. He had hidden it when his parents were still together, because he was afraid his father might end up killing his mom, or maybe all the family in one of his drunken rages. His mother had taken the gun along with her when she fled from her husband along with her three children.

Aiden also went through his mother's purse, taking what cash she had and her bank card and credit card.

The next morning, Aiden headed out to stop at the bank ATM machine where he withdrew most of his mother's money, and to take the car somewhere. He was thankful that, when his mother had gotten sick, she had told him her pin number for her bank card so he could pay their bills, get groceries and other necessary things for the family. He ended up driving three hours away, then caught a bus back to their hometown. He had paid for the gas he needed with his mother's credit card but paid for his bus ticket with cash so it couldn't be traced. Then when he got back to his hometown, he stopped at the grocery store to pick up some food they could take with them. And because he'd been buying the family's groceries since his mother had gotten sick a month ago, he knew buying groceries would not raise any suspicions.

He walked home from the grocery store glad they didn't live more than three miles outside of town. When he entered the house, the girls had quite a few things laid out in the living room. He was proud of them and all the things they had gathered. They had packed a lot into a couple of suitcases and other things in trash bags.

Aiden went over their lists to make sure they didn't forget important things. Now he instructed the girls to sack up mostly non-perishable food but also a little perishable food they could eat soon, while he went to pack his own clothing and toiletries, including first aid things. After everything was gathered into the living room, he asked the girls about such things as toilet paper, paper towels, and wash cloths, towels, soap, shampoo, raincoats and boots. The girls took off to gather those things they had not thought of. While they were out of the room, he smiled when he saw Izzy had packed her teddy bear.

He also told the girls to bring their phones, mother's phone, and I-pads.

"Why should we bring those things, we won't have connections, or any place to charge them?" Lottie asked.

Aiden answered, "Because if anyone comes to search the house, if they find our phones and I-pads, they'll know something is wrong, because no kid would go away without their technology items."

Aiden told the girls to get their showers and go to bed, while he went to find long poles and tarps to attach to the poles. He decided he should make two racks instead of one with everything they had laid out to take. He found tarps to use to cover all their supplies on the racks in the morning after they loaded everything up and ropes to tie it all down. He couldn't help but be grateful for the training he'd gotten in the Boy Scouts because he would need all the skills he'd learned to get them through this time now, although he was very unsure of the future for all three of them. He went to bed that night worrying about whether they were doing the right thing or not. He tossed and turned all night and woke feeling groggy the next morning.

After rising, he instructed the girls to eat a good breakfast before they began carrying their supplies out to the racks built by Aiden.

The racks were attached to the saddles on his and Lottie's horses after they were saddled, and everything was loaded and tied down. Each of them mounted and took one long look at their home before leaving. Lottie and Izzy both had tears in their eyes.

Aiden purposefully led the girls in the opposite direction from where his mother's abandoned car was. They stayed away from the roads, cutting through fields and open ranges. When they came across a lake, they stopped to rest a while, eat, and give the horses a chance to graze. Aiden was surprised to find the girls had fixed several sandwiches, something he hadn't thought of. After eating and relaxing a little, he said before they continued, "Get your phones and iPads and let's throw them all into the lake."

Lottie, startled responded, "What!? Why?"

"Because we can be traced through them."

"Oh, I forgot they can do that."

Izzy responded, "But I don't want to throw mine away. I need my I-pad, it's got my games on it."

"I know," Aiden said, "But for now, let's get rid of these and I'll try to get you another phone and I-pad, but not until I'm eighteen at least, because then I'll be considered an adult and maybe I'll be able to be your guardian, get a job, and we will be able to find a decent place to live."

"Do you promise?"

"I promise."

Izzy then asked, "When you turn eighteen, will we be able to go back to our house and live there?"

"No, because it will be repossessed and sold by then."

They rode on until around four o'clock when Izzy began to complain that her butt was getting sore. Therefore, Aiden began looking for a place to bed down for the night.

Eventually he spotted a clearing that was surrounded by trees. He set up the tent and spread their sleeping bags out in it. After downing another sandwich, they crawled into the tent early because of the mass of mosquitos that seemed intent on having their bodies for their evening meal.

As they lay in the tent, but before falling to sleep, Lottie said, "Let's make a pact between us three that nothing will ever separate us from each other, no matter what." They all agreed. Then each declared their love for each other before falling asleep. Aiden told the girls how proud he was of them. "I know this has been the hardest day of our lives. But you two have done very well in helping with our plan."

The next morning, Aiden had to wake the girls. He knew they were sleeping so soundly because of the long ride the day before, but they needed to get moving again. Izzy declared she would get up whenever she wanted, and no one was going to make her move until she was ready.

"Ok," Aiden said, "You can catch up with us down the trail. Charlotte and I will go on."

With that she unzipped her sleeping bag and crawled out, and declared, "You can't leave me behind! Remember our pact last night. So, you can't leave without me. So there!" She stuck her tongue out at Aiden.

"Then you'd better get a move on. Let's eat something and get going." They found dry cereal to munch on before saddling up.

Aiden chose to change directions to throw off their trail. However, he knew the racks they pulled behind would make an obvious trail, but hopefully no one would be searching for them anytime soon and eventually their trail would become hidden again by rain and wind.

This day was a repeat of the day before, and again Izzy complained that her butt was hurting. Aiden added a blanket underneath her in hopes that would help. But that evening, he told Lottie to take Izzy into the tent and look to see if she had developed saddle sores. She came out and asked Aiden to find the first aid kit so she could put salve on Izzy's bottom.

The next day, Aiden once again added the blanket to her saddle for padding. She assured him it helped.

On the fifth day, they entered a dense wood, dark from the overhead canopy, only allowing a dappling of sunlight to stream through here and there. In places, it was so dense they had to get off their horses and have Aiden use his machete to cut a path for them. In late afternoon they came to a clearing, and there stood an abandoned cabin.

"Aha!" he cried, "Look what we've found!" He went to gently push open the door to inspect the inside, careful of what creatures he might encounter. When he was certain it was clear he motioned for the girls to come and see it. There was plenty of dust and cobwebs, which was to be expected with a cabin that had been abandoned for some time. There was one bedroom up a narrow stairway, a small kitchen, and a living room, but no bathroom, which was usual since it was in the middle of the woods. There was a small table and two chairs, all old and handmade of wood that had turned gray with age. The unfinished cabinets had also turned gray with age. A wood burning stove sat along the back of the living room, which Aiden was happy to see. They wouldn't freeze next winter. Aiden figured it had been a cabin for hunters to use, so that was why it was crude without electricity or running water.

Aiden told them to look in his camping gear for some rags to dust with and to find a stick to knock the cobwebs down. He wanted to go find some water. He knew they would need water and was certain no one would build a cabin without access to water.

He set out in search of water with his horse and rifle, just in case he came across a bear, wolf, or other creatures wanting to do him harm. He eventually found the water down a slope, a little way from the cabin, a river. Satisfied, he headed back to the cabin.

The girls tried to clean the cabin with what they had, although it wasn't to either one's liking. Aiden scouted around outside and found a shovel and a bucket behind the cabin. He took the bucket and walked down to the river and returned. As he entered, he asked, "Do you think a little water might help?" The girls were delighted to see there was water and went to dig out the soap they had brought. Now they felt they could get the cabin very clean, but wished they had a brush to use to scrub the floor with. But at least they were thankful for the soap and water. They would make do.

After they finished, they came outside to find Aiden unpacking their things. He had laid everything on the ground, unhooked the racks from the horses, and unsaddled them allowing them to graze.

He instructed the girls to take all their food inside to the kitchen. He rewrapped most of his camping gear inside the tarps, except for the pots and pans, a few metal dishes, and some silverware, which he took to the kitchen. He also left the kerosene lantern out. After the girls had all the food and dishes put away, they took their suitcases to the bedroom. Soon they were feeling good about the shape of the cabin, and glad they wouldn't have to sleep in a tent anymore.

Aiden went outside, tied a rope between two trees, tethered the horses for the night, and gave each some oats they had brought for them.

They dug out the remainder of the sandwiches, finished them off, and topped their evening meal off with a protein bar. Afterwards, Lottie asked, "So what are we to do for a bathroom? I'm not seeing one in here."

Aiden answered, "Guess you'll have to go behind a tree, just like we did while traveling. Maybe out back somewhere."

"Oh, that's great!" she replied as she rolled her eyes.

"Eew!" declared Izzy. "That's gross."

"Well, just think of yourself as a pioneer. What do you think they used when they were crossing this country in covered wagons? You do with what you have."

Izzy grabbed the toilet paper and headed for the door, "Ok, but just so you know, I'm not a pioneer, and I don't like your idea. I think we need to talk about doing something about this." After she left, Aiden looked at Lottie and they both began to laugh.

"Not sure what she thinks I can do about it. It's not like there's a Home Depot I can go to and get lumber to build an outhouse."

"That doesn't sound much better."

"I should have told Izzy if she has to do a big job, she needs to take the shovel I found out back so she can dig a hole to bury it. Bet she'll love that too."

The girls complained about feeling dirty, so Aiden had them get the soap and a couple of towels and he led them down to the river. He instructed them not to go in too deep, and he would hide behind a tree but stay close by in case they needed him.

Afterward, they spread their sleeping bags on the floor of the bedroom and turned in for the night.

The next morning Aiden rose first and smiled when he saw Lottie had snuggled down inside her sleeping bag so much that her head was completely covered. He went to the river to have his bath, and when he returned, both girls were awake and up, munching on dry cereal. "So, Lottie," Aiden asked, "why did you have your head completely covered? I would have thought that got pretty hot."

"Because I had something crawl across my face in the night! And tonight, I want to set the tent up in here so that doesn't happen anymore."

"And how am I supposed to set a tent up inside? I have to have dirt to set the poles in the ground."

"Well, I don't know but you've got to do something, I refuse to allow critters to crawl all over me at night."

"The only thing I can do is to bring the tent in and put our sleeping bags inside it and zip it up, but it will be flat on our faces."

"That's better than the alternative anyway, and it won't be as hot as my sleeping bag."

Aiden instructed the girls to brush the horses and curry their manes and tails, then untie them so they could graze on the tall grass. He would lead them to the river for a drink later. He got busy with the shovel scraping leaves into a pile a little distance from the cabin to make an area for a fire. After the girls were done with their chores, he asked them to gather sticks to add to the clearing. Tonight, he wanted a fire and intended to throw their potatoes they'd wrapped in aluminum foil into it for their evening meal.

Then he told the girls he was going hunting and they could relax but to stay close to the cabin. He grabbed his rifle and headed into the woods in hopes of finding a rabbit, bird, or something else a little larger, maybe a deer. However, he returned empty handed, but he wasn't worried because he was certain there had to be wild animals in the woods.

When he returned, he found the girls playing cards at the kitchen table. He said, "Good thing you thought of bringing cards. I'll have to see if I can beat you two at a game later."

"But we only have two chairs. What will you sit on?" Lottie asked.

"No problem, I can stand."

"That will give you an advantage."

"Well, if you'd rather stand, that's ok with me."

"No, I don't want to. You can stand."

Then Aiden brought up something he'd thought of while hunting. "Ok girls, there's something I want to talk with you about."

"You sound serious. What's up?" Izzy asked.

"Well, I know eventually we'll probably run into people, and we've got to be prepared ahead of time for that. I know I'll eventually have to go to a store to lay in more supplies, and maybe even look for some kind of work. So, I think it would be wise if we changed our names right now."

Izzy looked worried, "Change our names," spoken as a statement instead of a question. "I don't like the sound of that."

"Just think about it," Aiden went on. "If we use our real names, someone could realize we're the family they're looking for. You can't just disappear if you're using your real names. And you know we only traveled for five days on horseback, so we aren't that far from home.

"I was thinking each of us could come up with a new name that begins with the first letter of our real names. That might make it easier for us to remember our new names. And if we begin calling each other by our new names now, we won't have trouble coming up with one at the last minute when we run into someone."

"So, I need to come up with a name that begins with a "C", Charlotte said.

"Yes. And Isabelle, you need a name that begins with "I".

Izzy's response was, "Well, I don't know any girl's names that begin with "I".

"You don't have to have one right now. Just think about it. You'll come up with something."

Lottie said, "I like the name Chloe. I guess I could use that name. I looked it up one time. It means 'new plant'. So I'll be like a new plant planted here in the woods."

"Ok, but Chloe doesn't begin with "L". Are you sure you'll remember it?"

"Yes, I know I've always gone by Lottie, but because I've always loved that name and decided if I ever had a girl, I'd name her Chloe. And Chloe begins with "C" like Charlotte."

Aiden said smiling. "OK, Chloe it is then. I'm changing my name to Alex. And we need a different last name as well, so I was thinking of Ryan.

"You can't have a last name like Ryan, that's a first name not a last name." Lottie complained. "I know it has to start with "R", but not Ryan. But we could use Robinson. You know, like Robinson Crusoe."

They all laughed at that.

Aiden agreed and then added, "After all, we are on an adventure also, but I just hope ours doesn't turn out to be dangerous like his."

Izzy stated, "Ok, I've thought up a name for me… Emma."

Lottie said, "But that doesn't start with an "I"."

"No but the beginning sounds the same. Izzy, Emma, Izzy, Emma. See?"

Aiden added, "If you're going by sound only, maybe "Busy" would be a good name for you. It rhymes with Izzy."

Lottie laughed but Izzy looked perturbed. "Ok, stop it you two. Not funny."

Lottie looked at Aiden for confirmation that the name Emma was alright. He consented and stated that from now on they were all to call each other by their new names. He was Alex, Lottie was Chloe, and Isabelle was Emma, and they were all Robinsons.

That evening they started the fire, threw the potatoes into it, and sat back to watch and listen to the crackling sounds emanating from the fire. After digging their potatoes out, Alex stated that he wanted to save the aluminum foil to reuse, and he apologized for not having any butter or salt and pepper to put on the potatoes.

Chloe declared, "That's all right. But having a potato without that makes me think I don't really like potatoes."

"Me neither," agreed Emma.

"So, Alex," Chloe began, "What are we doing tomorrow?"

"Hey, good job, Chloe, you remembered to call me Alex. Ok, tomorrow, what do you say we go fishing? We could cook fish for tomorrow evening's meal."

Both girls agreed that sounded really nice. They became silent then, each in their own thoughts while watching the fire become embers. Eventually, it began to darken as the night began to set in. Alex rose to take the horses down to the river for a drink, carrying a bucket to bring water back to put the hot embers out. He gave each horse some oats, then he tethered them and headed to the cabin for bed.

The next day the girls rose to find Alex had already gotten out the fishing poles and gear and was ready to head down to the river. The girls seemed to be moving more slowly and Alex asked if they were alright.

Chloe answered as she stretched, "At least I didn't have anything crawl across my face last night. But the floor is still as hard as a rock."

"Well, we have more blankets that we won't need until winter, so why don't we add them under our sleeping bags to make it a little softer?"

"Good idea," Emma added.

"Ok, you two. You need to do some exercises to get the blood moving. Jumping Jax." He began counting them out, but the girls weren't following along. "Come on, move," he demanded.

"Do we have to?" Emma complained.

"If you don't, I'll throw you in the river to wake you up."

"Ok, ok," as she began moving her arms and legs. Soon Chloe followed suit.

They fished all morning long and had a good amount of wide mouth bass by noon. Alex stretched one tarp out on the ground when they returned to the cabin to get ready to clean the fish he had dumped on it. He headed to the cabin to get a pan to put the filets in just as Chloe screamed, "Bear!"

Alex yelled at the girls, "Run to the cabin! Quick!" When they got inside, Alex dashed to the window where he could see the bear, which was devouring their fish.

"Do something!" yelled Emma. "Get your gun and shoot him!"

"No, let him have the fish; we can always catch more."

"But we worked so hard and so long to catch them!"

"And if I shoot him, what am I supposed to do with his carcass? We'll be inviting all kinds of creatures to our cabin to eat it and who knows what kind would come calling, maybe wolves, big cats. Who knows?"

"Oh, geez, I never thought of that."

"But I'll tell you what. I made a mistake today of cleaning the fish outside where the bear could smell it. I won't be making that mistake anymore. So, looks like tonight's meal isn't going to be fish after all. So, what sounds like a good alternative?"

They decided on peanut butter and crackers. Emma opened her mouth to complain, "This really s…"

"No complaints," Chloe said, cutting her off. "We can go fishing again tomorrow. I'm sure we didn't catch all the bass in the river today."

"And tomorrow, I'll clean them inside with the door shut so the bear can't smell anything. Then I'll take the inedible parts and go throw them in the river. And now I have to go find our horses that ran away when the bear showed up. We need to figure out what to do with them in the future to protect them."

Emma answered, "I'm not letting them inside to live with us." Alex and Chloe laughed at that thought.

"Why not?" asked Chloe, but she already knew the answer.

"And have them pooping on the floor? No way! If you do that, you can clean up the mess."

The next day, Alex spent the entire morning looking for the horses, and upon finding them, he tethered them to the rope he had strung for that purpose. Then he and the girls set off to go fishing once again.

They fished all afternoon and again had a nice catch. That evening as they sat around their campfire waiting for the fish to finish cooking, Emma said, "I feel eyes watching me. I think the bear is still close just watching and waiting for us to turn our backs before he comes charging out of the woods to take our fish again."

"Just stay close to the fire and you'll be alright."

"Well, I'm still scared." But they were able to eat without an incident, and soon it was time for Alex to give the horses their oats and turn in for the night.

The next morning, Alex took his axe and headed into the woods to cut branches from the trees to build a fence for the horses. His shovel was the wrong kind for digging a hole for posts, but he'd do the best he could and hope it would hold.

He worked on building the pen for the horses for the next several days, and when it was complete, he was glad to be able to lead them through the gate into the pen. He just hoped the horses didn't realize how flimsy it was and how easy it would be to escape.

When he entered the cabin, he asked the girls, "Who's up for a swim?"

They both jumped up, exclaiming, "We are." They had packed their swimming suits to which they were glad, but at the time of packing they didn't believe they would really need them. Still because you never know what the future holds, they figured it was better to be safe than sorry.

After they swam and dried off, Alex said "I'm getting low on oats for the horses, so I'm going to have to go find a store somewhere. Do you girls remember the farmhouse we saw a little back off to the left? I could go there and see if they can direct me to a store."

"Oh, I don't know about that," said Chloe. "Do you think you should talk to anyone?"

"Well, I guess I could just wonder around and try to find a store myself, but what's the chances of going in the right direction? I could travel quite far only to find out later it was in the wrong direction. And all I'll be doing is asking directions. How sketchy could that be?"

"I know. I figured eventually we'd have to go to a town, but it scares me to think we could get caught and sent to different foster homes. So, just be careful out there."

"Don't worry, I'll be very cautious about what I say. I think I can be vague if asked questions."

"So, when are you going?"

"Hmmm, I haven't really decided, but it needs to be soon. Maybe day after tomorrow. What do you girls think about going into the woods to look for mushrooms tomorrow? This is the time of the year for them, but we'd have to go early in the morning before the sun shrivels them up."

"I'd like that," confirmed Emma, "as long as there's no bears."

"I'll take the gun along to scare any away if we need to. Maybe we could also look for some blackberries, although I'm not sure they're out yet."

The next day they did find a few mushrooms, but not as many as they would have liked, although they figured they could search in other places also.

Alex said, "Then why don't we search again tomorrow. We can't wait on mushrooms, or they'll be gone. I can put off going in search of a store till day after tomorrow."

"Sounds like a plan," Chloe stated.

After finding several more mushrooms the next day, they placed them in a pan along with some water and cooked them over the fire along with some more potatoes. Chloe declared the mushrooms made the potatoes taste better, but she still missed having any butter.

"I'll see what I can do about that, if I can find a store," Alex promised.

Alex saddled his horse the next morning and set off for the farmhouse they'd seen earlier. Emma said after he mounted, "Don't spend all our money, we'll be needing more supplies in the future." He saluted and rode off.

He reached the farm eventually and saw a man in the yard. He rode up to him and said, "Good morning, sir. I'm new around here and have no idea where the closest town is or a grocery store. Do you think you could point me in the right direction?"

"Good morning to you too," he responded. "So, you're new around here. We don't get that too much here. What's your name?"

"Alex… Alex Robinson." He was glad he already had that figured out ahead of time.

"Where do you hale from, Alex?"

"Hale from?"

"Yeah, where are you from?"

Alex wasn't happy with all the questions, but he understood how the southern people were about hospitality, and sometimes downright nosey. He said the first thing he could think of, "Paducah, Kentucky." He knew nothing about Paducah, Kentucky and hoped the man didn't ask him any questions about it.

Thankfully he didn't, but asked, "Well, why would city folk want to move down here to no man's land?"

"Uh, well, my father got a job here, so we had to move."

"That's understandable. So, where's your dad working?"

"I don't know, some factory."

"Must be the new Toyota plant they opened a while back."

"Yes, sir. Probably. I really need to get going; Mom's baking a pie and needs butter so she can get it in the oven."

"Oh, yes. Well, if you go about two miles that direction," he said pointing, "there's a store on the corner of the highway. It's got lots of things we folks in the country need. No sense going all the way into Tupelo."

"Thanks mister."

He started off but heard the man call after him, "Tell Charles that Mr. Simpson sent you." Alex waved that he got the message.

He arrived at the store, dreading the questioning he might also get once again from Charles. He looked around, picking up things he wanted and laid them on the counter to look some more. He asked if the store carried grain for horses, specifically oats, to which the man took him into a room in the back. There he found more than oats. He also found a wash tub so they could do laundry in, and a leaf rake.

Charles did ask him what his name was but nothing more, to which Alex was thankful. As he mounted his horse with the wash tub tied to one side and holding the rake on the other side along with a couple of sacks of groceries attached to the saddle, he started for the cabin. He also noticed out behind the store there were some boards that he filed in the back of his mind for future use.

He didn't want to go all the way back past Mr. Simpson's house in case he had more questions for him, so he decided to try to find a route away from the road and away from his farm. He entered the woods before coming to the Simpson's farm to ensure he wouldn't run into Mr. Simpson.

The girls were very excited to see butter and even milk in one sack.

Chloe asked, "How do you plan on keeping milk from spoiling right away?"

"We can tie a rope around the handle and drop it into the river. That should keep it for a little while."

"Good," said Emma, "now we can have milk on our cereal in the morning."

"And how did it go at the farm you went to?" Chloe asked.

"Well, his name is Mr. Simpson. He did have several questions he asked me, but I think I came up with some good answers. Now just so you know, we moved here from Paducah, Kentucky because our dad got a job working in the Toyota plant that opened recently in Tupelo."

"Oh, geez!" Chloe went on. "More stuff to remember. Well, if I just stay here all the time, I shouldn't have to memorize anything, except to answer when someone calls me Chloe."

"Me too," agreed Emma. Then as she finished emptying the grocery bags and pulling out a newspaper, she asked, "What's with the newspaper?"

"Well, I figured it might tell us some things about where we're living. I was glad to find we are still in Mississippi. I was afraid we'd crossed into Alabama maybe."

"Who cares what state we're in, it's all the United States."

"Yes, but there could be different laws in different states, and I know nothing about Alabama laws. I know in Mississippi I'm considered an adult at age eighteen."

"Oh," was her only reply.

"And," Alex went on, "Chloe, the paper has the date on the top, so why don't you get some paper, make a calendar, and keep track of the dates for us."

"Why? Who needs to know what the date is?"

"Well, I figure after it's June, I could look for a job of some kind for the summer."

Her heart sank because she knew if he got a job, it could mean trouble for them if… if what? She didn't want to think about the 'if' part of the future. So, she tried to put it out of her mind, but hoped Alex would forget about getting a job.

The next day Alex felt like it was much more humid than it had been which meant it might rain. Therefore, he got a tarp, stretched it out, and attached it with ropes around trees to make a shelter of sorts for the horses. He hardly finished his job before the first splatters hit the ground.

Eventually inside, rain began to drip through the ceiling in one place causing the kids to grab a pan to put under the drips. Alex knew he would have another job to do after the rain ended using one of the tarps, if he could figure out how to get up on the roof.

The next morning Chloe came out of the cabin to find Alex was already on the roof wrestling with the tarp. "How'd you get up there?" she yelled up.

"Around back," he replied.

She went around back to see his horse standing beside the cabin. She went back around to the front to yell up to him, "What does your horse have to do with you getting on the roof?"

"I stood on his back."

"You stood on his back?" she asked, laughing.

"Yep. Had to figure it out with what I have. I wonder if I could get a ladder at the store I went to and carry it home on my horse?"

"I'd like to see that one."

It wasn't long before he had finished his job and jumped off the roof, saying to himself, "Another job well done."

Alex had purchased chicken at the store, and that evening they threw it, wrapped with aluminum foil, into their fire. Chloe opened a can of green beans, dumped them into a pan, added some butter, salt and pepper and set the pan on embers at the edge of the fire. They were enjoying their meal when they heard growling. They turned to find a wolf had emerged from the woods, probably because he smelled the meat.

The girls looked at Alex with wide eyes. "Do we run and let him have our food?" Emma asked.

"No," Alex responded. "Stay calm, stay close to the fire." Then he took a stick from the fire, then walked toward the wolf waving the blazing stick back and forth. The wolf wasn't happy obviously, but Alex wasn't put off. He wasn't about to lose another meal even if the wolf was hungry. Soon the wolf gave up the argument and went slinking back into the woods.

However, as soon as they finished eating, Emma declared she was going inside because she was sure the wolf was still out there staring at her. But Alex stated he wanted to stay close to the fire a bit longer to make sure their horses were safe.

The next morning Emma stated that she wanted to go fishing again. They got their poles and tackle box and headed to the river. They caught a few fish and then Emma caught a fish so large she was pulled into the river by an obviously large fish. She was soon out into deep water and was in trouble. She was yelling at the top of her lungs for help. Alex went running up the hill, and when Emma saw him leaving, she yelled, "Aiden, help me! Don't leave me, help me!"

Alex came running back down the hill with a rope in hand, yelling, "Hang on, Emma! I'm coming."

The current had pulled her down river away from where she had fallen in. So, Alex ran down to where she was, threw the rope into the water and told her to grab it, but she was too far from it to grab it. He pulled the rope in and jumped into the river and swam to her. He grabbed her and was able to drag her to shore.

When he pushed her onto the bank, she laid down, closed her eyes, and thanked God for her life.

He laid down by her putting his hand on her back, and said "Are you alright?"

Her eyes came open and she replied, "Thank you, Alex. I thought you were leaving me to die."

He raised up on his elbow, looked her in the eyes, and said, "You know I'd never do that. I love you."

She wrapped her arms around his neck, "I love you too."

"You know you called me Aiden."

"Yeah, I know. I'm sorry. I wasn't thinking. I was so scared, I thought I was going to die."

"That's ok. Don't worry about it. And you know we lost a fishing pole."

"Yeah, I guess we did."

"But just think of how big that fish must have been if we could have gotten him reeled in."

"He was a whopper, right? We could have had fish for a month, if I could have reeled him in."

"Obviously. So, if you're sure you're alright, why don't you go get on some dry clothes. I want to do some more fishing before I come in."

That night they ate their fish wrapped in aluminum foil and seasoned with butter and salt and pepper. They all declared it was absolutely delicious with the seasoning on it. "And without sharing it with a bear," added Emma. They all agreed and chuckled.

They settled into a life of existence, trying to be content with what they had, and even though they were still saddened by what had happened to them, they were determined to make the best of the situation. Alex couldn't help but be proud of the girls for their resilience and bravery.

Eventually Alex decided to try hunting again and headed off into the woods in search of game. When he returned, he held up a rabbit to show the girls. They clapped their hands in delight, but he let them know, as sorry as he was, he would have to clean it inside the cabin so there would be no critter to come and wrestle their food away from them. Even though the girls weren't keen on that idea, they understood all too well.

Emma asked, "So what does rabbit taste like? I've never eaten it before."

"Trust me, you'll love it," Alex replied, even though he'd never eaten rabbit before either.

He was able to make a spit of sorts made of sticks. With a stick on each side of the fire with a "Y" at the top of each and a cross stick over the fire high enough that it wouldn't catch on fire, he was able to run the cross stick through the rabbit and roast it over the fire, occasionally turning the stick so the rabbit was cooked on all sides. The girls both said it was delicious and clamored for him to go hunting more often.

One morning he told the girls they needed to saddle the horses and take a ride. He explained, "If you don't ride a horse often, they get cantankerous and won't mind very well."

They set off on a ride through the countryside the next day. The girls were happy to be able to get away from the cabin for a while. Alex headed them in a different direction than where Mr. Simpson lived so they might not run into him. When they cleared the woods, the sun shone down on the land, making the gently rolling hills seem to come alive. Or maybe it just felt that way because they had been surrounded by so many trees shutting out a lot of the sun for so long it just seemed that way. Still, they were happy they had the shade of the trees because it was getting close to the end of the month of May, and it was getting hotter. They rode for about an hour before returning to their cabin. They had spotted a couple of farmhouses but skirted around them. Alex commented that one house must be owned by a wealthy family because of how large the house was and the excellent looking huge barn.

Once they were back to their cabin, they led the horses to the river for a drink and then let them graze in the cabin's yard.

"You know," Alex said, "I spotted what might be pecan trees when I went hunting the other day. If they are, we'll have pecans next fall."

"Oh, I hope you're right about that," declared Chloe, "I love pecans."

"Guess we'll have to wait and see. But it shouldn't be long before we'll be able to go blackberry hunting. I saw some on my way back from the store, but they aren't ripe yet."

"That's even better. But I'm not sure I like picking them, they have thorns."

"You're right about that."

Emma asked, "Can we go mushroom hunting again?"

"Well, we could try, but I doubt if there's any more around. They tend to like a humid morning, and I don't think we've had enough rain for that."

So, the next morning, they headed out to look for mushrooms, but came back empty handed.

One day it was windy, and Alex noticed that one corner of the tarp over the horse's pen had come loose and was flapping in the wind. He climbed up to reattach it to the tree but lost his hold and came crashing to the ground. He landed on his back, knocking the wind out of him. He laid on the ground trying to breath when Emma came running to see if she could help him.

"Are you alright?" she asked with great concern. Then when he didn't answer, she yelled for Chloe to come quickly.

Chloe heard the desperation in Emma's voice and knew something was wrong. She flew out of the cabin and over to Emma and Alex. "What happened?" she asked as she looked down at Alex.

"He fell out of the tree, and he's not talking."

Chloe bent down and took Alex's hand. "Alex, you have to be alright. You can't get hurt. We need you. Do you hear me?"

"I hear you," he squeaked. "Just…can't breathe."

"You can't breathe? Why not? Are you hurt bad?"

He began to try to get up but moaned in pain.

Chloe went on, "What's wrong? Where do you hurt? I'm afraid to touch you. I don't want to hurt you more."

He was finally able to get his breath back. "I'm ok. Help me up," he said as he reached up to her.

"I think I just hurt my pride."

"Well, from now on, take it easy. We don't need any broken bones."

"Yeah, tell me about it."

She walked with him to the cabin where he laid down on his sleeping bag. Chloe and Emma slipped out of the house where Chloe said, "I know he's hurt worse than he let on. He just doesn't want us to know it."

Emma asked, "So, what should we do?"

"Let's let him sleep for now if he can. When he wakes up, we'll see how he is then. But I don't want him doing anything at all tomorrow."

"For sure." Emma was quiet for a few minutes before asking, "Chloe, what would we do if he's really hurt bad? He could have broken bones."

Chloe thought about it for a minute before responding, "I'm not sure. If he could get on a horse, we could take him somewhere for help. But if he can't get on a horse, I guess we'd have to go for help."

"But then people would find out we don't have a mom and dad."

"I know. So, let's pray he's not hurt that bad."

The girls let him sleep and when he woke up, they asked him how he was feeling. "I'm ok. I got the wind knocked out of me. That's all."

Chloe said, "Well, tomorrow you're not doing anything but resting, and that's that."

"No, I'm really alright."

"I've spoken, Alex, end of discussion."

"Yes, boss."

Alex woke up the following morning feeling sore and was glad Chloe had insisted he rest. He ended up laying on his sleeping bag most of the morning reading a book he'd packed.

The girls took turns going to the river and bringing back buckets of water to pour into the wash tub Alex had brought home from the store. They had clothes to wash. After washing them, they took them to the river to rinse the soap out and spread them over tree branches in order to dry.

Afterward, Chloe grabbed her note paper and began to write up a grocery list of things for Alex to get on his next trip to the store, while

Emma sat on a stump in the yard listening to a Mockingbird. When Chloe saw her, she thought Emma was day dreaming, she looked small, daydreaming in her own world. She smiled because Emma seemed to be doing fine without her games, she used to play endlessly on her I-pad.

Later in the afternoon, Chloe checked and found the clothes had dried, so she and Emma folded them and put them back in their suitcases. Alex was up by then and declared he was feeling much better and wandered outside. Still Chloe was keeping a close eye on his every move, assessing whether he was in pain or not.

The girls searched and found enough sticks for a fire for the evening meal to be cooked on, although they both declared it was getting too hot for fires. Still, they had the meat Alex had brought from the store and it had to be eaten soon or it would spoil. Again, the meat was divided into individual pieces, wrapped in aluminum foil along with small potatoes, and corn on the cob. They all declared it was the best meal yet, but Alex reminded them they couldn't eat that way very often. Still, it seemed to be a celebration because Alex hadn't gotten hurt any worse.

The girls made sure the horses got their oats that night and carried water to put out the fire before turning in. Alex praised them for their abilities, stating they were becoming quite the pioneers. Emma replied, "Yeah, I'm beginning to feel more like a pioneer too."

Chloe added, "Just don't decide you want to start wearing long gingham-dresses like the pioneers and those funky looking bonnets." They both laughed at that thought.

The next morning Alex was feeling even better, but just to be sure the soreness was gone he began the day by doing stretches. He felt ready for the day afterward.

Later that morning, both Chloe and Emma began complaining. After listening to them a few minutes, he had heard enough. He decided to set them down and have a discussion with them about their attitudes.

When Alex asked what was going on with them, Chloe stated, "You know, at first this was fun, something different, exciting. But now, well … it's boring and a lot of work."

Emma added, "Exactly! I'm tired of trying to cook with a fire on the ground; I'm tired of trying to get clean in a river full of fish so that I smell kind of fishy when I get out; I'm tired of sleeping on a hard floor with a tent covering my face; I'm tired of not having electricity so we can't even have a fan to keep us cool; I'm tired of having to boil water to drink, and I'm tired…"

"Whoa, I get it. And I agree this is a hard way to live. And I'm well aware we don't have any of the comforts we used to have. I'm missing our former life also, but right now I don't see any alternative and complaining doesn't change anything. So, tell me what you think I can do to change things."

When both girls were quiet, he added, "Ok, then, just think about it and let me know what you want me to do. Let's work together on this. And if you want to leave here, I'm willing to do that."

"And go where?" Chloe asked.

"I have no idea. Just move on, find someplace else. But just know that if we do that, whatever different place we find could be worse than this."

He then left the girls to go hunting. This time when he came back, he had killed a wild turkey. The girls were excited about having a turkey to eat.

Then as Alex filled the washtub with water to submerge the bird in boiling water heated over the fire, the girls approached him and said, "We've talked it over, Alex, and we've decided we don't want to leave here. And we're sorry we've been grouchy, and we'll try to do better. But we think we need more chores to keep us busy."

Alex looked up at them after placing the wash tub over the fire, "More chores, huh? I was trying to make your life as easy as possible, but if you want more chores, I'm all in for that. Ok, let me ask you girls a question? Did either of you bring your schoolbooks?"

"We both did," Emma answered.

"Then why not try to finish studying those books so you'll be finished with this school year. And I can let you both take care of the horses, brush and curry them, take them to the river each day for a drink, watch over them when you let them out of the pen to graze, and give them oats each night. And if you notice anything suspicious about them, like they're getting sick or hurt some way, be sure to let me know."

"We can do that," Chloe said, "but I'm not too happy about the school work."

"Well, you asked for more to do, so there you go. Also, I noticed on Chloe's calendar it is now June, so what do you say we go out hunting for blackberries while this water is coming to a boil.

"Sounds good," Emma replied.

"And why are you boiling water?" Chloe asked.

"We have to dip the bird in boiling water for a few minutes until the feathers can be plucked out, and you girls can help in plucking out the feathers. Now go put on long- sleeved shirts and jeans so the thorns on the berry bushes won't attack you."

Soon they were out in the woods with their pans. It didn't take long to find the berry bushes since Alex had spotted them earlier from his trip to the store.

They eventually had a good amount and noted that there would be many more in a few days.

When they got back to the cabin, they found the water boiling in the wash tub. Alex added the bird to the water by lowering it into the water by a rope he'd tied around it's legs. He allowed it to remain submerged for several minutes before hauling it back out and placing it on a tarp he'd spread out. Then he showed the girls how to pluck the feathers from it.

"Yuck," declared Emma. "It stinks."

"Wet feathers, yes, it stinks terrible," added Chloe, "but if we want to eat it, the feathers have to come off."

It took them some time to get all the feathers plucked off, then Emma declaring, "Don't go hunting for turkey ever again, Alex. I never want to do that again. Then Alex told the girls to take the tarp to the river and dump the feathers in the river. When they returned, he began gutting the bird and cutting it into pieces. Watching him, Emma said, "This is the part of roughing it I really hate. Cutting open animals to remove their innards. It's disgusting."

Alex responded, "Maybe you should be a vegan then."

"Yeah, maybe, but I do like the taste of meat."

"It's protein, and we all need protein."

"Right, but I think I'll just go find something else to do so I don't have to watch."

"Me too," Chloe agreed.

"School work," Alex yelled after them as they headed to the cabin.

That evening they each put a piece of turkey inside aluminum foil and added butter and salt and pepper before throwing it into the fire.

Chloe found a box of Stovetop Turkey Dressing that she was able to fix along with a can of corn. They topped the meal off with blackberries. They declared they almost felt like they were dining like royalty that night.

The next day Alex stated he needed to make another trip to the country store.

"Can we come too?" the girls asked.

Alex thought about it a minute before answering. "Well, I guess you can, but remember your names, and if anyone gets nosey, we moved from Paducah, Kentucky and our dad is working in the Toyota factory."

When they got to the store, they went inside passing a young girl sitting on the bench out front. When the girl saw Chloe and Emma, who seemed close to her age, she jumped up and followed them inside. She went up to Emma and asked, "Hi. What's your name?"

Emma turned around to look at her. "Emma."

"Are you new around here?"

"Yeah."

"How old are you and her?" she asked pointing at Chloe.

"I'm twelve and she's fifteen, almost sixteen."

Emma wanted to get away from her before more questions came rolling out of the girl's mouth.

"I've got to help my brother get some groceries," Emma began to move away, but the girl followed her.

"My name is Erin," the girl said. "I'm fifteen too. I'm going into tenth grade next fall in Tupelo high school. What about you? What grade will you be going into?"

"Eighth."

"So where do you live? I live just around the corner in a huge house. Have you seen it?"

Emma had noticed the huge house when they went horseback riding, but didn't want the girl, Erin, to know they lived close by, so she answered, "No," and ignored Erin's question asking her where she lived. Then Emma added, "Look my brother's ready to go. I've gotta go."

"Your brother is really cute. How old is he?" Erin continued the questions as she followed Emma out the front door.

"Seventeen. It was nice meeting you, Erin. Bye."

"Hey, maybe we could get together some time if you don't live too far from me."

Emma just looked at her without responding but shrugged instead.

On the way back to the cabin, Alex said to Emma, "Looks like you've made a friend."

"More like I've made a pest."

"So, what did you learn about her?"

"Her name is Erin, she's fifteen going into tenth grade at Tupelo high school and she thinks you're really cute."

Alex threw back his head and laughed. "She was pretty good looking herself," he replied.

"Well, she lives in that huge house we went by when we went horseback riding. So, if you're interested, I guess you know where to find her."

"I said she was good looking, not that I wanted to date her."

"Well, just be careful because I think she's got her eye on you."

"Yes, ma'am."

They ate turkey every night for the next week until they all declared they didn't want any more for the next year.

Later Chloe said to Alex, "I need to talk to you about something."

"Ok, what's up?"

"Well, I've been thinking about school. Will we be able to go to school next fall? I mean, if we don't go to school, I'll get set back a year and I won't be able to graduate when I'm eighteen, and I don't want that to happen."

"I wish I knew the answer to that. I really do, but we'll just have to wait and see, I guess. I won't turn eighteen until October third, so I don't see how you could begin in the fall when school starts because I won't be able to see about becoming yours and Emma's guardian until I'm eighteen. But I guess we'll just have to wait and see what transpires over the summer. And actually, I have no idea how to go about becoming a guardian for you two, so I'm going to have to try to figure that out, and I have no idea how long the process will take."

"Well, think about it. I'm sure Emma feels the same way."

"I will, I promise."

Alex told the girls he needed to make a quick trip to the store again, but this time he needed to go alone. When he got there, he asked the store owner if he made deliveries, to which he found out the owner did offer to deliver but only up to three miles away. In that case, Alex said he wanted to purchase some of the lumber out back. After the purchase, he made arrangements for it to be delivered just down the road two miles, and promised he'd be waiting for them at the designated time.

He rode back home, attached one of the racks he had made to his horse's saddle and headed back to the road leading to the grocery store. He waited by the road until the truck slowed and pulled over to the side of the road. The kid who brought the boards helped unload them onto Alex's rack. Alex thanked him and waited until the truck was out of sight before he headed into the woods, so the kid couldn't see where he headed.

When he got to the cabin, the girls clamored for an answer to what the boards were for. All Alex would say was that it was a surprise. Then he got busy unloading the lumber, box of nails, and a bag of lime. He went and got the shovel and began digging a hole in the ground. He dug for two days until he had a pretty deep hole. Then he began assembling the boards over the hole.

Chloe came outside and saw what he was doing and declared, "Its an outhouse. Am I right?"

"Yes, but don't tell Emma yet. I want to see if she can figure it out."

It took him a couple of days before it was complete and when Emma went inside the small building, and figuring out what the building was, she let out a yelp. "Whoopee!" she yelled, "No more pooping in the woods. Thank you, Alex."

Alex then showed the girls how to sprinkle some lime after using the outhouse in order to keep down the flies and smell.

"We are downtown now," Chloe exclaimed. "No more going out in the rain."

"Well," Alex replied, "You'll still have to go out in the rain to get to the outhouse."

"I can run pretty fast, so no problem. At least, I won't have to stay in the rain."

Next day was blackberry picking day again, and when they got home the girls declared they were eating them right then and not waiting till after supper. Then because they were sweaty, they all decided to go swimming. Emma was still a little hesitant to go into very deep water after her experience of being pulled into the river by the large fish. But they all had fun splashing each other and after they got out, they decided to lay on their towels and allow the sun to dry them off.

There were still chores to be done after they got dressed, and each of them got busy. The girls had to take care of the horses, and Alex carried water from the river to boil for drinking water. Then he gathered his hunting gear and set off into the woods. He wasn't gone long before he came back with two squirrels. As he was butchering the squirrels, the girls played cards.

Soon the squirrels were on the home-made spit with Alex turning them when needed. After supper all three decided to play cards in the cabin by lantern light.

The next day Alex noticed Emma scratching her arms and asked what was wrong with her. She pulled up her sleeve to show him, and he declared, "That looks nasty. It could be poison ivy or poison oak. Let me see what we have to put on it. He found some salve and rubbed it on her rash. Later in the day she declared it wasn't helping. "Why not go jump in the river. It might not cure it, but maybe the cool water will make it feel a little better."

The mosquitos arrived in mass the next day. But with horses needing tending, bathroom duty, hauling water up the hill from the river, and other things needing to be done, they couldn't stay inside. But Alex did tell the girls to wear long sleeved shirts and jeans whenever they had to go outside. The windows to the cabin had to be closed which caused the air inside to become stifling. They all three found they were waking up in a puddle of sweat.

Alex declared they needed to get out of the woods, and they should take another horse ride. They rode the same direction they had before, and when they saw the large house they had noticed, Erin was outside. She also spotted them and waved. Emma waved back as they rode on. Because Alex didn't want to run into her again, he decided to ride on to the next road, turned left toward the store, and turned back toward their cabin.

The following day Chloe woke up with a fever. Alex felt her forehead and went for some water and aspirin. When she reached for the water, he noticed a swelled place on the back of her hand. "What's that? Did you get bitten by a mosquito?"

"I think so. It itches like hell."

He jerked his head up at hearing her language, something he'd never heard from her mouth before. "Well, that could be why you have a fever." He went to get the salve. "Didn't you spray yourself down with mosquito spray?"

"I didn't think I'd need it since I was all covered up."

"Yes, but your hands weren't covered up. And have you looked at Emma's rash today?"

"No, but I see she's still scratching like crazy."

"Yes, I know. And that's the worst thing she can do. She could be spreading it."

"Well, it looks like I need to make another trip to the store to see if they have anything for it." He was soon back with a bottle of pink stuff he handed to Emma and told her to apply it to the rash, "And for heaven sake, stop scratching. You're only making it worse. Charles, the store owner, said this should dry the poison up within a couple of weeks, but to keep putting it on whenever it begins itching again. And if you're thinking of scratching, try slapping it, then wash your hands."

After Emma put the lotion on her rash, she declared, "This looks awful. But at least it doesn't stink."

"What is that stuff?" Chloe asked.

Emma replied, "Calamine Lotion. Maybe you should try it on your Mosquito bite."

"Not a bad idea, fork it over."

Soon both girls looked a little pink and Alex couldn't help but comment, "You two look like you're in the pink today."

"Not funny," Emma complained. "And just for your information, I'm never going blackberry picking again."

"I don't blame you one bit," said Chloe. "I'm never going outside again where mosquitoes can attack you."

Emma and Alex laughed because they both knew that would never fly. "Yeah, right," Emma said, "and how do you plan to accomplish that?"

"I'll just make both of you my slaves, so you'll be the ones going out to get me water and bring my food in."

Alex added, "OK, I'll volunteer to go to the bathroom for you too, then."

Emma began to howl with laughter. "Good one, Alex. Wish I'd thought of that."

The next morning Chloe's fever was gone, but Emma was still having a hard time dealing with the rash. Alex encouraged her to go down to the river and get a bath and wash the lotion off. Then she could reapply it afterward. She grabbed her towel, soap, and shampoo and headed off down the hill leading to the river.

Chloe declared she was doing the same. "I need a good bath after that fever making me sweat even more than the temperature inside the cabin."

After the girls returned, Alex said they could get busy with their homework, while he went to get his bath. Afterward, he got the axe and went to look for more wood for their fire. He worked most of the morning gathering, chopping, and stacking the wood.

He noticed the horses inside the pen hadn't been let out in order to graze, so he went to brush and curry them and let them out. He knew the girls had neglected them because of the mosquitoes, and even though he couldn't blame them, the horses still had to be tended.

After he finished, he went into the cabin and asked the girls, "So, have you girls brushed the horses?"

"Are you kidding?" Chloe replied. "And get eaten up by mosquitoes?"

"Well, I've taken care of them for you today, but we can't stop taking care of them. What if you were the ones out there, needing help, but no one came because they were too busy taking care of themselves? What if I decided not to go hunting for food, haul water to boil so you'd have drinking water, or..."

"Ok," Chloe interrupted, "we get it. Sorry, it won't happen again."

"And you know, I could be eaten up by mosquitoes too, if I have to do my chores and yours too."

"Yeah, yeah, yeah, I said we're sorry. Emma and I will just have to figure out how to do our chores some way so we won't get devoured."

"Devoured," repeated Alex. "Maybe, if you let the horses out a little later in the morning after the sun is heating things up more, get them into the sunshine to brush them, there might be fewer mosquitoes because mosquitos prefer the shade and cooler spots." Then he turned to go back outside.

"Hey," Emma stopped him, "why don't you get chewed up by them like we do?"

"I've read that mosquitoes only attack people who have something wrong with their body system. So, what can I say?" Then with a smile, he added "I'm perfect, but you two must be a little rotten."

"What?!" Chloe declared, "You just made that up."

"No, I didn't. I really read that. Your systems might be more acidic or maybe mine is, I don't know. But there is obviously something different about our systems."

"So maybe you're the one that's rotten and they don't want any part of you."

He laughed, "Yeah, you might be right."

The girls got busy on their schoolwork while Alex raked the ashes from the fire pit and prepared it for their fire that evening. Then because he had scrap wood left over from building the outhouse, he decided to see what he could do to repair the roof with it.

Even though his wood didn't match the wood shingles on the roof, he felt certain he'd done a satisfactory job when he finished.

When he entered the cabin, Emma asked, "What are you doing out there? There was a lot of pounding going on."

He explained he was fixing the roof and hoped it wouldn't leak anymore. Afterward Alex asked the girls if they wanted to go swimming to which they agreed heartily.

After getting into the river, Alex said, "Emma, you need to learn to swim. So come here."

He held her up to the top of the water with his hands under her and instructed her to kick her feet. When she did, he said, "Kick harder. If you don't kick hard, you won't go anywhere."

She began kicking much harder. Then Alex stood her up and using his own arms, he showed her how to use her arms. He told her to imitate him, which she did just fine while standing. Next Alex held her up on the top of the water again, and said, "Ok, now kick and use your arms like I showed you. Kick hard, Emma, like your life depended on it."

She did very well, and soon Alex lowered his hands and let her swim on her own. She did pretty good for the first time trying. Soon she began to yell for help. Alex said, "So, stand up. You're only in waist high water. She did it and laughed because she thought the water was over her head.

"Guess I'm still scared of deep water."

"All you need is a little more practice. You keep practicing and next time a fish pulls you into the water, you'll be able to swim out on your own. Just remember if you get into a stream that's trying to pull you downstream, swim sideways."

"Thanks, Alex."

That night, because they had no meat to eat, Chloe fixed a box of Mac and cheese and opened a can of peas.

While they were eating, Chloe said, "Hey, Alex, next time you go to the store, can you see if they have lettuce for a salad? I'm missing salads. And we'll need salad dressing of some sort too. Oh, and eggs and bacon. I'd like to have a nice breakfast besides cereal for a change."

He agreed to see what he could do.

A couple of days later, they were cooking their evening meal when a man walked out of the woods. It frightened them because of the way he looked. He was obviously a tramp, and Alex didn't trust him. He wished he had his gun at his side, just in case it became necessary.

"Hello, folks," he said.

"Can I help you?" Alex replied.

"I saw your smoke and was wondering if you might have some food for a poor man down on his luck."

"We don't have much, but I think we might be able to share," he said looking at the girls. "What do you girls say?"

Chloe rose to go inside for a plate, but when she handed it to Alex, her face showed she was not happy about this.

He ate, saying it was the first hot meal he'd had in a long time. Alex decided to see what he could find out from the man.

"So, what's your name, mister."

"John Smith."

"Nice to meet you, John. You said you're down on your luck, so are you homeless?" Alex felt certain that wasn't his real name. It just seemed too generic, but why would he give them a phony name unless he was wanted by the police for something, and he was on the run? He trusted this guy even less now.

"Yeah," he replied as he hung his head. "Lost my job, lost my house, then I lost my wife. I ain't got much to live for."

"So, are you headed someplace in particular?"

"Not really. Just decided it was too dangerous to live on the streets of Tupelo, so I just decided to take off walking and see where it led me."

"I'm sorry to hear about your predicament. But I'm afraid all we have to help you with is that plate of food, so after you're finished eating maybe you should move on."

John looked at Alex and said, "No problem. But I sure do thank you for this." He took another bite and asked, "What about you kids? You live here?"

Alex had to think about what to say. He hesitated to think and then said, "Temporarily. My dad will be back soon from work and he won't be happy to find a stranger here." He figured he had to let the man know they were living in the cabin in case the man had thoughts of coming back to stay, because if he had said they were just camping out for a night or two, he might come back thinking he could stay in the cabin. He hated to lie about having a father but felt it would be safer for them if the man believed a man would be arriving soon.

"Hmph," John said.

Soon the man was finished eating and without a word, picked up his backpack and headed into the woods.

After he left, Chloe said, "He gave me the creeps. And he looked dirty."

Emma added, "I'm sure he smelled good too, but I wasn't about to get close enough to check that out. And I sure wasn't giving him our soap and a towel. He probably has critters all over his body." She shivered, "The thought gives me the heebie-jeebies."

Alex decided to have a little fun with her, "We could have let him spend the night with us. You could have shared your bed."

"Alex! How could you even think such a thing?"

He laughed. "How about you Chloe, you could have shared your bed if Emma wouldn't?"

"Alex! Stop already!"

That night, Alex felt like he needed to secure their door in case John came back, so after he hammered a nail part way into the doo-jamb he bent the nail around to hold the door. Then he put one of the chairs under the doorknob, grabbed his gun, and laid it by his sleeping bag. He didn't sleep much that night worrying about their safety. Up until this incident, he hadn't thought they were in any danger, but this changed things.

After the incident with the man, John, or whoever he really was, Alex kept his gun close by. He was more concerned about the man invading their living space than he was about the bear or the wolf. He knew the animals only wanted food, but a man would be more apt to do bodily harm, especially since there were girls. He pondered other possibilities as well. Did the man have a gun, knives? If he was really running from the law, what had he done to cause that? Was he a violent man?

The next morning, he had a talk with the girls. "Ok girls, I think we should stay together as much as possible for a while. I know that guy, John, left, but I'm not sure he's left for good. I just don't like it that someone has found us."

Chloe looked Alex in the eyes, "You don't trust him, do you?"

"Do you?"

"Are you scared?"

"I wouldn't say scared, but I think we need to be cautious. Now that someone knows we're here and there's a cabin, what if he decides this is a good place for him to live, out of the elements." Alex was trying to say what needed to be said without frightening the girls half to death. He didn't want to tell them about how deeply he was concerned, even afraid.

"Just stay close to one another and be aware of your surroundings. That's all I'm saying. It's better to be safe than sorry."

They tried to keep busy with their chores but each of them couldn't help but stop every once in a while, to take a look around.

Chloe went into the cabin later to find Emma crying. She went to her, put her arms around her, and asked, "Emma, what's wrong?"

"I hate it here. I hate the way we're living. I want to go home."

"Oh," was all Chloe could say. She understood exactly how Emma was feeling because she felt the same way, but she'd kept it to herself so she wouldn't discourage the others. So, she just sat with Emma, holding her close.

"Do you know what I do to help me with our situation right now?" Chloe said. "I keep telling myself this is just temporary. Eventually things will change, and our life will get better."

"But it doesn't change," Emma complained. "Every day it's the same."

Alex came into the cabin then and saw Emma crying in Chloe's arms. "What's wrong?" he asked.

"Nothing," Chloe answered. "Emma is just missing Mom. Go back outside and let us girls have our privacy." She didn't want to tell him the real reason Emma was crying because she knew Alex was trying very hard to make their life as comfortable as he could, and she knew it could hurt him if he knew how the girls really felt about things. It seemed to Chloe that guys loved roughing it, but girls liked the finer way of life. She didn't think Alex would understand even if she were honest about her feelings anyway, so she kept it to herself.

After he went back outside, Emma looked up at Chloe and said, "Thanks. And I really do miss Mom."

"I know. Me too. Do you remember the time she took us to the indoor ice-skating rink?"

"Yeah. I remember we both fell on our butts so much our rears were freezing."

They began to laugh then, and Emma dried her tears. Then Emma said, "Do you remember when Alex, excuse me, but I'm going to call him Aiden, brought a friend home from school and he fell in love with you?"

Chloe chuckled, "Yeah, what a nerd he was."

"What was his name?"

"Um, Jeremy, Jerry, Jered, something like that. I don't remember. He wasn't anyone I wanted to remember, and I thank you for bringing him up.

"And do you remember when Mom took cupcakes to your class for your birthday only to find out that night that it was my birthday, not yours?"

Emma laughed, and added, "Yeah, but I didn't care. The chocolate cupcakes with chocolate icing were great. All the kids loved them."

"I'm sure they did. And Mom didn't even save one for me."

Then Chloe began to tickle Emma and soon they were rolling around on the bedrolls laughing and having a good time.

Alex entered the cabin again to check on them to see if they were alright, and when he saw them laughing and wrestling around, he just stood there shaking his head. He would never be able to figure a girl out as long as he lived. Crying one minute and laughing the next.

A couple of days later, midmorning it began to get dark outside. Alex looked at the sky and knew a storm was brewing. The wind picked up so he began gathering up loose things, the wash tub, shovel and rake, some of his tools laying by the cabin, and the camping gear they weren't using wrapped in a tarp. He called the girls to help him carry everything inside. The wind picked up even more becoming a gale. It began blowing strongly before they got everything in. Then Alex put halters on the horses and pulled them inside the cabin just as the rain came down in sheets. The thunder and lightning were ferocious, causing the horses to panic.

"Girls, try to keep your horse calm. Grab the halters so they can't rare up. Talk to them in soft tones." But it didn't help much.

"I can't hold him down," yelled Emma. "He's too strong." Alex reached out and grabbed her horse's halter to give her a helping hand.

"Keep talking to him softly, pet him."

The storm continued for what seemed like the rest of the day. The horses were screaming, they were so scared. The kids could see the terror in their eyes. The wind was very strong, and Alex couldn't help but worry that a tree could topple onto the cabin. He felt totally helpless to ensure the safety of his sisters and himself.

Eventually the thunder and lightning began to abate, but the rain kept coming down hard. And with the thunder and lightning moving away, the horses began to settle down. Alex said to Chloe, "Why not give them some oats. That should get their minds off the storm." She did so and began to curry her horse. Emma followed suit, and then Alex. He was glad to see that by tending the horses, it also kept the girls calmer than if they had nothing to do. It took their mind off the storm as well. Otherwise, he was pretty sure they would have been panicked just like the horses.

After the rain slowed to a steady gentle rain, Alex led the horses back outside. But the pen he'd built for them was knocked down, so he had Chloe hold the reins while he tied a rope around two trees to tether them. After they were taken care of, he looked around and saw the outhouse had been blown over, leaves were scattered everywhere along with sticks. He could see a limb down from a tree a short way into the woods, and he thanked God it wasn't one close to the cabin. There would be plenty of work to do to clean things up, and now they would have plenty of wood for the fire.

He went back inside the cabin to wait for the rain to stop. Emma immediately blurted out, "Now see what happened? I told you if you brought the horses inside, they'd poop on the floor!"

"Well, I have the shovel in here, so why don't you use it?"

"Me!? No sir, you brought the horses inside, you clean up the mess."

"What a big baby. Ok, I'll shovel it up, but you girls get the job of scrubbing the floor."

"Yuck!" Emma replied. "I think I'm going to throw up."

"Gotta grow up sometime. Might as well start now. How will you handle having a baby someday when it gets diarrhea?"

"Easy, I won't get married."

Alex and Chloe both laughed at that one.

"Another thing," Alex said, "our outhouse got blown over, so I'm going to need help setting it back up."

After the rain quit, he got busy outside picking up sticks and stacking them by their firepit and raking leaves into the pit to burn. Later he would take his axe to cut up the limb that had blown down. He felt the first thing he'd need to do was get the outhouse lifted back into place. He called the girls to help him. They wrestled with it until they finally got it back up.

The girls went back inside to finish moping the floor while Alex got busy fixing the horse's pen.

The next day he told the girls he thought it was time for him to find a job.

"What kind of job are you going to look for?" Chloe asked.

"I thought I'd try working on a farm around here. I figure any farmer is going to want to know a few things about me, and that's the one thing I'm hesitant about in getting a job. They'll probably ask my age, so that's why I wanted to wait till June to get a job. A lot of kids get summer jobs after school is out. So, if I get a job working on a farm, I guess it'll only be a summer job because they'll figure I'll be starting school again come fall."

"What about the store? Did you think about checking there?"

"Well, I think that's pretty much a one-man job. He does have a young boy to make deliveries for him, but I think that's probably enough employees."

"So, what farm are you going to check out for a job? Mr. Simpson's or Erin's father's farm?"

Alex answered with a smile, "Wouldn't you like to know?"

The next day, Alex set off on his horse and headed to the large farm where Erin lived. He figured it would be the most probable place needing farm hands.

He tied his horse to a hitching post and knocked on the door. It was answered by Erin. He asked if her father was home.

"Yes, he's home," she responded, but just stood there.

"Can I speak to him?"

"I suppose that would be fine," but again she made no move.

"Would you like to get him for me?"

"He's in the barn."

He turned to leave, and Erin followed him toward the barn. "So, you must be Emma's brother."

He knew she already knew that, but he answered anyway, "That's right."

"What's your name?" She almost had to run to keep up with him, his stride was long because his legs were so long.

"Alex."

"Alex what?"

"Robinson." She was turning into a pest.

"Hi, Alex Robinson. My name is Erin Wilshire."

"Ok."

"How old are you, Alex?"

"Old enough to know I should stay away from you."

She lowered her head to hide her smile.

"So, what do you want with my dad?"

He stopped and turned to her, "You sure ask a lot of questions." Then he began walking again.

"Well, I have to ask questions because you sure aren't offering any information."

"I give information based on the need to know. You know my name, that's enough."

"You're a turd, you know that?"

He smiled, "I try." He had a hard time stifling a belly laugh at her remark, but inwardly he was enjoying the banter with her.

When he got to the barn, he stopped at the door and looked around. He had never seen such a huge barn. There were horse stalls down through both sides of a wide aisle. Farther down the aisle on one side was a pen full of sheep. Across the aisle was another pen with llamas. There was a stairway to the hay loft on one side directly inside the door to the left. And to the right directly inside the door was a machine shop that looked complete with every kind of tool imaginable. Under the stairway on the left was a door that led to an office. He was in awe.

"So, I thought you said you wanted to talk to my dad."

"I do. So, where is he?"

"I don't know. Why don't you go looking for him, that's what I'd have to do?"

He began walking slowly down the aisle, looking both this way and that on his way. He counted eight horses in stalls, four on each side, with a tack room on each side in the middle of the four stalls. The horses were beautiful, putting his and his sister's to shame.

He kept walking until he came to the sheep and llamas. He had never seen llamas and just had to stop and stare at them. They stopped eating, raised their heads to take a gander at him. Then one of them came to where Alex stood. Before he knew it, he was covered in spit. He jumped back, looked down at his clothes, and said, "What was that?"

Erin was rolling in laughter. He turned to look at her and said, "Why didn't you warn me?"

"And miss the opportunity to see this?"

"Well, now I'm covered in snot, so maybe I should go home and come back to talk to your father another time."

"No, come on," she said, as she turned to lead him back up the aisle.

He followed her into the office, where she went to a door and extracted a rag and handed it to him. After he wiped himself off the best he could, he looked up to see Erin smiling broadly at him. "You think that was funny, don't you?"

"I sure do." She laughed out loud before adding, "Look, I'm sorry about that. I know I should have warned you, but I just couldn't resist."

"I might be a turd like you called me, but you're pure evil." Then he couldn't help himself, he broke out in a hearty laugh as well. "Your dad will notice my wet clothes and decide he doesn't want to talk to me."

"No, he won't. I'll tell him what happened. Come on, Dad's not in here, so he's probably outside on the side of the barn where the milking stalls are for the cows."

He followed her outside and Alex noticed the entire long side of the barn was filled with stalls with a roof over them. It was used for cattle to be hooked up to machines for milking.

They eventually found her father. She began, "Dad, this is Alex Robinson. He wants to talk to you. Oh, and he got spit on by a llama, so that's why his shirt is wet."

Alex was embarrassed, but her father just smiled knowingly. He held out his hand to shake Mr. Wilshire's hand. "Glad to meet you," Mr. Wilshire said taking Alex's hand. "How can I help you?"

"Well, I'm out of school for the summer and was hoping I might find some work before school starts next fall."

"I see. Have you ever worked on a farm before?"

"Well, my family lived on a farm before, but it wasn't anything like what you have here."

"Did your family have animals?"

"Horses, yes sir. But that was all."

"He rode his horse here, Dad," Erin put in.

Alex looked at her wishing she would disappear. He didn't need any help from her.

Her father then asked, "You're new around here, aren't you?"

"Yes, sir."

"So what brings you here?"

"My dad got a job in the Toyota factory."

"I've seen Alex and his sisters riding their horses across the road before," Erin added.

"So, you live around here?"

"Yes, sir."

He then asked, "So where do you live?"

"Well, we rented a house on a road over that way." Alex answered pointing. "Look, Mr. Wilshire, I might not have done a lot of farm work, but I'm a fast learner and I don't think you'll be sorry if you let me work for you."

Mr. Wilshire rubbed his chin, "Ok, I'll give you a week to prove you're worth it. Can you start tomorrow?"

"Sure can. What time should I be here?"

"Eight o'clock. See you then." Then he turned his back on Alex to get back to work.

Alex headed back to his horse with Erin on his heels. "So, you want to work here," she said.

"That's what you just heard."

"That means I have to look at your ugly mug every day all summer long, I guess."

He stopped, turned to her and said, "Look, what's your problem with me? What have I done to you?"

She laughed, "I was just kidding. Can't you take a joke? I was just being sarcastic."

"Oh, sorry, guess I'm not used to jokesters who are sarcastic." He began walking again.

"Actually, I'm glad you'll be working here."

"Why's that?"

"Because I get to look at your ugly mug every day."

He stopped again and laughed out loud. "You're a strange one, you know that? I've never met anyone like you before."

"I hope not. I want to be the one who stands out in a crowd."

"I bet you do." He arrived at his horse, turned to her, and said, "See you tomorrow, Miss Erin."

"Miss Erin," she repeated. "So formal."

"Just kind. Not sarcastic like some people I know." With that he mounted, but before he left, he said, "Oh, and thanks for the compliment."

"What compliment?"

"You said I was good looking."

"I did not," she declared defiantly. "I said you have an ugly mug."

"Yes, but if you're sarcastic, you really meant the opposite, so in reality, you said I was good looking." With that he turned to ride away.

"Goodbye, Mr. Robinson," she yelled after him smiling. He waved without looking back and continued on his way.

When he got back to the cabin the girls wanted to know if he found a job. "Yeah, I did," he replied, but without elaborating.

"So?" Chloe asked.

"So, what?"

"Where did you get a job?"

"Over at the Wilshire farm."

"Where's that?"

"Where Erin lives."

"Oh, you're going to be working at that large farm. That's great. When do you start?"

"In the morning."

"And what will your salary be?"

"No idea."

"What? You didn't even find out if they're going to pay you anything?"

"He wants to try me out for a week to see if I'm worth keeping on."

"Wonderful. So, that means you work for a week without pay. That's not good."

"Well, it is what it is. We'll see what happens." He got busy chopping wood to stack for fires with his mind on Erin the entire time. Then went in search of something to eat and drink.

After lunch he outlined extra chores for the girls to do since he would be working. "I know I'm not going to be able to pull my weight around here, since I'm working full time, so I hope you girls don't mind doing more around here."

"Looks like we don't have a choice," Emma replied.

"Would you rather be the one going to work every day then?"

"No, thank you."

Chloe added, "We don't mind, Alex. I just hope you make enough to keep us afloat."

"If Mr. Wilshire doesn't pay me enough, I'll go looking for another place to work."

"What about Erin?" asked Emma.

"What about Erin?" he repeated.

"Was she there? Did you talk to her?"

"Yeah."

"So, what did you think about her?"

"She's a pest who asks too many questions and is sarcastic. She said I have an ugly mug." He looked at the girls to see their reaction.

"What?!" Chloe asked. "You're not ugly. You're very good looking."

"Yeah, well, that's when she said she is sarcastic."

"Oh," the girls both laughed. "In that case I'd say you have an admirer."

He ignored that statement and went outside to gather water for the girls.

He showed up at the right time the next morning and headed to the barn. Mr. Wilshire was busy inside his office. When he saw Alex, he said, "Oh good. I think I've got some things lined up for you for today."

He rose and came around the desk, and said, "Follow me."

He led Alex up the stairway to the loft. "We need to get a few bales of this hay down and drive them out to pasture for the cows. Do you know how to drive?"

"Yes sir, I have my license."

"Good, so you can lower them out the window over there with that pulley," he said as he pointed. "The tractor is in the shed to the South of the barn. Keys are in it. The pasture I want it in is the one to the East of here. You'll see where the cows are. When you've finished that, put the tractor back in the shed and come and find me."

"Yes sir."

"Oh, and one more thing. There's wire cutters in the storage room downstairs to cut the wires off the bales. Keep the wire though, I recycle."

"Yes sir."

He left and Alex got busy lowering bales of hay. He had no idea how many bales Mr. Wilshire wanted in the pasture or which direction was South or North. He lowered several bales out the window, went downstairs and looked around for the shed. When he saw three sheds, he went to see if one had a tractor inside. He hit the jackpot on the first one he tried, for which he was thankful. He didn't want to look like an idiot because he didn't know which direction was south. He acclimated his directions figuring if this shed was South of the barn, then that told him which pasture was east to drop the hay in.

He found the keys were in the tractor ignition and backed out, headed to the barn, ran the runners under a bale, then loaded three more bales on top, and slowly began toward the pasture, only to realize he had no idea where the gate was. He turned off the tractor and went in search of the gate, which he finally found at the far end of the pasture.

After arriving at the gate with the hay, opening it, entering, then getting off the tractor to close the gate, he headed to where he saw cows grazing together. He dropped hay off in three different places close by, and it didn't take long for the cows to find them, after he cut and removed the wire.

He put the tractor back in the shed, pulled the overhead door down, and went in search of Mr. Wilshire with the wire and cutters in hand. He found him still in his office. Mr. Wilshire looked up, and said, "Done already? That was fast. Just take that wire into the storage room where you found the cutters. Make sure you put the cutters back where you found them and there's a bin labeled, 'Recycle' on it for the wire."

Alex did what he was told and went back into the office. Mr. Wilshire stood and said to follow him. He went to the storage room and chose a tool hanging on the wall that looked like a rake with long slots cut out of the metal shovel part but attached across the ends. Then he took Alex to the horse stalls.

"We need to muck out all the stalls, and that's something that has to be done every day. There's a wagon right there you can use," he said pointing along the wall of the first stall, "and when it's full we dump it out in back of the shed on the West. You'll see the big pile. Start a new pile not far from the pile that's there. We use the dried manure for fertilizer, and since this stuff here will be wet, we don't want to mix the two.

There's a four-wheeler in the shed where you found the tractor. You can hook the wagon to it after you have it loaded to drive it behind the shed to dump. The wagon has a lever right here," he touched it to show Alex, "just pull it and it will dump for you.

"And after you get the horse stalls mucked out, we have to do the same with the sheep and llama pens."

Alex's heart sank, he had no desire to go around the llamas again. So, he asked Mr. Wilshire a question, "Mr. Wilshire, can I ask you a question?"

"Sure."

"Why do you have llamas? I mean, they spit on you."

He chuckled, "Yes, I guess they do. I have them for two reasons. Those are high quality llamas, show llamas. I make good money from them for show, but also, I sell their wool. The coarse hair is used for making rope or rugs, things like that, but the underbelly hair is fine and used to weave clothing. You can also use llamas as a pack animal, but we don't use them for that. They spit on you, if they don't know you, they might think you're a competitor. That will stop after they get to know you as their caregiver. Have you ever done any herding?"

"Do you mean like herding cattle?"

"Any animal really."

"Well, no sir, I've never done that, but like I said, I'm a fast learner."

"And don't call me sir, or Mr. Wilshire. My first name is Daniel."

"Yes, sir…er, Daniel."

"After you muck out the horse stalls, we'll go have some lunch."

"Oh, I brought my own lunch, sir…uh, Daniel."

"Ok for today but starting tomorrow we provide lunch. And after lunch, we'll move the sheep and llamas to pasture. That will keep you from getting spit on."

Alex moved the wagon to the first stall and began trying to move the manure out but was having trouble with the horse in the way. Erin showed up shortly, and said, "You need to move the horse out of the stall first. Here, let me show you." Alex watched as she removed a rope on the wall in the aisle and attached it to the horse's halter, moved him into the aisle and tied him to the bars on the top of the stall walls.

"Thanks for that," Alex said.

"So, I'm supposed to let you know that lunch will be ready in about forty-five minutes."

"Oh, I have my own lunch."

She just stared at him. Then, "Bet you won't have something as good as we'll have."

"Probably not, but that's ok."

"Well, what do you have in your lunch."

"Why does it matter?"

"Because my dad believes if a worker doesn't eat well at noon, he won't get diddly squat out of him in the afternoon. So, I suggest you take your lunch home, and eat with us for lunch."

"No, I've already told your father I have my own lunch, and he said that was ok for today."

"Well, I can change that easily enough." She turned and marched down the aisle. Soon she was back, and Alex stopped work to look at her, "Ok, Dad said to eat with us for lunch today. So, take yours home."

"Ok, then, if you're sure? Forty-five minutes you said."

"That's right, and if you're not inside by then, we eat without you."

"Wait! Just one question. How do I know when forty-five minutes is up?"

"You don't have a watch?"

"No," holding up both wrists.

"Well, I guess you can look at the clock on the wall in the office then."

"Ok, thanks."

She strode off, and he got back to work. Within forty-five minutes, he had all the stalls finished, and had hauled the manure where Daniel told him to dump it. He really enjoyed driving the four-wheeler and wished he could own one. What would the girls say if they could see him now?

He showed up on time at the house, knocked on the door, and Erin admitted him stating that he didn't have to knock, if he was coming into lunch. Other times though, yes, he needed to knock.

"Yes, ma'am," he said and removed his hat as he entered.

"Hat rack is over there," she nodded in the direction.

He was ravenous, and tried to eat slowly, but just barely. "Do you like the food?" Erin asked.

"Oh, yes, ma'am."

"Better than what you brought?"

"Yes, ma'am."

"Told you." Her parents both laughed along with her older brother, Dane.

And because he hadn't met the rest of the family, Erin offered to introduce him. "Mom and Dane, this is Alex Robinson."

"It's nice to meet you," Alex replied.

Dane continued, "So Dad's using you as a slave I see."

Daniel said, "Now, Dane, be fair."

"Just kidding."

Alex then said, "You must be sarcastic like Erin."

Dane looked at Erin before answering, "Looks like you know her pretty well already."

"Not really. She just told me she was sarcastic. Before that I thought she was serious when she said I have an ugly mug."

The family all laughed at that. Mr. Wilshire said, "That's Erin. Don't believe anything she says."

"This food sure is delicious, Mrs. Wilshire. What do you call it?"

"Chicken pot pie. Family loves it, and it makes a nice one-piece meal, except for the salad, that is. Erin made it today."

He stopped eating, fork midway to his mouth, and looked at Erin, before saying, "Then, thank you Erin, it is delicious, and that's not sarcasm."

Again, the family laughed.

After he finished eating, he grabbed his hat and headed outside. After he left, Mrs. Wilshire said, "I think he's going to fit in with our family just fine. He's witty."

Daniel added, "I agree, but I think we'll need to keep our eye on Erin. I think she's very interested in our new guy."

Mrs. Wilshire agreed and Erin blushed.

After lunch, Alex got his first lesson in herding animals. First Daniel called for the dog, Shep, explaining he helped with the herding.

In the barn, Daniel raised the overhead door in the back of the barn, Shep took up his position which he already knew well. When Daniel opened the doors to both pens, Shep took over. Alex was already mounted on his horse, and just watched in amazement as the dog went to work, running back and forth across the aisle, barking at the llamas and sheep. They immediately went toward the open door. Daniel mounted his horse, and he and Alex followed them out. Shep already had turned the animals to the right chasing them along the side of the barn. The animals instinctively knew where to go and headed for the correct pasture.

Daniel rode along after them, then as they neared the pasture, Daniel rode ahead to open the gate for them to enter. Afterward, he closed and locked the gate.

"That's it?" Alex asked. "Doesn't seem like much herding to me. The dog did all the work."

"If you have animals to herd, you need a good working dog. Sure makes the job easier. And before you leave this evening, which, by the way, is six o'clock, you herd them back into the barn. Just call Shep and he'll come running."

"Yes, sir. Now I'll get busy in their pens in the barns." He rode back to the barn, and Daniel couldn't help but smile. He felt certain the boy would work out just fine.

Alex tied his horse up inside the barn's aisle and got busy mucking the stalls of the sheep and llamas, glad to be able to work without the llamas spitting on him.

After he hauled the last of the manure to the latest pile, he went in search of Daniel. He said, "Are you finished already? You're a good worker. I like what I see. Ok, so now, take each horse to the washing area out by the shed out back and give them a good bath, and you might include your own horse. He looks like he could use a good washing as well."

Alex headed to the first stall, clipped the lead rope on his halter and led him to the wash station. Afterward, he washed the others and his own. He sensed that his horse really enjoyed his bath, Alex talking softly to him.

After he completed that job, which took him quite a while because there were seven horses to wash, Daniel said, "It's time to bring the sheep, llamas and cows in."

Alex called Shep who came running. "Let's see if you can bring them in alone," Daniel said. "Although it will take a little more work to drive the cows in. Shep will still be able to help you with that, but just take a rope wound into a circle to shake toward the cows when you drive them. It helps move them along a little faster. If you have trouble come and get me."

Alex saddled and mounted his horse, while Shep led him out of the barn, already knowing what his job was. When he opened the gate, Shep went to work, making a wide circle around the llamas and sheep and easily herded them to the barn. After Alex had them locked inside their pens, he and Shep went to the cattle pasture, opened the cattle pasture gate, and once again Shep circled the cattle bringing them into a tight mass. Alex rode around to the back of the herd just like Shep and began waving his rope and slapping it against his leg to help get them moving. With Shep's barking and his slapping, the cattle eventually made it to their milking stalls."

He went looking for Daniel. "Ok, cows, sheep and llamas are all in their pens and milking stalls."

"Ok, then today I'll do the milking, but I think we need to show you how to become friends with the llamas, so they won't spit on you. Erin told me about your little accident with them yesterday."

Alex smiled, "I got a second bath yesterday."

"So, I heard." He led Alex down the hallway, stopping by a large bin along the wall. "This is the llama food. If you feed them, they will love you."

Then he showed Alex how much to pour into the feeding troughs, stopping every once-in-a-while to pet one."

"Got it?" Daniel asked.

"Yes, sir."

"Do the same with the sheep, and eventually, they'll look at you as their shepherd, and follow you without you even asking them too."

"That's cool."

"After you feed both of them, give the horses some oats, and you can go home."

"Yes sir."

Daniel turned to walk away, but stated, "Sir! Will you ever stop calling me that?" He turned to look at Alex who just smiled.

When Alex got home that night, he was beat. He hadn't worked so hard in a long time, maybe he never had. He flopped onto his bedroll to rest. The girls plied him with questions for quite some time and were surprised when he handed them his lunch. He explained that he was to eat with the family every day.

"What a lucky duck," was Emma's reply.

"Lucky duck, my eye. You should see what all I had to do today."

"Did you see Erin today?"

"At lunch. She has an older brother that I think is sarcastic just like her. Must run in the family."

Chloe chimed in with, "An older brother, huh? How old is he?"

"I don't know. Around my age I guess. I wonder why he wasn't working on things at the farm today?"

"What does he look like?"

Alex could see she was interested, so he decided to play with her a little. "He's ugly with pimples all over his face."

"Ew," Emma added.

"I have to be at work by eight every day, but I don't have any way to tell time, so I guess I'll have to play it by ear. I'll just get up every morning, eat a quick bite and head out. I sure don't want to be late, or he might not keep me on."

The next morning, he got to work earlier than eight which surprised Daniel. "Ok, he said, "today you won't have to work as hard as yesterday. We'll have the help of Dane today."

Alex was happy to hear that. "So today, first thing, I want you to take each horse out for a ride. Take your time getting back. They need to be ridden on a regular basis or they get cantankerous."

"I'm aware of that. All horses get the same way."

Soon he was saddled and mounted on his first horse, only to see Erin enter the barn. "Hey, wait for me, I'll ride one of the horses." *Oh, great,* thought Alex. *Trouble.*

As she was saddling her horse, Alex asked, "So when you ride your horse, where do you usually go?"

"Just follow me, I'll show you. Dad has lots of land, so we'll ride through his pastureland."

As they headed out of the barn, Daniel called after them, "Alex, while you're riding your horse, check the fences to make sure there aren't any broken wires or leaning fences. We'll fix whatever needs fixing this afternoon."

"Will do," Alex answered.

He took the first horse completely around one pastureland, then back to the barn to change horses to inspect another pasture's fences. And when he changed horses, Erin decided she needed to go inside and help her mother with lunch. She felt Alex wasn't very talkative because he had a job to do and was intent on doing a good job. She had wanted to get to know him better and came up with a plan to do something about it.

Alex hurried around each pastureland checking the fences, because he wanted to get the job done by lunch. He was looking forward to lunch, if each day was going to be as good as yesterday's lunch. He wished he could take some of the left-overs home to the girls and felt bad they weren't eating as well as he was. But under the circumstances, he knew there was nothing he could do about it.

Lunch was, indeed, delicious, and something he'd never had before. They told him it was called Fajitas, a Mexican dish. He watched the others at how they loaded everything into the soft taco shells, and when he took his first bite, he thought he'd died and gone to heaven. He kept letting a hum escape his throat with each bite, and Erin couldn't help but smile. She was really enjoying Alex, if only he would talk more about himself and his family. That was frustrating her, and she couldn't wait to put into action her plan.

After lunch, Daniel handed Alex some tools and gloves and, after they mounted their horses, they headed out to the place where Alex had seen one of the breaks in the wire fence

Daniel proceeded to show Alex how to mend the fence by stringing a new wire from one post to another and attach the ends to the posts and wrap the ends around the existing wire on both ends. Afterward, Alex went to repair the other two breaks he had noticed in the fences.

When he returned to the barn, he replaced the tools where they belonged, and went in search of Daniel. When he found him, he asked, "So how do the fences get broken?"

"Usually, it's cows that get their horns tangled up in the wires reaching for grass on the other side."

"Oh, that makes sense. I just wondered. So, what else can I do?"

"Well, I think it's time to bring in the cattle for milking. You need to learn how to milk them."

"Yes, sir. My horse is still saddled up."

"Well, let's use a different horse. Let that one rest."

"Yes, sir.

He saddled up a different horse, the all-black stallion, his favorite, and called for Shep. He found the job very easy with the help of the dog, since Shep did most of the work.

When the cows were into their stalls, Daniel already had their food loaded into their feeding trough, and he showed Alex how to hook up the machines to the cow's teats. After they had that accomplished, he showed Alex where to turn on the machine. Daniel explained that there would be a semi come the next day to take the milk to the factory. Alex had noticed a semi pull into the barn yard the day before and wondered why.

"So how often will the semi come to get the milk?" he asked Daniel.

"Comes every day," Daniel said as he led Alex to a door in a room on the side of the barn where the cow stalls were. He opened the door and entered. "This metal silo is where the milk ends up after milking, inside this refrigerated room, but we still don't want the milk to stay here very long. And we have enough milking cows to need a truck every day."

Daniel then asked Alex to go feed the horses, sheep, and llamas before going home for the night.

He was excited to explain to his sisters when he got to the cabin how the cows were milked, something he'd never seen before. And with the amount of cows Mr. Wilshire owned, he was glad to see he didn't have to learn how to milk a cow by hand. He figured it would take all day, if that were to be done.

He also told the girls about the rest of his day, and about eating Fajitas, apologizing that the girls couldn't have some also. Then he asked the girls about what they'd done for the day. They began telling him about their day, but soon he butted in because he was so excited with his job.

He told them how impressed he was with the Wilshire's dog, at how he was strictly a working dog, and how well he knew his job and performed it.

The girls told him they took their horses for a ride and had gone past the Wilshire farm in hopes they might get a glimpse of Alex but were disappointed that it didn't happen.

He grabbed his rifle and headed into the woods to hunt for something the family could eat for a couple of days. It wasn't long before he spotted a deer, but because it would be such a chore to dress it out, he decided against shooting it, and to look for something smaller. It wasn't long before he found a couple of rabbits he was able to bag.

The following day when he arrived for work, Erin came into the barn to saddle a horse. Soon she was gone, and Alex was busy mucking out the stalls. Erin was on a mission. She headed up and around the corner toward the store only to turn left at the corner. She rode down the road and dismounted when she got to the place where she had seen Alex enter the woods the night before, when she had followed him home after work. She had wanted to figure out where he lived.

She walked through the woods until she entered the open area where the cabin was. She stopped while she was still in the woods to watch and see what she could determine if he really lived in the cabin, which was on her father's property.

She noticed the girls come out to brush down the horses and let them out of the pen so they could graze. She watched as they carried water from the river up and fill the wash tub. She watched as the girls built a fire and heated the water, wash some clothing, and hang them over a rope Alex had strung between trees.

Yes, she realized Alex must be living here. But why? Were his parents also living in the cabin? There was no drive to the cabin, so if his father worked in Tupelo, where did he park his vehicle? Did he park it out on the road somewhere, and walk out of the woods each morning to go to work? And because she saw the girls doing their chores, was their mother inside the cabin? Or was there no mother at all? She had so many questions and no answers. But she planned on finding out what she could, if she could just figure out how.

She headed back to her home trying to figure out her next move. Her curiosity was certainly peaked. She had a mystery to solve and needed to outline what her plan was. Who was Alex and his family? She knew her father was really pleased with the work Alex was doing. If she solved the mystery of Alex and his family, would Alex lose his job working for her father? She found she was very interested in Alex as a boyfriend, but if his family was living in their woods, were they hiding from something or someone? Could they be trusted? She knew her father knew nothing about them using his cabin, so should she tell him? She had so many questions and no answers, and she wasn't sure what to do with the information she had already gathered and hoped to still find. Should she tell her father? No, she decided she would wait to see what else she might figure out about this strange situation.

At lunch that day, she couldn't help but look furtively every once-in-a-while at Alex, although he didn't notice. She hung on every word he spoke in hopes he might reveal something about his family. If only she could figure out a question or two to ask him about them. But she decided that would have to be away from the earshot of her family, because he would surely clam up if she embarrassed him with questions while in their presence.

Alex had driven the llamas and sheep out to pasture and mucked out their respective pens in the morning. And left them in the pasture until later in the afternoon. He was glad that the llamas were becoming accustomed to him since it was his job to feed them each morning. He hoped Daniel was correct that feeding them would help the llamas to stop spitting on him.

After lunch Dane took Alex into the tool room to show him how they inspected all the tools from time to time, sharpening what needed sharpened, oiling and greasing what needed it. They worked most of the afternoon inspecting, sharpening, oiling and greasing what tools needed it.

While they were working, Dane asked Alex how old he was, and after finding out he was seventeen, he asked if he had one more year of high school left. Alex answered in the affirmative.

Then Alex asked Dane how old he was, to which he replied that he was eighteen and had just graduated high school and was taking college courses over the summer to get a head start on it.

Alex then asked, "What do you want to be?

"Well, I figure I'll eventually take over the farm, so I'm taking courses in business, so I'll be able to run the farm. I just need to understand the business end of the farm. But I'm also taking courses in the veterinary line so I will be able to take care of the animals better. That's something dad doesn't really know about except for what he has learned from his father."

"That sounds really nice. So do you want to get your license as a vet?"

"Hmmm, maybe. I definitely want to understand animals better, and if I have to go to the point of becoming a vet, then that's what I'll do."

"That would be awesome to be a vet and have this farm also."

"So, what are you going to study in college?" Dane asked.

"Uh, I doubt if I'll be going to college."

"Really? Why not?"

"We are too poor. But I do love to work with my hands, and I've already learned a lot in the few days I've worked here. I like working on the farm because every day is different, so it never gets boring."

"You're right about that. But since I'm taking classes at home this summer, that's why I only help on the farm two days a week."

"That's understandable. How do you feel you're doing with your classes?"

"Well, so far, I'm just taking classes in the business end of things, but I'm really more interested in getting into the animal part. However, Dad spends a lot of time in his office, so I know I've got to learn about business. And I'm hoping I might eventually learn some ways to make the business end of farming easier for dad, and maybe even a way to make more money."

"Well, it looks like your dad is doing alright in the money department. Do you think he needs to make more money?"

"Well, you've probably heard the advice to 'Work smarter, not harder.' Maybe I can help lighten the load on my dad some way. After all, he's not getting any younger."

"That's certainly commendable." Alex felt envy to see the relationship Dane had with his father and how his desire was to help his father. He wished he had that kind of relationship with his own father, but he knew that would never be. His admiration for Dane increased quite a bit.

Alex ended the day by herding the llamas and sheep back into their pens inside the barn, then feeding all the animals before heading home.

The girls told Alex upon his return that they worked on their schoolwork and felt sure they finished the school year. He told them he was very proud of them for that. They also told him they felt they were up on all their chores including brushing and currying the horses, except for his horse. He let them know he would take care of his own horse, because he could do it while he was at the Wilshire's.

Chloe then asked, "So what are we supposed to do with our time now?"

"Well, do you need anything at the store?"

"We always need things at the store."

He then gave her some money, and said, "Then here, take this, but be frugal with it. Don't buy anything we don't absolutely need."

"OK, Emma and I will make a list tonight that you can look over."

"Good, now I need to know if you girls need more water hauled up the hill. And I plan on chopping more wood for the fire."

"We hauled water today, so we're fine with that."

After Alex arrived at work the next day, once again Erin saddled her horse and rode off. Alex wondered that she would ride her horse two days in a row, but he thought perhaps it made Erin happy to ride, so he put it out of his mind and got busy with his work.

Because it was the end of the week, Daniel came to Alex and handed him a check. Alex looked down at it and was surprised at the amount.

Obviously, Daniel was a very generous person. His eyes widened as he looked back up at Daniel.

Daniel responded, "You earned it. You're a good worker, Alex. I want you to stay on for the summer, if you would."

"Oh, I'd love to. Thank you, Mr. Wilshire. But can I ask you a question?"

"Sure."

"Do I need a bank account in order to cash this, because I don't have one?"

"No, but you can cash it at my bank."

"But I have no way to get to a bank. I have no car."

"Well, don't your parents have a car?"

"Yes, but they use it every day to go to and from work, and they don't get home until late. So, is there a way you can maybe pay me in cash?"

"Oh, I see. Sure, I'll be happy to do that. Here give me back that check."

Soon he was back with cash that he handed to Alex.

"Thank you, sir."

Erin had ridden her horse to the woods across the road from their house, but this time she didn't go around, past the store, and down the way she had when she followed Alex home. She rode to the edge of the river across from where the cabin was, dismounted and while her horse was drinking, she sat on a rock and hoped one of the girls would come to the river for some reason.

Eventually Emma came down the hill toward the river, but upon seeing Erin, she stopped and stared. What should she do? Should she turn and run back up the hill? But Erin had seen her and waved. So, Emma waved back.

Erin wanted to start a conversation, "Hi, Emma. How are you?"

Emma slowly continued walking down to the river's edge with her bucket that she lowered into the water. "I'm fine," she replied. "How is Alex working out at your farm?"

"We all love him, especially my dad. He was on trial for a week, but dad's keeping him on for the rest of the summer he said." She paused before continuing, "Emma, I know you and Alex live in the cabin over there. Do you care if I come over to visit a while with you?"

Emma shrugged her shoulder, "I guess."

"I'll have to go around and come into the woods from the other side since it's too deep to cross here. I'll be there in a minute." With that she mounted her horse and rode off.

Emma hurried up the hill to let Chloe know what had just happened and to ask her how they were going to handle the situation.

Chloe said, "Just stay calm. We haven't done anything wrong. And remember where we supposedly came from, and I'm sure she'll ask why we're living here so we need an answer ready to give her."

She thought a minute, "Why don't we tell her we lost everything in a fire in Paducah, and we had no money to rent a place and we found this cabin, and since it wasn't being used, we decided to live here until we can afford rent."

"Ok, so if she asks, you can tell her that. Not me."

Erin soon emerged from the woods, walking her horse. She walked over to Emma and Chloe and said, "It's so good to see you." She then looked around and asked, "Is this your home? How quaint. I love it."

"You do?" Emma asked.

"I really do. I've often wished I had lived years ago in a more primitive time period."

"You can have it," offered Chloe. "It's a lot of work."

"So, what kind of work?"

Chloe went on, "Well for one, washing your clothes in a wash tub and rinsing them in the river."

Emma added, "Carrying water from the river up the hill to boil for drinking water."

"Well, I guess it doesn't really matter what time period you live, there is always chores."

Soon the three girls were chatting, laughing, and having a great time. Erin eventually said she had to go, but she was so happy to have girls her age who lived close by, and she asked if she could come back again. The two girls were thrilled that she was so accepting of where and how they were living, non-judgmental, and heartily agreed that they'd love her to visit any time she wanted.

After she left, Chloe and Emma, both felt it would be best not to say anything to Alex about their visitor.

When Erin returned home and took her horse into the barn to brush him down before leading him into his stall, Alex was there. "Did you have a good ride?" he asked. "You were gone for quite a while."

"I had a great ride, and I plan on going riding more often."

"Good for you." Alex hadn't really spoken a lot with Erin after first meeting her and going through her litany of questions. In reality, he liked her, thought she was extremely pretty, but was terrified of her. He'd never been afraid of any girl before and had no trouble conversing with them. He had asked himself, why was he afraid of her? He decided it was because he himself had something to hide and was afraid she might find out his secret life. It was also because he felt drawn to her, and that in itself was enough to terrify him.

The next afternoon, Erin could hardly wait to go visit the girls again. When she walked into the clearing with the cabin, she didn't see the girls, so she knocked on the door. It opened and the girls invited her in.

Chloe spoke first, "Did you say anything to Alex when you got home yesterday? Because I don't think he would be happy to find out you know where we live."

"No, I didn't say anything to him." She hesitated before continuing, "Look, can I be honest with you?"

Chloe looked at Emma, then Erin went on, "I needed friends. Living here in the country, it gets pretty lonely when school is out. I was so happy to see you that first day at the store, I wanted to find out where you lived, so we could get to know one another. I was hoping we could become friends. So, the other night, I followed Alex home and knew you were here at the cabin. I wasn't sure if you were really living here, but I decided to find out one way or another, so that's why I was down there by the river yesterday, to see if one of you would come down to the river so we could maybe become friends. I hope you're not mad at me for that."

"Oh, no, I'm not mad at you. I think we both needed someone to be our friend too, but Alex doesn't want anyone to know we're here," stated Chloe.

"Why not?"

"Well," Emma looked at Chloe. "Should I tell her?"

Chloe gave her a warning look, but Emma went on, "I'm sorry Chloe, but I trust Erin. I think our secret is safe with her."

Chloe answered, "Emma! I can't believe you just said that!"

Erin put in, "Look, your secret, whatever it is, is safe with me."

Emma looked at Chloe then, and said, "Well… It's just us three living here, Alex, Chloe and me. Our parents are dead and because we are under-age, we were afraid we'd be split up and put in foster homes, so we left to live somewhere, wherever we could find, that would keep us private and keep us together. We don't want to be separated. That's all."

"I think that's admirable, and it shows how much you mean to each other. Believe me, I won't say a word to anyone, not even to Alex."

After that discussion, the girls taught Erin how to play the card games they loved. Erin was having so much fun with them she didn't want to go home, but knew it was time.

When she returned to the barn, Alex was just finishing up mucking out the stalls, and again he asked, "Did you have a nice ride," mostly because he didn't know what else to say to Erin.

"Yep," she replied, "I'm just exploring lots of stuff." She felt she could say that truthfully because she was exploring the lives of the three kids. She had learned more about them today, and quite frankly, she was in admiration of all three. She wished there was some way she could help them, and then she thought of a plan to do just that.

After Erin left the barn, Alex finished mucking out the llama and sheep stalls, replaced the straw in them, and called Shep to help herd them back inside the barn. He then fed all the animals once inside and used Shep again to go herd the cattle in from the pasture. He connected them to the milking machine, turned it on, and went in search of Dane to see if he would finish the milking because it was time for him to leave.

When he got home, the girls seemed to be in a much better mood and he couldn't help but wonder why, but he was happy that they were. Soon their evening meal was ready, and once again they saw a wolf at the edge of the woods staring at them. Alex told the girls to just stay calm, but he kept his eyes on him. He felt sorry for the wolf because he knew he must be hungry to show up while they were eating, but he also knew if he threw him some food, it would encourage the wolf to come back again seeking more food. And after all, a wild animal is wild, aren't they supposed to hunt for their own food? Alex knew there were squirrels and rabbits, so wolves should catch their own food.

The next day Erin went to see the girls as soon as she was done eating lunch, and this time she packed up left-overs from her lunch to give to the girls. The girls were elated that she thought so much of them to give them food.

Even though they had eaten some crackers and peanut butter, they devoured the food Erin brought them.

Erin requested to play cards with them again, and soon, they were having a wonderful time and laughing a lot. Before Erin left, she told the girls, "Actually, I have a little secret also I can tell you girls."

"Oh, I love secrets," said Emma.

"Well, just so you know, this cabin you're living in was built by my grandfather. He built it for hunters, and my dad owns the cabin now."

Chloe looked shocked, "Oh, Erin, we are so sorry to be living here then."

"No, don't worry about it. Dad doesn't go hunting any more, and he doesn't allow hunters to hunt on his property either, because there used to be so many hunters that they depleted the wildlife way too much. So, no one uses this cabin, you're fine here. I doubt if anyone will ever know you're here, except me, of course."

"But Alex has been hunting in the woods."

"Well, I doubt if he will hunt to the point of extinction of all animals."

"Right you are. So far, we've seen a bear, a wolf, and rabbits and squirrels. But still.... if your dad doesn't want anyone hunting here..."

"Well, I won't tell if you won't."

"Alex doesn't hunt for sport, but just to get us some meat to eat. And he doesn't hunt every day, just once-in-a-while."

"So don't worry about it. I mostly just wanted you to know you're on our property, so you're probably safer here than anywhere else."

"Thank you for telling us that."

"Look, from now on I will bring some food from our house, so don't eat any lunch before I get here."

The next day Chloe decided to go to the store to get a few things. While she was there, Charles, the owner of the store asked her, "So, what's you girl's name?" Chloe and Emma, both gave him their first names. "Do you live around here? I've seen you here before."

"Yeah, we do, and because Mom and Dad both work, we try to go to the store for them from time to time."

"Well, you both seem to be very respectful kids. I'm sure your parents are very happy to have you two help them out. You be sure to tell your parents I think you're a couple of fine young ladies."

"We'll be sure to do that. Thank you, sir."

They couldn't wait to get away from him before he started asking more questions.

That evening Alex and the girls decided to do some fishing for their evening meal. They had lost one of their rods when Emma was pulled into the river, so Alex had cut a long stick and fashioned a line on it to use it as a fishing pole. He figured if Tom Sawyer and Huckleberry Finn could make their own poles, he could too.

Alex noticed that the girls didn't seem to be very hungry that evening and commented about it. The girls made up an excuse that they must have eaten too much for lunch.

The next day Erin showed up with food for their lunch. She told them a funny story about Alex washing the horses that morning and ended up so wet it looked like he'd had a bath with his clothes on. At lunch, Dane took one look at him, and took Alex up to his bedroom and gave him a change of clothes. Alex took his wet things to stretch out into the sun to dry, but Erin's mother stopped him, threw his clothes into the dryer, and he was soon able to change back into his own things.

When Alex got home, he told the girls about his escapade, and both girls acted like they knew nothing about it. Chloe asked him, "So what happened that got you all wet?"

"The nozzle on the hose coming down out of the ceiling broke. So, then I had to fix it. And guess what? Daniel was so impressed that I was able to fix it without his help that he said I deserve a raise. So, now I'll be bringing home more money."

After lunch the next day, Erin was loading some leftovers into plastic containers when her mother saw what she was doing. "What are you doing with that food? I've noticed for the last few days we were either eating more or someone was doing something with the leftovers."

Erin had to think fast. Then she said, "Well, I've found out Alex is from a very poor family, so I'm sending leftovers home with him. I hope that is ok."

"Oh, I had no idea about that. Then yes, of course, let's try to help out. And I can send a few extra things along as well, stuff from the garden. I have some jars of tomatoes, salsa, pickles, and I'll see what else I can find."

"Well, let's don't load them up with too much, or it could hurt their pride."

"Nonsense, people like that usually appreciate all the help they can get."

Soon Mrs. Wilshire handed a basket full of things to give Alex. Therefore, Erin had no choice but to send the basket home with Alex instead of taking it to the girls herself. She went in search of Alex.

She saw him mowing the lawn out close to the pastureland where the cows were grazing, so she took the basket back inside the house to wait until he was finished. Eventually, she saw him hosing the tractor down to clean it up before putting it back into the shed.

She walked to him and handed him the basket of food. "What's this?" he asked.

"My mom likes to share food with neighbors all the time. She told me to give you this to take home."

"Wow, thanks. I didn't expect that. Be sure to tell your mother thank you."

"Sure," she replied as she turned to leave.

"Uh, Erin. Have I done something to upset you?"

"No, not at all. Why do you ask?"

"Well, it just seems like you've been avoiding me lately. You used to hang around quite a bit, but I don't see that anymore from you."

"I've just been busy, I guess. Really."

"Oh, ok. I see. Too busy going on horseback rides."

"Alex, don't read into it more than it is. I like you, really."

"Really? You mean that? I like you too. I like your entire family. I think you're all great."

"Why thank you, Alex. So, if you really like me, what are you going to do about it?"

"Uh-uh. You're fixing to get me in trouble with the boss. I've got work to do, so get out of here."

He watched as she walked slowly away, aware of her feminine figure. He looked from head to toe and was ashamed when she turned around and caught him staring at her. She smiled at him, aware of his staring at her backside. Girls! He figured they were the ruination of every man they came in contact with. He looked down and got busy working but took one more glance her way just as she headed out the door.

She ran into Dane as she entered the house. He had two bottles of water, one for him and one for Alex. "Where do you go every afternoon?"

"Wouldn't you like to know."

"Yeah, I would. You're gone for hours, and I doubt you're riding your horse that long."

"What if I told you I'm at the store, just watching the foot traffic."

"I'd say you're lying. Come on, Erin. Fess up."

"I can't, Dane."

"Why not? You're up to something, I can smell it. What is it?"

"I promised not to tell, so stop pestering me."

"Promised who?"

"Dane!" she complained. "I… I…" she hesitated.

"Come on, Erin. We've never kept secrets from each other before."

"You have to promise not to tell anyone."

"Cross my heart and hope to die."

"Well, I followed Alex home one evening, just to see where he lives, because I knew he had two sisters when I first saw them at the store. I just wanted to see if I could get to know the girls, so I'd have someone to do something with this summer."

"And?"

"Well, you'll never guess."

"No, I don't suppose I could."

"They live in our woods across the road, in the cabin grandpa built for hunters."

"What!? Are you sure?"

"Positive. And you'll never guess why?"

"Come outside so Mom doesn't hear this." He then led the way out the back door. "So, tell me what's going on."

"Well, I have been able to make friends with his sisters and I've gone over to the cabin to spend time with them. They told me both of their parents have died, and because they didn't want Child Family Services to split them up into different foster homes, they decided to run away, and when they found our abandoned cabin, they decided to stay."

"That's awful. Erin, we've got to do something to help them."

"I know, and I've been taking them food, and today I got caught fixing to take our leftovers to the girls, but Mom caught me. Of course, she wanted to know what I was doing with the food that's been disappearing in the frig, so I had to make up a story. I told her Alex's family was poor and I wanted to share some of our food with them which really wasn't lying. They are poor. So, she goes and fixes up a whole basket of stuff for me to give Alex. Now I think Alex is suspicious of something."

"Erin, this is bigger than you or me, we need to tell Mom and Dad."

"No, Dane. I promised I wouldn't tell."

"Look they need help. I'm not sure what we could do to help, but we need Dad involved for sure."

Erin held his arm so he couldn't go to their dad. "Let go, Erin. I'm going to do the right thing even if you won't. I understand your loyalty to the girls, but if someone is in need, our family has always been willing to help." He hesitated then, but eventually said, "Look, I won't say anything while Alex is here, but tonight you and I need to sit down with Dad and Mom and explain what's going on."

"The girls will hate me now because I blabbed when I told them I wouldn't."

"I doubt that. And even if they get mad about it, I doubt they'll stay mad for long."

That evening, Daniel looked puzzled when Dane said he needed to speak with him and his mom. He went and got Erin and forced her, against her will, to come with him to talk with their parents.

After everyone was seated in the living room, Dane began, "Erin and I need to tell you two something. Erin didn't want to talk to you about this, but I think it's something you both need to know. It's about Alex and his family."

"What about them?" Daniel asked.

Their mom interrupted then, "I know. Erin told me. I've fixed a basket of food up to take to Alex for his family."

"So, what's going on that everyone but me knows about."

"Ok," Erin said, "I told Mom that Alex's family was poor and she made up a basket of food for me to send home with Alex today."

"But that's not all," Dane added. "It seems that Alex and his two sisters are living without any parents in the cabin across the road."

Daniel looked floored. "You mean, in our cabin across the road?!"

"Yes."

"And without parents?!"

"Yes."

"Where are the parents?"

"The girls told Erin they are dead, and because the three kids didn't want Child Family Services to separate them and put them in different foster homes, they decided to run away."

"Oh, my," Mrs. Wilshire said. "Daniel, we have to do something. Those poor kids. They need help."

"And so, they've been trying to survive alone in the woods for several months now. Is that right?" Daniel asked, rubbing his chin.

"Right," Erin put in. "The girls said Alex has done some hunting to get meat for them to eat, and he got this job here so they'd have some money for other things. But my guess is they're barely surviving. I promised I wouldn't tell on them, that it was alright for them to stay in the cabin, but I'm worried about them."

"As well you should be," Daniel added. "Thanks for telling us about this. I'll talk things over with Mom here and see what we might be able to do to help."

"Oh," Erin put in, "and you should see the way they have everything fixed up. The cabin is as clean as a whistle, Alex has built a pen for the horses, and stretched a tarp over it so they have plenty of shade, and he's even built an outhouse."

"But they need other things. There's no electricity in the cabin, nor running water."

"Yeah, they have a gas lantern, and they carry water up the hill to the cabin. I suppose they have some way to make it safe to drink, unless they just buy bottled water. I'm not sure about that. And I've seen them wash clothes by hand in a wash tub, rinse them in the river, and hang them over a rope they have strung between trees."

"Oh, my, Daniel. What should we do?" Mrs. Wilshire asked, startled.

"Let me think about it. Thanks kids."

The kids went to their rooms, and Daniel turned to his wife, "I'll go see our attorney tomorrow, see what he has to say. We're not going to have those kids barely existing in our woods, that's for sure."

She put a hand on his arm, "Did I ever tell you how thankful I am that I married such a loving guy? You have such empathy for people in need. It makes me love you more."

He leaned forward and kissed her and rose to go to the barn to finish anything still needing to be done before dark.

The next day, Daniel headed out early to go to Tupelo to see his attorney. He had called ahead to let the secretary know he was headed her way. When he entered the attorney's office, first he had to flirt with the secretary. "Hi, Shirley, you look as beautiful as ever." She blushed, and said, "Go on in, he's waiting for you." He entered and held out his hand to shake, "Hello, Jake."

Jake rose from his chair, shook Daniel's hand, and said, "Good morning, Daniel, what brings you to town? I don't see enough of you these days."

"Seems I've got a bit of a problem that you might be able to help me with."

"Well, have a seat. What can I do?"

"Maybe nothing, but I need some advice. You see there's this boy who came to me a few weeks back and asked for a job working on my farm during the summer before school starts next fall. He said he has one more year of school before he graduates high school. I tried him out for a week to see if he was fit to keep or not. Turns out he's an excellent worker, he sees what needs to be done, and he digs right in and gets it done. And he's a fast learner too. So, I kept him on, and I've even given him a raise, he's so good, respectful too. He even calls me 'sir'."

"Ok, I'm not seeing much of a problem with that," Jake said with a smile.

"Here's the problem. My kids have found out he's living with his two sisters in a cabin in our woods across the road from us. It's not much of a cabin. My grandfather built it back in the day just for hunters, but it hasn't been used in years. Anyway, nothing wrong with that, but then the kids said they have no parents."

Jake leaned forward on his elbows, listening intently.

"My kids believe their parents are both deceased, and the kids ran off because they didn't want to be split up into different foster homes. Jake, the kid working for me is Alex, and he's the oldest at age seventeen, and his two sisters are younger than that, but I don't know their ages.

"I want to help those kids, not only because it's the right thing to do, but especially to help Alex out. I'm sure he's trying to do everything he can to keep them together, and to survive."

"I see," Jake sat back in his chair. "So, what would you like me to do?"

"Help me out here. What can I do? I need legal advice on how to help them without them being separated."

"You say the boy has another year of high school?"

"That's what he told me."

"So, he must be about sixteen or seventeen, probably seventeen, or will be soon. Well, if you really want to help them, you could file for custody, but you'd have to get them out of the woods. Do you have room for them at your house, all three of them?"

"Come on, Jake, you know I do."

"Ok then let me draw up the paperwork for you. We'll file for custody and see what Child Family Services says. I'll need all three of their legal names."

"Good. I'll get their names and give you a call."

"Are you sure this is alright with Miriam?"

"You should have seen how concerned she was when the kids told us what was going on. I think she was ready to go get the three of them right then and there."

When Daniel left his office, he was feeling good about the situation and couldn't wait to get home to tell Miriam. He ran a couple more errands and stopped at the bank for a withdrawal of funds to pay Alex his wages for the week. Now he understood why Alex wanted paid in cash. There were no parents to get him to a bank to cash the check, no ride except his horse he showed up on each day at work. Alex had no bank account and was living on only what he made at his farm and was trying to take care of his two younger siblings.

He arrived back home just before lunch, and when he entered the house, there were Alex's sisters with Erin in the kitchen. They stared at him, and he stared at them. Finally, he broke the ice and said, "You two must be Alex's sisters. I'm glad to meet you."

"Yes, sir." was all he got out of them.

"Alex is a fine brother to have. I'm sure you are both very proud of him."

"Yes, sir."

"I hope you're planning on staying for lunch, because if I know my wife, there's going to be quite a spread and plenty of food."

"Yes, sir. Thank you, sir."

Erin had the girls help set the table, and soon Alex came inside and was shocked to see his sisters there. "What are you girls doing here?" he whispered to them.

"Erin came and said we were invited to lunch here at her house. That her mom insisted we come."

"How did Erin know where you lived to come and tell you?"

"We'll explain later. Not now."

Dane couldn't keep his eyes off Chloe, she was so beautiful. She caught him staring at her and blushed, then kept her eyes down the rest of the meal.

After the meal was over, the girls thanked Mrs. Wilshire for a wonderful meal, and said they needed to get back home. After they left, Alex went back to work, but was very concerned that Erin knew where they lived. He couldn't wait to get home that evening to have a talk with his sisters.

Later in the afternoon, Daniel called him into his office in the barn and asked him to have a seat. He was afraid he'd done something wrong and was about to get fired.

"Alex," Daniel began, "I like you, and I think you're a fine worker, and I respect that."

"I'm sorry, Mr. Wilshire. Whatever I've done wrong, I'll gladly make up for it, work longer hours, whatever you want. I'm sorry my sisters came for lunch when they shouldn't have. I'll see to it that doesn't happen anymore.

"You haven't done anything wrong. And your sisters were invited to lunch here today with us. I need to talk to you about something else.

"Dane came to us and told us about your living arrangements in my cabin across the road."

Alex cut in, "We'll move out right away, that's no problem. And I'm sorry, I had no idea it was your cabin. We had no right."

"Wait! Slow down. You're not in trouble here. What I wanted to say is that we want to help you kids. From what I've been told, it's just you and your two sisters. Right?"

Alex hung his head. "Yes, sir," he almost whispered.

"And your parents are dead. Is that right?" Alex knew that was only partly true, but he figured the girls had told them that, and he didn't want anyone to know his dad was still alive.

"Yes, sir."

"And you're trying to make sure you three are not separated and sent to foster homes. Is that right?"

"Yes, sir."

"Ok, I went to see my lawyer today to see what can be done about your situation. Here's what I'm going to do. I'm filing for custody of you and your sisters. My lawyer will file the request right away with Child Family Services, but I don't foresee any problem with that. But I need to get you kids out of my cabin and moved here into my house."

"But, sir, we couldn't impose on you like that. It's too much. You people are wonderful people, and I thank you for the offer, but I can take care of my sisters and myself. Really, I can." He became terrified when Daniel had mentioned contacting Child Family Services. He just knew now since they'd been caught, they'd be sent away and separated from each other. His heart began pounding against his chest in fear.

"I'm certain you can. You're a very responsible young man, and I've been very proud of your work ethic. But you are all underage, and I'm afraid you just can't continue to live as you have been. Besides Miriam and I want to help. We've talked it over and we both agree that we'd love to have you three come and live with us."

Alex began to tear up. He tried to blink back the tears, but found it was no use. One trickled down his cheek, and he swiped at it with his sleeve.

Daniel went on, "All I need is the names of you three kids, your parents' names, and previous address."

Alex began to sob then burying his face in his hands. "You don't understand."

Daniel looked puzzled, "What do I not understand?"

"I haven't been honest with you."

Daniel sat up a little straighter at hearing that, "What have you not been honest with me about?"

Alex lowered his hands, but hung his head, "My name."

"Your name isn't Alex Robinson?"

"No,"

"So, what is your real name?"

"It's Aiden Roberts. You see, I figured they'd come looking for us when we ran away, and if we used our real names, we'd get caught, so we all changed our names."

Daniel sighed and was relieved that was all he was dishonest about. "Ok, I don't see that as a problem, since no one around here knows your real names. I'll just give your real names to the lawyer."

"But there's more."

"OK."

"I…I don't want to tell you the rest."

"Why, Alex? I want to help you. Nothing you tell me will hurt you, I promise."

"It's my mom. She got COVID. It was real bad, but she couldn't get into the hospital. I kept calling to see if they had a bed for her, but every time they said 'no'. And then she died. I didn't know what to do." He was crying again, and Daniel's heart was breaking to see the hurt and desperation that must have put in the kid's minds.

"My mom, she… she… no one knows she's dead. At least, I don't think so."

"So, your mother died at home?"

"Yes."

"And did you call the police or 911?"

"No, because I knew they'd call Child Family Services."

"So, you just ran away? Is that right?"

"Yes, but we buried mom in the barn in a horse stall and covered it with straw so no one would find her. We made it look like we just went away on a trip."

Daniel took a deep breath. He wasn't sure how this was going to impact things. He knew it was against the law to just bury someone on your property without notifying the proper authorities.

"Ok, tell you what. I have to get your name and your sister's names to the lawyer, so why don't you give me their names. I'll call him and see what he says to do about your mother. Don't worry, Alex, we'll get things squared away. I know how difficult all of this has been for you, and you've been quite the man of your family, stepping up to take responsibility of your two sisters. I'm going to do all I can to help you. Just trust me."

"Thank you, sir," he said as he sniffled and wiped his eyes on his shirt sleeve.

"And I've called you Alex so long, I'm not sure I'll ever get used to calling you Aiden," Daniel said with a chuckle.

Aiden smiled and wiped his tears again with his sleeve. Then he gave Daniel the real names of his sisters, Charlotte, and Isabelle Roberts. Lottie, as they called her, and Izzy, short for Isabelle.

Daniel then told him to go home, pack everything up and get his sisters and move back to their house.

18

The girls were surprised to see Alex come home so early. He sat them down and explained everything that had happened to them. They cried because they were both fearful of what their future might hold. He cried with them. They were all so frightened.

"Oh, Aiden, what are we going to do?" Charlotte asked. "What if Child Family Services say we can't stay with the Wilshire's? What if they take us away?"

"I don't know right now." He was emotionally drained.

"We're so sorry about Erin finding out where we live. She told us she followed you home from work one evening. That's how she found us."

"It's not your fault. I guess it was bound to happen eventually." He took a deep breath.

"Well," Izzy stated, "I for one, am glad we're leaving this cabin. I don't want to live here anymore anyway."

Lottie answered, "Well, you don't have to be so honest."

Aiden smiled and said, "Since we're being honest, I don't want to live here anymore either." They all laughed at that.

"So, from now on, I guess we go by our real names?" asked Lottie.

"I guess so. Mr. Wilshire has to give them to Child Family Services."

"Yeah, Child Family Services! That's what we're afraid of."

"Mr. Wilshire promised he was going to do everything he could to help us, and I believe him, so, let's get everything packed up, and moved to their house.

Soon they looked like three Indians riding their horses down the road, dragging their homemade racks behind them. They were met in the yard by Dane and Erin. Dane stared at Charlotte and Charlotte stared at him. Aiden noticed but said nothing.

Erin and Dane took charge immediately, helping them unpack their things. Clothing and personal items went into the house, along with left-over food. Camping gear, and tools went into a storage building out back.

When they were walking back toward the house, Dane fell in beside Charlotte and asked, "So your real name isn't Chloe. Right?"

She just looked up at him but kept walking. "So, what is your real name?"

She wasn't sure if he was making fun of her or if he was asking in disgust because he'd been lied to when first introduced to him, or what. She answered, "Charlotte is my real name," she stated defiantly as she jutted her chin out.

"I just wondered so I'd know what to call you. So, I just call you Charlotte then?"

"Well, you could call me Lottie. That's what my friends used to call me."

She walked with her head down, ashamed that they'd been caught and not sure exactly how they would be received in the family. Then Dane said, "We're really glad to have you here with us, you know."

Her heart lifted a little and hoped he was telling the truth.

"Really?"

"Really. Stop worrying. Everything will turn out all right. You'll see." She hoped he was right.

Then Dane turned around and said to Izzy, "And what's your name?"

"Isabelle, but you can call me Izzy."

"Ok, then, Izzy. Glad to meet you."

"We already met once."

"No, I don't think so. I met someone named Emma." She glared at him, and he continued, "Just kidding. Don't kill me."

Erin was walking beside Izzy, and said, "Well, I like the name Izzy better than Emma anyway. And I'm thrilled you're going to live with us."

Izzy added, "Yeah, me too." But she wasn't very enthusiastic because she was still very frightened of what Child Family Services would decide to do with her, Lottie, and Aiden.

"Let's go see your room," Erin added. "You and Lottie are going to share a room, and Aiden is going to share a room with Dane. Dad's going to get bunk beds added so they won't have to sleep with each other."

When the girls entered their room, they walked around looking at everything first. Then Izzy sat down on the side of the bed, "Oh, to sleep in a real bed again. Isn't this wonderful, Lottie?"

She smiled at Izzy. Just then Erin entered the room carrying hangers for their clothes. "The closet is empty since this was the guest bedroom, the dresser's also empty so you can use it too. After you get everything put away, come downstairs, and I'll show you around the farm. Oh, we're going to have so much fun together," she said with a giggle. The girls wished they could believe that, at least for a while, before Child Family Services ended it all.

Erin took them to the barn to see the animals. They petted the horses, even their own that were standing in the aisle. Then when they got to the Llamas, Erin warned them not to try to pet them until the llamas got used to them or they might get spit upon. So they chose to pet the sheep instead.

She showed them all the rooms in the barn, including the office, tack rooms, tool room and hay loft. Next, she showed them her mother's garden and declared they would probably have to help work in the garden like she did. While they were walking, she explained that every day her mother cooked a nice meal for the family and workers, and they'd probably get to help with that as well, along with the clean up after eating. "Mostly, we kids do whatever we're told to do. You'll get on it soon."

"We're used to doing chores. We're not afraid of work, and we wouldn't feel right if we weren't given chores to do anyway."

Erin giggled.

"Well, with you two here to help, it will make my work lighter. We'll also have plenty of time for games, horseback riding and things like that."

Soon it was time to go to bed. The girls found Aiden and told him good night. "Do you really think we'll be alright here?" asked Izzy.

All Aiden could say was, "I hope so."

"Do you mind sharing a room with Dane?"

"No, I like him."

"Good night, then. See you tomorrow."

The girls made their way to their room, and after crawling into bed, they laid in the dark staring up at the ceiling. Eventually, Izzy asked, "Are you asleep, Lottie?"

"No."

"I'm scared."

"Me too. But Aiden trusts Mr. Wilshire and we trust Aiden, so we have to believe things will be ok."

"What do you think about the Wilshire's?"

"So far I like them. They seem nice. What about you?"

"I like them too. I just don't understand why they want to help us."

"Maybe because they are nice people. I don't know, but I know there are still nice people in the world."

"Well, I'm going to do everything I can to make them like me so they won't kick us out."

"Me too. Now go to sleep, we'll probably have chores to do in the morning."

It was quiet then, but eventually Izzy whispered, "Lottie, are you asleep?"

"No. What do you want?"

"They have air conditioning."

"Yeah, I figured that out."

"No more waking up in a puddle of sweat. Geez, we didn't even have air conditioning at home."

"The Wilshire's are obviously wealthy. Better say a prayer and thank God for this all as long as it lasts."

"Right. Well, goodnight."

"Goodnight, Izzy."

It was quiet for a little while longer before Izzy again whispered, "Lottie."

Exasperated, Lottie said, "What now?"

"They have running water and hot water."

"Yes, I know."

"No more cold baths in the river."

"Goodnight, Izzy."

The next morning, Izzy woke and stretched. She didn't get up immediately but laid there looking around at the beautiful room with the white ruffled curtains, the pink flowering wallpaper, pink chair in the corner, the nice dresser and bed and thick carpet on the floor. She had never seen such luxury and decided to enjoy it as much as possible for as long as she could.

She realized Lottie had already risen, so she began to move as well. She dressed, went to the bathroom, taking her toothbrush and hairbrush. Afterward, she went in search of her sister. She found her in the kitchen making toast.

She went to Lottie's side and whispered, "Can I have some too?"

"I assume so. But I'm not making it for you. You'll have to do your own. And there's honey and jam too."

"Wow!" Izzy exclaimed.

They each enjoyed two pieces of toast, and was just finishing eating when Erin walked in. "Good morning," she said. "You two are up early."

"We're used to getting up early. We've eaten our breakfast and ready to do our chores, if you know what we are to do."

"Mom will let us know what she wants done today."

"Good morning, Erin." Mrs. Wilshire said as she walked in. "Nice of you to get out of bed. These girls have been up for a while. I hope their ways rub off on you soon."

"Oh, Mom, it's summer. I'm supposed to be able to sleep in."

"Well, summer or not, there's chores to be done, no one will do them for you. So, girls, any dirty clothing needing washed?"

Lottie answered, "I'd like to wash all our clothes, because even though we had soap and got them clean, we had to rinse them in the river, and I feel like, well, like they kind of smell like fish."

"Then go get them and bring them downstairs. Let's get them washed today. I'll show you how to use the washing machine and dryer."

"Oh, we know how to use a washing machine, but Mom didn't have a dryer, so, we might need a little help with that."

After the clothing was sorted and into the washing machine, all the girls and Mrs. Wilshire got busy making lunch. And what a wonderful lunch it was! The girls were sure they had never tasted anything so good before. They made two large cake pans of lasagna, and served it with salad, and Texas Toast.

When the guys all came inside for lunch, the girls greeted Aiden, "Hi, Aiden."

Dane spoke up, "What? Don't I get a 'hi Dane'?"

"Oh, sorry," Lottie said, "Hi, Dane. You boys better wash up, we're putting food on the table right away."

Daniel entered just in time to hear that last instruction, and opened his eyes wide to Miriam, but she just smiled at the way Lottie had taken charge. "You too," she said to her husband.

"Yes, ma'am."

Soon they were all washed up and sat down at the table ready to dig in. The girls had the salads already dished up in each one's bowl, while Miriam dished their portions of lasagna onto their plates, and they passed the toast.

Everyone expressed delight with the meal, and all too soon the guys finished their meal and headed back to work.

The girls cleaned up and kept busy with the laundry in the afternoon. Later in the afternoon, a truck arrived hauling a set of bunk beds into the house and up to the boy's rooms. They removed the larger bed and took it with them when they left.

Daniel called Aiden into his office again to talk with him. He told Aiden he needed the names of his parents, and their last address. So, Aiden gave his parent's names and the last address where he lived with his mom.

Daniel said, "You mentioned that your mother died of COVID, and you buried her in the barn."

"Yeah."

"What about your father?"

Aiden hesitated, not sure what he should reveal about his dad. He decided to tell Daniel the truth. "My dad left our family when I was only nine, Lottie was seven and Izzy was two. Izzy doesn't even remember dad, and Lottie and I don't want him back in our life. I have no idea where he is, or even if he's alive. He was a drunk who beat Mom, Lottie and me. So, I really hope he's not alive. And if Child Family Services should track him down and say we have to go live with him, we will just run away again. We won't live with him. I'd rather live in a foster home than to live with him."

"Hmm," he thought about that, then said, "OK, if he is alive, and if Child Family Services should find him, we'll explain things to them. I wouldn't think they would want you three to go live any place that isn't safe.

"I think you can go back to work now. Oh, and one more thing, did your mom rent or own her house?"

"She was making payments on it to buy it."

"Ok and how long has it been since you kids ran away?"

"We left right before May, so a couple of months. Why do you need to know that?"

"Just wondered how many payments have been missed on the mortgage. The lender has probably sent a letter explaining that the payments need to be made, but I doubt if they've begun repossession yet, so if the payments are made, you could sell the property and have a little extra cash. So how do you feel about me garnishing your wages to pay those mortgage payments for you?"

"Yeah, sure. And I have a little money saved up I can give you to add to my wages. I never thought about making those payments or trying to sell the house. I was just going to let the bank have it back."

"Well, if we can bring the payments up to date, then we can sell the property, although I'm not certain about leaving your mother buried in the barn. We'll need to see what we need to do about that before it's sold."

After Aiden left, Daniel got on the phone with his lawyer to give him the names and address of where they lived. He explained about the kid's father leaving the family and being abusive, and that they'd run away again if given back to him. "That's good to know. I'll add that to my filing for custody," Jake stated.

"And Aiden says his mom was buying her house. So, I was wondering if you have a good investigator that I can hire to see what I can find out about that house, and about the kid's father?"

"Sure do. I'll share his contact information with you, so be looking for my text."

"Thanks, Jake. I'll let you know what the investigator finds out. Talk to you later."

Daniel was able to reach the investigator. He told him what he needed from him, and the investigator said he'd get back with him right away about the house because that would be easy enough to find out but finding the father would be another matter that might take some time.

Soon Daniel got a phone call from Jake. He said, "Your petition to take custody of the children has been filed. Now we wait to hear back about it. But I've done some checking around about their mother being buried in the barn, and the police want to talk to Daniel. I've set it up for them to pay you a visit tomorrow. They need to question him about that."

"Alright, I'll be looking for them. I know Alex, I mean, Aiden will be scared to death to meet with them, but I know it has to be done, but I'll be here for him. Hope it goes well."

"Me too. I'll be in touch."

As suspected by Daniel, Aiden was very afraid to meet with the police and asked, "Will I go to jail?"

"I doubt it. You were traumatized by the death of your mother. You had no one to guide you about what to do. You did your best under the circumstances. I wouldn't worry too much about it."

The next day the police arrived at the Wilshire farm mid-morning. Daniel showed them into the living room and sent Erin to tell Aiden to come inside. When he entered, he hung his head and walked slowly to the couch to sit. Daniel thought he looked like a whipped dog.

He explained that his mother was very sick with COVID, and he had tried several times to get her into the hospital but there were no beds. He tried to take care of her the best he could, but she died. He explained that if Child Family Services had come, they would have taken all three of her children away, probably put them in different foster homes, and they'd never see each other again. All they wanted was to be able to stay together. There was no malicious intent.

When he finished telling his story, the policeman looked at Daniel, sighed, and said, "Well, I can understand why you did what you did. But did you realize it was against the law to bury your mother on the property without notifying the authorities?"

Aiden answered, "I never thought about it. I was thinking that people back in time often had family burials in the country. I didn't really know it was against the law. I just didn't want our family to be split up. Us kids needed each other, and even more so after Mom died. That was why I didn't call anyone after she died. I knew if I got the police involved, they'd call Child Family Services, so we ran."

Daniel entered the conversation then, "I've got a lawyer here in Tupelo that has filed for custody of the three children. We're waiting to hear about a ruling on that."

"I see. That's good. So, son, just so you know, your mother will have to be dug up and taken to a mortuary. They'll do an autopsy to make sure you're telling us the truth. And if everything checks out, she'll be cremated, and you or your guardian, will have to pay for that. I don't see any reason for an arrest here, unless it turns out her body shows signs that she died of other causes. Do you understand?"

"Yes, sir." Aiden said without looking at the policeman.

"Now what was your mother's name?"

"Mamie Roberts."

"I'll write a report and let you know later what the autopsy report shows," he said this more to Daniel than to Aiden.

He rose to go, but Aiden stopped him by saying, "Thank you, sir."

He turned to look at Aiden and Daniel couldn't help but notice the pained expression on the policeman's face, and he wondered if he had children of his own and was thinking of how his own kids might handle a situation like this one.

The policeman put his hand on Aiden's shoulder and reassured him that he felt certain everything would be alright.

After the police left, Daniel said, "Aiden, after the autopsy, and cremation, if you three want to go back to retrieve her ashes, I'll be happy to take you back."

"I'd like that. Thank you."

The following day, Daniel received a call from the investigator who had the information about the house the kid's mother owned. He gave Daniel the name of the lender, and the amount still owed on the property, then he asked, "Do you have any idea where the kids last saw their dad, or where he might be living? I need a starting point."

"I'll see what they know about that and get back with you right away."

After they hung up, Daniel went in search of Aiden. Aiden told him the address where they lived in Arizona, but that he had no idea if his dad still lived there or not.

Daniel got back with the investigator and gave him the address.

"Thanks, that helps," he answered.

Aiden was still working as usual, but his mind was distracted because of everything that had transpired and still was transpiring. He worried and worked, worried and worked. He hoped his work was satisfactory because he was so distracted. And he worried about how his sisters were dealing with everything. He felt like he had the weight of the world on his shoulders.

He thought he had done the right thing for himself and his sisters, and now to find out he had broken the law. The policeman was kind, but would his boss see it differently? Could he still be arrested for burying his mother in the barn? And when they dug her up, what would they do if they found some mark on her body or a bruise? Could he be blamed for maybe murder? He wished he knew the answers to all his questions. He was frightened. He needed to think. Yet thinking only made him feel worse. He just wished it would all go away.

Dane found him later and said, "Hey, man, you look awful. Are you alright?"

"I don't know. Things are a mess. I've made a mess of everything."

He came to stand in front of Aiden, and said, "Don't worry, Dad will take care of everything. He's smart. He'll know how to handle things."

"I hope you're right."

"Trust me, I know what I'm talking about. You'll see."

20

The next day, Daniel had another talk with Aiden. He said, "Aiden, I've been thinking about your future. What do you intend to do after high school?"

"I don't know," was his reply.

"Well, your senior year will be the deciding factor, so you need to be thinking about after high school."

"I didn't think I'd go back to school. I figured I would just find a job and try to take care of my sisters."

"Not good enough. I want you in school come fall. Think about what you want. If you get good grades next year, you could earn a scholarship for college."

"I figured I wouldn't go to college either. Mom certainly couldn't afford it, and now I have my sisters to think about. And I figured I wouldn't be able to go back to school next fall because of needing to work to provide for them."

"You can leave your sisters up to me to think about, I want you to think about you. I can tell you're a bright kid, and I don't want that brain of yours to go to waste. So, just try to figure out what you want to do with the rest of your life, and maybe I can help you achieve it. And I definitely want you to start high school next fall."

"Thanks, Mr. Wilshire."

"Now get back to work," he said with a smile.

"Yes, sir."

"And stop calling me sir."

"Yes, sir," he said with a smile and walked out of the office.

Daniel was able to contact the lender, find out the amount of money needed to bring the kid's mother's mortgage up to date. It wasn't as much as Daniel thought it could be. He called Aiden inside, and said, "It looks like the house payments are only behind two months so far. To bring it up current we need to pay $1050. You said you have some money saved up, so how much do you have."

"Nowhere near that much. I have around $400."

"Ok, give it to me, and I'll pay the balance, and garnish your wages until you pay me back or until it's sold, whichever comes first. We need to get it paid up before they repossess the house."

Aiden smiled, "Thank you…s…"

Daniel interrupted, "Don't say it."

"Thank you, Daniel," Aiden said with a smile. "Do you have any idea how much we could sell the house for?"

"No idea. But after your mother's body has been taken care of, we'll get a real estate agent involved."

"Ok, thanks again."

Aiden didn't tell the girls about everything going on. He wanted to keep them from worrying like he was. Besides, he figured he should shoulder the responsibility of taking care of them, and the less they knew the better right now.

He watched the girls as much as he could, and he felt they were settling in very well, and were even happy to be living with the Wilshire's. Of course, he was happy to be living with them as well. Actually, he wished they could live with them forever, but he knew that was unrealistic. He hated not knowing what would happen in the future.

The girls were helping with chores, as well, weeding the garden, picking vegetables that were ready to be picked, cleaning the house, doing laundry, washing, drying, and ironing. And when they had no other chores needing to be done, they went to brush and curry their horses. They would pet the Wilshire's horses, and wander back to pet the sheep, but they were afraid to get close to the llamas, even though they wanted to pet them as well. Erin would get her horse, and the three girls would go horseback riding. It was turning out to be the best summer of their lives.

One day Erin got out the four-wheeler, and they took turns riding it around in the pasture. This was a new experience for Lottie and Izzy, and they were thrilled. Alex was mowing, but he took a few minutes to watch them zipping around, and it made him smile, because he knew exactly how they were feeling.

A week later, Daniel got a call from the investigator he had hired. He asked Daniel to come to his office, which he did that afternoon. He sat down across the desk from Mr. Wildman, who opened a folder and took out a page.

"I want to go over what I've found about the kid's father, George Morgan Roberts." He handed Daniel a picture of the man. "I began with the last known address in Arizona, and was able to track him to San Diego, California." Daniel took the picture and noticed how much Aiden looked like his father.

Mr. Wildman went on, "He wandered around San Diego holding down first one job and then another. He was arrested a few times for public intoxication. He shacked up with a couple of women over the years, but never married. That's a good thing, because he and the kid's mom never were divorced. He checked himself into a couple of detox centers to try to kick the drinking addiction. But he went back to his old habits upon being released. Eventually, he was drunk one night walking along a highway, and was hit and killed.

"They've been looking for next of kin ever since he was killed in 2019 in San Diego. The county cremated him and buried his urn in a pauper's grave inside the city. Here is his death certificate," he said handing over the paper.

"Now here's the kicker. When he died, even though he was a drinker, he had $108,000 in a bank in San Diego. He was a gambler, so he probably won a windfall at some point, but he died before he was able to drink it up. Here's the name, address and phone number of the bank." He handed another paper to Daniel.

"Looks like your kids have a nice little inheritance. So, here's the person to contact about that." He handed another piece of paper to Daniel. He was floored, this was totally unexpected.

He thanked Mr. Wildman and when he got to his car, he made a call to his attorney. He needed to get the information to him and let him take care of the inheritance. Jake told him to come right over, so Daniel handed all the paperwork from the investigator over to him. He kept the picture.

When he got home, he called Aiden into his office to relay this latest information to him. He handed the picture of his father to him. Aiden just sat staring at his dad's face. He knew the picture was not recent and probably from when his father was in the services because, even though it was just a head shot, it looked like he might have a uniform on.

Then when Daniel told him about the inheritance, his eyes widened, "What?! You're saying my sisters and I are inheriting $108,000? I can't believe it!" He was stunned.

"Looks like it. I've given the information to my attorney to finalize the exchange. I think we need to get you a bank account opened up. And you'll be able to pay me back the balance of your mother's mortgage payments sooner than we expected."

"I can even pay off Mom's house, all of it," Aiden said ecstatically.

"I know you could, but I don't think I'd do that if I were you."

"Why not?"

"Because you don't know what's going to happen in the future. You might end up needing the money for something, maybe one of you will get hurt and there would be medical bills. And when you sell your mom's home, there will be closing costs to pay at closing. And you might decide to go to college if you don't get that scholarship. So, I'd put the money in the bank and sit on it for a while and wait and see."

"Yeah, that's probably a good idea. Wow! I just can't believe this. Just wait till the girls find out."

"Then why don't you go tell them. Off with you now," Daniel said with a chuckle.

Aiden ran out of the barn and into the pastureland where he'd seen the girls last. They were still riding the four-wheeler and he went running and calling both their names. They thought something was wrong, looked at each other, and went running toward him.

When he told them the good news, they were ecstatic. They were screaming and dancing around, hugging one another, jumping up and down. Erin came riding up on the four-wheeler, shut it down and asked what was going on. When they told her, she joined into the celebration, jumping up and down and screaming just like the other three.

That night, the family celebrated with a special dessert of Rum Cake slathered with rum sauce and topped with whipped cream. Aiden stuck his finger into his whipped cream and dotted it on Izzy's nose which brought a round of laughter.

Daniel took Aiden to Tupelo the next day and helped him open a checking and savings account. Aiden gave them $5.00 to deposit into each account, since a deposit was required.

Aiden found it hard to concentrate the next day as he worked. He wanted to chuck it all, take time off from work, and just spend the day celebrating wealth. But he knew he wouldn't because of his loyalty to Daniel. He felt so indebted to Daniel for all his help. But his elation was soon to change to worry once again.

Soon Daniel got a call from his lawyer about Child Family Services wanting to meet with all three children. Daniel asked if the meeting could be set up in Jake's office. Jake said he would set it up and get back with Daniel about it.

Daniel also received a call from the police wanting to set up another meeting with Aiden about his mother's body. Daniel sighed. Things were getting very busy. He set an appointment for the police to come by the following day.

Aiden was ready, although he was fearful. The same policeman came that had come before, and he was shown to the living room where Aiden and Daniel were waiting. He shook hands with both of them and was offered a chair. He began, speaking to Aiden, "I wanted to come by to let you know about the autopsy of your mother. The toxicology report shows she did have COVID, and there were no other things found like excessive liquor or illegal drugs, nothing to indicate a suspicious death, so there was no reason to believe she died of any other cause. Therefore, she's been released to be cremated, and we need to know what you want done with her afterward."

Aiden looked at Daniel, who spoke up, "We'll come and get her ashes in a couple of days if that is alright."

"Of course." He then looked at Aiden, "I'm very sorry for your loss, son. And if I might say so, I think you've landed in some pretty fortunate arms here with the Wilshire's."

"I couldn't agree more," he replied. "And thank you, sir."

The officer smiled, looked at Daniel, and said, "And he's so mannerly, very respectful. Is he always like that?"

Daniel replied, "I still can't seem to get him to stop calling me sir."

They laughed, Aiden smiled, they all shook hands, and the officer left.

Jake called Daniel to let him know the appointment with Child Family Services would be at his office tomorrow. Daniel said they'd be there at the appointed time.

All three kids were dressed in their best. They were scared and sat quietly the entire drive to Jake's office, each afraid to voice their thoughts openly. Daniel led the way into the conference room. They quickly glanced at the three people already seated at the table in Jake's conference room, trying to assess if they were friendly or not before looking down at the floor.

After introductions, Daniel began the conversation, "I want to make sure each of you are fully aware of these children's situation."

The woman, Mrs. Drew, said, "I believe your attorney has done a good job of explaining it very well in his filing."

"Well, there's more information I've learned since he filed for custody of the kids. I hired an investigator to see if he could find their father. He found their father is deceased, and Jake has his death certificate."

"Yes, he's passed that on to us. Therefore, we'd like to talk to the children to see just how they feel about you having custody of them, so if you don't mind, Mr. Wilshire, we'd like to talk to them without you present."

"Not a problem," he rose to leave the room, but was happy that his attorney was still in the room.

After he left the room, Mr. Waltrip, one of the three from Child Family Services, asked, "So I take it you are Aiden?" looking at Aiden.

"Yes, sir."

He then asked which of the girls was Isabelle and which was Charlotte. After that was cleared up, he asked Isabelle first, "May I call you Isabelle?"

She said, "Yes, sir."

What do you think about Mr. Wilshire?"

"I think he's wonderful. He has already helped us so much. I love his family."

"Good, thank you for that. And Charlotte, what are your thoughts about living with the Wilshire's?"

"I hope we can live with them forever."

To Aiden he asked, "Aiden, do you feel the same?"

"Absolutely."

"And am I to believe you are already staying with the Wilshire's?

"Yes, sir."

"And you've been living with them for a few weeks so far. Is that right?"

"Yes, sir, but I was working for them several weeks before we began living with them."

"I see. And what kind of work do you do for them?"

Aiden squirmed in his chair, he was so excited, "Well, sir, I have lots of things I can do. Mr. Wilshire trained me, and he leaves it up to me to do whatever I want. I get to feed horses, llamas, who will spit on you if they don't know you, and sheep. I get to herd the cows in every evening. I get to mow. I get to clean and repair things. There's always plenty to do. It never gets boring."

"So do you feel like he's using you as slave labor?"

Aiden was incensed that he would even ask such a question. "No, not at all. I'm very happy to be working for Mr. Wilshire. He's the best. He's even given me a raise because he said he's so happy with my work ethic. I'm never overworked, I start work at a set time, and I'm to quit at a set time.

"Slave labor would be awful. And people who use kids for that are awful to be around. Mr. Wilshire and his family are fun to be around. Ask the girls."

He then turned to the girls, "Charlotte, how do you feel living with the Wilshire's?"

"It's the best place we've ever lived, including with our mother. We loved our mother, but we were poor. She did her best to provide for us, and she was very loving, but I can't imagine what would make people do as much for strangers as the Wilshire's have done for us. They are very kind people. We do have chores to help with, but I'd be bored if I didn't have anything to do. I like to work, and I enjoy learning more things, like Aiden does. I'm learning how to raise a garden and we'll be able to help Mrs. Wilshire put up food like canning and freezing. I'm very excited about that."

He then looked at Isabelle. She didn't wait for a question, "I want to live with the Wilshire's and if you don't let me, I'll just run away from wherever you put me."

They laughed at her straightforward statement, "Well said."

They called Daniel back into the room. He saw them all smiling and knew it would be good news. They let him know they had no problem with the children staying with his family, to which the children broke out in "Hurray's," "Yay" "Thank you, thank you," and a few other expressions of elation.

When they left Jake's office, they were all talking at once, a far cry from their somber attitude when they first arrived.

Back home, Daniel declared they needed another celebration, to which Erin, Dane, and Miriam were elated.

"Then I say we take tomorrow off and do something fun," Daniel declared. "Put your heads together and decide what you want to do."

They decided they would go out to eat in Tupelo and find a good movie to go to. Everyone was happy and left the theater laughing and joking around. Dane said, "Here's one for you: Why can't my nose be twelve inches long?" No one answered, so he said, "Because it would be a foot."

Aiden then said, "What is a pig's favorite karate move?" Silence. "A porkchop."

Charlotte said, "What do you call a belt made of watches?" "A waste of time."

Izzy had one too. "Which animal is the most untrustworthy?" Silence, "Cheetahs."

Aiden had another one, "Why did the little girl hit her birthday cake with a hammer?" "It was a pound cake."

And it went on and on all the way home, everyone laughing until their sides hurt.

The next day, Daniel took all three children back to their hometown to get their mother's ashes. Daniel paid for the cremation, again causing the children to thank him over and over again for his kindness.

"While we're here," Aiden asked, "do you think we could go by our house and see if there's anything else we want to bring with us?"

"Sure, I was going to ask if you wanted to go see the house one more time anyway."

It felt strange and sad for the children to enter the house. So many memories, both good and sad. After somberly walking through it and looking at everything, they eventually made it to their rooms where they found a few more pieces of clothing they wanted to keep.

Aiden went into their mother's bedroom where he found a picture album he wanted, and a picture of all three kids with their mother inside a frame he couldn't stop staring at.

Daniel could see how poor the family had been. It was a very old house, just a few miles from the edge of town, and in need of much repair. He thought the living room sloped to one side even. He figured their mother had gotten it at a very low price, but at least it was a roof over their head, and a barn for their horses, albeit needing a lot of repairs also.

When they were ready to leave, Daniel stated, "I've found a REALTOR in this town. Should we stop at the office to see about listing the house for sale?"

"Why not?" Lottie replied. "We're never living here again."

They found the real estate office and talked with the Realtor. She wanted to look at the property first before discussing a price. They left the keys with her and told her to get back with them after she saw it.

Aiden asked before they left, "Do we have to come back here to sign the papers?"

"No," she said looking at Daniel. "I can email the papers to your email. You can sign everything online."

He replied, "I'm not the owner, these kids are. Their parents are no longer living, so we'll get their death certificates to you. My attorney has them, so text me your email so he can send them to you. You'll have to email the paperwork to my attorney who will represent the kids as their Power of Attorney." He then texted her Jake's email and gave her his own phone number in case she needed anything from the kids.

On the way back home, Daniel said, "Well, we're slowly making headway. We've gotten the information needed about your father, taken care of your mother, set up a bank account for you, and talked to a REALTOR about getting your mom's house listed and sold."

Aiden said, "We can't thank you enough, Mr. Wilshire."

"Now what do you want to do with your mother's ashes?"

"Well, we haven't talked about it yet, but I propose we dump her ashes into the river across the road in the woods."

The girls both agreed, so Daniel said the entire family would go with them when they decided to do it.

Lottie said, "I think Mom would love the river. It's so beautiful." Izzy agreed.

The next day, the Realtor phoned Jake and said her CMA showed the market value of the house was $79,000. The mortgage showed she still owed around $15,000 on the house, so the kids would have a nice chunk after closing. Jake talked with Aiden and Daniel by phone about the price the Realtor recommended listing the house for, and they both agreed it sounded reasonable, especially with the condition of the property.

That Sunday Miriam roasted a turkey for dinner. She added mashed potatoes, with turkey gravy, dressing, green beans, homemade dinner rolls, and slaw for a salad. When the kids came inside to eat, Dane declared, "Wow! What's the occasion?"

"Well, I figured we're still celebrating that the Roberts kids will not be sent to foster homes," declared Miriam.

The three kids all declared they had never had a more wonderful meal. And couldn't thank Miriam enough. They topped the meal off with Blackberry pie and ice cream.

While they were eating the kids regaled the Wilshire's with their recollection of having to pluck the feathers of the turkey Aiden had shot, and Izzy reenacted the smell of the wet feathers with the most God awful face, bringing a round of laughter from everyone.

"Ok," Miriam said, "But this is the last of the celebration, tomorrow we get back to chores. And you girls need to pick the green beans, onions, and carrots. We'll can some of it, some of it we'll freeze, and some we'll give to neighbors."

Everyone was so stuffed they laid around all afternoon, too full to move.

That evening all five of the kids decided to go horseback riding. They rode up to the corner and headed left over the bridge above the river and to the store. Charles was beaming to see customers on Sunday evening.

"Just in time, I'm getting ready to close for the day. So, looks like you kids have made some friends," he said speaking with Dane.

"Yes, we have. Have you met the Roberts kids?"

"Sure, they shop here," he nodded toward Aiden.

Aiden greeted him, but bumped Dane in hopes he would understand not to say anything further about him and his sisters. He still had his pride and didn't want the entire countryside to know the details of their lives.

Dane got the point and moved on to the candy aisle where he loaded up on candy bars, sweet and sour discs, peppermint patties, and a few other things. They left with a nice sized bag. He stuffed them into his saddle bag, after divvying some out to the others.

They rode down the road and Dane declared he wanted to see the cabin. Soon they were all tramping through the woods single file, walking their horses behind them. At the clearing, Dane said, "Wow, looks like it's been taken good care of."

He went into the cabin, looked around and came back out, "You guys did a good job on things." Then looking around, he stated, "And you've even built an outhouse."

"Something I never want to use again," declared Izzy.

"What's with the fence?"

"Horse pen," answered Lottie. "We had to have some place for them so they wouldn't run away."

"Good job, Aiden. You're very resourceful."

"It's called family survival," Aiden answered.

Next day the girls got busy in the garden, while the boys headed to the barn. Aiden began mucking out the stalls, while Dane threw bales of hay out of the loft to take to the pasture.

They kept busy all day doing first one thing and then another. That evening the Roberts kids taught the Wilshire kids how to play Hand and Foot, the card game they loved. It wasn't long before Daniel and Miriam asked if they could join in as well.

Aiden was so happy to have a nice family to live with, and to see how close a family could and should be. He stopped playing cards and just sat looking around the table at everyone. So happy to be among such wonderful people. He just wondered how long they'd be able to live with the Wilshire's. He knew his sisters felt the same way.

A few days later, Daniel received a call from Jake telling him he had deposited the $108,000 inheritance from the kid's father into Aiden's bank account. Aiden let Daniel know he would write a check to pay him back for everything he owed him, attorney's fees, the cremation of his mother, the investigator's fee, and the money Daniel had kicked into the mortgage payments in arrears on his mother's house.

"I believe the only thing we agreed on was that you'd pay me back for the money I kicked in on your mother's house payments. The rest is my expense. You keep your money. I want you to go to college.

And by the way, have you thought any more about what you want to do with your life after high school?"

"Yes, sir, I've thought a lot about it, and I'd like to have a ranch like this someday. I really enjoy working on your farm."

Daniel was taken aback. "But you don't know what you're asking. I inherited this farm from my father and added more land to it later. It would take you years to build up a farm by yourself."

"Well, I wouldn't need a big one like this, just someplace of my own in the country. Just a few acres, big enough to have a house and barn, a garden, and a little pasture- land."

"Are you sure?"

"I believe I am. Ask me again half-way through my senior year. But I doubt if I'll change my mind."

"Well, if you're sure, talk to Dane about the classes he's taking because he plans on taking over this place someday."

"I've already talked to him about his classes. So, I just need to know what electives I should take next year that could help me."

"Well, have you thought about entering 4H?"

"That's a good idea. I'll look into that."

"I'm not sure what electives the high school offers, but again Dane might know. If he doesn't, then I guess you'll just have to wait until we get you kids enrolled in school."

23

Soon they got a call from Jake that the Realtor had an offer on the kids house. It was an investor who was offering $70,000 cash and a close within two weeks. Jake had countered at $73,000 and the investor agreed. The kids were elated that the house had a contract on it so quickly.

The paperwork was emailed to Jake who signed for Aiden and the girls, and within two weeks they had close to another $70,000 to add to Aiden's bank account.

Shortly afterward it was time to enroll for school for all the kids except Dane, who was heading off to college. Aiden realized with Dane being gone, it would mean more work for him, and hoped he might get a raise, if he could carry the load.

Before Dane left for college, he cornered Lottie in the barn, and said, "Lottie, I might be leaving, but before I go, I want to let you know something."

"Ok, what?"

"Well, I… uh…," this proved to be harder than he had expected. "I want you to know about my feelings for you."

Lottie's eyes grew wide. "Your feelings?"

"Yes, in getting to know you, I find I'm drawn to you. I know I have four years of college but what I'm asking is… what I'm asking is… this is so hard to say."

"Just say it."

"I was wondering if you would consider waiting for me."

"Waiting for you? Waiting for you to do what?" she knew exactly what he was asking but she enjoyed making him squirm.

"Wait for me to finish college. Wait to marry me."

"You want to marry me?"

"Yes, if you feel for me the same way I feel for you."

"How do you feel about me?"

"I… I… I love you," he finally blurted out.

"Oh, Dane, that's the most romantic thing anyone has ever said to me." She hesitated before continuing. She looked up into his eyes, "I love you too, Dane."

He pulled her close to him, looked into her eyes, raised her chin, and lowered his lips to hers. They pulled apart and he said, "I've wanted to do that ever since I met you. God, you are so beautiful."

She chuckled at this and didn't want to leave his arms. "I love you to hold me like this."

"I love holding you."

"Please don't say anything to Aiden about this. He might punch you out. He's pretty protective of us girls."

"No problem. But Aiden and I are friends, so I don't think he'd be very upset."

"Well, he might not punch you, but I'm sure he'd give you the third degree. Four years of waiting then?"

"If you really love me, you'll wait."

"You know I'll be in school with a lot of other guys." She enjoyed teasing him, but she knew there could be no one else but Dane.

"I know and that scares me. If you feel like you can't wait, you've got to promise to let me know. Do you promise?"

"I promise."

"Good, now kiss me one more time. I'm leaving in the morning, and I want to remember this kiss while I'm gone."

He kissed her ardently. He kissed her again and again, running his fingers through her long hair, pulling her as close against his body as he could.

While they were still locked in each other's arms, Aiden walked into the barn and saw them.

"Lottie!" he yelled. "What are you doing?"

They pulled apart, and she turned to look at Aiden. "Aiden, don't get mad."

"Dane?" he asked, looking at Dane.

Dane spoke up, "I plan on marrying your sister."

"That's funny. I thought you were going to college."

"I am, but Lottie says she'll wait for me. We love each other."

"That's a long wait. I hardly think that's fair to her."

Dane was flustered. "She said she'll let me know if she decides not to wait for me. I'm not tying her down to just me. But if she finds someone else, I want the chance to discuss it with her."

"And what about you being around all those pretty girls at college?" Aiden asked.

"Charlotte is the only one for me. Look, Aiden, I'm not going to do anything that will hurt her. You know me. I'd never hurt her in any way."

"You'd better not or you'll answer to me. And, Lottie, are you sure you want to wait four years for him?"

"Yes, Aiden, I do. I'll only be twenty when he's through with school. It's ok, Aiden."

Aiden stood staring at Dane. Eventually, Dane said, "It's ok, Aiden. Trust us."

Aiden then turned and walked back out of the barn. He needed to think about this.

Dane and Lottie looked at each other. "That went well," Dane said.

"I don't know, Dane. I've got the feeling that Aiden thinks I'm doing the wrong thing to wait for you."

"But he doesn't know how much you love me, and I love you. We'll be good for each other, I'm certain of it. You love living here, and I'm to inherit Dad's farm, so you'll end up staying here for the rest of your life. Do you think you'd like that?"

"Oh, Dane, you know I would. I just don't want Aiden to worry about me."

"Well, after I get settled in, I'll call you as often as I can. And here," he handed her a wad of cash, "get yourself a mobile phone."

"But I can't pay a monthly bill. All of our money is in Aiden's bank account which I don't have access to."

"Then I'll pay your bill each month. No problem. I just want you to have your own phone so we can talk privately. I don't want you to use Dad and Mom's phone where everyone in the family can hear our conversation."

"So, do I put the phone in your name?"

"No, go ahead and put it in your own name. They won't care who pays the bill, as long as it gets paid."

She took the money then and tucked it down her bra. He watched with delight, wishing he could go dig it out. No, he had to keep his mind out of the gutter. Eventually, he told himself, be patient.

Aiden couldn't get it out of his mind that Lottie wanted to marry Dane. He knew Dane was in line to inherit the farm, and if Lottie and Dane did get married, he knew she'd be well taken care of. And so far, he liked everything about Dane, and would be happy if Lottie married into the Wilshire family. Charlotte Wilshire, the sound of her name being linked with Dane's made him smile. Yes, he felt it could be a good thing for them to get married, but he had reservations about Lottie waiting four years for Dane.

Later Lottie caught Aiden and asked him to please keep it to himself about her and Dane. She wasn't ready for Izzy to find out.

He promised to keep it a secret, but said, "I just hope you know what you're doing."

She smiled and replied, "I think I do. And you should marry Erin."

"Now there's a thought, me and Erin."

"You like her, don't you?"

"She's alright." Even though he was secretly in love with Erin, he had no intentions of admitting it.

"Well, I happen to know she's in love with you."

He jerked his head up, "How do you know that? You don't know that."

"Oh, but I do. She told me so."

"When?"

"A long time ago when she was visiting us girls in the woods. She thinks you're gorgeous."

"Ha-ha, that was a long time ago. She's probably changed her mind now that she's gotten to know me."

"I'll find out."

"Oh, no you don't. You keep things to yourself, or I'll tell Izzy about you and Dane."

"Spoil Sport. You ruin all the fun. Ok, I won't say a word, but just pay attention to the way she looks at you, and the way she finds ways to be where you are."

He had to admit that was something he hadn't noticed. Could he really be so dumb as to not pick up on when a girl was interested in a guy? Had he been so intent on doing his work that he'd totally missed her true feelings for him?

24

ottie was sad to see Dane leave the next day. Dane couldn't help but look at her longer than he'd intended. He winked at her, which brought tears to her eyes. She blinked them away, and then he was gone.

Izzy picked up on the emotion between the two and decided to speak with Lottie about what she'd noticed. The first chance she got when they were alone, she said, "So what's with you and Dane?"

"What? Nothing."

"Come on, Lottie, I know you. You almost cried when he left. You love him don't you."

Lottie sighed and grudgingly said, "Yes, I love him. But he's gone and that's that, so no more talk about love."

"Well, I saw him wink at you, so I know there's some electricity between you two. It's not all you, is it? He's in love with you too."

"You're imagining things, Izzy. Now drop it."

"Ok, you can play that game if you want to, but we both know the truth. Secretly, I hope you marry him. I don't believe you could find anyone any nicer. And look what you'd have," she said as she spread her arms wide. "All of this."

"Well, he's gone now, so nothing will probably come of it anyway."

"Does Aiden know?"

"Yes."

"What does he think about it?"

"He thinks four years is too long to wait."

"Yeah, he might be right about that. So, in the meantime you could find someone else, get married, and go back to live in the cabin in the woods."

"Izzy!" Lottie declared. "Honestly!"

"Well, you never know. People fall in love with the wrong guy all the time and live in misery for the rest of their lives. Look at mom."

"Well, I for one will not do that. I've known Dane long enough to know the kind of man he is, and I believe he's a lot like his dad, whom I admire greatly. So, if he stays that way, I couldn't do any better. Now get out of here and find something useful to do."

Soon Erin knocked on Lottie's bedroom door. When she entered, she flopped on the bed and said, "So when's the wedding."

"Not you too."

"Oh, come on, Lottie. Everyone in the family can see Dane is in love with you, and I'd love to have you as my sister-in-law."

"Everyone in the family? You mean your mom and dad too?"

"Sure, they were just talking about it. Mom said she'd be happy if the two of you got married, and Dad said you'd make a great wife for Dane."

"Oh, Lord!"

"Oh, Lord, what? I think it's great. I plan on marrying Aiden and that will make the two of us even closer, connected through marriage."

Lottie said, "Now there's a thought. Our families tied together with two marriages. So how are we supposed to tie Izzy into that mess?"

"Hmmm, never thought of that. Looks like she'll be the odd man out."

"She's too young anyway, and so are we, as a matter of fact. Who knows what will happen in the future?"

"Oh, don't be so negative. You know it's going to happen. I know Dad's been talking to Aiden about going to college too. I'd hate to have to wait that long for him to marry me."

"Won't we both feel like old maids by the time they're out of college?" They both giggled at that thought.

Later as the girls were helping Miriam fix lunch, Miriam turned to Lottie and said, "I think it was hard for you to say goodbye to Dane. Am I right?"

Lottie stopped working and looked at her. "Yes, ma'am."

"You know when Dane first met you, that day you girls came to lunch, he told us you were the girl he was going to marry."

This shocked Lottie. She had no idea he was interested in her that long. "Really?" she asked, as she felt her face turn red, she was embarrassed.

"Yes, and Daniel told him to leave you alone."

Lottie laughed at that. "Well, he did a good job obeying then. Until yesterday, I had no idea he was interested in me at all."

The girls laughed. Izzy said, "The girl is always the last to know. I just hope I'll find someone for me like Dane when I'm older."

"Yeah," said Lottie, "too bad the Wilshire's don't have another son about your age."

"Yes, wouldn't that be great," Izzy put in. "And Mrs. Wilshire, I've heard Aiden plans on marrying Erin."

Erin jerked her head up. "Izzy! Keep things to yourself. You don't know that for sure."

"Well, don't you think your mom needs to know so she can keep an eye on you? You need to stay away from Aiden just like Dane had to stay away from Lottie."

Mariam spoke up, "Absolutely right. Thank you, Izzy."

Aiden took the advice of Daniel and took electives in school to help him in the future if he was ever able to obtain a farm of his own. He took a financial course, and biology in hopes he'd be able to understand the anatomy of animals better. And even though he wasn't really interested in math, he figured he'd need an advanced course in that as well, although he wasn't exactly sure what part math would play in ranching, except to keep the books. He also signed up for woodworking because he knew there would be things to build or repair. He felt good about the classes he'd be taking and was sure it would put him on track to reach his goal of being a rancher someday. And he vowed to try to be a straight A student and maybe win a scholarship.

Now that they were registered for school, Miriam said she wanted them to do some shopping for school clothes, and supplies. All of the kids, Erin, Aiden, Lottie, and Izzy got new clothes and Miriam insisted she would pay for them. The girls were ecstatic at getting new clothes, especially Lottie and Izzy. It had been a very long time since they got anything new. They were used to the second-hand clothing their mother always bought them.

They oohed and aahed over their choices in clothing, jeans, tops, shoes, and even pajamas and underwear, as-well-as, backpacks. The other items, for school, pens, pencils, and paper were essential and not very exciting. So eventually they felt sure they had everything they needed.

"No, you don't have quite everything you need," declared Miriam.

"What did we miss?" asked Erin. "I think this is enough."

Miriam then looked at Aiden and said, "You kids don't have any electronics, do you?"

He hung his head, and replied, "No, ma'am."

"It's nothing to be ashamed of."

"It's not that ma'am. It's just that…well, it's that we threw them into a pond we came across when we ran away from home."

"Oh, and why did you do that?"

"Because we could be traced through them. We didn't want anyone to be able to find us."

"I see. Well, you'll need iPads in school, so I suggest we go shopping for those as well."

Lottie spoke up, "Dane gave me money so I can get a mobile phone so he can call me."

"That's fine. But you'll still need an iPad."

So, after they got all that taken care of, which seemed to take forever, they headed for home.

25

One day, while Aiden was hooking the cows up to the milking machine, he got kicked by a cow. He went down screaming. Soon Daniel heard him and came running. Aiden told him what had happened.

"Where did he kick you?" asked Daniel. Aiden showed him the place on one of his legs. "Can you move it?" Daniel asked.

Aiden tried but could not without screaming. Daniel told him he would bring his truck over to where Aiden was and get him to the hospital. Aiden was screaming the entire time Daniel was helping him into the truck. The girls heard him all the way inside the house and came running.

"What's happened?" asked Lottie.

Daniel explained and let them know he was taking Aiden to the hospital. His sisters said they wanted to go with him. They loaded Aiden into the back seat to lay down and the girls jumped into the front.

Erin said she wanted to go too, but Daniel said she had to stay home because there was no room for her in the truck.

Soon they were in the emergency room. The girls were on each side of his bed holding his hand, trying to pacify him with kind words. It wasn't long before they came to take him to get an X-ray of his leg. While he was gone, Daniel took the girls down the hall to a vending machine to get them each something to drink.

When the doctor entered the room again, he explained that the leg was broken below the knee, but it was a clean break, not a compound break, and that all Aiden would need would be to have it set. He would get pain meds as well.

Soon they were on the way back home, along with a prescription for pain meds, and instructions to go to see his primary doctor in a week to have the temporary cast replaced because after the swelling would go down, the current cast would be too loose.

Daniel joked in the truck, "Some people will do anything to get out of work."

"Hey!" Aiden replied, "I'd rather be working than this any day."

"Yeah, I know. I was just joking. But it looks like you'll be laid up for a while, so, you girls are going to have to take over some of Aiden's workload. Do you think you can do that?"

"I don't think we have a choice," Izzy replied.

"Don't worry, Mr. Wilshire. We don't mind. We'll be happy to help out more," Lottie put in.

They got the prescription filled, got Aiden home and into the house and onto the couch. He let the girls know what still needed to be done in the way of chores.

The girls left to go to the barn to saddle up horses to get the llamas and sheep brought into the barn for the night. They too, marveled at Shep and thought they really weren't needed to do anything. They actually thought the job was fun. Then they fed the animals for the night, staying well out of reach of the llamas, and headed to the house, glad to be finished with their work for the day. But they knew tomorrow would be another story and would need Aiden to lay out his work schedule. They were glad school had not started yet so they would get used to the work and know what they were doing before homework kicked in.

They got Aiden up the stairs to bed, but before he would be able to go to sleep, he asked for more pain medicine.

The next morning Aiden stayed in bed, Erin bringing up his breakfast. She sat down on a chair in the bedroom, and asked, "How are you feeling today?"

"A little better, I guess."

"I'm so sorry, Aiden. How did it happen?"

"I was hooking the cows up to the milking machine. I went around behind one cow to the next one, and he just kicked."

"Well, I'm sorry. I know how bad it must feel. And I know how much you have enjoyed your work here. I just hope this doesn't turn you off from wanting to continue working for Dad."

"No, nothing like that. But I sure will give a cow a wide birth from now on when I have to walk behind them."

"Horses too. You just can't trust an animal. If they can't see you, they don't know what you're doing."

"Right, I'll remember that. Can't trust a llama either. They spit on you."

She laughed, "Yeah, I remember that one well. You were so astonished when that llama spit on you. I should have warned you ahead of time. The expression on your face was hilarious."

"It was so gross."

"I know. I've been spit on also. Once that happens to you, you don't forget it." She rose to go and told him she'd come back to check on him later.

Before she left the room, Aiden said, "Erin, come here." She went to his bedside, where he held out his hand to her. "Thank you. You make a good nurse."

She laughed again and headed to the door. At the door she turned to look at him and couldn't help smiling as she saw the smile on Aiden's face.

She went to help the girls with the work in the barn. Daniel was there to make sure they understood what to do, and how to do it. He let them know, he would also help out. He was going to take hay out to the pastureland for the cattle, while the girls began brushing down the horses and mucking out their stalls.

They worked until noon and were very thankful for the break. Erin took a tray of food upstairs for Aiden and to check to see how he was doing. He let her know he needed more pain medicine and thanked her for the food. She said, "I'm sorry I didn't come back to check on you sooner. I was busy doing your work for you."

"Yeah, and I thank you very much for filling in for me. I hope I'm not laid up for long."

"Believe me, after doing your work for you, I hope you aren't laid up very long either. And give me time and I'll figure out a way you can pay me back."

At the table for lunch, Lottie said, "I sure respect the men for all they do, now that I've done their work. And may I say, I'm glad I'm not a man."

Others at the table laughed, and Izzy agreed she'd rather do women's work than mens.

Erin headed back upstairs with a bowl of ice cream for Aiden and to get his tray. "Hey, thanks for the dessert," he said as she handed him the bowl. She moved his tray to the bedside table and sat down to talk to him while he ate. She took his ice cream bowl after he finished, sat it on a tray, and leaned down and gave him a kiss.

His eyes widened and he asked, "What was that for?"

"No special reason. I just think you're a great guy and I feel really sorry for you right now."

"Do you want to show me how sorry you are?" he asked, as his arm reached out for her waist.

She leaned down once again, and he held her as close as he could. Her lips lingered on his.

When she pulled away, he said, "You'd better get out of here before I invite you into the bed with me." She smiled, picked up the tray, and left the room.

At the end of the day, the three girls marched into the house, flopped onto the couch and declared Aiden had to get well overnight. They were exhausted and wasn't looking forward to doing it all over again the next day. They all went to bed early that night and slept like a log.

26

The next morning when Erin brought his breakfast up to him, he declared he wanted out of the bed. He was tired of laying around doing nothing. She got his crutches for him and helped him stand up. He said before heading down the stairs, "Thanks for the help. Now I think you need to kiss me so I can get through the day."

"No way buster. If you're up and around you're doing better."

"It's your kisses that make me better, and I need more so I'll get even better."

"Nice try, but if you want to eat this breakfast, I suggest you get downstairs."

"Aw, you're taking all the fun out of the day."

He was able to navigate down the stairs, but slowly, and to the table where his food awaited him. He took his time eating alone since all three girls were already out into the barn.

Aiden hated being laid up like he was. His house pants had one leg cut off just above the knee and he was basically living in them day and night. He wanted to get back into his jeans and get back to work.

As time passed, he eventually was able to go to the barn using his crutches. He would heckle the girls, telling them they weren't doing a good enough job, until they threatened to take him to the washing stall for the animals and turn the water on him. And if he didn't stop it, they'd ban him to the house. He laughed and said he was actually enjoying watching them shoveling poop.

It became a habit for Aiden to show up in the barn mid-morning to oversee the girl's work, correcting them if he felt it wasn't done well enough. Daniel showed up in the doorway viewing the exchanges between him and the girls and smiled.

Eventually Aiden decided he needed to get back to work and his leg had stopped hurting. Therefore, with his temporary cast changed to a permanent one, he put his crutches away and hobbled with his cast out to the barn. He let the girls know they could go back to the house to their own chores, and he would take over the barn work. The girls were relieved. "Are you sure?" asked Erin.

"Yeah, I'm sure."

When the day came that Aiden was to go to the doctor to have his cast removed, you couldn't have found a happier man. "Relief at last," he declared.

The girls took the time to fix his favorite dessert for him that evening, a pecan pie with ice cream. When they brought it to the table, he said, "I'm so fortunate to have girls who love me." He had a big cheesy grin on his face.

He got his cast off just in time to begin school. And now that school was in session, he had to get up earlier than usual to get some chores done before getting on the bus. The girls pitched in to help him each morning.

Homework each night meant he stayed outside even longer to get his chores finished for the day. Sometimes he didn't come inside until after dark. He worked hard to make good grades trying to qualify for the scholarship that Daniel had told him about. Erin didn't like not having as much time to spend with him, but it was better that they didn't spend as much time together anyway, because the closer they became to each other, the harder it would be to wait until Aiden finished college to get married.

Lottie was spending time several times a week on the phone with Dane. He would tell her about his classes, his homework, the trouble he had finding his way around campus, that sort of thing. She would tell him about Aiden's broken leg and all the extra chores the girls had to do to help him out.

"I wish I'd been there to help out," Dane said.

"I wish you were here too, but for a different reason," Lottie replied with a smile.

"I know, but I'll be home for Thanksgiving, and I want to spend every minute I'm there with you."

"I miss you."

"I miss you too but keep busy till I'm back and we'll have some fun then. So, how's Aiden's leg now?"

"He's doing well. I think he had planned on going out for football, but now his doctor said he probably shouldn't since he got his cast off just a couple of weeks ago. Even though he's healed up, the doctor said it could still be a weak spot for a while longer."

"He wouldn't have time for football anyway, what with his workload at home. Football would require practice after school, plus games in the evenings and weekends. If he wants to be a rancher, he needs to concentrate on achieving that goal instead of chasing a ball around a field. That won't help him in real life anyway."

"Well, I think he was thinking of all the ways he might be able to get a scholarship and if he failed in the grades department, maybe he could get it through sports."

"Nah, he's smart enough, he'll be fine if he just concentrates on his grades."

One day, Aiden got a B on an exam, and he felt it was the end of the world. He went to the teacher and explained that he really needed the chance at a scholarship and was there anything he could do to bring his B up to an A. He was certain he'd never qualify for a scholarship unless he was a straight A student.

The B grade he received was in biology, so the teacher told him he could get extra credit if he could catch enough frogs for the class to dissect. "How many frogs will you need?" he asked his teacher.

"About thirty I suspect, but if you can't get that many, I can assign two students to one frog, so that would be fifteen needed."

Aiden wasn't sure he could even get fifteen and was certain he could never get thirty.

That evening at the supper table, he told the family what he had to do. The girls immediately offered to help. "We can go over to the river," offered Izzy. "I bet there's plenty over there."

"But how are we supposed to catch them. Alive or dead?"

"Teacher didn't say, so I don't think it matters. And after we dissect them, they'll be dead anyway."

"Eew, that sounds gross," Izzy proclaimed. "Do I have to touch them?"

"You could wear gloves," Aiden said.

"Believe me I will. And what do we put them in?"

Miriam spoke up then, "I think I have some gallon jars with lids I can supply."

The next weekend, the three girls and Aiden gathered the jars and a fishing net and headed for the river. Aiden had cut some small straight limbs from some trees, whittled points on the ends to make them into spears. They could hear the frogs before they even reached the river's edge.

"Look along the edge of the water. Frogs like to be in the water," Aiden said. "But I want as many as possible to be alive, so don't spear them unless you have to."

Soon they were each squealing in delight when they were able to capture one. Aiden cautioned them to try not to mess them up too badly if they had to spear them or they might not be usable.

Eventually, they heard a loud scream and jerked up to find it was Izzy. She had accidentally stabbed her foot when she was aiming for a frog. It began to bleed, and Aiden sent Lottie back to the house with her to bandage it up.

"Wouldn't you know it, stabbing her foot! I can't believe it! I mean, how does someone stab their own foot aiming at a frog?" Aiden asked.

"She's a girl, Aiden," Erin explained. "This is not something girls would normally ever do. And I'm pretty sure it's not something Izzy has ever done before."

"You're right. I just hope in losing her, we won't come up short on frogs."

"I don't think she actually caught very many anyway. She's too girly girl for this kind of thing."

Soon Lottie was back stating that Miriam was tending to Izzy. After they were finished, they counted up how many frogs they'd caught only to find they had a total of seven.

"We need to come to the river either early in the morning or later in the evening," Aiden declared. They all decided that on Sunday they would try again in the evening.

When they got back to the house, they found Izzy sitting with her foot wrapped up and an ice pack on it. "How's Crip?" Aiden asked.

"It's not funny," Izzy blurted out. "It hurts."

"Who's laughing. Do you want to use my crutches?"

"Stop it, Aiden. I didn't make fun of you when you were crippled with a broken leg."

"Hey, I'm just trying to be helpful. And now that you're hurt, we probably won't make my quota, thank you very much."

Lottie jumped in then, "Lighten up, Aiden. You'll get your stupid frogs. And you'd better be thankful we helped at all."

"Oh, believe me, I'm very thankful. I just might buy you all a milkshake after school if this brings my test score up to an A."

"I'm holding you to that," Erin declared.

Lottie, Erin, and Aiden went to catch more frogs the next evening, and by nightfall they had caught all fifteen Aiden needed. He couldn't thank them all enough for their help.

On Monday morning, Aiden entered the classroom carrying a box filled with the frogs. He walked up to the teacher's desk where she was sitting, opened the box, and dumped the frogs out on her desk. The frogs began croaking and leaping all over the place. At least the live ones did. One landed on the teacher's chest. She screamed, and in trying to get up as quickly as possible, she almost fell backwards in her chair. Pandemonium broke out in the classroom. The boys jumped up to rush up front to help catch the frogs, while the girls jumped up, screaming, to rush to the back of the room, as far away from the frogs as they could get, while Aiden stood beside the teacher's desk with his arms crossed just watching the melee.

The teacher said, "Aiden Roberts, I should give you an "F" for this."

Aiden stated, "You can't do that. You promised an A on that test if I got you fifteen frogs, and here they are."

"I know what I said, but I should give you an F." She could hardly keep from smiling. She was trying to be stern, but the antics were really quite funny she had to admit.

Time was moving quickly, Aiden raised his grade up with the fifteen frogs he was able to produce, and soon Dane arrived for his Thanksgiving break from school. Everyone was very happy to have him home, especially Lottie. She felt she had gotten to know him so much better while he was gone, because even though she had been living at his house for most of the summer, he had followed his father's instructions and stayed away from her. Now that she had a phone of her own, and they talked often, she could get inside his head and come to know the real Dane. She was still very interested in him.

His time with the family was limited and it wasn't long before he was saying goodbye again.

Aiden had never seen time race by as quickly as it did during his senior year, and he attributed it not just to school and homework, but also the chores on the farm. Christmas came and went with another visit from Dane, and before long it was May and graduation time for Aiden.

He just missed getting his scholarship by a couple of points, but he knew he had done his best and Daniel and Miriam told him how proud of him they were. He declared he didn't really want to go to college anyway, but he'd wanted to please Daniel since Daniel wanted him to go. Actually, all he really wanted was to just work on the farm. It was in his blood, and he was tired of schoolwork anyway.

"Besides," he declared, "I can always pick Dane's brain since he's learning how to run a farm. I'm just not sure someone really learns as much going to school to learn that stuff, as you are by actually doing it."

Daniel had to agree. "And since you've graduated now, maybe I'll begin showing you my books and you can help in running the farm. You can learn how to order supplies, feed, hay, vitamins for the animals along with medicine for them, and other things needed. You can see who our contracts are with for cattle, horses, sheep, and llamas. What do you think about that?"

"I'd love it. Now that's really learning the ropes."

Aiden soaked the training up, learning easily everything Daniel did, who his contracts were with, who his vendors were. He was trained in how to maintain the equipment; tractor, four-wheeler, mower that could be attached to the back of the tractor, as-well-as, the riding mower and push mower. He learned how to clean the milking machine. He learned how to take care of all the tools and leaf blower and weed eater. He learned how to shear the llamas and sheep, as well as, when it should be done, then who the vendor was to buy the wool. He learned how to take care of the books and balance the budget. He was shown the bank statements and learned how to balance that also.

Daniel took him with him to the show where he paraded his llamas in front of judges, and always won ribbons and cash. Aiden could see why his llamas were so important and he vowed to take better care of them.

With all the training Daniel had given him, he was flying high. He felt like he learned more under his tutelage than anything he could ever learn in a book. He didn't envy Dane going to college to learn what he was learning at home.

Dane was home for the summer, to Lottie's delight, and Aiden was glad to have his help with the farm. Cows had babies in the spring, and he wanted to watch them closely and give them the necessary shots from the vet in order to get them started on the right foot in life. One cow had a baby that wouldn't come when it was due. The cow was in trouble in trying to give birth. Eventually, Daniel had to herd her into the barn where they hoisted her up off her feet and pulled the baby from the mother. Even Aiden had gotten long gloves on and helped in reaching inside the mama to pull the baby out. When the little female cow was born, Aiden declared its name was Erin. Everyone laughed at that.

Daniel was glad the ordeal had worked out well, but he let Aiden know that it doesn't always end well. There will be a death here and there, and if that happens, he explained how the corpse was disposed of.

With summer's arrival, it was time to sheer the sheep and llamas. Aiden and Daniel were both happy Dane was home to help. They took the sheep outside one at a time, one holding them down while one did the clipping. The wool was gathered up and thrown into a wagon with tall sides. It was a dirty job, and not one that Aiden relished, but it had to be done, and it made them money. They would take the wool the next day to the company Daniel used to purchase it. After the sheep were sheared, the llamas would be next, and they were harder to do because of their size. They had a halter they put on them, and with one holding the halter, another holding the back steady, the third one did the shearing. Next, they made the llama lay down, they turned it on its back and sheared the underbelly. They bagged the underbelly wool to keep the soft wool separate from the stiffer wool. The bags were thrown into the back of the truck. Then it was off to market with the wagon, full this time with the wool from the llamas. The llamas at first, were afraid of the sound of the clippers, and fought, struggling to get free, but eventually they settled down.

"You'd think the animals would love to be sheared," declared Aiden. "With summer here, they'd get pretty hot with all that wool hanging on them. The heat could actually kill them."

Dane declared, "Yeah, but they're just dumb animals."

After their job of shearing was completed, Daniel said, "And, we have one very old horse I think we need to sell and purchase a younger one." Then to Aiden he said, "If we get a young one, you can help train him."

Aiden was looking forward to that. Soon they herded the old horse into a trailer and drove her to an auction house for farm animals. They came home with a young filly, which Aiden asked Erin to name.

She looked the young horse over. She was black with four white socks, and a white stripe down her nose. Erin decided she needed to think about it before deciding on a name because, as she said, "This is a name that will stick with her for the rest of her life, so I have to get it right."

Aiden responded, "Are you going to have to take a long time to decide on a name of your own baby when we have one."

She stared wide eyed at him, "Did you say, 'when WE have one'?

"That's what I said."

"Is that a proposal?"

"Well, I'm going to marry you some day. But first you have to finish high school. But as soon as you graduate ..."

"Oh, I like the sound of that," she interrupted.

"I'll do a proper proposal someday. But just don't go falling in love with someone else while I'm waiting for you."

She just smiled at him.

Aiden noticed, as well, that Lottie seemed to show up quite often wherever Dane was. He thought he'd better keep a close eye on them because Dane still had three years of college to go. He knew how hard it would be for them to wait because he had to wait one more year for Erin to graduate high school. At least as soon as she graduated, he planned on putting a ring on her finger even if they might have to wait to marry until he was more settled so he could provide properly for her. He wanted a place of his own. He didn't want to work forever for the Wilshire family.

Erin spent quite a bit of time with the new filly. Watching it, letting it out into the pasture along with the other horses to see how she reacted with them and they with her. She noticed that the little thing loved to run. She would run all over the pasture, kicking up her heels. So, Erin decided her name had to be Dash, because she seemed to always be dashing around here or there. Everyone agreed it was a fitting name. And she immediately declared Dash was going to be her personal horse. But each day it was Aiden who took the filly to the coral to train it.

Aiden caught Lottie aside one day and decided to take advantage of the time. He said, "Lottie, I know you love Dane and that he's only home for the summer, but you need to leave him alone so he can get his work done. You're not helping him by always seeking him out. It's going to be hard enough for him to leave you this fall, but you're building up more passion in him, and that will make it harder for him to leave. I'm sure you don't want to make him depressed to go back to school."

"Oh, gee, Aiden. I never thought about me being around him so much having that effect on him. I can see how that could happen. I'll be more aware of my actions. I certainly don't want to be the cause of him becoming depressed. I was just thinking about how he'll be leaving again, so I wanted to be with him as much as possible while he is here."

"Yeah, well, if you don't stay away from him, you and he won't be able to wait till he's out of college, and something could get really out of hand, and you could wind up in trouble. So, play it smart. Three years might be a long time to wait, but if you both can wait until you're married, it will be much sweeter and with no regrets."

"Ok, Aiden. I'll be more careful. Promise."

"That's my girl."

And after thinking more deeply about it, he knew he needed to take his own advice, regarding Erin.

Summer flew by and before everyone was ready for it to be over, Dane was off to college and the three girls were back in school. Aiden was busy doing all the chores again without Dane's help, and he was helping Daniel run the farm, taking on more and more responsibilities.

Daniel was pleased at how quickly Aiden had picked up the business end of things.

Dane was calling to talk with Lottie more often this year than last year, which pleased Lottie well. However, she was concerned that he might not be getting his studies completed because of how often he called her, although he promised he was doing well. She finally told him she only wanted him to call her three times a week and one of those times had to be the weekend. She told him she didn't want to be the cause of him falling behind. He wasn't happy about that, but she said if he called more often than that, she wasn't going to answer the phone.

Aiden was glad when school began so he wouldn't be tempted to be around Erin as much. And the faster school began, the faster she would be graduated, and he'd be able to propose properly.

After all of his training and Daniel overseeing his foreman's position, for that is what he truly believed he was, he was given raises right along. He was making very good money and decided to open another bank account so he could keep his money separate from his other account that had the three kid's inheritance and money from the sale of their mother's house. That money had to be split three ways.

One day Aiden came to Daniel to tell him he needed to buy his own vehicle. At first Daniel protested that he didn't really need one because he could use Daniel's any time he wanted, but Aiden had his heart set on having his own truck. So, Daniel took him shopping. When they finally found one Aiden liked, he was disappointed that he'd have to pay cash for it because the dealer wouldn't finance it for him, since he had no credit.

Therefore, Daniel said he would cosign for him so he wouldn't have to pay cash. Daniel didn't want him to spend so much money for a truck knowing Aiden had his heart set on buying a place of his own someday. If he paid cash for the truck, it would take him longer to purchase his own farm.

When the girls got home from school, they ran to see his truck and heartily agreed it was nice. Lottie said, "I'm so glad you were able to get your own vehicle. I know that means a lot to you.

"And I've wondered, what do you think ever became of Mom's car?"

"I have no idea," Aiden replied. "It probably got hauled off and sent to the auto auctions they have."

"Yeah, probably. Too bad we didn't go back to see if it was still there."

"Wasn't worth much anyway, and I drove it several hours from home. I wouldn't have asked Mr. Wilshire to drive that far just to see if it was still there."

"You're right. What does it matter anyway?"

Miriam did her part to train the two girls. She had them help her can things from the garden and freeze some things. One Saturday she took them to Tupelo to a store for them to pick out patterns to sew something. She instructed them that, what they picked out couldn't be something complicated since they had never been taught how to sew.

The girls were excited about learning something new. Izzy picked out an easy dress to make and Lottie chose a robe. Next Miriam helped them choose the correct material for each. She wanted their first project to be as easy as possible so it wouldn't frustrate the girls and make them decide they didn't like sewing.

The next day after lunch, Miriam began with Izzy while Lottie looked on. They went to Miriam's craft room, laid out the pattern, cut it apart, and Miriam showed her how to position the pieces on the material, so none of it was wasted. Then the sewing began, and Miriam showed her how to read and follow the directions of the pattern.

She got a good start and eventually it was Lottie's turn. The girls didn't complete their projects in one day, and Miriam told them not to worry because they'd get them completed Monday after school, as long as the girls weren't loaded down with a lot of homework.

After the girls finished their projects and declared they liked sewing, Miriam asked, "So would you girls like to learn more crafts? What do you think about making some jewelry?"

"Oh, I think I would love that," Lottie declared.

"Me too," Izzy added.

The following weekend they were all seated around the large table in the craft room. Miriam said she had enough supplies that she didn't believe they'd need to run to the store. She brought out all her beads, and the girls got busy digging through them to choose what they wanted to make.

Lottie chose red beads, Izzy chose turquoise, and Erin decided on a pastel pink. Erin had made jewelry before, so she helped one of the girls while Miriam helped the other. Miriam and Erin took their time to show them how to string them, attach the ends to a fastener, and soon the girls had their necklaces finished. They all wanted to make earrings to match, and Miriam agreed that was a good idea, but they'd have to do them another day because it was time to get cooking for their supper.

When it was slated for Dane to come home for Thanksgiving, Daniel declared he wanted to have a bonfire and invite friends for a wiener roast and hayride. The girls were delighted and vowed to help write out invitations to give to their friends and the neighbors.

Dane arrived on Tuesday evening before Thanksgiving and the bonfire was set for the coming Saturday. Things were in a flurry to get everything ready. Daniel chose a spot in a pasture for it and hauled wood for the fire and bales of hay. He sat the bales in a circle around the wood for everyone to sit on.

The girls went to the store to lay in the food, hot dogs, buns, and marshmallows. Potato salad and baked beans would be made at home. Others would also be bringing food and desserts, and all the paper products needed along with silverware. Daniel said he would provide beer, water, and soft drinks.

The guys strung lights around poles, and Dane hooked them up to long electric drop chords attached to one another end to end.

The girls asked if there was some way they could have a dance floor and music. Therefore, the guys went to Home Depot and got lumber and made a nice dance floor. Dane said he would have no trouble providing the music. They all couldn't wait for Saturday night.

People began arriving around five and by six they were roasting hot dogs over the fire on the sticks provided by Daniel.

Everyone had a great time, and the kids all danced the night away while the adults sat around the fire and talked. Lottie was so happy to be held close to Dane when a slow dance came on. Dane looked down into her eyes and said, "I wish I didn't have to go back to school. I wish I could stay home to be near you."

"Me too. But you've started it, you need to finish it."

"I suppose. You feel so good in my arms."

She smiled up at him, "Right where I want to be."

Aiden had his arms around Erin also as they swayed to the music. She rested her head on his chest, enjoying the feel of his hard body and the beat of his heart.

Daniel and Miriam were keeping a close eye on both couples.

Eventually Daniel got the tractor and wagon loaded with the bales of hay for the hayride. The young people scrambled up onto the wagon immediately. Dane settled down into the hay with his arms wrapped around Lottie, and Aiden did the same with Erin. The girls snuggled down and soon they were off, being pulled along country farm roads back along tree lines, and across pastures. The sky was clear, stars twinkling above, and a gibbous moon shone brightly. When they returned to the campfire, the kids were all singing and laughing at the top of their voices, having such a good time.

The week end quickly passed and Dane headed back to school. Life settled down to the daily routine on the farm. Aiden ordered more hay and oats for the animals, called the veterinarian out to check over all the animals, gave shots to all that needed them, and got a bill of health on them all.

Aiden took a horse out to ride the fence rows to check them out and found a tree limb had fallen on one of the fences breaking the barbed wire. He also noticed places where brush had grown up around the fence row swallowing the fence up so he couldn't even check to see if the wire was intact or not.

Therefore, he let Daniel know what he had found and that he intended to repair the fences. He took his truck, loaded it with a chainsaw, loppers, clippers, a roll of barbed wire, and gloves and drove back to remove the brush and cut up the tree limb. Then he repaired the fence wire, loaded the tree limbs into his truck bed, and stopped to throw the logs onto the place where they'd had a fire for the bonfire. He stopped to wipe the sweat from his brow, downed a jug of water, and headed back to the barn.

Before he reached the barn, he heard a cow bellowing and went to inspect it to see what the problem was. There was a stock pond in one of the pastures, and as he reached it, he saw one of the young calves had gotten into the pond in water over his head and was having trouble getting out. His mother was at the water's edge calling to the little guy, and the young calf was crying for his mama. Aiden turned his truck toward the barn racing back to get his horse, and rope.

He rode back to the pond, was able to lasso the head of the calf, and back his horse up to pull the calf out of the water, while the little thing was screaming the whole time. As soon as Aiden got him onto dry land, he dismounted, removed the rope from his neck, and noticed the mama was licking her baby as he rode away. He couldn't help but feel proud in rescuing the little guy, especially since he realized the calf was the one he had helped pull from his mama a few months ago, the one he named Erin.

One day, he saw on the news that there was a storm headed their way and would hit in a couple of days. He went to Daniel to ask what should be done about the cattle in the field. He knew the llamas, sheep, and horses would be alright in the barn, but what about the cattle?

Daniel said, "Cows are resilient, they'll be fine. They usually take cover under a tree out there and ride it out."

Aiden thought about that but wasn't satisfied. It bothered him that they didn't have proper shelter for the cattle. Therefore, he went back to Daniel and said, "I've given it a lot of thought about the cattle being out in the storms. What do you think about me building a shelter they can run to for protection? Nothing elaborate maybe just a roof they can get under."

"Sure, if you want to do that. That's fine with me. When did you want to build it?"

"I'd like to get the lumber and begin on it right away. I'm sure I won't get it finished in time for this storm, but maybe it will be ready for the next one."

"Ok, but you'll have to rent an attachment for the tractor to dig the post holes. It's too hard to dig them by hand."

"Yes, sir." Aiden headed into town to get what he needed. But instead of renting the attachment for the tractor, he ordered one and paid for it himself. He figured it was a piece of equipment that would always come in handy on a farm. He also ordered metal roofing for the shelter. So, because he had to wait for those things to come in, he decided to wait to get the lumber closer to delivery time for the other items.

Christmas came and went, and soon it was spring. More cows were being born, along with sheep and llamas. Aiden was busier than ever and wished Dane was home from school to help out. And the more Aiden considered it, the more he was convinced they needed another work hand on the farm. But because in just three months, Dane would be home for the summer, he decided to wait until fall to bring the subject up to Daniel about hiring more help.

Even though Aiden didn't like the idea of getting rid of any of their animals, Daniel said they needed to load up a cow to take to have it slaughtered for their freezer for the next year. He knew this was a part of ranching, but he didn't have to like it. He looked at his cattle more like pets than a business product. Also, Daniel said they needed to load up a couple of the young bulls born a few months back because you can't have more than one bull or there'd be trouble between them.

Summer arrived and Dane came home from college, much to the delight of Lottie, of course, but also of Aiden, because he needed help on the farm.

Lottie graduated high school and the family celebrated.

Aiden went over the books with Dane shortly afterward, to show him where they were financially, took him out to see how many more cows they had after the spring birthings. He went over the additions as well with the sheep and llamas.

Dane said, "Looks like we'll have to build a bigger barn if this keeps up. God must really be blessing you."

"Oh, I don't believe that. But I do think we need to talk about the sizes that the herds are increasing to. Daniel's been pretty much leaving things up to me as far as running the farm, which I appreciate, but …."

"But you don't feel adequate. Is that it?"

"Not that so much as I just feel short-handed, and if I'm to run the farm while you're gone, I don't think I can handle it if it grows much larger. And if we want it to grow, then when you head back to college come fall, I'm thinking we need to hire more workers."

"Have you had this conversation with Dad?"

"Not yet, but I wanted to run it by you first. You're the one who will inherit your father's farm, so I guess I thought I'd see what you want, a larger farm, or to keep it about the same size that it is?"

"I see. Well, if we decide to keep all the cattle and allow even more, we do have more land for pastures, but it would have to be cleared. There's a lot of brush on it. More help would mean more salaries to pay. More cattle means more expense in feed and vet bills, and we'd have to build more milking stalls. Sounds like a lot of work and expense. So, I think for right now, I'd say let's get rid of some of the extra animals, keep things about where we are now, and I'll address what to do about it after I graduate. That will keep it from putting too much on your plate. After all, you're still pretty new to this ranching business."

"That sounds great to me. I just have a hard time getting rid of some of the animals. I guess I'm getting too attached to them. But I don't have as much trouble selling them as I do butchering them."

Dane laughed, "Yeah, I know what you mean. I remember when I was little how I would cry when dad had to get rid of some, especially the sheep. Those little lambs are so cute you hate to see them go. I wasn't as upset when he had to put down an old one, but the babies, yeah, it upset me.

"I remember one time Dad had a cow that had a terrible time giving birth. She got torn up inside very badly, and the baby died before being born. That mama cow was laying down in the pasture and couldn't get up. We poked and prodded to try to make her get up, but she just couldn't. Dad let her lay there for a week before he gave up trying and had to shoot her. I think I cried for a week. But the longer you're in the business, the easier it becomes. It's just part of the business that you know you have to accept, like it or not.

"Now I know you gave that little calf you helped pull from the mother a name, and that makes it special to you, and that was alright for the first one you were able to save, but a piece of advice: Don't name a calf. It makes it much harder to put it down if it needs to be put down or sell if it needs to be sold."

Aiden had never thought of that, but it made sense. "Oh, I never thought of that. I agree that's a bad idea. No names in the future."

Dane laughed, slapped Aiden on the back, "You'll get the hang of everything. You're doing a great job already. I know if Dad is letting you pretty much run the show around here, it means he has confidence in your abilities."

"I hope so. I try, and I really like the work." Aiden then asked, "So how is school going for you? Do you think it's worth it to go to college to run this place?"

Dane had to think about it for a few seconds. "Worth it? Not really."

"Then why go?"

"Dad was insistent on it. He thought it would make me a better rancher than he is, but I don't think so. Anyway, if it makes him happy, I'm glad to do it. But I think you're learning as much as I am without college."

"That's pretty much what I had decided too, that hands-on was the best teacher. I'm just a greenhorn who needs the training though. But someday, I want to have my own ranch, or farm, whatever you call it."

"Well, Dad always called it a farm, but I call it a ranch. To me a farm is someone who goes out, plows the ground up, and plants a crop, but a ranch is animal raising, which is what we do."

"Yeah, I kind of agree with you. Well, anyway, someday I want a ranch of my own." He hesitated then, and asked, "So tell me how things are going between you and Lottie. She tells me nothing."

Dane laughed, "We're good. I have two more years of school, and then we're getting married. She's a super girl. I can't believe how fortunate I am that you guys came into our lives."

"No, we're the fortunate ones. If we hadn't stumbled across your cabin, there's no telling where we'd be right now. I feel like we three owe your family our lives. And just think, after you and Lottie marry, and Erin and I get married, we'll be brothers-in-law."

"So have you proposed to Erin already?" Dane asked.

"Not in so many words, but I let her know that someday I will. She's got to graduate first. But as soon as she does, I plan on getting a ring on her finger."

"Well, don't tell Lottie, but I've already bought the ring for her."

"Nice. And just so you know, now that you're home for the summer, I had a talk with her last summer not to smother you so much because it would make it harder for you to go back to school in the fall. You wouldn't want to go."

"I already don't want to go, and speaking of Lottie, here she comes."

"Looks like I'm going to have to have that talk with her again." Then Aiden turned and walked away.

Erin showed up to the office with a glass of sweet tea when Aiden was working on the books. He stretched, and said, "Aw, how sweet of you to bring me some tea. I'm needing a break. This is the one part of ranching I really don't care for."

"Why not?" she asked while sitting his tea down on the desk.

"Give me a horse, cows, anything to be out working with my hands and I'm fine, but stick me behind a desk, and I shrivel up."

She came to stand beside him, wrapped her hand around his upper arm feeling his muscle, and stated, "You do feel shriveled up."

He pushed his chair back, grabbed her around the waist and pulled her onto his lap. She giggled. Aiden said, "Oh, I am, am I?" as he held her tight.

She leaned back to look into his eyes, and he lost control. Staring into her beautiful eyes, he slowly lowered his lips to hers. Her arms immediately wrapped around his neck. They kissed a couple more times, and then he released her and said, "You'd better get out of here, Miss Wilshire, before daddy sees you messing with the hired hand. You don't want me to get fired, do you?"

"Daddy would never fire you. He loves you."

"Well, let's keep it that way. Now get. I have work to do, but thanks for the tea."

She rose from his lap, headed to the door, but as she reached it, she turned and blew him a kiss.

Both boys found it harder and harder to keep their resolve to stay away from the girls. The flame of passion grows strong between two people who are in love, especially when you're young, and having self-control becomes one of the hardest things you can do.

Dane was wondering why they couldn't get married while he was home, and Aiden was wondering why he had to wait for Erin to graduate before getting married. Life was hard to figure out sometimes. Both boys were torn. They wanted to do the right thing, but their resolve was waning. Aiden was thinking how Erin wasn't even eighteen yet, nor out of high school, and Dane was thinking how unfair it would be to marry a girl only to head off to college for another year.

Daniel arrived back at the farm with money in his pocket from the sale of a couple of his llamas he'd sold after the latest show. Aiden hadn't gone with him this time because of all the work to do at home, but Dane had decided he'd like to go.

One day Aiden went into the house during the morning and found Erin busy working to prepare lunch. He began teasing her. She tried to ignore him, but he didn't act like he wanted to go back to work. She told him the animals were calling his name.

"Ha, ha, nice try. I just needed a break and to come and see what you were up to."

"I'm still working, and you're interrupting me. So go away."

"My work can wait. I have more important things on my mind." He reached out to take a carrot she had peeled but got his hand slapped.

She said, "The Bible says, 'if anyone doesn't want to work, neither should he eat'.

"What? You just made that up."

"No, I didn't. Look it up. It's in 2nd Thessalonians 3:10."

"Ok, ok, I can take a hint."

He left to go back to the barn, and when he got there, he found a Bible on the shelf in the office. He looked up the Scripture in 2nd Thessalonians, and sure enough, Erin was right. That was exactly what it said. So, he began searching through the Bible to try to find a Scripture he could use on her.

Soon it was time for lunch, and everyone gathered around the table. After lunch was over and before Aiden headed back outside, he leaned down to Erin and said, "The Bible also says, 'Love is patient and kind'. Look it up in the Bible."

She just smiled, and Aiden turned to head out the door.

He used the afternoon to take stock of supplies for all the animals and ordered what things that were needed. Dane got busy cleaning the milking machine. The weather was getting warmer each day, and soon Dane was sweating profusely. He came into the office to get a little relief in the air conditioner and found Aiden in the office just hanging up the phone.

Dane said, "So I overheard you spouting Scripture to Erin on the way out the door. What was that all about?"

"Well, she did the same thing to me earlier. I was just giving it back to her. So, tell me, is she one of those Bible thumpers, always spouting off something in the Bible?"

"Not really. But she does read her Bible. Not sure how often, but if there's a Scripture that she can gouge you with, she'll use it on you, so beware."

"Yeah, I will. I think I'll find another one in the Bible to use the next time she tries to corral me with something from the good book."

Dane laughed and said it was time for him to head inside to change his shirt.

The next Saturday, Dane and Aiden asked all three girls if they wanted to go to Tupelo for the evening. The guys really didn't want Izzy along but knew it would be rude to not include her. They ordered a pizza in a New York pizza joint, then decided to see what was playing at a theater. Nothing looked interesting so they decided to go to a park and just walk around.

The air was warm, but not sultry thankfully. They strolled along under the canopy of trees, stopping occasionally to look up at the full moon shining brightly. Aiden and Erin separated from the other three, walking over to enter the gazebo. Erin walked to the railing, Aiden came up behind her and slipped his arm around her waist. She was quiet. He whispered, "What are you thinking?"

"I'm thinking how beautiful this night is. I'm thinking about how glad I am that I have you." She turned around to look at him, "I'm thinking I never want this night to end. I'm thinking how in love I am."

"Oh, Erin," he said taking her face in his hands, "I love you so much." He lowered his lips to hers. He held her close to him, feeling the curves of her body against him. He wanted to marry her right away. He didn't want to wait.

After they kissed a few more times, she pulled from his embrace, looked up into his eyes, and said, "We'd better get back with the others. I'm sure Dane and Lottie would love to get away from Izzy for a few minutes."

He dropped his arms, and said, "I guess you're right. I'm glad they're along with us, or I'd put you in that truck and we'd find a lonely road somewhere."

"Not a good idea, Aiden."

"I know. God, this is so hard."

"I know, but just one more school year, and we can get married."

They walked slowly back to where Dane and the girls were. They walked on and eventually Dane and Lottie disappeared. They were gone for a while and when they came back, Lottie was wearing a ring. She kept it hidden from the others, but the smile on her face told everyone else what had happened. Izzy was the first to walk up to her, take her hand to look at the ring. Izzy and Lottie hugged, "I'm so happy for you, Lottie," Izzy said.

Aiden shook Dane's hand and said, "I knew you wouldn't wait until you graduated. Congratulations!"

Lottie said, "We still plan on waiting until Dane's out of college, but at least now everyone will know I belong to him." She smiled up at Dane, who had one arm around her waist.

The next day, Aiden left mid-morning to head into Tupelo. Dane suspected he knew where he was going but said nothing. Soon he was back but was quiet, saying nothing to anyone else. He worked all day but that evening he asked Erin to meet him out behind the house shortly. He left the house, and shortly she showed up.

She began, "Aiden, I just don't think we…"

"Shh," he said, as he walked slowly toward her. He wrapped his arms around her holding her tight.

"Aiden," she whispered. "We can't."

"Shh, you talk too much." He kissed her over and over. And even though she complained, she never resisted him.

Aiden then took the box out of his pocket and got down on one knee. Erin's eyes widened, and her hand flew to her mouth, she was so shocked. This was totally unexpected so early in their relationship.

Aiden said, "Erin Wilshire, will you become my wife."

"Aiden," she whispered, and stood staring at him.

Aiden's heart did a flip flop. She wasn't saying anything, and he thought sure she wasn't ready. He knew he had made a mistake by rushing her.

After what he felt was at least an hour, he said, "My knee is getting pretty sore here. If you don't want to marry me, please let me know."

"No, I do. I just…I just…This is so unexpected."

Aiden put the ring on her finger, took her hands while he rose, then rubbing the back of her hand with his thumb. He said, "Look, I know this is a little early…"

"A little? How about a lot."

"We can still wait until you've graduated if you want, but at least, with a ring everyone at school will know you're spoken for, so it will be hands off to the guys."

He smiled at Erin, and she was smiling at him. Eventually she said, "Are you sure about this?"

"Sure? You're all I think about every minute you're away from me. Dane and Lottie are planning on waiting too, so I figured why can't you wear my ring too for a few months before we tie the knot?"

She slipped her arms around his neck and lifted her face to his. He lowered his lips to hers, brushed her lips with his gently before kissing her with all the passion he possessed. He moved down to her neck, caressing her, and she let her head fall back to allow him to have his way.

When they went back inside, Erin headed upstairs, so excited to show Lottie and Izzy her ring. She wasn't ready to show her parents just yet, afraid they would not approve of her getting engaged before she was eighteen. But she reasoned that it was only about four months before she turned eighteen, so she saw no problem with the engagement at all. However, she decided not to wear the ring to school. At least not yet.

One day, Aiden heard something and went out of the barn to see what it was. He was drawn to the pasture where the sheep and llamas were. It sounded like the llamas and sheep were all screaming. The llamas were running around all over the place while the sheep had huddled together toward the far end of the pasture.

Aiden ran back into the barn, grabbed a gun from the gun case, mounted his horse that was still saddled, and headed to the pasture.

When he entered the gate, he could see the problem. Coyotes had attacked one of the sheep and were tearing it apart. Aiden rode his horse toward the coyotes, shooting above their heads to scare them away. They jerked their heads up, and seemed nervous, but wouldn't run away. So, Aiden aimed at one of the coyotes and fired. It went down which caused the other ones to run away.

When Aiden got to the fallen sheep, he could see it was too late for the sheep. It was still alive but just barely. The coyote Aiden shot was dead. Aiden put a bullet through the sheep's head to put it out of her misery.

He then roped both dead animals, dragged the coyote to the burn area, loaded wood on top of it and went to get fuel to add to the wood and light it. He felt bad about losing one of his sheep but at least he could butcher it and the family could eat it. He was glad it was only one sheep lost.

He butchered it right there in the field, tossing the skin, and innards into the fire, and loading the edible parts into a plastic bag and into a wagon to haul to the house.

He let Daniel know about the incident, and Daniel said he knew coyotes were becoming more of a nuisance, and he decided to put out traps outside the pasture to catch some and move them far from the farm before releasing them. If you didn't keep the numbers down, they could decimate a heard quickly. Aiden agreed and set about setting traps with some of the sheep parts he had just butchered. He rode back into the woods beyond the pastures and set the traps.

31

Aiden was not far from Erin one day when her phone rang. From the conversation he was able to hear, he knew it was a boy interested in dating Erin. After she hung up, he went to her, turned her around to look at him. He put his arms around her, pulled her to him, and said, "So other wolves are circling."

"Nothing to worry about. I can handle them."

"So, who was it?"

"Just a boy from school. He invited me out, but I said, no."

"Did you tell him you are already engaged?"

"No."

"Why not? And where is your ring?"

I'm not wearing it during the summer. And I don't plan on wearing it until I'm eighteen."

"Why not?"

She looked down, "I haven't told my parents yet."

"Why not?"

"Because I don't think my parents would look favorably about it until I'm eighteen. They'd probably tell me I'm too young to know what I want."

"Really? You really believe that? I can't see that after knowing how your father loves me. He'd probably be very happy at your choice."

She smiled up at him. "Maybe. But I'm not taking any chances. I'd hate to be forced to give the ring back to you."

"Do you really think they'd make you do that?"

"I don't know, Aiden, but I love you and I want to marry you, so I'm not going to let anything stand in the way of that. Don't worry. After I turn eighteen, I'll tell my parents, and start wearing your ring."

With that he pulled her to him, looked deeply into her eyes, and said, "Well, I like that. Just remember you've promised your heart belongs to me."

"Not to worry," then she raised up on her tiptoes and kissed him. He held her tighter in his arms and holding the back of her head with his hands, kissing her with all the deep feelings he felt deep within his heart.

When they pulled apart, she said, "You said 'other wolves.' Does that mean you're also a wolf?"

He smiled down at her, turned and walked away.

She called after him, "Wait! You didn't answer my question."

He just waived at her without turning.

Another night as Dane lay awake in his bed, he heard horses crying. "Aiden," he said, "get up. Something's inside the barn. Come on."

They pulled their jeans and shoes on, Aiden grabbing his father's rifle from the bedroom on the way and heading down the stairs. They met Daniel at the back door heading out, as well, holding a rifle.

Daniel led the way into the barn, moving carefully, quietly. The boys were close behind him, and soon they all noted someone coming out of one of the horse's stalls. Daniel raised his rifle and pointed it at the man, "Hold it right there."

The man dropped the reins and held up his hands. "Don't shoot!" he cried.

As the boys and Daniel neared the man, they noticed someone staring at them in the adjacent stall. The boys pointed their rifles at the stall and yelled, "Ok, we see you, come on out."

The second man emerged with his hands in the air as well. They saw the men were just boys no older than seventeen or eighteen.

"What were you thinking?" asked Daniel.

They looked at one another and one said, "We just wanted to go for a joy ride. Honestly. We would bring them back, we promise."

"Do you realize taking a horse without the owner's approval is stealing? There was a time when stealing a horse merited the death penalty."

The boy's eyes widened with that information. "We didn't mean no harm, mister."

Daniel told Aiden and Dane to search the boys to make sure they had no weapons, and when they said the boys were clean, he lowered his gun.

"Mister," one of the boys said, "we like horses. Just wanted to go for a ride. That's all."

Daniel was quiet, contemplating this. "Ok, here's the deal. I won't call the sheriff this time. And if you really want to go horseback riding, come back during the day, and my boys here will take you horseback riding."

"Really?" they were astonished. "You mean it?"

"Yeah, I mean it, now get home before I decide to call your mama's."

The boys ran out of the barn, jumped into their beat-up truck and headed out of the barn yard. Daniel looked at Dane and Aiden and all three burst out laughing.

"At least it wasn't any worse than that," Dane said.

"Yes, but I think we need to start locking the barn door at night," Daniel said. They headed back to bed. They had scared the daylights out of the two kids, and by offering to allow them to come back to ride their horses, Daniel hoped he had averted possible theft charges against the boys in the future. He knew boys often started thieving at young ages, but if caught in time and handled lovingly, they could be kept from going down that road.

On the way back to the house, he said to Aiden, "If they come back, take them horseback riding until they are saddle sore, then offer them a job here for the rest of the summer."

"Do you think that's wise? Won't we have to watch them like a hawk to make sure they don't try to steal something else?"

"Maybe, but I want to give them a chance to show their true colors. If they mess up, you can always fire them, but if they don't, we'll work them hard enough they won't feel like going out getting in trouble at night after work."

Dane and Aiden laughed. "I sure like the way you think, Mr. Wilshire," Aiden said.

When they got back into the house, all the girls were up and looking out the window to see what was going on.

Daniel and Miriam immediately went to bed, but Dane and Aiden went to talk to the girls about what had just happened.

They couldn't help but notice that the girls were in their night clothes. Their minds did a one-eighty from what had happened outside to what they saw inside.

Lottie wrapped her robe tightly around her after realizing Dane was staring at her bare legs protruding from her skimpy sleeping shorts. He smiled, and she said, "Let's all get to bed. It's late."

The girls made the guys go up the stairs first ahead of them for obvious reasons.

When Lottie and Izzy entered their bedroom, Izzy said, "Better lock the door. I saw how Dane was staring at you."

"You're imagining things, Izzy."

"Oh, really?"

The two boys who had broken into their barn the night before came the following day to go horseback riding. Aiden groaned because he felt he had a lot of work needing to be done, but since Daniel had told him what to do if they came back, he let his work slide.

He said to the two, "First, what are your names?"

"I'm Tom Tuttle," said the more vocal of the two, "and he's Cody Thompson."

"Have either one of you ridden a horse before?"

"No," they both admitted.

He then decided which horses they should ride because they would need gentle ones. He showed them how to bridle and saddle a horse, as well as, how to make the horse turn the direction they wanted to go. He didn't really think they'd need that too much because he knew if he led the way, the other horses would naturally follow.

They all mounted, and he led the way out past the pastures to a clearing. He kept them on the horses most of the morning, and when they returned to the barn, the boys dismounted and Tom said, "I feel like I'm bowlegged."

"Me too," agreed Cody.

Aiden made sure they brushed the horses down, curried their tales and manes, and got them a drink from the horse tank outside before putting them into their stalls. Then before they left, he said, "So you boys must be bored this summer before school starts. Am I right?"

Cody said, "Summer can get pretty boring."

"Then what do you think about coming to work here for the rest of the summer. You could earn a little cash, and it might help keep you out of trouble."

The boys both looked at each other. Tom hesitated, but Cody said, "I'd love that."

"Ok, then, when can you start?"

"Tomorrow. Come on, Tom, this will be fun, and we'll be making some money to boot."

Tom finally agreed to work as well.

"I'll see you both here at eight o'clock tomorrow morning. And wear old clothing."

Aiden couldn't wait to let Daniel know his plan had been implemented. They both laughed because they knew city boys rarely worked hard enough at anything. Daniel hoped this might teach the boys the value of hard work, plus keep them out of trouble.

Tom and Cody showed up the following morning, and Aiden put them to work mucking out the stalls. He showed them how to tether the horse outside the stall, load the poop into the wagon and where to pull the wagon to dump it.

As the boys were working, Izzy came out to meet them. "Cody Thompson, is that you?" she asked as she saw him. She knew him from school. "So, you were trying to steal our horses last night?"

He looked up and stopped working. "Izzy?"

"Yeah, it's me. Why would you try to steal the Wilshire's horses?"

"I wasn't stealing. Just… borrowing."

"Yeah, whatever."

Tom had stopped working as well to stare at Izzy. Then he looked at Cody and said, "When I agreed to work, I didn't think I'd be shoveling crap."

"Watch your mouth," Izzy replied. "Daniel doesn't allow foul language." She looked at Cody then, and continued, "Work hard and you'll have a job here every summer if you want it."

"Well, I don't believe I'll be coming back next summer," Tom put in.

"Your decision," she said walking away.

Cody watched her go, then said to Tom, "I think I'll keep working for them. She's a looker that I'd like to get to know better. Do you know her from school?"

"No. Never had any classes with her."

"She was in my algebra class last year, but I never really got to know her. But I think I'd like to get to know her better," Cody said, smiling at the thought.

After they finished with the horse stalls, Aiden pointed out which shed had the four-wheeler in, and Cody went to bring it to the barn to pull the wagon to the dumping grounds.

While he was gone, Tom walked down the length of the barn, inspecting the sheep and eventually the llamas. One llama walked over to him, and spit in his face. "Ack," he cried, turned and ran to the horse trough to get the snot off him.

When Cody returned, he put the wagon back where it was, and found Tom still rinsing his face off. "Hey, Tom. You don't have to drink the horse's water. I'm sure they have stuff for people to drink."

"I'm not drinking the water. I'm washing the snot off my face. That blasted llama spit on me."

Cody laughed, "Maybe you deserved it."

Aiden found them, and said it was time to drive the llamas and sheep to pasture, but Tom said, "Look, I don't need this. I'm out of here."

"Come on," Cody said, "Let's do this."

"You can stay if you want, I'm going home. You'll have to find your own way home when you're done here."

Tom walked off, and Cody just shrugged his shoulders. "That's ok," Aiden said. "We'll have some fun without him. I think you'll like your next job."

He told Cody to saddle the horse he rode yesterday, and Aiden did the same. Then Aiden called Shep. He opened the gates to the llama's and sheep's pens, and Shep went to work. Cody was enthralled. Aiden rode in front and Cody was bringing up the rear. Soon Aiden realized Cody wasn't with them, and he turned back to see what the problem was. He found Cody on the ground and the horse standing beside him with the saddle on the side of the horse.

"What happened?" asked Aiden, even though he already knew.

"The saddle slipped around the horse and that threw me off."

Aiden laughed. "Yeah, that can happen if the saddle isn't cinched up tight enough. Sometimes a horse will bloat his belly up to make the saddle do that if they don't want to be ridden. They can be ornery sometimes. So, if you think the horse has bloated his belly up, you have to knee them in the gut. That will release their air, then you can get the saddle tight enough."

Cody saddled his horse again, mounted, and by the time he and Aiden got to the pasture gate, the sheep and llamas were huddled up, ready to get into their pasture. Aiden opened the gate, and Shep herded them in.

When they got back to the barn, Cody said, "That dog is amazing."

"Yeah, he knows his job, and he loves it. They have him as a working dog, not as a pet."

Aiden told Cody to take his saddle off his horse, then take her over to the wash station and wash the horse. He showed him where to find the wash station, while he decided to muck out the stalls of the sheep and llamas for Cody.

After Cody brought his horse back to the barn, Aiden let him know he had to wash the other seven horses. "Geez, I'm going to be soaked by the time I'm done."

"Let me tell you something, Cody. The first time I washed all the horses down, I had it finished by noon, and didn't get wet at all. Of course, when the shower head broke, I was really soaked then. But if you get soaked, I've got clothes you can wear.

"Oh, and by the way, the Wilshire's provide lunch, so hop to it and get your job done before lunch. Then after lunch I can show you another interesting job you might like."

This pacified Cody, and he got busy on the rest of the horses.

During lunch Cody kept sneaking glances at Izzy and she noticed. "Where's Tom?" she finally asked him.

"After a llama spit in his face, he decided he didn't want to stay."

Everyone laughed at that, and Izzy couldn't help but continue smiling.

"Hey, Aiden, I didn't get soaked after all washing the horses. Did you notice?"

"Yeah, good for you. I knew you could do it. And the horses stand pretty still because they like getting a bath."

Cody thanked Mrs. Wilshire for a wonderful lunch, but she let him know all the girls helped, so he also thanked them too.

After lunch, Aiden took Cody to inspect the fences for breaks in the wire. They each had a four-wheeler and rode along all the fence rows. Aiden noticed only one place that needed repaired. So they went back to the barn, got the necessary tools and wire, and went back to repair the break.

Afterward, Aiden said, "Let's take the four wheelers for a ride." He took off with Cody in hot pursuit. They went round and round in the pasture where the cattle were grazing, careful to stay far away from the cows so as not to spook them but racing from one end to the other end of the pasture. The cows kept grazing, taking no note of the guys as if they weren't even there.

After they put the four-wheelers up, Cody said, "That was great. I loved it."

"Yeah, you've probably heard the saying, "All work and no play, makes Jack a dull boy." Gotta have some fun a little along with work."

"I've never heard that saying, but I can agree with it." They both laughed, and Aiden slapped him on the back.

"Let's go feed the horses some hay," Aiden said.

"That's fine, but I don't want to feed the llamas."

"No problem. After we bring them back into the barn, I'll feed them. But at some point, you need to start feeding them, because after they get used to you, they won't spit on you."

"But how do I feed them without getting spit on?"

"I'll show you this evening."

Next Aiden wanted to inspect the cages he had set to catch a coyote out in the woods in order to see if they'd caught anything. He took Cody with him on the four wheelers. Cody loved it. They parked the four-wheelers at the edge of the woods and walked in. Aiden noticed one of the cages had been sprung, but it was empty. "Looks like it might be working," he said. He inspected the latch to make sure it would easily close behind the animal once he was inside the cage.

"What's going on with these cages?" Cody asked.

Aiden then explained how they lost one of their sheep to coyotes, and that Daniel had noticed how the coyotes were increasing in number and needed to be thinned out. Otherwise, if they didn't do something with some of the coyotes, soon there wouldn't be enough wild animals for them to eat, and more and more, they'd be seeking out the herds.

"How do you know all this stuff?" Cody asked.

"Believe me, I didn't used to know any of this. Daniel and Dane have taught me everything I know."

"So how long have you been working here?"

"This is my third summer here."

"So do you work during summer like I'm doing?"

"No, I live here, so I worked while I finished my last year of school."

"Wow, that would be great. Do you think I could work here while going to school?"

"If you do a good job, I'm sure you can. Dane will be going back to college this fall, and I'll be needing another hand. Just try to learn as much as you can this summer and come fall, you'll be ahead of the game.

"But I need to ask you about what kind of grades you get, because we'll expect you to make good grades, or you'll be spending more time studying than working on this farm."

"I'm a B student with a few A's thrown in. But look, I can do even better with my grades. I can do most of my homework in study hall and still work here after school."

"We'll see. Let's play it by ear and see how things go. You'll have to show me your report card."

"Sure." He thought a minute and then added, "I think my grades slipped after I began running around with Tom. He's a wildcat who'd rather be out running the streets instead of doing homework."

"So why would your parents allow you to run the streets at night?"

"My parents?" He looked sad, "My mom works two jobs because my dad is gone, and she's never home in the evening. So, she doesn't know what I'm doing."

Aiden's heart hurt at hearing about his home life, it reminded him of his own before the Wilshire's got hold of him and changed everything. "I'm sorry to hear that, Cody. You know that sounds a lot like my home before I came here. My mom was working more than one job to try to provide for me and my sisters too."

"Then how did you come to live here?"

"It's a long story, I'll tell you sometime."

When they inspected another cage, they found it had a coyote in it. "Hurray!" yelled Aiden. "Tomorrow, we take this guy far away, and release him into a different woods.

Soon it was time to herd the sheep and llamas back into the barn. Aiden called Shep; they mounted their horses and headed out. Soon the animals were all in the barn. Aiden showed Cody how to feed all the animals, although Cody wouldn't go near the llamas. But he did notice that after Aiden put the feed into the feed trough for the llamas, the animals were more interested in eating than in spitting, and Aiden reached out and petted each one. He knew this was the way Aiden was becoming their friend.

Cody headed home, tired. Tom called him to see if he'd go out with him to stir up trouble, but Cody begged off, he was much too tired. He took a shower and headed to bed early.

The next morning, he couldn't wait to tell his mother about his job. "How much money are they paying you?" she asked.

"Gee, I don't know. I forgot to ask."

"What? You're working at a job to make money, but you didn't even think to ask about a salary?"

"I just wanted to work on the farm. It's so fun, and I'm learning a lot. I just didn't even think about money. I'm sorry Mom, I know you need more money. I'll ask tomorrow."

"You'd better. And if you like the work, I'm happy for you, son."

She asked about the family he was working for, and he explained how kind they seemed. They even provided his lunch. He left out the part about Tom and him trying to steal their horses, of course. No need making his mother worry about him, she had enough on her plate without knowing about the sins of her son.

He couldn't wait to go to work again today.

"Say, Aiden," Cody said, at work, "my mom wants to know how much I'm being paid to work here."

"Oh, she is, huh? How does $500 a week sound?"

Cody's eyes widened, he'd never had a job and never dreamed his first one would pay that much a week. It just didn't seem right to take pay for something you enjoyed doing. But still, he knew his mother needed help with expenses.

He swallowed, "That...that sounds fine," he replied.

"Do a good job and you might even get a bonus."

"Gee, thanks, Aiden."

Aiden wanted to help his family because he knew what it was like to be poor. He knew his mother must be working like a dog to provide for his family.

As they worked together, Aiden finally decided to see what he might find out about Cody's family. He asked, "So, Cody, you told me you don't have a father around. What happened to him?"

"Got killed in Afghanistan."

"He was a military man?"

"No, a government contractor. Mom was devastated when dad died."

He decided to say a few things about his own life so Cody would feel more comfortable opening up to Aiden. "Yeah, I understand. I had to become the man of the house when my mom left my dad."

"That's a lot of responsibility."

"Don't I know it. So do you have any siblings?"

"No, thankfully. If I had brothers or sisters, I suppose I'd be the one to take care of them."

"That's what I had to do when mom died."

"Your mother died?"

"Yes, COVID."

"Oh, I'm sorry to hear that." He hesitated before going on, "But it looks like you're doing alright now living here.

"Purely by accident that we ran into the Wilshire family. Look, Cody, I know how hard your life probably is right now, but if you stay with this job, I guarantee you, you won't be sorry. The Wilshire's are the kindest people I've ever met. You can learn everything there is to know about ranching right here, and after high school, you'll have a skill that you'll be able to get a job on any ranch or farm."

Cody smiled, "Do you think I'd be able to stay here and work?"

Aiden smiled also, "Probably. Just don't try to take our horses again."

Cody laughed, "You got it."

Aiden and Cody collected the cage with the coyote inside, loaded him into the back of the truck and headed off to a distant place to release him.

While they were on their way, Cody asked, "Can I ask you a question?"

"Sure."

"I know Izzy's last name is Roberts, so she's your sister. Right?"

"Right, and you can stay away from her. She's only fifteen, sixteen September fifth, and has two more years of school to go."

Cody smiled, "Yes, sir. I just wondered."

"What grade are you in, Cody?"

"Just graduated eleventh. Why?"

"Just wondered. So, you'll graduate next spring."

"Yeah, why?"

"No reason, just thinking." Aiden knew he was interested in Izzy, but they both needed to mature before dating. *And look at me*, he thought, *ready to propose marriage to a girl who still has one more year of school as well.*

A couple of nights later, once again, the family was awakened with noise coming from the barn, and once again, the guys grabbed their guns and headed to the barn.

They heard rustling in one of the horse stalls, and the horse didn't like it one bit. They edged over to the door of the stall, and Daniel burst out laughing, because there was an opossum scratching around in the straw. The boys began laughing too and headed back to the house. They slept well the remainder of the night.

Cody had a good laugh about it as well the next morning. "I bet you thought Tom and I were stealing your horses again."

"The thought did cross my mind," Daniel said, "but I didn't want to believe you'd be that stupid."

"No, sir. I learned my lesson."

"Glad to hear it."

One Thursday evening Aiden got a phone call from Cody. "Hey Aiden. How you doin' man?"

"Fine, Cody. What's up?"

"Well, I was just wondering if I can have tomorrow off work."

"I guess so. Are you ok?"

"Yeah, it's just that the Elvis Festival is going on this week, and I'd like to go tomorrow."

"The Elvis Festival?"

"Yeah, it's every year, because Tupelo is the birthplace of Elvis. Live music all day, and vendors selling their wares, and lots of food trucks."

"Sounds great. Maybe we'll see you there. Is it downtown?"

"Yeah, they block off streets and all."

"Well, I'll talk to Dane and the girls and see what they have to say about it. If we come, what time should we get there? And where can we meet up with you?"

"Come around ten o'clock. That gives us time to look at the vendor's tables before lunch. Let's meet at the courthouse."

Dane and the girls agreed that they wanted to go. Dane drove his dad's truck. They had no trouble finding Cody, and soon they were walking the streets looking at everything for sale. Lottie and Erin found earrings that they purchased, and each of the boys bought pocket-knives. Aiden also bought a large knife similar to what Jim Bowie carried. He was sure it would come in handy on the ranch someday.

They found food at the different food trucks, each choosing what they liked best. Afterward, they found a picnic table to sit on while eating. Cody stated, "It was great that ya'll came, sure would have been boring to come alone. And I didn't want to run into Tom and his gang. I've gotten away from that crowd, and I'd like to keep it that way. You guys are way cooler than they are."

Aiden agreed, "I'd like you to stay away from him as well. Just hang with us and you'll go places."

They all laughed at that. Then Cody added, "Someday we should go to Tombigbee State Park. It's so beautiful and has trails to hike. And there's a picnic area we could take a lunch to eat there."

"Tombigbee State Park?" asked Lottie.

Dane answered, "Yeah, it's a pretty great place. Let's plan on it soon, before school begins in the fall." He was looking at Erin and Izzy.

After lunch Dane and Lottie separated from the others to go their own way. While they were walking, looking at all the vendor's wares,

Dane said, "Lottie, what do you think about getting married this summer before I have to go back to college?"

"What? I thought we both agreed to wait until you were out of school?"

"I know but it's getting pretty hard to wait."

"And we get married and then you go off to college?"

"You could come with me. I could find a place to live off campus."

"And what am I supposed to do all day while you're in school?"

"Well, you could get a job."

"Look, Dane. Aiden, Izzy, and I made a pact after mom died that nothing would separate us. I'd hate to go back on my word."

"We could come home often. Old Miss isn't that far."

"Izzy and I are very close. I just don't want to leave her alone."

"But she wouldn't be alone, she'd have Erin."

"Yes, but she wouldn't have me. It's not the same thing. I just don't want to leave her, or Aiden either."

Dane dropped his head in defeat. "Ok, I understand. It was just a thought."

Lottie put a hand on his arm, "Dane, I'd love to get married right away too, but I only plan on getting married once in my life, and I don't want to rush it. If we were to marry this summer, it would have to be rushed. It takes time to plan a wedding, and I don't want to rush my marriage and mess it up."

He smiled then. "Well, if we wait, I'm sure by the time we're getting married, you'll have it all planned out perfectly, just like you want. Especially if you let my mom help."

"Are you kidding? I couldn't do it alone. Of course, I want her to help."

They walked on looking at all the vendors wares, and Dane seemed quiet to Lottie. He had hoped she would agree to his plan, but now he had no choice but to wait. But the waiting was killing him. He figured he'd have to take more cold showers this summer.

Aiden and Erin were walking along looking at vendors also, along with Cody and Izzy. Aiden was holding Erin's hand, and eventually he noticed Cody was holding Izzy's hand as well. Aiden pointed his two fingers to his own eyes, then pointed them at Cody, as if to say, 'I'm watching you'. Cody just smiled.

Later after they got home, Aiden said to Izzy, "What are you doing, Izzy?"

"What do you mean?"

"Holding hands with Cody?"

"Oh, that didn't mean anything. You and Erin were holding hands, so we just wanted to look like a couple too. Stop worrying."

"Well, I don't want any sneaking around. He's going to continue working on the farm all summer, so I suggest you stay away from him. No accidentally showing up where he's working."

She laughed, "Yes, Dad. Aiden, you worry too much."

"Just want to keep you safe until you're old enough to think about marriage. You still have two years of school, and I don't want you distracted from your studies."

"Ok, Dad."

"Stop it, Izzy. The Wilshire's might have custody of you, but it's still my responsibility to make sure you're safe."

"Ok, ok, I get it. Now don't worry, we're good."

The next day Cody arrived for work, and said to Aiden, "You know there's something else you might be interested in seeing close to Tupelo."

"What's that?"

"There's a buffalo park and zoo. What do you think about seeing buffalo?"

"Really? It has buffalo?"

"Yep."

"I would be very interested in seeing them. When should we go?"

"I can take you this Saturday if you'd like."

"I'd like very much. But let's keep it just us two. No girls. I doubt if buffalos are something girls would get excited about anyway. I'll see if Dane wants to go too."

34

Dane did want to go. He'd been there before, but knew this was a treat for Aiden, something he'd never seen before. And he was right, Aiden was thrilled to be able to get up close and personal with such beasts. He felt like a little boy in a candy shop.

"Wow, can you believe these guys?" Aiden asked. He was in awe of such huge beasts. He knew buffalo would be larger than a cow, but he had no idea how large their heads would be. The grunting noises they made thrilled him. "I'd love to raise buffalo."

Dane said, "I've heard they can be pretty cantankerous. And I don't believe their heads would fit into the milking stall's metal bars that are supposed to fit on each side of the cow's head. And besides, would you really want to try to milk one?"

Aiden laughed, "Yeah, you're probably right. Not a good idea, but I was just dreaming."

The boys got some feed to try to coax one over to the fence, but the bison ignored them.

"So much for that," Cody said, "but at least you got to see them. I thought you might like to see them."

"You're right," Aiden agreed. "They're awesome. but actually, those are bison not buffalo. Do you know the difference?

"No, I thought those were buffalo."

"It was actually bison that roamed the West. Do you see the hump at the shoulders?"

"Yeah."

"And how short their horns are?"

"Yeah."

"That's a bison. Buffalo don't have the hump, and their horns are long, not short. Maybe you've seen pictures of water buffalo, that's a true buffalo."

"How do you know that?"

"I had to do a report on an animal in eighth grade, and I chose the American bison. Can you imagine huge herds of them like they used to be out west? I've even read somewhere that the herds were so huge that it would take days for them to cross a particular place. There were over sixty million around 1800."

"Wow. What happened to them?"

"Hunters. They were hunted for their hide and slaughtered them in mass. The United States and England encouraged the hunting, and eventually the Indians even got involved in the slaughter. With Indians eventually having horses and guns, it made it easier for them to kill the bison. They used their hide as barter for things they wanted like pots and pans, guns, knives, horses, and other metal items. Before the white man got involved in killing the bison, the Indians killed them just for food, and used every part of the beast. Things changed with the white man."

"That's not surprising."

"The slaughter was so great. That's why there aren't many left in the United States. The estimate now is that there's only about three hundred sixty thousand."

"Thankfully we have places like this, so they don't completely disappear."

"Yeah, the largest number are now found in Yellowstone National Park, where they roam free instead of in fenced fields like this."

"Well, at least we get to see them here in Mississippi. Just glad we don't have to travel to Yellowstone."

"Hey, look. There's a little one. He must have been born just this past spring. He's cute," Dane put in.

Cody then said to Aiden, "You sure remember a lot about what you learned about them. No wonder you were interested in coming to see them."

"Yeah, this was great. I'm glad you told me about this place."

A week later, the family was all woken again at night by the horses being bothered by something or someone. Something was obviously inside the barn. Again, the guys grabbed their guns and headed out. The front door was locked, so they all headed to the back of the barn. They had not locked that overhead door because they didn't think anyone would think to go around to the back.

They tromped to the back and peeked around the open door, to find Tom and another boy putting halters onto two of the horses.

Daniel entered, pointing his gun at the boys, and yelled, "Tom! What do you think you're doing? You didn't get by with it before, what made you think you could now?"

Dane and Aiden then entered coming up behind Daniel.

The boys both dropped the reins and held their hands up in defeat. "I'm getting pretty tired of your antics," Daniel went on. "I tried to help you out the last time by offering you a job, but you didn't want the job. It's pretty stupid to come back and try it again. Who's your friend?"

The other boy said, "I'm Derek Johnson."

Daniel went on, "Aiden go inside, and call the sheriff." Aiden left and Daniel went on, "I didn't really want to do this, but now you've given me no choice. So, boys sit down on the floor, and intertwine your fingers behind your head and stay that way until the sheriff arrives." Then Daniel sat down on a bale of hay and told Dane to go unlock and open the overhead door in the front of the barn.

Soon the squad car arrived without the siren but had the flashing lights on. When the two officers entered the barn, one of them looked at the boys, and said, "Well, well. We meet again Tom Tuttle. So, you're up to no good again. What's it going to take to get it through your thick skull that you're in deep do-do again."

"Yeah, so?" Tom said.

"You've been sent to JuV before, do you want to go through that again?"

He just shrugged.

"If Mr. Wilshire presses charges against you, you will go away for a while, maybe a long time this time. No more friends to do your dirty work with you. That certainly sounds like fun, doesn't it?"

Daniel spoke up and said, "Officer, he's done this before here, not just breaking into my barn, but trying to steal my horses. I offered a job to him in hopes he'd learn the value of hard work, but it didn't work obviously."

The sheriff took out his handcuffs, made the two boys stand, put their hands behind their backs, and he cuffed them.

Daniel then said, "Officer, can I have a word with you in private? Dane and Aiden can keep an eye on the boys for a few minutes." He led the sheriff into his office and closed the door.

He said, "I really don't want to press charges against these boys. I know boys will be boys and do stupid stuff. But I don't want them to try this anymore either. I'd rather see if the law could make those boys work off their charges here at my farm if that's possible. But I don't want to have this show up on a record for either one. I'd rather see if these two can be rehabilitated instead of slapping them in Juvenile Detention. I believe that putting people in prison doesn't do anything except make them worse when they get out. I can see Tom is heading down that path, but I'd like the opportunity to see if he can be turned around.

"So, you believe Tom is the lead instigator, and the other boy is just going along for the ride. Am I right?"

"I don't really know the other boy" the sheriff stated. "But that's what I suspect. I'll take them in, and we can get together with the judge tomorrow and see what he says. But let's let them cool their heels tonight in lockup."

"That sounds fair. I'll meet you in Judge Lacky's chambers tomorrow at whatever time he has available."

"Sounds like you already know him."

"He's a friend of mine. Known him for years, and he's fair."

Judge Lacky told Daniel and the sheriff he had some time to meet them at one thirty. Daniel arrived on time and shook the judge's hand. The judge asked, "So how are you, Daniel? I haven't seen you in a coon's age."

"Busy as ever on the farm. You know how that goes."

"And how's the rest of your family?"

"They're doing well. What about yours?"

"As mean as ever." They both laughed. The sheriff arrived then.

The judge began, "Ok, I only have about fifteen minutes, so how can I help you two?"

The sheriff answered, "Daniel here got his barn broken into last night. Two young boys trying to steal his horses."

The judge looked at Daniel. "That's right," Daniel said. "One of the boys had tried it a couple of weeks ago and we caught him. I didn't press charges then, but offered him a job instead, hoping it might make him see the error of his ways, but he quit shortly after he arrived.

The sheriff put in, "The two boys are locked up in my jail now."

"Now this time you want to press charges. Is that right?" the judge asked.

"Not exactly," answered Daniel. "I was thinking, if I don't press charges, but they were made to work off a certain amount of time on my farm, some community service, I'd be satisfied with that. I just don't want to ruin the boy's future by having an arrest on their record. And from what the sheriff says, one boy's been in Juvenile Detention before. I'd like to see if a little hard labor might change their attitude about stealing horses in the future.

"I mean, I could offer them a job, but that one boy would probably just quit like he did before, but if a judge ordered him to do community work on my farm, he couldn't quit, and maybe it might help turn them around."

"I see your point," the judge said. "So, let's let them think you're pressing charges, they meet before me tomorrow morning at nine o'clock, and I'll sentence them to work on your farm for a month. Do you think that's enough time?"

"Let's hope so. And thank you for your help."

The judge replied, "Your heart is too soft, you know that don't you, Daniel?"

Daniel, rose, shook his hand, smiled and said, "I suppose you're right, but I just hate to see young ones hauled off to JuV, with that on their record, and not rehabilitated. And I feel young ones are born into a hard world, and if an adult can help them any, it might make a better person out of them."

"You're a good man, Daniel. I admire your ambition. I just hope it works out alright."

"Me too, and thanks again."

The sheriff and Daniel left his office, and as they were walking out of the courthouse, the sheriff said, "See you tomorrow morning at nine, and when he releases the boys into your care afterward, I'll drive them out to your place."

"Thanks. Tomorrow then."

When he got home, he called Dane and Aiden into his office and explained that they would have two more ranch hands for the next month. Aiden looked at Dane and could read the expression on his face that he wasn't happy.

The boys left the office and Dane said, "Have fun with that. I doubt if that Tom will learn anything, but dad always thinks he's a savior."

"Well, he was a savior for me. Not sure where I'd be right now if he didn't have such a big heart. Maybe we need to emulate him. I'm of the opinion that kindness will go a lot farther than hatred."

"You're right. But be prepared for trouble, especially with that guy Tom."

The next day the sheriff deposited the two boys to the Wilshire farm early after they met with the judge. Aiden met them and got them busy brushing down the horses and currying their tails and manes.

Derek enjoyed working with the horses. He would pet the ones he was working on, talking softly to them, while Tom worked without making a sound. He was still smarting from having been brought back to the farm to work.

Cody walked into the barn and was surprised to see Tom working. "Hey, did you change your mind about working here?"

Tom looked up, "Something like that."

Cody spoke to Derek as well since he knew him from school, and he wondered why he was working on the farm. He would ask Aiden about Derek later.

Aiden got Cody busy mowing, then he got Tom and Derek busy mucking out the horse's stalls, and Tom began complaining to Derek about having to do that job. But before long, they had their job completed, and the horses back in their respective stalls. Aiden brought the four-wheeler into the barn, hooked the wagon up to it, showed the boys the lever to dump the manure, and told Derek where to take it to dump. Derek was smiling at Tom when he got on the four-wheeler. He knew Tom would be envious because he was chosen to drive the four-wheeler instead of him.

Soon he was back in the barn, driving too fast, but was able to stop in time before running into Aiden or Tom. While he was gone, Aiden and Tom had saddled a couple of horses. Aiden told Tom and Derek to get on them, then he called Shep, who came running. He opened the sheep and llama gates to their stalls, and Shep went to work. He told the boys to just follow the dog, open the gate when he herds them to the pasture, and let the animals enter. "And make sure the gate is closed and latched after they're all in," he added.

When the boys got back to the barn, Derek dismounted, bent down and ruffled Shep's fur, calling him a good dog, and wished he had a dog like him. Aiden couldn't help but notice that Tom was quiet and wasn't enthused about the work as Derek seemed to be.

He told Derek to begin mucking out the llama and sheep stalls, while he took Tom to the loft. While they were in the loft, before Aiden put him to work lowering bales of hay out the window, Aiden decided to see what was going on in Tom's head. He asked, "Tom, so how do you feel about working here for a month?"

"Not happy."

"Well, it could be worse. You could have been sent to a JuV detention center. The only reason you weren't is because Mr. Wilshire didn't want that on your record. He's such a great guy. I hope you'll end up enjoying it here, like I do."

"I doubt it."

"You know, I'm surprised I haven't ended up in JuV." Aiden said this to see what Tom's reaction would be.

Tom jerked his head up, "Why would you end up in JuV?"

"I was on my own for a while, without a mother or father. I could have gotten in a lot of trouble."

Tom looked at him, quiet for a minute. "So, what happened to your parents?"

"Both of them are dead."

Tom looked shocked, "Dead? So, you were on your own after that?"

"Yes, and as a teenager, I had choices to make, all alone, without parents to help me." Tom was quiet, without a word, just standing there looking at Aiden. Aiden had given him enough to think about, then showed him how to lower the bales of hay out of the window.

He kept both boys busy all day until it was time to bring the sheep, llamas, and cattle in. He got the boys to call Shep, he showed them how to feed the animals, and then it was time for him to drive both boys home.

They dropped Derek at his house first, and Tom directed Aiden to his home. While they were alone, Tom asked, "Can I ask you a question?"

"Sure."

"Have you ever been in trouble with the law?"

"Nope."

"So, when you were on your own, you never did anything bad?"

"Well, not sure what you mean by bad, but yeah, I guess I did, but it worked out ok."

"So, what did you do?"

Aiden looked at him, not sure he wanted to open up to him. But he finally decided that if it might help Tom, he would. "I buried my mom in the horse barn."

"You what?! Really?" Tom said in shock.

"Yeah, I did, but I didn't know at the time it was against the law."

"Hey, man, why did you do that?"

"Because I didn't want my sisters and me to be sent to foster homes. Our dad was out of our life, and I knew we'd be separated and put in foster homes after mom died, if I called the police."

"And did you get caught."

"Yes."

"What happened then?"

"Well, we three kids had run away, and wound-up living for a while in a cabin in the woods until Daniel found out about us, and now he has custody of us three. He's a really super nice guy. If he hadn't helped us, I have no idea where I would have wound up.

"And the sheriff said you've been in JuV before. What did you do to merit that?"

"I robbed a house and got caught."

"Oh, I see. And if you don't mind me asking, why steal?"

"You'll see why when you see my house. I'm living with my grandparents. They're poor and I just want more out of life than what they have to offer. And I don't have any money to buy things, so I steal things to sell."

"Hey, man, that's a bad way to get what you want. Why not work, make your own money, so you can buy what you need?"

"And who would hire me with a record now?"

"I believe Daniel would, as long as you don't steal his horses," Aiden said with a smile. "And honestly, I think even though you're working now at his farm, because the judge said you have to, I wouldn't be surprised if he paid you for your work."

"Do you really think so? That would be great."

They arrived at his grandparent's home, and Tom was right, they were poor, very poor, and it showed from the looks of their home. It definitely was dilapidated, even junky looking.

Before Tom got out of Aiden's truck, Aiden asked, "Hey, Tom. How old are your grandparents?"

"Not sure. Probably close to eighty, maybe even into their eighties. Why?"

"No reason, just wondered."

Aiden decided to talk to Daniel about Tom. He wanted to try to see if Daniel would pay him for his work now that he knew Tom's situation.

He sought Daniel out that evening after he got home and asked if he could speak with him alone. They headed to the office in the barn.

"What's up?" Daniel asked.

"I want to talk to you about these two boys."

"Did they cause problems today?"

"No, nothing like that, but I did get an opportunity to talk to Tom when I took him home tonight. It seems the reason he's getting into trouble is because he's been caught stealing. He steals in order to sell things because he's living with his grandparents who are dirt poor. You should see their house. It's in pretty bad shape. He says they have no money to get him things he needs."

Daniel rubbed his chin. "You know, I figured the kid had some kind of rough life."

"What I would like to do," continued Aiden, "is to pay the boys for their work. What do you think about that?"

"I think that would be a good idea. So come Friday, I'll hand them each some cash, and maybe that will be the incentive to work harder while they're here."

"There's something else I want to talk to you about. When Dane goes back to college this year, I'd like to hire another hand to help with the work here. What are your thoughts about that?"

"Well, we have Cody and he's working out well, but if you feel like you need more help, then I'm all for it. Maybe if one of these boys work out well while they're here, you could hire him."

Aiden added, "I'll think about that. I guess I'd need to know their ages. Not sure they are out of high school. Thanks for talking to me about this. I just think paying Tom for his work here just might be what he needs to turn him around from the road he's heading down."

"Let's hope so."

Derek and Tom showed up in Derek's car for work. Aiden let them know they needed to do the same thing they did the day before. The boys got busy brushing down the horses, but Tom let Derek know that today, he was the one driving the four-wheeler to dump the manure.

When Tom got the four-wheeler out of the shed, he took a spin around the barnyard with it. Aiden saw him and motioned for him to bring it into the barn. When Tom did so and turned it off, Aiden said, "This isn't play time. If you want to ride the four-wheeler after all your work is done today that's fine, but when you're on the clock you work."

"Aw, Aiden," Tom said, "I was just having a little fun."

"Like I said, after work. And that's only if you get your work done in record time, so I suggest you get at dumping the manure, it's almost lunch time."

The boys hooked up the wagon to the four-wheeler and Tom drove it out behind the shed and dumped it. Afterward it was time to eat.

The girls fixed their plates and headed out to the patio to eat. There were only so many seats around the dining room table, and they really didn't want Cody, Derek and Tom to sit gawking at them while they ate.

As it was, Daniel was glad to have the girls away from the boys. This gave him an opportunity to talk to Tom and Derek. He began with, "So Derek, tell me a little about yourself. How old are you?"

Derek stopped eating, and took a drink of his tea before answering, "I'm seventeen."

"So, you're still in school, I take it."

"Yes, I'm going into my senior year this fall."

"And what do you plan to do after high school?"

"Well, my parents want me to go to college, so guess I'll be putting in my applications sometime this school year. Not sure where yet."

"And what do you plan on studying in college?"

"Uh, maybe business of some sort. My granddad was President of a bank, and Dad thought I might get a job in a bank after college and work my way up like granddad did."

"That's an admirable goal to work toward. But you realize you have to keep your nose clean in order to achieve that goal."

He looked sheepishly at Daniel, "Yes, sir."

"Try not to screw up anymore and I'm sure you'll do fine. But just know that if you mess up after you turn eighteen, you'll have a record then, and no one will want to hire you, even after you graduate college."

"Yes, sir. I think I've learned my lesson."

"I hope so, because you could have a bright future ahead of you. Don't mess that up."

"Yes, sir."

He then asked Tom, "And Tom, what about you? What is your age?"

"Eighteen. I graduated last year."

"And now that you've graduated, what do you plan to do the rest of your life? Any goals?"

"No, sir."

"Why not?"

"Well, I can't go to college, so I guess I'll just get a job."

"Did you take any classes in high school to prepare you for a job after you got out?"

"Well, I took woodworking and really liked it."

"Would you like to be a carpenter?"

"I guess so."

"Ok, then I might have some work you can do for us while you're here. That is if you want it."

"I guess it depends on what kind of work it is."

"Well, we have that huge barn out there. Of course, we put the straw and hay up in the loft, but there's plenty of room left over that we don't use. I was thinking if Aiden hires someone come this fall, we might need a room built in the loft for someone to stay in."

"I'd like to work on that if you think I can."

Dane spoke up, "I can help him, Dad."

"Ok, then I'll order the lumber, and you two can get on it right away. And Cody how do you feel about swinging a hammer?"

"I haven't had a lot of experience building things, but if Dane doesn't mind teaching me, I'm willing to help."

"Good, then you three can work on that together."

Tom really seemed to perk up about this opportunity. He smiled the rest of the meal.

On the way back to work after lunch, Cody fell in beside Tom and whispered, "Hey, what Daniel said back there, something about Derek screwing up. What did he do?"

"We came back here to steal a couple of their horses and got caught."

"Again? Are you nuts? So that's why you're working here again?"

"The judge said we have to work here for a month."

Cody whistled, "Man, you've got to quit that stealing stuff. You'll end up in jail for sure if you don't."

Tom walked on without another word, but it weighed heavy on his mind about what Cody had said.

Tom and Derek were able to complete their work assignments early and Aiden told them they could take the four-wheeler out to the pasture for a little fun. "Just don't wreck it, and don't tear it up," Aiden told them. The boys, Tom, Derek, and Cody all had such a great time.

The next morning the lumber was delivered, and Dane, Tom, and Cody got busy hauling it up to the loft. Daniel had included a wall air conditioner/heater and one window to be added to the outside wall. He went up to the loft to help the boys know where he wanted the room built. He took his tape measure and marked on the floor where he wanted the walls built.

Before the day was done, they had the room framed in. Daniel ordered more supplies, such as a door, insulation, electrical wiring, junction boxes, and an electric panel, outlets, and a light switch, a fan with a light for the ceiling, and tongue and groove boards for the ceiling and walls of the inside of the room.

This took the boys most of two weeks to get it finished, except for the tongue and groove boards for the walls. They still had to install the air conditioner/heater in the outside wall, and the window, but soon, those two things were in as well.

Aiden offered to help with the tongue and groove siding, and with all four working together, even that was soon finished. The only thing left was to finish the outlets, light switch, and hang the ceiling fan. They had decided to include a closet in the room also.

Dane went to his father after the room was completed, and said, "Dad that's a great room for a hired hand. He'll be close to the animals if they should need anything, but what about bathroom facilities?"

Daniel answered, "Well, we do have the half bath downstairs he could use. There isn't a shower though, but we could take a little room out of my office and add a shower there, don't you think?"

"Let me do some measuring." Dane hurried out of the office to get the tape measure and was soon back.

However, after measuring for the shower, thinking about it and what that would do to the office, he went outside to see about taking some of the room from the refrigerated milk room. After measuring, he decided it was a better idea than to take room from the office. Daniel went to see what that might do to the milk room, and he agreed that's where the shower should be added. And there was room to cut a door from the half bath into the shower room.

Daniel liked the idea of having a shower in the barn even if they didn't end up hiring another hand, because there were times someone would get pretty dirty, and could shower outside before going in.

O ne day Lottie asked Miriam, "Can I ask you a question, Mrs. Wilshire?"

"Sure, what is it?"

"Do you ever get tired of doing all the things you do? I mean, the cooking, cleaning, laundry, stuff like that?"

Miriam thought a minute, "Well, the way I look at it is, if I really love my family, I want to do things for them. So, no, I guess I don't get tired of doing those things. But every once in a while, we do something fun for the entire family. We go to the beach, or fair, or the Elvis festival. Things like that. But now that Daniel has your brother as ranch foreman, I've told him I'd like to take a cruise."

"Oh, that would be fun. Where would you go?"

"We haven't gotten that far yet, but eventually maybe. Why are you asking if I get tired of doing all the things I do for the family?"

"I don't know. I was just thinking about getting married to Dane. I know he will take over running this farm eventually, and I feel like you have so much to do. I was just thinking about all that I would have to do in the future."

"Well, if you like what you do, it really isn't work. But if you decide you don't like doing those chores, then maybe you shouldn't get married," Mariam said this while looking at Lottie to see her reaction.

"I know a lot of girls think they'll get married and live happily ever after without thinking about anything but having fun with the one they love," Lottie responded. "I don't feel that way. I know with marriage comes responsibility, and I don't mind work. I guess I was just thinking about change once in a while."

"Then if you marry Dane, and you need a change once in a while, like you said, you have a talk with your husband, and let him know how you feel. You need to have fun also in your marriage. It can't be all work and no play, or the marriage could very easily fall apart. Open communication between two individuals is very important."

"I believe that too. Thank you for talking with me. I don't see how our marriage would ever be boring because Dane is so kind, like his parents, and I'm sure he'd do anything to keep me happy."

Mariam just smiled before returning to her ironing.

Tom and Derek were working out fine, making good money, and at the end of the month, Tom asked if he could stay on, although Derek and Cody had to get ready to go back to school. Aiden spoke to Daniel about it, and he agreed that Tom was working out very well and he'd be happy to keep him on. However, Aiden didn't tell Tom about their decision until after he and Derek met with the judge once more after the month was up. The judge wanted to see how things had worked out for the boys. Satisfied with their attitudes, he let them know he didn't want to ever see them back in his court again and told them they were free to go.

After that was taken care of, Aiden told Tom that he could stay on as a ranch hand, if he wanted. Tom said, "That's great. And I have a favor to ask."

"Oh?"

"Do you think I could move into the loft bedroom?"

"Well, I don't see why not. We built it for a ranch hand, and I don't believe you have a vehicle to get to and from work without Derek, so that is fine with me. But let me run it by Daniel first. I'll get back with you about it."

Daniel was fine with it, and Tom moved in right away. He was so happy to be moving out of his grandparent's home. It wasn't that he didn't love them, he did. But he felt it was time for him to be on his own. He wanted to be more independent, and he was really happy to be working on the farm. He'd learned so much. Especially did he like working with the animals.

When he needed time to think, meditate on his life and where he was headed, he would take a horse out to ride. He let on with Aiden that he needed to check the fences but in reality, he just needed time to himself.

As he spent time with the animals, he realized they were able to help him become more caring and understanding. He felt the anger inside him evaporate. Yes, he'd had a hard life, but he'd learned that hard work, enjoyable work, brought rewards. He began to realize how anger had held him back, was crippling any growth toward maturity. He thought about Aiden and all he'd been through. To see his mother die like she did and be able to step up to the plate and take the responsibility on in taking care of his sisters was commendable, and he was pretty certain he could never have done that. As it was, his parents were both out of his life, not by death, but by their own choice, left him feeling unworthy of love. Now as he meditated on that situation, he came to realize that he wasn't the problem, but that his parents were the problem, and if they didn't love him enough to stay with him, he was better off without them.

He felt he'd found a good family, one that was willing to put themselves out to take him in, help him learn a trade, and even paid him while he was learning. He felt indebted to them all. And it didn't hurt that Aiden had a little sister just a couple of years younger than he was that was extremely good looking to admire once in a while.

He looked her up and down every chance he got, and he wasn't exactly sure, but he thought he caught her eyeing him a couple of times as well. Maybe if he played his cards right, someday if he proved his worth, he might even have someone to love him the way he'd always wanted and needed to be loved other than his grandparents.

Summer was coming to an end, Dane was getting ready to leave for college, and Erin, and Izzy were preparing for school. Erin would be a senior this year and Izzy was going into tennth grade. Cody was going into his senior year of high school as well, but his mother agreed to allow him to continue working for the Wilshire's if they would let him.

Dane brought to Aiden's attention that they had never taken the opportunity to go to Tombigbee State Park during the summer like they'd planned and wondered if they still wanted to go before school started.

Aiden agreed, and at lunch he brought it up to everyone. All the young ones clamored to go and, since time was running out for the summer, they should do it soon, like maybe tomorrow.

So, the next day, Mrs. Wilshire had a picnic basket of food prepared for them all. Dane drove his truck and Aiden drove his. Lottie and Izzy and Cody piled in with Dane, and Tom, Derek and Erin crawled in with Aiden. Daniel and Miriam decided to stay home and have a day to themselves.

On the way to the park, with windows rolled down, and radios blaring, the party began. They found a good place to park, and headed down a trail, laughing, singing, and just having a great time together.

They followed a trail into the woods. The woods were thick with trees that were so tall they seemed to reach the sky. They followed the path, until they found a clearing with a picnic table, so they stopped to eat their lunch.

Soon they were back on the trail again. After an hour or so, Dane and Aiden heard angry words coming from behind them. They stopped to see what was going on, and as they turned back, they saw Cody land a punch on Tom's jaw.

"Hey, you two," Aiden said, as he looked down at Tom sprawled on the ground. "What's going on?"

Tom spoke, "He punched me because he found out I like Izzy. He says he saw her first."

Aiden spoke up, "She's not for sale to either one of you guys, so I suggest you two try to get along. Izzy, come up here and walk with us."

He helped Tom up and asked him if he was alright. "I guess so," Tom said, looking at Cody with a smirk while rubbing his jaw.

Aiden finished by saying, "Cody you and Tom can bring up the rear, alone. And try to have fun. That's why we're here. Don't ruin it for everyone."

Dane sighed deeply, leaned down to Aiden and said under his breath, "Told you so."

Aiden whispered back, "Keep an eye on those two."

Eventually the trees gave way to a huge lake, spread out before them, calm and serene. The sun glistened across the water, reaching right up to the bank where they stood. Soon someone picked up a stone to skip across the top of the water, and everyone joined in, scouring the ground in search of the perfect rock to do the same.

There was no further incident between the boys the remainder of the day, and the crowd arrived back home at dusk, tired but happy to have had the day off work for a little R & R.

When the girls got to their rooms, Lottie said to Izzy, "Geez, I've never had two guys fight over me like that."

Izzy just rolled her eyes.

"You didn't do anything to cause that I hope."

"Like what?" Izzy asked.

"Like lead one or both of the boys on that you were interested in them."

"Come on, Lottie, you know me better than that. I was furious with those two. I wanted to punch them both in the face."

"So… tell me how you feel about those two."

"Feel?"

"Yeah, do you like one over the other?"

"Um, I'd have to think about that. I really haven't gotten a chance to know Tom very well yet. Guess time will tell."

38

Next morning, Aiden caught Izzy before heading to the barn. "Hey, I think you should steer clear of all three of those boys. I don't want any more trouble."

"Don't worry, I will. Honestly, why do boys think they need to fight over a girl anyway?"

"Too much testosterone." Then he turned and headed out.

The girls decided to take the day and go shopping. Lottie borrowed Aiden's truck and soon the girls were in the stores. Midmorning they went to a tearoom where they had coffee and tea, and soon decided they should get back to the farm to help make lunch for the guys.

When they entered the house, Izzy couldn't help but glare at Tom and Cody and hoped they saw. She wanted them to know how disgusted she was with both of them. She was the first girl who got her plate filled and flew out the door to eat on the patio.

When Lottie came out, she stated, "Well, I guess you showed them. Your face said it all."

"Good, I hope they realize they both just ruined any chance they had with me."

"Atta girl, stick to your guns."

School started shortly afterward, and Erin and Izzy got on the bus early in the morning each day and didn't get home until a little after four. Cody showed up shortly after school to work. Aiden said, "Do you have any homework to do, because if you do, I want it done before you get to work?"

Cody said he will be able to do his homework in study hall in school and doubted he'd ever have homework this year.

"That's fine, but if you don't get it all finished in school, just remember, school first."

"Sure, no problem."

Dane had left for college, so that meant the work was up to Aiden and Tom during the day and Cody after school each evening. The girl's chores were left up to Lottie alone with Miriam. Lottie worked as hard as she could each day so she would be free to take phone calls from Dane in the evenings.

Cody came to the Wilshire's one evening after school, and said to Aiden, "I have an assignment for school that I could use your advice on."

"Ok, what's the assignment?"

"I have to do a report, complete with pictures, of my career choice for the future. So, I was thinking about writing about working on this ranch. So, while I'm working, if you could dog after me, and take pictures while I work, I could use that for my report. What do you think?"

"Ok, I guess I can do that."

Cody got busy brushing down the horses, mucking out the stalls with Aiden snapping pictures. He also took pictures of Cody mounted on a horse, herding the llamas and sheep out to pasture with Shep helping. He had Cody get on the tractor and Aiden took pictures of him mowing. Some of the pictures were just for show and Cody wasn't really doing the work, but it showed the jobs that he would do on the farm. Cody was pleased with how the pictures turned out. He promised to show Aiden what his grade on the report turned out to be, although he was certain he would get an 'A'.

Tom was busy working but was worried about Cody being at school possibly around Izzy every day while there. He hoped Cody wouldn't be able to turn Izzy's attention toward him. When she would come home each night, Tom watched the way Izzy acted to try to determine if her affections toward Cody had changed. He was behaving properly toward her, staying away from her, and he wanted Cody to dothe same at school. And if he happened to come across Izzy for any reason on the farm, he made certain he treated her with proper propriety. He felt like he was turning into a proper gentleman, and he hoped Izzy noticed. He didn't want to do anything to make her want to turn away from him. He was walking on pins and needles. He had been in trouble with the law before, yes, but that was behind him now. He was learning a new life, and so far, he was enjoying every minute of it. Yes, he had to learn hard work, but he had to admit it made him feel more like a man and he liked what he was seeing and feeling. Maybe he would be able to put his hard sad life behind him forever.

Lottie had picked the remainder of vegetables growing in the garden, and she helped Miriam put them up. However, Miriam let her know, they had plenty already, and this last batch was to be given to some neighbors. Therefore, she prepared a basket of corn on the cob, carrots, lettuce, cucumbers, and green beans, and sent Lottie off to deliver the food to close neighbors.

Lottie went first to Charles at the store around the corner. He was happy to have some produce that he declared he would allow customers to have, free of charge, of course. She went to the Simpsons, the farmer Aiden had met the first day he went to the store and asked Mr. Simpson for directions. He was glad Mr. Simpson was out in a field and she was able to meet Mrs. Simpson.

She said to Lottie, "You say this produce is from the Wilshire farm?"

"Yes, ma'am," Lottie replied.

"But you're not Erin. She usually brings me produce from Miriam's garden."

"Yes, ma'am but she's in school, so I'm delivering for Mrs. Wilshire today."

"Then who are you?"

"My name is Lottie. I work for the Wilshire's."

"I see, well, come in and I'll pick a few things out of your basket. I just love the home-grown vegetables instead of store bought. Don't you?"

"Yes, ma'am."

Lottie stopped at a couple of other houses before heading back to the Wilshire's.

Aiden called Daniel into the barn to talk to him. He had an idea that he needed to run by him. Daniel said, "What's up, Aiden?"

"Well, I've been thinking. I know you have a lot more land than just what you use for pastures. What do you think about clearing a field and plowing it up for a crop?"

"Hmm, I've never done any farming. I'll think about it, and let you know."

Aiden decided to call Dane that evening to see what his thoughts were about doing a little farming. Dane said, "Have you talked to Dad about this?"

"I brought it up today, but he said he wants to think about it."

"Yeah, I talked to Dad about doing that a long time ago, but he wasn't interested. He said he was no farmer and didn't intend to become one."

"Oh, I didn't know that. It's just that he has all this land that he's not using, and it seems like a waste not to use it somehow."

"I agree, that's why I talked to him about planting a crop. I figured if we planted wheat, barley, corn, oats, or something like that, it would take care of the horse's feed and would save us having to buy feed.

"I agree, it just doesn't seem right to have that land just laying fallow not bringing in any income, or saving us on feed, but draining money in taxes from us."

"I'll wait a little while to see what Dad says about it, and then I'll talk to him if he's still against the idea. Maybe we could just start with a small field, get him used to the idea before plowing under any more land."

"Sounds like a plan. I'll let you know what he says to me about it. And I think while Daniel's thinking about it, I'll do a little research on farming in Mississippi."

Dane laughed, "Good idea."

Daniel called Aiden into his office and said, "I've thought about your proposal to plow up some land for a field, and I just don't think I want to do that."

Aiden was disappointed, but after talking with Dane, he wasn't surprised. But he was ready for a rebuttal. "Look, Mr. Wilshire, I've spoken with Dane about this, and we both feel like not only will it save us money in feed for the animals, but it will make the land more usable."

"I know, but I don't want to be labeled as a dirt farmer. There's a stigma attached to farmers I just don't like."

"And you care about what people say about you? You've had your reputation established here in this community for years, even generations, so I really doubt it will matter now what you do. But I guess I can understand, so what do you think about this idea? We could build a fence around more pastureland and get black angus cattle to sell for the meat instead of milking cattle. I think you have enough of those already."

"Now that idea I like."

"And what if Tom and I built a small pen and house for some chickens? The girls could take care of them."

"That's a good idea. Where would you build that?"

"Why not out behind your house by the shed there. We could use one side of the shed and build a cage for the other three sides."

"Sounds good, but you might also want to put a roof over the entire cage because there are coyotes that might get into it and eat the chickens."

"Good idea," Aiden agreed, "And I'll put a walk-through door with a latch on it."

Aiden and Tom went to town for supplies to get started on the chicken coop right away. They could wrap the pen with chicken wire after the coop was completed.

The coop was large and tall enough to stand up inside it, with a little house built for the hens in the middle of it. One side of the coop had small doors that could be dropped down to extract the eggs from the nests inside made with straw. They even built a ramp for the chickens to walk up to enter their coop. When it was completed, Aiden stood back to admire it and said, "Reminds me of Foghorn Leghorn."

Tom responded, "Foghorn Leghorn? What's that about?"

"The rooster. Haven't you heard of Foghorn Leghorn?"

"No."

"Man, you haven't lived." Then he mimicked Foghorn Leghorn saying in a deep voice, "Listen, son. I say…I say listen, boy."

Tom laughed. "So, who is Foghorn Leghorn?"

"Cartoon. He was a Looney Tunes character. He was one of my favorites. You should look it up on the internet. I loved Looney Tunes. Watched them every Saturday morning when I was little."

"Yeah, I'll do that."

"We just have to make sure Wiley Coyote can't get in here to eat our chickens."

"Now I've heard of him. Isn't he always trying to catch the roadrunner?"

"Yes, and I have no idea how many times he blew himself up trying."

They both laughed as they carried their tools back to the barn.

Aiden called Dane to tell him the latest news about not being able to plow any land under to plant a crop. But Dane was at least happy that they could increase their cattle herd, and he liked the idea of a chicken coop. Another chore for the girls.

"And if we get enough chickens," added Aiden, "we'll sell eggs and make a little more money."

Dane laughed, "The girls will have their own business. Maybe we can let them pocket the money they make from the eggs."

"That's a good idea. I'm sure they'll love that. Wages for their work."

Aiden had the girls put an ad on social media for laying hens, and soon they had all they needed. The girls seemed excited and even decided to name their hens. They had Rhode Island Reds. And Aiden couldn't help himself, he had to purchase some called White Leghorn layers. And come to think of it, Foghorn Leghorn was white too although Foghorn was a rooster instead of a hen.

The following week, Aiden ordered fencing materials to be delivered for the fences. He ordered a third four-wheeler and that is what they drove to the new pastureland each morning to work on the fences. Tom thought that was great fun. Each day when they headed back to the house for lunch, they would race to see who would get there first.

Aiden was proud of the changes he was seeing in Tom, no longer the angry boy he once was. He was even fun to be around, and he was becoming a good carpenter. Altogether turning out to be a great hand on the farm. He was happy to have Tom living in the loft bedroom as well. He knew Tom couldn't afford to purchase a vehicle and he certainly didn't want to have to go to town every day to bring him to work and take him home every night. He knew at Tom's age, living in the loft also gave him a sense of independence.

But one day after their lunch, while they were working on fences, Aiden asked him, "Hey, Tom, have you been by to visit your grandparents lately?"

"No."

"Don't you think you should."

"I guess so. Yeah."

"And I've been thinking about them lately. How would you feel, if after we get these fences finished, we get a few supplies and do some repair work on their house for them?"

Tom's eyes widened, "You'd do that?"

"Well, you said they are poor, so I figure they probably don't have the money to do some repairs. We'll look their house over and decide what needs repaired first."

"Gee that's great. I know they would love that. And I'm sure they're wondering how I'm doing too."

"So, let's don't tell them what we plan to do. Let's make it a surprise. We'll go visit them, and while I'm there, I'll look the house over."

"That's wonderful. I'd really like to do something for them."

Eventually they had fenced in about 25 acres for the cattle, and they went to the auction to pick their cattle. The Black Angus were delivered by semi, drove right up to the gate to the pasture, lowered a ramp from the truck, and unloaded them. Aiden had used the tractor, attached the front scoop on it and dug out a pond in the back of the pasture for the cattle to get water. He figured at first the cattle could graze on the long grass but eventually he would need to have enough hay ordered for them. Even though, some clearing was needed in the pastureland, Aiden wanted to leave some in order for the cows to have a little shelter before he could build them something to get out of bad weather.

He was glad to have more farmhand with more cattle to care for. He told Tom that they would need to build a lean-to in the pasture for the cattle to get under in case of bad storms. After another trip to town for lumber and roofing, it wasn't long before that too was finished. Soon they'd have to do more clearing.

Aiden was ready to take Tom to see his grandparents. Because Tom had called ahead to let them know he and Aiden would be coming, there was iced tea waiting for them. Aiden shook hands with Tom's grandfather before sitting down.

They talked and Aiden assured them that Tom was working out very well on the farm, pulling his weight with the chores, and even becoming quite a good carpenter. His grandparents were beaming at that information. "Of course, we keep him busy on the farm, and without a vehicle, he can't go anywhere to get into trouble," Aiden laughed.

Tom smirked at him. "Now you know I'm the best ranch hand you have."

Aiden laughed again and said he had to agree with that.

"We're very happy that he's doing well," his grandfather said. "We were worried about him. He's a good boy, but just needs a little guidance."

Aiden noticed a bucket sitting on the floor, glanced up at the ceiling, and noticed a water stain on it. Therefore, he realized they had a leak in the roof.

On their way back to the Wilshire's, Aiden said, "I noticed that they have a leak in the living room ceiling. What do you say we put a new roof on the house for them?"

"They have more than one leak. That's a good idea. I know they'd appreciate it. But do you think Mr. Wilshire will agree to doing this for them?"

"I'm going to pay for it, not him. Let's keep this as our secret. No one but us needs to know anything about it."

"Wow, that's great. But I feel ashamed," Tom said it as he hung his head.

"Why would you feel ashamed?"

"Because I should be the one taking care of them, not you."

"But you just graduated high school. How could you possibly take care of them?"

"I'm ashamed that we are so poor?"

"That's nothing to be ashamed of either. Things happen in life. I don't know the whole story of your family, but I'm sure they're doing the best they can. And even though they are poor, they made room for you to live with them. They provided food, and shelter for you. Just be proud that you have grandparents that love you that much and want to help you."

"Yeah, you're right. I guess I never looked at it that way. And I know they really do love me."

"You see? That's what I'm talking about. And because of their love for you and trying to provide for you the best they could, that's why we need to do something for them, to give back a little."

"Yeah, I really do want to help them. I feel sorry for them. It must be hard to grow old."

"Then just don't do it."

They both laughed at that.

The girls would go to the chicken coop and feed them each morning before school. Then each evening they would collect the eggs. Izzy got busy making up a sign to stick in the ground by the road to advertise that they had eggs for sale. It wasn't long before people were stopping to buy some. If the girls were in school, Lottie took charge of the transaction, and gave the girls their money when they got home.

One day Daniel was hauling bales of hay to the pastureland, when one of his back wheels on his tractor dropped into a deep hole. The hole had been hidden by tall grass and weeds. It tilted the tractor to one side causing Daniel to be thrown off his seat. He tried to hold onto the steering wheel, but with his weight thrown to the side, it caused the front wheels to be sharply jerked in a different direction, and the entire tractor rolled onto its side with Daniel pinned beneath. He was crushed by the weight of the tractor. He died instantly.

Eventually Aiden saw the tractor on its side and went running into the pasture. When he found Daniel, he checked for a heartbeat but found none. He was devastated. What could he do? He went running back to the barn, yelling for Tom and Cody. He also yelled for Lottie. She heard and came running out of the house. He told her to call 911. He had the boys each get a horse and rope, and with no time to saddle them they mounted, and rode them out to the pasture. They tied their ropes to different parts of the tractor, and using all three horses, were able to pull the tractor back into an upright position.

Aiden jumped down and again tried to feel a heartbeat on Daniel, but again felt nothing. Then he began CPR. When the EMT's arrived, along with two squad cars, Aiden was still giving Daniel CPR. They took over, but eventually they had to pronounce him dead.

Dane, Aiden, Lottie, and the boys were devastated. Lottie turned to look toward the house and saw Miriam standing in the yard with her hand over her mouth. Lottie could see the terror on Miriam's face and took off running to her. Miriam already knew it was bad and was crying uncontrollably.

The EMT's loaded Daniel's body onto a stretcher and into their vehicle but stopped in the farmyard where Miriam and Lottie stood. They allowed her to see her husband, giving her privacy and all the time she needed to say her goodbyes to him. She leaned down and kissed him on the mouth, smoothed his hair, and held his hand. The entire time Lottie stood by her with her arm around her waist, tears streaming down her face.

After they drove away, Miriam turned to Aiden, "What happened?"

"Miriam, I am so sorry," he began. "I have no idea what happened. I just saw that the tractor was on its side and ran out to see what was going on."

"I'm just so, so..." she broke off unable to finish her statement. Lottie wrapped her arm around her, walked her to the house, and put her to bed.

The uniformed officers questioned Aiden and the boys, but being assured it was an accident, they left.

Lottie waited until they were finished questioning the guys, then went to Aiden, who was still standing in the barnyard with the other boys, and asked, "Do you think we should get her to a doctor's office? I think she needs a sedative."

Aiden thought that was a good idea. He went to the office to see if he could find the Wilshire's doctor's phone number. He eventually found it and called his office. The doctor was not only their doctor, but a friend as well. He said he would be right out.

Aiden hated to have to make the next phone call, but knew it was up to him to do. He dialed Dane's number. Dane knew it must be important for Aiden to call him during class time. He stepped out of the class to take the call.

When Aiden told him what happened, Dane slid down the hall wall and cried. The phone line was silent for a long time, Dane holding it to his chest while he cried. Eventually he was able to tell Aiden he would be right home and hung up. He drove like a madman all the way and arrived within two hours.

Aiden also went to the high school and collected both Erin and Izzy. Aiden was quiet until they were inside his truck. The girls knew something was wrong or Aiden wouldn't have come to get them during school hours. After he told them, they were in tears all the way home. Erin ran into the house and straight to her mother's bedroom. They cried together, holding each other tightly. The doctor had given Miriam a sedative, but it didn't seem to be working. She couldn't rest, she couldn't sleep. Nothing could console her.

When Dane arrived, Aiden could see he also had been crying. He ran to his mother's bedroom without saying a word, closed the door, and the three Wilshire's remained together, alone, crying, trying to console one another. They never came out of the bedroom the rest of the evening.

Aiden, Lottie, Izzy, and both Tom and Cody sat stunned in the living room, unable to speak, not knowing what to do. The doctor was sitting with them, and he soon got up and left the room, made a few phone calls, and before long, friends and neighbors of the Wilshire family began to come by bearing food and offering condolences.

People were encouraging them to try to eat something, but none of them wanted anything. Later Cody rose to go home. He knew his family would worry about him if he stayed any longer. Aiden didn't realize he had left. Tom eventually went to the barn to his room, and again no one noticed he had left the room.

The next day, cars began arriving and asking Aiden what needed to be done. He accepted their help, because he didn't feel that he could do any work. He pointed them to the barn and said Tom could direct them. There seemed to be people everywhere, fixing food, tending to the animals, sitting everywhere in the house, in the yard, chatting about how terrible this accident was, and how wonderful the family was. Aiden didn't care if things weren't done according to his fixed routine, he didn't want to think about anything. He just wanted to be near his sisters and the Wilshire's. He had nothing of comfort he could say to them, but just to be near them brought him a measure of comfort.

A few people had stayed the night, catching snatches of sleep here and there in chairs in the living room. Aiden, Lottie, and Izzy occupied the couch all night. Eventually the whispers stopped and there was an eerie silence that spread through the room.

The next morning, Dane and Erin came slowly out of their mother's bedroom, leaving Miriam to sleep. They had spent the night in her room, and they looked like they had been put through the wringer. Their faces were puffy and tear streaked, their clothing wrinkled, because they had slept in them.

Aiden rose from the couch, went to Dane and Erin and embraced both of them. This brought another round of tears from all three. Lottie and Izzy had also came to them and Erin fell into their arms. Aiden led them upstairs away from the people congregated in the living room and kitchen.

Aiden, Dane, Erin, and Izzy all went to Dane and Aiden's bedroom. Dane flopped onto the bed, Aiden sat in the chair and Izzy sat on the floor. Erin laid on the floor with her head in Izzy's lap. Soon Lottie appeared carrying a tray of hot steaming coffee for them all. However, Dane and Erin would not touch it. No one said a word, they just needed to be together.

After what seemed like eternity, Dane roused himself and leaning on one elbow, he said to Aiden, "I'm so drained, exhausted. Would you all mind leaving the room so I can get a little sleep?"

Everyone began to move, and Dane added, "Erin, you should do the same. Go take a nap." They all left the room, and Erin went to her bedroom, closed the door, and slid between the sheets with her clothes on.

Aiden and his sisters went downstairs, and out the back door to the patio. They sat under the trees overhanging the patio, and even though it was hot, they felt they'd rather be alone together than inside with people they didn't know. Eventually, Aiden ambled over to the barn where he found Tom and Cody working.

"Hey, guys," he said, "thanks for working. I know there's some guys that know the Wilshire's that want to help out, but I don't think I'm up to helping them. Would you two tell them what needs to be done?"

"I've already been doing that. And one of the things I told one of the farm neighbor's to do is take the backhoe to the land beyond the pasture to bring dirt and fill the hole that caused the accident," Tom said. "Aiden, how is the family doing?"

"Everyone is in shock. Dane and Erin spent the night with their mother in her bedroom, and now they're both asleep in their own rooms. I'm not sure about anything other than that. I'm going back up to the patio with my sisters, if you need anything."

"Sure, we'll take care of things here, you just need to take care of the Wilshire's."

"Yeah, as soon as they're up to it, I'll help them make arrangements for his burial."

41

Later in the afternoon, Dane came wandering out of his bedroom. He came outside where Aiden was still sitting, and said, "Aiden, I need to talk with you. Can we go into the office?"

Aiden rose immediately and followed him. When they entered, Dane sat down in his father's desk chair. He rubbed his hands up and down the wooden arm rests, feeling where his father had put his hands many times. He looked down at the desk, something he'd seen his father do many times. His father had spent so much time here in his office. He wanted it to make him feel closer to his father. Then he covered his face with his hands and took a deep breath.

"I'm totally lost, Aiden. I don't know what to do." Tears sprang up into his eyes, and he swiped at them with his sleeve.

"I understand. If I can help in any way, you know I will."

"You're a good friend."

"How is your mom doing?"

"I don't know. I think the doctor went in to see her when I came outside. I'll go check on her in a minute. But I need a little direction here."

"I'm not sure I'm the one to give direction, but I thought you might like to go see your father and I'll be glad to take you, if you do."

Dane groaned, "I don't know. I'm not sure I can. I just want to find a hole I can crawl into and hide."

"I understand, but Dane, you've got to think about Erin and your mom. They are going to need someone to take charge, and…and I think *that* someone has to be you."

"I know, but to step into my dad's shoes now. I just never thought…" his voice trailed off.

"When my mother died, I knew I had to step up to the plate and help my sisters. They had just lost their mother, their best friend and provider. I'm sure you feel the same way. I had no one to help me get through it, but I'm here for you. Dane, you have to do the same, you have to step up to the plate and do what needs to be done. There are arrangements to be made for your father's funeral. You need to find out if your father had a Will. Tell me what you want me to do. I'm here and ready to help."

Dane rose and headed to the door, "I've got to go see how Mom and Erin are doing."

Aiden knew how hard this was for Dane. He hoped Dane would be up to the task of becoming the head of his family as *he* had when his mother died. He sat in the office just meditating on life, how unfair it is, to everyone really, no matter if they had riches or not. Life seems so unfair to everyone, no matter who they are. Tom had been dealt a bad life, and so had Cody. He knew his own life could have turned out badly had it not been for Mr. Wilshire, and now he was gone. He felt like once again he was on his own, trying to figure life out all over again for himself and his sisters. What would become of them? Would the death of Mr. Wilshire change everything for him and his sisters, for Tom and for Cody? Would Dane have to let all the ranch hands go because of financial difficulty? He was running the business for Mr. Wilshire and knew the ledgers well, and it seemed to him that everything was running smoothly, as far as financially goes, but would Dane see it that way? He wondered if this would have any effect on his relationship with Erin, or Lottie's engagement to Dane? Could everything fall apart now that things had changed? He took a deep breath, shook his head, and decided to go back to the patio with the girls.

However, the girls had left the patio, so he headed for the back door. When he entered the kitchen, it felt like he was entering a different world. The entire house seemed to have changed. People were busy moving about, but with no place to go. He just stood and stared. Izzy saw him and came and took his hand, leading him to Mrs. Wilshire's bedroom door. "She's asking for you," she whispered.

He looked surprised, but slowly opened the door. Dane and Erin were on each side of her bed. When she saw Aiden, she motioned for him to come closer. She looked so sad, even withered. A different person entirely to Aiden.

She spoke softly, "Aiden, I want you to know I don't blame you for what happened. I hope you're not blaming yourself."

Aiden looked bewildered and hung his head without speaking. He knew the accident had not been his fault and he never even considered that someone might think *he* was responsible for Daniel's death.

She went on, "Accidents can happen any time and any place. I know it was just an accident, and I don't want you to carry any burden if you feel you're responsible in any way. We all have jobs to do around here, and Daniel was always ready to jump in and help."

All Aiden could think to say was, "Thank you, ma'am."

"We have all valued your work here, and no one valued you more than Daniel. I want you to know, your place here is secure, as well as your sisters. I know there's things we need to do now, and I hope you won't take it too hard, if me and my kids lean on you a lot right now for support. Right now, we are pretty fragile, and I think we've come to know you well enough to know you'll stand by us to help us in our time of need."

"Yes, ma'am. I'll be glad to do whatever I can to help."

"Good," she reached out and took his hand. "One thing I'd like to ask of you is to help Dane make the arrangements for his funeral. Do you think you can do that?"

"Yes, ma'am."

"Thank you, Aiden."

Aiden turned to leave the room, glancing at Erin and Dane. He reached for the doorknob, and with his hand on it, he turned and said,

"I'm so very sorry about Daniel. I loved him so much." When he turned to open the door, he had tears in his eyes.

Lottie and Izzy were just outside the door waiting for him. He wrapped his arms around them and held them close. Lottie then said, "Is everything ok? I mean, with us living here? They don't blame you for this, do they?"

"No, nothing like that. They know it was just an accident, and Mrs. Wilshire said our place here is secure. Dane is having trouble coming to grips with this and she asked if I would help him make the arrangements for his funeral."

"Whew," Lottie said, "I was afraid they might decide they couldn't keep us anymore. I'm glad they trust you to help them."

"Miriam said they might lean on us quite a bit because they feel pretty fragile right now, so let's all try to do more around here than we've been doing. I know Mrs. Wilshire usually does most of the cooking for the ranch hands, but you girls will probably have to step in and do a lot of it. And speaking of cooking for the ranch hands, it's about lunch time. Why don't you both take a plate of food and glass of tea out to Tom and Cody. Tell them they can eat in the office or up in Tom's room, wherever they want really."

The girls headed for the kitchen, and loaded up two plates and tea for them, even including a pitcher of tea for refills. Tom and Cody were thrilled that they brought the food out to them, because neither one really wanted to go into the house. They felt that they were just the hired help and that the family needed to be alone without having to take care of them.

Lottie and Izzy stayed with the boys while they ate, mostly because there really wasn't any other place they wanted to be at the moment. After the two finished eating, the girls picked up the tray and headed back to the house. Lottie said, "You know we need to feed the chickens. We haven't done that today."

"I'll do it," Izzy said. She headed toward the shed to get the feed, while Lottie went on into the house.

Aiden was sitting on the patio again and Lottie came out to sit with him, setting two glasses of iced tea on the table for them. Eventually, Dane came out and said to Aiden, "Mom wants me to go to the funeral home and make the arrangements. Do you think you could drive me?"

"Sure," Aiden said as he rose.

42

Before they headed into town, Aiden said, "Do you want to get some clothes to give to the funeral director for your father to be buried in?"

"I never thought of that. Let me go ask Mom."

When he came back outside, Aiden had already brought his truck around to the back door, and Dane came out carrying a set of clothes. When he got in, he said, "Mom wants him buried in his jeans and golf shirt, clothing he wore every day. She doesn't want him in a suit. That just wasn't Dad."

He then asked, "Do you think I should go see Dad?"

"That's entirely up to you. If you don't want to now, you will see him in his casket later."

Dane looked over at Aiden, "I think I'd rather wait then."

They found the funeral home Mrs. Wilshire said she wanted to use and met with the funeral director. It seemed, in speaking with him, that everyone in town knew Daniel Wilshire, and Aiden was proud that he had such a sterling reputation and was so well known. But it really didn't surprise him with the kind heart that he had. People like him always drew people to themselves. The area had just lost the greatest man around according to Aiden's way of thinking. He couldn't help but wonder if he could ever build up such a fine reputation as Mr. Wilshire's. He vowed he would do everything in his power to try to live up to what he knew Mr. Wilshire had seen in him.

The funeral director explained that because Mr. Wilshire was so well known and respected, it would be a large funeral. He took notes as Dane answered his questions for the obituary for the paper. The funeral was set for the next Saturday, five days away.

When they left the funeral home, Dane asked if he could go see Daniel's attorney. When they arrived, the secretary said she wasn't sure if Jake had time to see them because they didn't make an appointment prior to arriving. But when Jake heard who wanted to see him, he came out of his office, extending his hand to Dane.

"I heard about Daniel. I'm so sorry, Dane. Come in. And it's nice to see you again Aiden. I wish we were meeting under different circumstances."

Dane and Aiden sat down across the desk from Jake. Dane was glad he didn't have to say anything, Jake took charge of the situation.

"I'm sure you're here about your father's affairs," he said it more as a statement than a question.

"Yes, sir."

"I'll get with your mom, you and Erin after the funeral and go over his Will. I have a copy of it. So have you made arrangements for the funeral yet?"

"Yes, sir. We just came from the funeral home. It will be this Saturday at three in the afternoon. It should be in tomorrow's paper."

"I'll be there. And let's get together next week. I'll be in touch to set up the meeting. Again, I'm so sorry about Daniel. He was one of the kindest men I've ever met."

He stood and shook both Dane and Aiden's hands. Aiden thanked him to taking time to meet with them.

There was still a crowd of people at the Wilshire's when they got back to the house. Aiden parked his truck, and said, "Dane, are you alright with all these people here?"

"It's ok. I know they want to help in any way they can. They're our friends and neighbors and some day they might need my help in turn."

"I'm only asking because I don't want it to become a burden on you and your family."

"No, but thanks for asking. It's alright."

"One thing's for sure. No one will go hungry around here. I think there's enough food in there to feed an army." Aiden had hoped his statement might lighten the mood, but it fell flat. Dane was too preoccupied with his own thoughts to have even heard Aiden.

Dane went to his mother to let her know about the funeral arrangements and said that the funeral director said to expect a huge funeral.

She smiled at him, "I'm not surprised. Daniel was loved by everyone. Now I have something to ask you. Do you think you would feel like saying a little something about your dad at the funeral?"

"Oh, Mom. I don't think so."

"What about Aiden. Do you think he would?"

"I'll ask him. It's not that I don't want to, I just… don't think I can."

"I understand. And if you decide to write something out, we could ask someone else to read it for you."

"I'll think about it."

"And one more thing, Dane. Your father had a favorite song I'd like them to sing at the funeral. It's called "Our Strength, Our Hope, Our Confidence." You know the song don't you?"

"Yeah, I'll call the funeral director and tell him."

He found Aiden again on the patio, sat down by Lottie, and took her hand in his. He said to Aiden, "Mom wants to know if you would say a few words at the funeral."

Aiden was shocked. He didn't know what to say. He thought a minute, then finally, "I'll do whatever your family wants me to do." But he was terrified. He'd never spoken in front of a crowd before and definitely never in front of one as large as this one might turn out to be. He definitely would need time to put something together.

He only had a few days to get a speech written and it kept him awake at night trying to figure out what to say. Finally, he began to put pen to paper. He wrote:

> Daniel Wilshire was not only my mentor, I look at him as my savior and father. The reason I call him my savior is because he saved me from a life of uncertainty, a life riddled with doubt, a life with no future. He took me and my sisters into his family when we had no family. He took care of us like no one ever had before. Daniel Wilshire was the kindest, most generous man I've ever known. He didn't have to help my family when we were in need, but he did. My sisters and I owe him and Miriam our very lives. We have grown to love them and their two children with all our hearts. I'm sure everyone here knows him better than I do, and probably have wonderful stories they could get up here and tell also, but then we'd be here until 'the cows come home' as they say. So today we are here to say goodbye to the greatest man who ever lived, outside of Jesus, of course. May you rest in peace Daniel Wilshire, you will be greatly missed, more than you will ever know.

When he finished writing his speech, his eyes were watering, and no matter how much he swiped at them, he couldn't help but cry. He folded his paper and slipped it inside his shirt pocket.

Tom and Cody were able to keep busy with all the chores needing to be done, and they guided other men where they were needed to help out as well. When the milk semi came to get their milk, there were so many cars in the drive and barnyard, that the boys had to go find whoever owned the ones in the way and ask them to move them.

The driver finally pulled in, got down out of the cab, and said to Tom, "Looks like you folks are having a party."

When Tom explained what was going on, the driver said how sorry he was to hear that Daniel had died. He had known him for years since he was a regular driver in picking up the milk at the Wilshire's. He said he always liked Mr. Wilshire, said he always seemed very friendly toward him, had even helped his family once when his wife had gone into labor early and had lost the baby. He said he had missed several days of work, and Mr. Wilshire knew that was something that would hurt his family, so he made out a check and handed it to him to help out.

He asked when the funeral was, and let Tom know he would be there, and he would make sure his company knew as well.

Soon it was Saturday and time for the funeral. The Wilshire's, Aiden and his sisters, and Tom and Cody arrived early in order to spend a little alone time with Daniel before others began to arrive.

Miriam had decided she didn't want a visitation the evening before. She felt it would be too much for her kids and her to endure.

It was very hard for Miriam to see her husband, but especially hard for Dane and Erin. At least she had the opportunity to say her goodbyes when the ambulance took him away from his home, but the kids hadn't seen him yet.

Dane broke down at the sight of his father in a coffin. He had to grab the sides of the coffin to steady himself. Tears welled up into his eyes, and he tried to blink them back. Hands folded across his chest, with his work clothes on, Daniel looked like he was ready to head to the barn for work. His face was serene, he was at peace. Dane leaned down to kiss his father on the cheek, and Erin decided to do the same. She stood arm in arm with Dane, just staring at their father. The last time they would ever see him. Erin fumbled in her purse for a tissue and handed one to Dane. The tears could not be held back.

Dane spoke to his father, "I hope I can be at least half the man you were, Dad. Just know I'm going to try."

Erin said, "I'm going to miss you, Daddy. I always looked forward to coming to talk to you after school in your office. It was our special time, just you and me. I'll miss that."

Miriam stood by their side, they hugged each other, not wanting to let go of the last time their family would be all together. When people began to arrive, they took their seats, with the Roberts kids beside them on the front row. Tom and Cody were right behind them.

The funeral director was right. It was going to be a huge funeral. As it turned out, there was a line two blocks long, and after the funeral home seats were filled up, others stood in the back, and others filled up a second room in the funeral home. When there was no more room, people stood outside, wanting to be a part of Daniel Wilshire's life just one more time.

When it was time for Aiden to get up and read his eulogy, he got so choked up he hardly got through it. When he sat down there was not a dry eye in the crowd, including his own.

After the funeral and grave side services people headed to the Civic Center that the town allowed them to use for a final meal.

Miriam came to Aiden and said how much she appreciated what he had said about her husband. Dane gave him a hug, thanking him for doing what he himself could not do.

The funeral was over, people went home, food was packed into cars to be driven to the Wilshire's home, and then it was over. But not for the Wilshire's nor the Roberts. Miriam found she had no desire to do anything. She seemed lost. She would sit at the kitchen window and stare outside to the pasture where the accident had happened. Eventually Erin and Izzy had to go back to school, but Dane let his mother know he had no intentions of going back to college, except to get his things out of his dorm room. She didn't protest, and Aiden was glad to have him back to help with the farm.

Dane took over many of the financial chores that Aiden didn't really like anyway. And the next week after the funeral was over, Jake called their house and spoke with Dane about setting up an appointment for the reading of Daniel's Will.

Aiden was surprised when Dane told him he was to be there for the reading as well.

The Wilshire's arrived at Jake's office at the designated time and sat around his large conference table holding hands.

Jake began, "We are all here to hear the reading of the Last Will and Testament of Daniel C. Wilshire, written and filed on September 29, in the year 2020, witnessed by me and my secretary, Jane Winslow."

He then read that Miriam was to inherit the house, and all its furnishings. He read that she could live in the home for the rest of her life. She also was to inherit Daniel's stocks and bonds, as well as his personal bank checking and savings accounts.

His son Dane was to inherit all the livestock, including the cattle, llamas, sheep, and horses, except the horse that belonged to Erin named Dash. He also was to inherit fifteen hundred (1500) acres, the area that had been surveyed and marked off, as well as the barn and outbuildings, along with all Daniel's liquid assets for the business. Amount unknown at the time of writing at death.

Erin was to inherit her bedroom furniture, and two hundred fifty (250) acres of unimproved pastureland and some woods, also surveyed and marked off. He read off the legal description which meant nothing to her. The only part she understood was that it was on Pine Meadow Road, the next road over from her parent's home. She also was to inherit her horse named Dash.

Aiden was to inherit two hundred fifty (250) acres of unimproved pastureland running from Pine Meadow Road and alongside the acreage allotted to Erin, also surveyed and marked off. He read the legal description to his acreage as well, but again Aiden didn't understand it.

Jake told Aiden and Erin that there would be survey markers on Pine Meadow Road marking off the property, so when they went to look at the property, they could easily see the boundaries.

When he finished, they all sat stunned. Dane knew he would inherit the farm, and knew when his mother died, he would also inherit the house, but he had no idea how much farmland his father owned. He knew it was a lot, but this information floored him.

Aiden was in shock that he would inherit anything at all.

Jake began speaking again, "Daniel said your land, Erin, is on another road called Pine Meadow. You'll see the survey markers. And Aiden, he gave you land that runs alongside Erin's property on the same road. Daniel said he figures some day you and Erin will get married and when you do, you two will have five hundred acres together.

Mariam, as I read, you can live in the house for the rest of your life and Dane will inherit the home at that time, unless your Will specifies otherwise at the time of your death.

"I think that's everything. May I say again how sorry I am for your loss. Daniel was a great client of mine, but more than that, he was a great friend. I know we'll all miss him. And I'm speaking for the entire town when I say we'll all miss him."

Miriam had tears in her eyes, she rose, held out her hand to Jake, who gave her a big hug. Then she turned to the door.

Jake also hugged Dane, shook Aiden's hand, gave Erin a hug, and said, "Stay as long as you like. No one needs the room. Take your time."

Aiden was still in shock and looked bewildered. He said, "I don't know what to say. I'm not even a blood relative!"

Dane spoke up, "Now you know what Dad thought of you. He never would have put you in his Will if he didn't love you."

Erin added, "And he already guessed we are getting married and wanted his little girl taken care of well. And it looks like he felt you are the man to do it." She smiled as she looked up at Aiden and hooked his arm with hers.

Miriam added, "We talked about you two getting married, and, of course, we already knew about Dane and Lottie. But we weren't entirely ignorant of the feelings going on between you two. We felt certain that someday you'd be a part of our family, Aiden."

He gave her a hug. He knew she was as much responsible for his inheritance as Daniel was. Then she turned to Dane, and said, "And just so you know, I'm never moving out the house, so you'll have to take care of me in my old age."

They all laughed at that. Dane said, "And kick out the best cook this side of the Mississippi River?"

They laughed again.

Work resumed on the farm. Dane let Tom and Cody know how much he appreciated them stepping in when they were needed, taking over the daily chores and helping the men who came to help out to know what to do. He told them that he wasn't going back to school and would be in charge of running the farm now that his father was not around.

He also let Tom know he could continue living in the loft bedroom, and that he and Cody still could count on their jobs. They both thanked him and told him how grateful they were to help during the family's time of need.

A few days later Dane announced that he had to go back to get his things out of his dorm room. Before he left, Lottie said to him, "Are you sure you're doing the right thing by not finishing college? You only have one more year after this year is up."

"I'm sure. Mom will need me even more now. And I really didn't want to go to college anyway. I was only doing it for Dad?"

"What do you think about finishing college online? That way you'd have your degree under your belt."

"I don't know. I'll think about that." Then he pulled Lottie close to him and kissed her again and again. "I'm so glad to have you…here. And now that I'm going to be home permanently, what do you say about getting married soon?"

"Oh, Dane," she wrapped her arms around his neck, reaching up to kiss him. "I love that idea. Should we set a date, or do you think it's too soon after your dad's death?"

"We need a little happiness in our family, don't you think? I say we get married as soon as you can get things put together."

"You know, I think that's a good idea. I will need your mother's help, and right now she doesn't seem to have any drive to do anything, so this just might be what she needs to help get her moving again. I don't want her to waste away pining for her husband."

"Let's set a date in the summer, the girls will be out of school then."

"That's a good idea. Why don't you announce it at supper this evening?"

That evening while they were dining together, Dane took his knife and rapped it on the side of his water glass. "Ladies and gentlemen, I have an announcement to make. Actually, I have two announcements to make. One; I'm going to finish college online. That was Lottie's idea," he smiled at her. "Second; Lottie and I have decided we're getting married this summer."

Everyone was elated. The girls were excited and said they wanted to be in the wedding. Dane said, "And Mom, Lottie will need help and she's counting on you because you're so good at organizing things. So, what do you say?"

At first, she began to shake her head and say she wasn't sure she could. Then Dane said, "No begging off. She can't do this alone, and she really needs your help."

She finally relented, and after supper, the girls put their heads together to help decide color schemes, where the wedding might be held, and the reception. Things like that.

Miriam said she could contact the Golf Club Daniel belonged to, to see about securing the club house for the reception. Izzy suggested pink dresses for the girls, but Lottie said, "Even though I know a lot of summer weddings are pink, I want something different."

Izzy then said, "What about ice blue?" All the girls agreed that would be beautiful. It would bring out the blue in their eyes.

The next day Aiden and Erin took a drive around to Pine Meadow Road, where both of their acreages were they had inherited. It was a very good piece of land. Aiden noticed there was plenty of open pasturage, a little wooded area too, and easy access onto the property from the road. They walked the property, deciding where they could build a home, and what should be pasturage. They decided they wanted their home to back up to the woods, which would give them shade in the hot afternoon/evening sun, with plenty of room for the barn away from, but beside the house, and the pastureland would lay further past the barn and backing up to the tree line and projecting out to the open area. They would have plenty of land for everything they wanted to do, and Aiden said after they were married, he would have the two plats of land combined into one large plat of five hundred acres.

They headed back to Aiden's truck parked along the road arm in arm. They were so happy about their future plans.

A couple of days later, Dane noticed Aiden was in the office and went in and shut the door. "I want to talk to you about something, Aiden," he began.

He sat down across the desk from Aiden and continued, "I know Dad didn't want to plow up any ground for a crop, but I do. I assume you still want to also."

"I think it's a good idea. Daniel said he didn't want to be known as a dirt farmer. He said people would talk. I couldn't believe he cared anything about what others thought about him, and I let him know he already had a good reputation in the area, and nothing would change that. I think we saw how people thought about him at the funeral."

"Right, and I don't believe plowing up a little dirt will make people look down on us either. So, let's do it. There's a great piece of land to the left of the llama/sheep pastureland. I believe it's about thirty acres or so. What do you think about starting there?"

"That's a pretty large chunk to begin with. What if we decide it's more work than we want? I was thinking more about the open land beyond our new Black Angus pasture."

"Yeah, maybe you're right. Let's start with the smaller acreage and see what we think. Then if we want to enlarge, we can use the other land."

"So, what crop do you think we should plant?"

"Not sure. Let's think about that. But we're going to have to purchase some equipment to attach to the tractor; plow, disc, planter, and fertilizer spreader."

"Ok, do you want to order that, or should I?" Aiden asked.

"Go ahead, you can do it?"

"Ok, how soon do you want me to do that?"

"Now, tomorrow, whenever you want."

Aiden did his research online for the equipment they would need, and the more he thought about it, the more he didn't want to purchase the equipment in case it turned out that they didn't want to be farmers. Therefore, he caught Dane and talked with him about the possibility of just paying someone to plow the field and plant the crop for them for this first go round to see how it went. Dane agreed that was a good idea, so he called a friend and neighbor just down the road from them, George McCleary, and hired him to do it for them.

Dane and Aiden got on their four wheelers and had George follow them to the field they wanted plowed. On the first day, George got all the soil turned over and said he would come back the next day to disc the soil. That took him quite a while because he had to go over it several times to break up all the large clods. The third day he came back pulling his manure spreader. Aiden scooped their pile of manure up and dumped it into the spreader. Afterward, George disced it once more. He soon had that job completed. It was time to plant seeds. Aiden and

Dane had decided on planting oats as their first crop since they bought a lot of it for feed.

After the field was finished, they stood back to admire the way it looked and said now they just needed to pray for rain. The rest was up to God.

The boys headed back to the barn, happy that they got a good start on being a dirt farmer. Dane joked that they needed to get some bib overalls to look the part. They had a good laugh at that.

When Dane entered the barn, Aiden asked, "So you and Lottie are getting married this summer. Have you set the date?"

"Lottie and the girls are plotting and planning. But I think I need to nudge her to set the date. I'll let you know."

"Well, congratulations again. I think something wonderful like that is just what we all need. And did I tell you Erin and I went around to Pine Meadow Road to look at the land Daniel left to us?"

"No, I hadn't heard that."

"It's a great piece of property. There's plenty of pastureland, and we decided where the house and barn should be built."

"Well, good for you. So have you and Erin set a date for your wedding?"

"No, she still has one more year of high school left."

"Hey, we could have a double wedding," Dane declared.

"Nothing doing. Lottie would kill me if I took some of the attention away from her special day. So, you two enjoy your day, and maybe next summer it will be our turn."

45

Dane said he wanted to talk to Lottie one evening so they sat out on the patio drinking iced tea. He began, "So I was wondering how the wedding plans are coming along."

"Pretty good. Well, maybe not as fast as I'd like, but it's a big event, so I guess it takes time."

"Is Mom being any help?"

"Yes, actually. She's come up with some good ideas."

"Have you thought any more about setting a date? That could speed things along."

"Hmmm, well, this is April, and it won't be long till summer is here. What do you think about sometime toward the end of June? You know, June is typically the month a lot of marriages take place."

"I didn't know that." He looked at his calendar on his phone. "Well, what do you say we set it for June 25?"

"Sounds good. Your mom and us girls plan on going shopping this Saturday for dresses and other things we'll need. And since Erin and Izzy both want to be in the wedding, you'll have to pick a couple of guys to stand up with you as well. I'm sure you'll want Aiden, but you'll have to pick another guy."

Dane already had in mind who the other guy would be but didn't say anything to Lottie about his choice.

"I hope you don't mind renting tuxes, because I want you guys in long tails."

"Oh, wow, you are going really formal."

"Like I said, 'you only get married once' so I want it perfect, memorable."

"Oh, you know it will be something neither will ever forget for as long as we live." He leaned over and gave her a kiss, looking deeply into her eyes. She smiled at him. "I love you Lottie Roberts, don't you ever forget that or doubt my love for you."

"I love you too, Dane Wilshire."

"Lottie Wilshire. I like the sound of that. Just think in a little over two months we'll be husband and wife."

"I can't wait."

"Me neither."

They found dresses for the two girls and Miriam. But Lottie hadn't found a wedding dress, so she declared she would look online for one. They found invitations to be sent mid-May which Erin and Izzy declared they would take care of. Miriam suggested they hit a flower shop to pick out flowers for the wedding while they were in town. It seemed everything was coming along nicely.

As they got in the car to return home, Miriam asked Lottie if she'd like to go by the country club and see the room she'd booked for the reception, to which Lottie agreed that she'd love to do that. It was a huge room that could easily hold two hundred and fifty people, but Lottie stated that she didn't want a reception that large. She knew most of the guests would be friends of Dane's, but she planned on inviting some of her old friends from her former high school, as-well-as, some she'd made friends with in her new high school.

That evening she informed Dane that he had to get his guest list made up soon and they agreed that two hundred invitations were plenty enough to invite. Lottie said she wasn't sure she even had half that number to invite, and she didn't mind if there were fewer than two hundred.

They discussed the country club and since there was a dance floor, Dane said he would order a band for the evening. Lottie stated, "So we haven't discussed a church for the wedding yet."

"Yeah, I've been thinking about that. I don't know, we've never been churchy people."

"Us either. So why don't we do something totally different. What do you think about getting married at that national park we went to? What was it called? I never can remember."

"Tombigbee National Park. Hey, that's a great idea, and guess what? They have a large building there that can be rented. Why don't we go tomorrow and take a look at it?"

That was agreed upon.

"And we need a preacher," Dane said. "I'll call the guy who did Dad's funeral."

They loved the building at the park, and Dane asked, "So why couldn't we also have the reception here after the wedding?"

"Well, we could, but setting up for the reception might interfere with the wedding or the wedding might interfere with the reception. Your mom has already booked the Country Club for the reception. I really don't want to disappoint her. It might make her feel like her suggestions aren't good enough, and I don't want to hurt her feelings, so let's keep the reception at the Country Club."

"Ok, it was just a suggestion."

She put her hand on his arm, and said, "You understand about your mom, right?"

"Sure, I do want her involved as much as possible."

"Speaking of her being involved, what do you think about asking her to come up with the food menu for the reception."

"She'd like that. Just don't let her decide to do all the cooking. I can just see her offering to do that."

Lottie laughed, "No way would I let her do that. This is supposed to be a day of family fun, not work."

They spoke to the park's conservator and booked the room for June 25th.

Lottie went online and found a wedding dress she loved and ordered it. She and Miriam went to order the tuxes for the guys. Dane had chosen Tom to stand up with him and Aiden. Tom was elated, it made him feel like for the first time in his life he was important to someone. Aiden slapped him on the back, and said, "I told you if you stick with the Wilshire family things would turn out well for you. And I haven't told you this, but you're turning out to be a really nice guy."

Tom dropped his head, and said, "Thanks, Aiden. That means a lot to me."

"So looks like we have an appointment to get measured for our tuxes.

"What? We are wearing tuxes for the wedding?"

"That's what Lottie said."

"I'm not sure I can afford that. What do they cost?"

"Well, we won't have to buy them, just rent. So it shouldn't be that much. We'll ask when we go to get measured. And if it's still too much, I'll make sure you have the money."

"Thanks, Aiden." He was quiet for a minute before saying, "I've never worn a tux before."

"Yeah, me neither. And it's supposed to be with tails. Pretty formal."

Tom smiled at the thought, then added, "I want a picture of me in mine."

"Oh, don't worry about that, I'm sure they'll have someone taking pictures."

Izzy soon got busy stuffing invitations into envelopes and mailing them out. Dane hadn't liked the idea of having to get up a guest list complete with addresses, but with the constant coaxing from Lottie and Izzy, he finally accomplished the task.

Miriam was thrilled to take charge of the food menu, and after she finally decided on everything, she ran it by Lottie who approved of it heartily. Miriam knew a good caterer in town, and soon all those arrangements were complete.

One evening Izzy proclaimed she was happy that Lottie was getting married first so it would make preparations for her own someday that much simpler.

Lottie came to Aiden and said, "I have a problem I need help with."

"Ok, what's up?" Aiden asked.

"I have no father to give me away."

"Oh, you're right. I guess I could do that."

"But how can you do it when you're standing up with Dane?"

He thought a minute before answering, "Guess I can walk you down the aisle, then take my place by Dane, couldn't I?"

"That's a little weird, but yeah, I guess that would work. You know, I had thought Mr. Wilshire would be the one to walk me down the aisle." Tears sprang up in her eyes.

Aiden wrapped his arm around her shoulder. "I know, and it's sad that he won't be around to see either of his kids get married. But don't say anything about that to Miriam."

"Oh, I won't. I just wish he was here." She sniffled and wiped her eyes with her sleeve.

"We all wish he was here. This wedding is going to be a bittersweet event. But I'm like Dane, I think it will do Miriam good to see a happy occasion. I'm sure she will miss her husband not being there as well, but let's try to portray a smile through it all."

"Of course, I'll be smiling, it's my wedding."

"You know what I mean. Let's try to put the tragedy behind us and not think about it on your wedding day. If you see someone crying, give them a hug, but you need to keep on smiling."

"Right."

The day arrived for the wedding. The weather was sunny and warm. The girls were upstairs getting ready. Dane, Aiden, and Tom were dressed in their tuxes and downstairs.

"Not sure I like wearing a tux," Dane stated.

"Gee, I kind of like it," Tom put in. "I feel really important. A starched white shirt with cuff links, long tails, and this blue cummerbund. Even got a flower in my lapel."

Aiden and Dane laughed. He was enjoying everything about this wedding.

Dane asked, "Aiden, did you order the limousine to pick us up after the wedding?"

"Done. And now you need to get your boutonnière pinned on. And let's get out of here before the girls come down."

They left in Aiden's truck and headed for the park. Miriam would bring the three girls.

Aiden was waiting by the door when Lottie arrived ready to walk her down the aisle. Approximately two hundred people were already seated. Everything went as planned, except that Lottie whispered to Aiden that he needed to hold her up because she was weak in the knees. Dane couldn't help but notice she was trembling during the ceremony, but they got through it without her fainting, which he was worried about.

After the wedding was over, Lottie was surprised that Dane had ordered a limo to take them to the reception. On the way, Dane asked, "So how does it feel to be Mrs. Dane Wilshire?"

Lottie repeated, "Mrs. Dane Wilshire. I guess it will do."

Dane laughed and pulled her into his arms. He turned her chin toward him, looked deeply into her eyes, then cupping the back of her head, kissing her over and over. Softly, gently but becoming more passionate. Her dress had an open back, and soon Dane was running his hand up and down her skin. He loved how smooth it felt under his touch. It sent shivers down Lottie's spine. They eventually pulled apart, and he said, "Can we skip the reception and go straight to our motel room?"

Lottie laughed, "No way, Dane Wilshire!"

"You know I can't wait to get you alone. I've waited so long to have you to myself." His eyes sparkled in delight.

"You definitely have a one-track mind. And by the way, where are we going on our honeymoon?"

"Honeymoon? Oh, no, I forgot about a honeymoon."

"What!? You mean we're not having a honeymoon?"

He smiled at her then mischievously.

"Dane, you're terrible. I should have known you were teasing me. So where are we going?" He didn't reply.

During the reception, Aiden and Tom left their table in search of iced tea. Aiden grabbed a second glass for Erin. On their way back to the table, they ran into Mr. Simpson, one of the Wilshire's neighbors. He said, "Hello Alex. Good to see you again."

Aiden said, "Oh, hi Mr. Simpson."

"Looks like you've made friends with the Wilshire kids. I saw you at their house when…uh, the accident, you know. I was going to say something to you then, but this guy here," he said putting a hand on Tom's shoulder, "kept me pretty busy out in the barn. I thought you'd come out to help in the barn, but…"

"Yeah, nice seeing you," Aiden interrupted. "I've got a lady waiting for her drink." Then he moved on.

Tom said, "Did he call you Alex?"

"Yeah, he probably didn't remember my name. I met him a long time ago." Aiden was afraid Tom had caught the name Mr. Simpson had called him. He tried to smooth over the discrepancy so Tom wouldn't wonder about it any further.

The girls were happy to have a band so they could dance. Aiden was happy to be able to hold Erin close to him, to feel her body sway to the music along with him. Tom danced several dances with Izzy as well, and Aiden could see he was becoming interested in her.

When Aiden got home, he caught Izzy and said, "Thanks for warning me that Mr. Simpson was invited to the wedding."

"What? Who is Mr. Simpson?"

"The farmer who lives on the same road as the grocery store. Don't you remember, he's the farmer I stopped to ask directions to the store, and he asked me my name, and I told him Alex Robinson?"

"Oh, yeah, I forgot."

"Well, I ran into him at the reception, and he called me Alex in front of Tom, and Tom caught what he called me?"

Izzy laughed, "Oh, no. What did you do?"

"I kind of cut Mr. Simpson off and hurried away and when Tom asked me about it, I sluffed it off, acted like Mr. Simpson just didn't remember my name."

"So, you've never told Tom about your past?"

"Just a little of it. Not much."

After the reception was over, the limo took the bride and groom to the airport. They hopped on a plane and soon landed in Orlando. They booked into a suite at Disney World. Their suite overlooked a lake on the property, and Lottie went immediately to the patio door to peer at the beautiful landscape. The room service had a bucket of champagne on ice waiting for them.

"Are you happy about going to Disney World?" Dane asked, coming up behind her and wrapping his arms around her.

"Are you kidding? Disney World was only something I read about, but never dreamed I would ever be able to afford to come here."

"I hope to give you everything you've ever wanted but could never afford," he whispered, turning her to face him.

They stayed in Orlando for two weeks, visiting Disney World, and Epcot, of course, but other things as well in the city. They had a wonderful time, but both agreed that after two weeks of running here and there, it became exhausting, and they were ready to go home.

When they got home, Miriam told them they were to take her bedroom. Dane complained that he couldn't do that, but she said, "Nonsense. I have a new bedroom. Come see." She led them to her craft room beyond the kitchen, and when she opened the door, they found it had been turned into a bedroom for her.

"Wow! Mom. How did you…?"

"Aiden and Tom did it while you were gone. You don't think I was going to have Lottie and you share a bedroom with Aiden, did you?"

"I figured we'd kick Aiden out into the barn to bunk up with Tom."

"Well, I figured different. Actually, I didn't want to stay in my room anyway. There are too many memories of Daniel."

Dane put his arms around his mother, rocking her gently back and forth. "I understand, Mom. And thank you. Lottie and I will have a great time making our own memories in that bedroom."

She pulled out of his arms, gently smacked him on the arm, and declared, "You men are all alike." He just smiled down at her.

Later when Dane saw Aiden in the barn, he said, "Hey, man, when did you get to be so handy?"

"What are you talking about?"

"The bedroom. Mom said you and Tom turned her craft room into her bedroom."

Aiden laughed, "Yeah, and we had to hurry to finish it before you two got back. I hope you're not upset that we spent money on supplies we needed for the project."

"Heck no. It's awesome. And you guys moved her furniture and everything for her. So now Lottie and I have an empty bedroom to sleep in. Guess we'll use your sleeping bags until we can get it furnished for us."

"No, you don't have to do that. Erin, and Izzy are sharing the bunk beds in our room now, and I'm bunking with Tom, so you two can have Izzy and Lottie's bedroom until you get yours put together."

"Sounds like you've got everything all figured out."

"Well, we didn't think it would be right to put you two in the bunk beds, so …?" He arched his eyebrows to see Dane's reaction to that.

"Ha ha, not on your life." They both laughed at that.

47

Dane said, "As soon as we get our bedroom furnished, I want to talk to you about what we're going to do about Mom's craft room. She's always enjoyed having a room she can do her crafting in, and I'm sorry she had to give that up for Lottie and me to have her room. We'll have to come up with a plan of some sort. She would probably go crazy if she couldn't sew or do whatever else she enjoys doing. So be thinking about it and let's do something for her."

"I sure will. You know Tom is becoming really good with a hammer and saw. He's careful, and meticulous with his work. He's becoming quite an asset. I can't find fault with any of his work. He's like a different kid altogether from what he used to be."

"Yeah, and thank you Dad for turning that boy around."

Aiden chuckled, "I told you your dad was a savior. I bet that gave him a lot of pleasure to be able to help troubled boys, and I was one of them."

"I'm sure it did. I sure miss him," Dane said as he ran his fingers through his hair, a gesture Aiden had seen him do before when he was upset about something.

"I think we all do. Life just doesn't seem fair sometimes. It seems we all have been dealt a rough life in one way or another, Tom, Cody, my sisters and me, and now your family. The road can get pretty bumpy along the way. Guess we all just have to make the best of it and try to move on. But, hey, I wish the best for you and Lottie. You make a great couple, and she couldn't have married any better."

"Thanks, Aiden. You're a great brother-in-law. When you three came into our lives, I had no idea we'd end up permanently joined together in marriage. And speaking of that, what are your plans for you and Erin?"

"Well, she's still not finished with school, but I've got the ring."

"I knew it. That day you went to town and were pretty secretive about it, I figured you went to buy a ring. And if I remember right, it was the day after I gave my ring to Lottie." Aiden just smiled.

The heat of summer arrived with a vengeance. Their crop was growing nicely in the field with the spring rains, but with the heat came a lack of rain, and Dane and Aiden began to worry about their crop. Now they understood the risk involved in farming, a risk every farmer took because no man can control the weather. Dane began to think possibly this was one of the real reasons his father never wanted to raise crops. What if a bad storm with high winds blew down the crop, or worse a hailstorm tore through the field? What if there was a drought and the crop shriveled up before producing? Why sink a lot of money into farming with so many things that could go wrong? He began to wonder why anyone wanted to be a farmer, but he was thankful some did, so there was plenty of food, not just for his animals, but more importantly, for people. He realized how he had always taken for granted that there would be food, but now he had a higher regard for the farmers of the world.

Aiden sought Dane out to talk to him about what to do for his mother's crafting. He proposed building her a separate building close to the house. He suggested, not only building a craft room, but adding another section on the side for her gardening supplies and adding a potting area inside. He said if they built it close to her garden, it would make gardening more convenient for her. Dane loved the idea immediately.

Soon they were in the office drawing up the plans, kicking around different ideas about how it should look. The drawings began to take shape, dimensions were discussed and changed until they felt it was perfect. They would make it look like a cute little cottage with gingerbread trim at the front eves, and sporting two windows, one on each side of the front door. The garden/potting room would be accessed at the side of the building. A long potting bench would be built along one wall, and shelves for supplies along another wall. Peg boards would be added to an interior wall to hang tools.

Dane took their drawings to an architect to draw it up professionally, then to Home Depot to get an estimate on materials. And even though it was going to cost more than he thought it would, he knew he still had to do it for his mother, not just because she had lost her husband and best friend, but because she was the best mother in the world in his mind and had given so much for her family over the years. After thinking about her further, he realized how she had always put everyone in the family ahead of herself in everything, no matter if it was where the family was going to take a vacation, or where they were going to eat out, or even which part of the chicken the rest of the family preferred. He realized his mother had always chosen the back of the chicken, a piece no one else in the family wanted because it was too much bone and not enough meat. He was certain it wasn't his mother's favorite piece, but she was once again sacrificing for the family so the others could have the choicest parts. He didn't remember a time when she insisted on having things her way over others. He couldn't help but admire her generosity and wanted to be like her.

Dane arranged for part of the supplies to be delivered so they could get started on framing up the building over the concrete flooring that had been poured. They knew Miriam had seen them working each day, but she had no idea what the building was for, and assumed it was to be another storage building of some kind.

They trenched in electricity from the house, and water from the well. They planned on putting an outside spigot so they would have easy access to water for the garden during times of draught.

One day in the evening, Aiden asked Erin if she'd let him take her out on a date the next weekend. She was more than agreeable. That weekend he made reservations at a high-end restaurant. Even though he wanted to order a nice wine, he didn't because Erin was still underage. But they had a great meal, talking about the craft building that was being built for Miriam, the furniture that Lottie and Dane had picked out for their bedroom, Izzy's growing interest in Tom, and whether that would cause a problem between Cody and Tom.

Then after the dishes were cleared away, Aiden reached into his pocket, got down on one knee, and proposed properly to Erin. Her eyes widened. She had no idea this was coming. She looked around the room, while Aiden was still kneeling, and every eye in the room was on them. She couldn't speak, she was shocked. Finally, all she could do was nod. As Aiden slipped the ring on her finger, the room erupted in applause, and Aiden hugged her tightly.

Shortly, a waiter came to their table with a small cake and a single candle, which was unexpected by both Aiden and Erin.

Aiden reached across the table and held her hand. "Aiden, I'm so surprised. I didn't expect this until after I graduate next spring."

"Yeah, well, I don't want you to fall in love with someone at school, so if you're wearing a ring, I know they'll keep their distance." He smiled at her.

She responded, "Like I would ever be interested in anyone but you!"

"I'm so happy you said yes. I can't wait for you to graduate. I want to marry you right now. This waiting is killing me."

"Why are we waiting until I graduate?"

"Well, I thought that was what we agreed on."

"No, that was what you said. We could get married while I'm out on Christmas break."

"Really? You want to do that?"

Why not? I've known other girls who get married before they graduate."

"Then let's do it."

"But there's one thing I want, or I should say, don't want."

"What?" Aiden asked.

"I don't want a large wedding like Lottie and Dane had. I think that's too nerve wracking. Lottie was a nervous wreck. I want a small wedding, just a few close friends and family."

"That's fine with me."

When they got back home, they broke the news to the family, and everyone agreed they'd have to celebrate the next day with a nice meal. They invited Cody to eat with them as well, even though he didn't work on Sundays. Of course, it was a given that Tom would be eating with them since he lived in the barn loft.

Lottie decided to set a place for Daniel, even though he wouldn't be with them. It just felt right to include him she explained.

Erin was happy to have the insight gained during Dane and Lottie's wedding. It would make her wedding less stressful, she figured.

In October, as Dane and Lottie laid in bed one night, she asked, "Dane, how do you feel about having children?"

He raised up on one elbow, looking her into her eyes, "I want kids, at least two, a boy and a girl, in that order if possible."

"Me too. So, if you had a son, what would you name him?"

"I have no idea. Guess we'll have to wait until that time comes. Wait! Why all the questions about having kids?"

"Well…. If you're going to be a father, that's why."

"What?! Do you mean now!? Are you sure?"

"I believe so."

He wrapped her into his arms, "How? No, I didn't mean that. I know we thought we'd wait a while longer after we got married, but… Oh, Lottie, I'm so happy."

"I believe it happened on our honeymoon. So, I suppose I'll be showing when Erin and Aiden get married. I hope she doesn't ask me to stand up with her."

"Don't worry. It will all work out. And if you don't feel comfortable standing up with her, I'm sure she'll understand."

"Should we tell the family right away or should we wait awhile?"

"Let's wait. We just found out about Erin and Aiden's engagement. Let's let them revel in the limelight a while longer."

"Sounds good."

A few nights later, Lottie couldn't sleep and went to the kitchen for a drink of water, only to find Miriam sitting at the table having a cup of tea. "Miriam, why are you up so late?" Lottie asked.

"I guess I can't sleep without that someone in bed with me."

"And I can't sleep with that someone in bed with me," Lottie replied, which brought a smile to Miriam.

"Won't you sit and have a cup of tea with me?"

"I'd love that," Lottie replied as she went to the cabinet to retrieve a cup. She sat down across from Miriam.

Miriam went on, "I just feel so lost. I wish I was young again with Daniel. I was remembering our wedding day, the horseback rides we used to take, the dances we went to, the jokes we'd play on each other. We even played hide and seek just like little kids."

Lottie listened without a reply. How could you say anything to memories? She thought how she wanted to build up memories like that with Dane. Miriam had years to look back on, but she and Dane were just beginning their journey through life together.

Miriam said, "I remember the day Dane was born. It was snowing to beat the band when my water broke, and with snow already heavy on the roads, there was no way to get to the hospital, so he was born right here in our bedroom upstairs. I was thankful that his mother was here to help deliver him, or I'm not sure what I would have done."

"That's a nice story. I had no idea he was born here at home."

She smiled, "Yes, and when it got close to time to have Erin, because she would also be born in winter, I made Daniel take me and Dane to a hotel room in town so I would be near a hospital. When both of my kids were born, I couldn't help but marvel at how beautiful they were. Dane had the dimple in his chin and cheek, just like Daniel did. Erin was born practically bald headed because she was so blonde you couldn't see her hair. But she had the most beautiful blue eyes and when she looked up at me, my heart just melted."

"She still has beautiful blue eyes."

"As you do also. I can see why Dane fell in love with you immediately."

Lottie wasn't sure she wanted to say it, but under the circumstances she felt she couldn't hold back. "So, Miriam, someday you'll have little babies again, grandchildren."

"I hope so. I want to live long enough to see them. Maybe even great grandchildren."

Lottie smiled, yes Miriam needed to know Dane and her secret. "You're still young, Miriam, and I happen to know you will live long enough to see one of your grandkids."

Miriam's eyes widened knowingly, "You're pregnant!"

Lottie smiled, "Yes, but please don't tell anyone just yet. We want Erin and Aiden to revel in the news about their engagement a while longer."

"My lips are sealed. But you must have gotten pregnant on your honeymoon. I think that's my fault."

"No, I think it's Dane's fault," Lottie said with a chuckle.

"But if I'd been a better mother to you, I should have gotten you birth control so you could have waited a little longer. I just wasn't thinking. I'm so sorry."

"Sorry that you're going to have a grandchild? No, we're not sorry at all, and you should have seen Dane's face when I told him. He wants a son. I hope I can give him one."

"So, when are you due? Probably next spring then, I guess."

"I think so. But I won't be standing up at Erin's wedding with her since I will be showing come December."

"Oh, don't worry about that. She'll still have Izzy, and she's already told me she wants a small wedding, so if Dane stands up with Aiden, and Izzy with Erin, I think that will make Erin happy."

"I suppose Dane will be giving Erin away, like Aiden did for me."

"They haven't said, but I'm sure that's the plan. Well, your pregnancy has made me very happy I want you to know."

She coughed then, and Lottie asked if she was alright.

"Yes, just allergies. Well, I think I'll try to get some sleep tonight," as she rose from the table.

"I need to do the same."

Miriam gave Lottie a hug before heading to her room. "You take care of yourself now, you hear? Take good care of that grandbaby."

"Yes, ma'am," Lottie said with a smile.

Miriam laid awake a long time after retiring, thinking of what all she could do for both Lottie's baby and Erin's wedding. She decided to have a talk soon with Erin about her wedding and what was needing to be done. She was also determined to make sure Erin didn't get pregnant on her honeymoon like Lottie. There was still plenty of time to prepare for Erin's wedding and Lottie's baby, but Miriam knew time didn't stand still, and in fact, seemed to be moving faster and faster the older she got.

Erin entered the kitchen the next morning to find Miriam fixing breakfast for all of them. Miriam coughed a couple of times, and Erin asked, "Are you alright, Mom?"

"Sure, just allergies."

Erin dismissed it and left to get Izzy up. Soon everyone was seated around the table including Tom, who normally came to the house to eat not only because he had nothing in his room to cook on except a microwave oven, but also because Aiden insisted he be included in all their meals.

Izzy leaned over to Lottie while they were cleaning up the table, and whispered, "I think Mrs. Wilshire should go see a doctor. She's doing a lot of coughing."

"No, she said it's just allergies. I'm sure she's taking something for it."

But at noon, when Dane heard her coughing even harder, he said, "Mom, what's wrong with you?"

"Allergies," was her reply.

"I've never known you to have allergies. I think you should see a doctor."

"I'll be fine, you guys are all fussing over nothing."

Then that night as Lottie went to the kitchen once again to get a drink, she heard Miriam coughing so hard she almost couldn't catch her breath. She immediately woke Dane up and said she felt like they needed to take his mother to the emergency room.

Dane bolted out of bed and threw on his jeans and shirt, shoes and socks. Lottie did the same. Miriam complained about their concern, but they wouldn't take no for an answer and soon they had her loaded into the truck and was on the way to the Tupelo hospital. Dane and Lottie sat in the waiting room while Miriam was put through a battery of tests. When the doctor came out to talk with them, he said, "I have good news and bad news. The good news is she doesn't have COVID. The bad news is she has pneumonia. We need to keep her here until she's better. I have her on oxygen, and antibiotics. I've given her something to make her sleep, but if you want to go in and see her now, that's fine. Then you two need to go home and get some sleep too."

He started to walk away but Dane stopped him, "Doctor, my wife is pregnant. Do you think she should go in to see my mom?"

The doctor looked Lottie up and down then, "Looks like you're in the early stages, but if I were you, I think I'd stay away from her for now. I'm not sure if her pneumonia is bacterial or viral related. If it's viral, I don't want you near her."

Dane then said, "Thank you, doctor." He then turned to Lottie, "I'll go say goodbye to Mom. I'll be back in a minute."

When he entered Miriam's room, he said, "Looks like you're staying here for now. We hope you're better soon."

"I have to be, I've got a grandson on the way to see."

"Lottie told you?"

"Yes, and I'm very proud of you. And I laid awake a lot thinking about it, and I have a favor to ask."

Dane raised his eyebrows in question, "Anything you want, Mom."

"Would you consider naming him Daniel if it's a boy?"

"I've already thought of that, and I haven't run it by Lottie yet, but I doubt if she'll object."

"You're such a good boy. Now take your lovely wife home to get some sleep."

The next morning, everyone was surprised to find out Miriam was in the hospital, and Izzy went to the phone to call the flower shop to send her two dozen red roses. Later in the afternoon, Erin asked Lottie and Izzy if they wanted to go to the hospital with her to visit her mom. Lottie didn't know how to respond. She couldn't be around Miriam according to the doctor, so she thought a minute before saying, "You two go ahead, I'll go later with Dane." That seemed to work, and both girls understood perfectly.

Miriam was sitting up in bed when the girls arrived, but still with oxygen on. She told them she was feeling better and hoped to go home soon, but the girls said she was to stay in the hospital until the doctor released her, because they didn't want her coming home too soon just to get sick all over again. They stayed for an hour chatting with Miriam, who asked Erin, "Now, Erin, you must tell me what things I can help you with for your wedding."

"Well, first things first, Mom. You've got to get well, then we can talk about that."

"But it seems to me like this is the perfect time to talk about it. You're here, and I'm stuck in this bed so …."

"Ok, well, I was thinking how you did such a beautiful job organizing the reception, the place to have it, the food caterers, decorations and all for Dane and Lottie. So I'm going to leave all that up to you. And I've decided on dark burgundy for the girl's dresses since it will be in the winter. We need dark colors, don't you think?"

Izzy and Miriam liked that idea, and Miriam, added, "Then I think we should begin the meal with a soup. Nothing heavy, just a broth with vegetables, maybe. What do you think about that?"

Erin replied, "It should warm everyone up before the meal."

Dane and Lottie headed to the hospital that night and Aiden insisted on coming along with them. Dane looked at Lottie, a look that said, 'how do we deal with Aiden?' because they didn't want him to find out about Lottie's pregnancy yet. She just shrugged as if to say, figure it out.

When they arrived at the hospital, Lottie said, "You two go on in, I'll wait here in the waiting room. I'm tired, I think I'll see Miriam tomorrow." That seemed to work, and the boys headed down the hall.

While Miriam was in the hospital for the next week, the boys decided to work long hours to try to get as much done on the craft room side of Miriam's cottage, for that is what they decided to call it, Miriam's cottage. They already had the siding installed on the outside. They hung the windows and doors, then on the craft room side, the girls helped as they insulated the interior, hung drywall, finished it, and painted it a cheery light green. Then while the boys were working on the inside of the potting room, the girls brought Miriam's furnishings into the craft room. The boys had brought her large table and chairs over from the shed where things had been stored. The girls brought over the rolling drawers of sewing supplies, along with her sewing machine. Next they brought over the buckets of beads and other jewelry supplies and slid them onto the shelves the boys had built along one wall. They stood back to admire the room, and knew Miriam would be surprised, and smiled at their handiwork.

The boys didn't get quite everything finished on the potting room side before Miriam was released from the hospital, but they were working on the inside where Miriam couldn't see, so she had no idea what they were doing. And when she was released from the hospital the doctor had given her instructions to rest and take it easy for a few weeks anyway, so it wouldn't be hard to keep her from snooping around.

They built the potting shelf along one wall, put up peg board over another wall for hanging the small hand tools on, and put the same on another wall for rakes, shovels, brooms, and any other larger tool. Shelves were added on a different wall for pots, bags of potting soil, fertilizers, or other paraphernalia Miriam wanted to add. They even decided to add a sink on the back wall so Miriam could wash up before entering the house. However, since there was no drain that had been piped in, they channeled the water to the outside and away from the building so it would run down the gently sloping hill behind the cottage.

Miriam was told she had to stay indoors to rest, supposedly in order to follow doctor's orders, and the girls let her know she was not to cook until her next doctor visit and was declared well.

Soon the boys were hauling all the garden tools from one of the sheds to the potting room. They bought bags of potting soil, and mulch, more fertilizers, sprays, garden gloves, seeds to plant, and a few other odds and ends.

Finally, Miriam went on her follow-up doctor's appointment and was declared healthy. When they got her back home, Dane opened her car door for her, Aiden, Tom and Cody, Lottie, Erin, and Izzy were out in the yard, and they broke out clapping when she climbed out of the car.

She stopped to stare at them all and declared, "Gee, I didn't do anything except go on a doctor's visit. Why this big welcome home?"

Erin rushed to her mother's side, "Because we have a surprise for you."

She guided her mother to the cottage, and opened the door, stepped back for Miriam to enter, and when Miriam entered, she gasped. The others rushed in behind her, and Erin couldn't help but notice the tears in Miriam's eyes. She just stood staring at everything. She took a walk around the big table in the middle of the room, letting her hand drift along the top of the table. Then she stopped, "I don't know what to say," she choked out, barely able to speak.

Dane said, "That's not all, come here." Next, they took her into the potting room to show it to her, and here she broke down in tears. "This is…this is…too much," she finally said as she swiped at her tears. "I've never had… I never thought," she finally chuckled, putting her hand to her mouth. She was in awe. Again, she walked around the room looking at everything. She eventually turned to all of them, standing waiting by the door, "You guys are…too, too much."

Dane came and put his arm around her, "We needed to do something for you. You gave up your craft room for Lottie and me. I didn't want that for you. Besides you've always been there for us, helping us in one way or another. It was time to give back."

She slid her arm around his neck, he bent down and held her in a bear hug. "You're the best mother in the world," he whispered. "We hope you like it."

"Like it? I love it," she declared as she pulled out of his embrace.

Dane said, "Good, I thought you would. And we still have a little work to do on the outside. We need to paint it, and we're going to put some gingerbread along the eaves on the front up over the porch, and maybe put a rocker on each side of the front door, if you'd like. I also want to put in a walk from the backdoor to your cottage. Oh, and by the way, we've named it, Miriam's cottage."

She smiled, "I like that."

Miriam decided to go to town a short time later. When she arrived back home, she headed to her cottage carrying a bundle. She laid part of her bundle on the table but hid the rest.

That evening she took Erin to the craft room and showed her the decorations she had purchased for the reception. There were white paper bells, silver bells, crepe paper to stream here and there, candy dishes to sit around on tables to be loaded with goodies, candles to display on tables, and other minor things. Erin was very happy. It made the wedding somehow seem nearer.

Miriam asked, "I don't know if they will let us, now that Daniel is no longer a member of the country club, but if they will, do you want your reception there like Dane and Lottie's reception?"

"I don't know. Let me think about that. I'll talk to Aiden about how he feels about it."

She found Aiden and as she walked toward him, his heart swelled with love. He looked her up and down, watching her hips sway. When she reached him, he reached out and played with a curl that had come loose at her temple. "Hi, love," he said.

"Hi," she responded, "I came to ask you a question."

"Aw shucks. I thought you came just to see me and maybe give me a kiss. If not, I'll steal a kiss anyway." Then he bent to brush his lips across hers. Her arms instinctively wound around his neck, and he pulled her close to him, kissing her more deeply, running his hands slowly up and down her back. "I love you so much. Can we run away and get married today?"

"Hmmm" she said while snuggled up against his body. "I wish we could."

He held her that way for a while, but then she said, "Mom wants to know if we want the reception in the golf club house like Lottie and Dane had."

He thought about it awhile, not so much what his answer would be, but rather just to hold her a while longer. She eventually pulled away, looking into his eyes. "Well?" she asked.

"I don't know. What do you think?"

"I don't want my wedding to be a copycat of Dane's, so I say no."

"Then no it is," he replied with his arms still wrapped around her waist.

"There's another thing I want to discuss with you."

"Ok."

"I need to know how you feel about having kids. I want kids."

He laughed, "I want kids too, but I want to have you to myself for at least two or three years before starting a family."

"Good, now that that's settled, I'd better go tell Miriam to look for a different place for our reception."

As she turned to walk away, again Aiden couldn't take his eyes off her.

Miriam agreed to search for someplace else for a reception when Erin told her their decision. Erin said, "In a way, I almost wish we were getting married in the summer. I'd love a wedding outside, maybe at the Tombigbee Park. It's so beautiful out there."

Miriam smiled, "I know, and if you want to change the date, you always can, you know."

"No, I think Aiden would kill me if I did that."

Miriam led Erin to the craft room, locked the door, and pulled out the bundle she had hidden upon her return from town. She showed Erin the material she had bought to make a baby quilt for the baby. And since she didn't know if it would be a boy or a girl, she bought pastel pink, blue, yellow and green for the squares, and another material with baby animals all over it, teddy bears, kittens, puppies, horses, and rabbits, which she explained would be appliquéd on the top of the squares. She had also bought batting, and white silk for the underside of the quilt, and a wide silk green ribbon to go around the outside edge of the quilt.

"Oh, mom, that will be beautiful," Erin said with wide eyes. "But no one's pregnant yet and it might be a long time before anyone is. Are you sure you should have gotten all this already?"

"Well, you never know when. And I want to be ready."

"Well, I hope when I get pregnant, you'll make a quilt for my baby."

Dane had ordered large pieces of rock to be delivered to make the walkway to Miriam's cottage, and soon the boys had dug a deep flat area for the walk, lined it with black plastic, and shoveled sand on top of it, leveled it, and began laying the stones on top, leaving space for mortar for the joints. The walk would be even with the ground so it could be easily mowed across.

Dane was just finishing hosing the finished product off when Miriam came outside carrying a tray of iced tea for everyone. "Oh, that looks so nice," she stated, "I'm so proud of you boys. You do fine work."

"Nothing but the best for you, mom," Dane replied.

She turned to go back inside after setting the tray on the table on the patio, but turned and said, "You know, that stone would look nice on top of the concrete patio, don't you think?" She smiled and Dane took the hint.

"Eventually, Mom, but give us a rest for a while first."

"Dinner will be ready soon, so better go wash up, and by the way, I think washing up in the potting room or the office bathroom from now on is a good idea."

"You got it," Aiden replied as he rose from his chair on the patio to go wash. "Come on boys, gotta follow orders from the chief cook and bottle washer."

While they were eating dinner, Aiden looked around at all the faces at the table, Miriam, Dane, Lottie, Erin, Izzy, Tom and Cody, and said to Miriam, "Do you ever feel like you're running a boarding house, Miriam?"

"Well, I never thought about it like that, but if this is a boarding house, I've got the best tenants in the world." She took a bite and continued after swallowing, "But the pay sure stinks." This brought a round of laughter from everyone.

Miriam told Erin she wanted to take her to the Civic Center in Tupelo to see if she liked it for her reception. When they got there, the concierge asked how many they would be expecting. Miriam looked at Erin and Erin said, "Maybe sixty or seventy."

He took them to look at a couple of rooms and said that the one room had a partition that could open the room to another room. Miriam stated that if they took that room, they could have the wedding in one room and open the wall afterward for the reception that would be in both rooms. Plenty of room for dancing, and tables for dining, as well. Erin liked that idea, and so it was decided. She was sure Aiden would like it as well. The room was bright with windows from floor to ceiling all along one wall. It had light colored stone for the walls. And the ceilings were twelve feet tall. Erin felt it could look very elegant. Miriam reserved the room and paid the deposit.

One day Erin walked into the house after school and could tell something was wrong with her mother. She noticed Miriam was roughly slamming pans around, opening cabinet doors, and closing them loudly. "Are you alright, Mom?"

Miriam was mumbling under her breath. "Mom?"

Miriam turned to look at her, she hadn't even noticed Erin had come inside. "Oh, hi, honey."

"Are you alright? You seem upset about something? Who was that I saw driving out of the driveway?"

"Nobody."

"So, it looks like "nobody" has you riled up about something."

Miriam slammed down her spoon, and said, "It was old man Bower, if you must know."

"Mr. Bower from over on Cripple Creek? What did he want?"

"If he thought he could fill Daniel's shoes, he has another think coming to him."

"Fill dad's shoes?" Erin was confused, she didn't understand.

"He was just after money, that's what I think. Thought he'd come here and propose, and I'd fall into his arms."

"Oh! I hope you told him no."

"I tried, in about ten different ways, but he wouldn't take no for an answer."

"Well, he's gone now, so you must have gotten through to him somehow."

"Yeah, after I got mad enough, I finally told him I wouldn't marry him if he was the last man on earth."

Erin laughed, "I'm sure that made him mad."

"I hope so. Now you better get your homework done before supper."

"I got it done in study hall, so I can help you make supper. And by the way you've been slamming things around, I think I'd better help before you break some dishes."

That made Miriam smile at Erin, and soon they both broke out in laughter.

At the dinner table that evening, Dane asked his mom a question, but she didn't answer, so he said, "Mom?" Erin looked up at her mother.

She jerked her head up and said, "What?"

"I asked if you are planning anything special for Thanksgiving this year?"

Erin spoke up, "Mom's not in a very good mood right now. Better tread lightly."

"What's going on. What's wrong, Mom?" Dane asked.

Again, Erin looked at her mother. "Oh, nothing," she said.

"Nothing? Mom, tell them what happened. It obviously upset you quite a bit."

Miriam sighed, "I was just propositioned by a neighbor."

Dane laid his fork down, "Propositioned? You mean sex?"

"No," Miriam looked at him, "marriage."

"Someone wants to marry you?"

Erin added, "Mr. Bower who lives over on Cripple Creek."

"That old man? What was he thinking?" Dane added with a laugh. "I hope you told him no."

Miriam answered with, "Yes, in about five thousand ways. But I don't think I'll be seeing anything of him again."

"Well, good for you. I've heard he's a womanizer. We certainly don't want someone with a reputation like that in our family."

"Not to worry. I'm a big girl. I can take care of myself. Now eat up, there's Lemon Cake for dessert."

After dinner was over, Aiden and Erin went out on the patio with their glasses of iced tea. Aiden started, "Looks like we need to keep a closer eye on your mom. She's still a nice-looking woman, and a wealthy one at that, and I'm sure the wolves all over the countryside will be circling soon, and we need to protect her."

"What do you propose we do? I'm still in school, I can't be here during the day to see what's going on."

"Well, if we see a car come into the drive and someone going into the house, I'll go investigate. And I'll also alert the other guys to do the same, in case I don't see it but they do."

"Good idea." She then thought a few minutes, "Lottie was home, why didn't she put a stop to what was going on."

"Good question, I'll ask her."

When Aiden questioned Lottie, she wasn't home at the time. She'd gone into town to run an errand, which satisfied Aiden, but he told her he wanted her to also be on the lookout for men interested in Miriam, and to step in if needed. She agreed to do so.

Erin came out to the barn next day after arriving home from school. She was missing Aiden and just wanted to spend time with him. Aiden looked up as she entered the office. "Hi, honey. What's up?" Aiden asked.

"Nothing. I just wanted to see you, to be near you."

Aiden rose and came around the desk, took her in his arms, and peering deeply into her eyes and eventually looking down to her lips, lips that were full, that were irresistible. "Thank you for that."

She stood looking into his big brown eyes, happy in the knowledge that she was his and his alone, and he belonged to her. Aiden ran his hands up and down her bare arms, feeling the smooth silky skin, and felt immense pleasure. Eventually Aiden felt something was wrong.

"Are you alright? Is something bothering you?"

"No, I'm fine. It's just that…well, I've been thinking a lot about Mom lately, and I know she's young enough to get married, but…"

"But you don't want her to, is that it?"

"Well, it would change everything if she did. Think about what that would mean. I would have a stepfather, and how would that change everything if Mom were to die before him?"

"Do you mean how would it change the inheritance?"

"Yes, would we all have to answer to him for what he wants done, or any changes he might want to make around here?"

"Well, your mom inherited the house, the furnishings of the house, and all of your dad's liquid assets, except your dad's business liquid assets. So, if your mother should die before someone she might marry, she would have her own Will. She wouldn't have a lot to Will to her husband, but if she Willed the house to him, he would have the right to continue living here, but he couldn't change the business. However, he might have the right to throw all of us out of the house. You know that is something to think about. Guess I never entertained that possibility. I think I'll run it by Dane. But before I go in search of him, do you mind if I kiss you? You're just so irresistible."

He lowered his lips to gently brush hers before kissing her passionately. He held her tightly against him, aware of her feminine curves. Then he kissed her eyes, her cheek, and when he began kissing her neck, she instinctively raised her chin and allowed him to caress her. He began breathing heavily and he knew he had to stop. He wished time would hurry so they could get married.

She pushed him away, and said, "You'd better go find Dane now. I'm heading inside."

He thought how Erin had a resolve of steel and he wished he could say the same for himself.

He eventually found Dane and told him about Erin's concerns. Dane felt it would be a good idea to have a little chat with his mother about it.

After dinner that evening, Dane asked his mother if he could have a word with her in private. She said, "Sure, but you'll have to come out to my craft cottage, I'm working on something."

He sat at her table while she cut material into squares. "Mom, Erin brought something to my attention that I want to discuss with you."

"Ok."

"She brought the question up that if you should decide to ever get married, how would things change around here?"

She laughed, "I'm not getting married. I thought I made that clear the other night."

"Yes, I know what you said, but we can never really know the future and what could happen. Right now, you don't want to ever marry, but in the future, you could change your mind."

"I'll never change my mind. Daniel was more than enough man to keep me in love with him for the rest of my life."

"But what if you got lonely."

"I have you kids around me, and soon I'll have a grandchild to help raise. I'm sure that will be enough to keep me busy for the rest of my days."

"And what if Mr. Right, Mr. Handsome, Mr. Perfect should walk into your life totally unexpected? Everything would change then."

"What would change?"

"Everything could. Think. If you should get married, and die before your new husband, you could Will the house to him, but then he could decide he doesn't want us kids to live here with him. What if he had family that he wanted to move in here with him? What would happen to Lottie and me? I had hoped we'd be able to stay here in this house running the farm."

She rose and came to Dane, put her hand on his cheek, and said, "Oh, honey. You don't have to worry about that. I'd never leave the house to anyone but you. I thought you'd have known that."

"But wouldn't your husband expect to inherit upon your death?"

"He could expect all he wants, that doesn't mean it would happen. Now stop worrying, there's no way I'll ever let anyone take this house away from you. This house belongs with the farm. It's been in Daniel's family for many years. And I'll never get married again anyway."

"You won't care if I hold you to that, do you?"

"Believe me, I don't need anyone else in my life. I have everything I want and need right here."

He stood up and gave her a big hug. "Did I ever tell you that you're the best mom anyone could ever have?"

She laughed, "Only all the time. Now get out of here, I'm busy."

"What are you making anyway."

"I can't say just yet. Now get. And son, to alleviate yours and Erin's fears, I'll go see Jake as soon as he has time and make sure my Will says you inherit the house."

"Thanks, Mom. I love you."

The guys enlarged the patio to extend across the entire back side of the house. They poured concrete, finished it, and when the stones were delivered, the concrete had hardened. The boys all got busy laying the stones over the patio concrete, cutting some to fit, and mortaring them down. When it was finished, everyone was pleased that the walk and patio now matched, and that the patio was now large enough to host a nice sized party.

While they were standing around appraising the fine job, Dane asked his mother, "What do you think about building an outdoor fireplace at that corner, and a kitchen over here?"

She clapped her hands. "Just think, if we had a fireplace, we could sit out here in the winter, and not have to go out into the field to sit around a bonfire."

"And with an outside kitchen, we could have more cookouts," Dane added.

"I like that idea. As a matter of fact, if you could build a nice roof over the entire patio, I could order new furniture for out here, some really comfy chairs and a couch."

"And I like that idea."

Dane and Aiden decided to hire someone to build the fireplace and use stone that matched the patio floor, while Dane, Aiden, and Tom got busy building the roof. As it was, they built a tall peak with open rafters above. Open on one side, but with it adorned with screens that zipped closed in the middle or could be tied back at each corner. That would keep mosquitos and flies at bay when the patio was being used.

The outdoor kitchen had a built-in grill and sink. The counter was granite and had two doors under the sink. On each side of the kitchen end, they built partial walls of stone to match the fireplace and floor.

After it was completed, Miriam bought the furniture, complete with side tables, a coffee table, and an outdoor rug for the front of the couch. It had all come together very well, and everyone couldn't wait to try it out.

"Let's have a party this weekend," Erin said. "Just us, and Tom and Cody included, of course."

The girls bought steaks, potatoes to bake, and salad. Lottie baked a pie. They enjoyed the evening, glad that it was becoming cooler in the evenings. They sat talking, singing, dancing until it was time to go to bed.

The next day the girls decided to go horseback riding. They ended up at the cabin in the woods, and marched down to the river, sat on a log, skipping rocks across the water. It was a beautiful day, sunny and bright. Lottie raised her face to the sun, soaking it all in.

"You look relaxed," Izzy said.

"Isn't life wonderful?" Lottie replied. "It just doesn't get much better than this. I'm so happy to be married, and especially to Dane. Erin you will be so happy once you're married, I just know it."

"I think we will. Aiden is such a great guy. He's so tall and handsome. Every time I look at him, my heart swells with love for him." She looked at Izzy then, "And I hope someday you'll find the perfect man too, Izzy."

Izzy just smiled. Lottie looked over at her and detected a secret in Izzy's heart that she wasn't telling. "You're in love with Tom. Am I right?"

Izzy replied, "Maybe, but I don't think he notices me at all."

Lottie said, "Nonsense. I've seen him watching you when you're around him. He's just not letting on yet how interested he is because you still have to finish another year in school after this year."

"Well, I'm not too young to date. If he was interested, why hasn't he asked me out?"

Erin put in, "He's probably afraid to."

"Why? Afraid of what?"

"Afraid you might say no. That would hurt his pride. Men are funny like that. They act like they're tough macho guys, but in reality, they're pussy cats."

Lottie added, "If you're interested in him, you'll have to give him a nudge."

"Like how?"

"Don't you know anything? Women have a charm they can use to catch a guy."

"So how do I use my *charm*?"

Lottie explained, "When you're around him, and you need to find reasons to do that, do a little flirting with him. Take him a nice cold glass of iced tea. Look him in the eyes, see what his reaction is."

Izzy thought about that, and because she had a shy streak in her, she wasn't sure she could do that. She had never needed to be outgoing because of Lottie. Lottie was the older one who would always take charge, so Izzy would stand back in the shadows and let her. And she always felt that the guy should be the one to take the first step toward a girl he liked. She didn't want to look too forward. She needed time to think about this. She picked up a flat rock and skipped it across the water.

December was just a few days away, and Erin was putting the final touches in place for her wedding. She had ordered her dress and the Civic Center had been booked.

Erin had asked Lottie and Izzy both to stand up with her, but Lottie had begged off. "But why?" Erin asked. "You had me stand up with you at your wedding."

"I know, but under the circumstances, I don't think it would be appropriate."

"What circumstances?"

"Look," Lottie lifted her top up to reveal her bulge in her stomach.

Erin's eyes widened in understanding, "You're pregnant?"

Lottie smiled. "Now you see why I shouldn't stand up with you at your wedding?"

"Lottie, I had no idea. Why didn't you say something?"

"Because I didn't want to detract from yours and the family's excitement about your wedding. This is a special day for you and the spotlight should be on you, not on me."

"Just wait till Mom finds out about this."

"She already knows, but I swore her to secrecy."

"Does anyone else know?"

"Well, Dane knows, of course."

"How does he feel about having a baby."

"He's excited. But I recommend getting on birth control right away if you don't want to get pregnant on your honeymoon like I did."

"That's a good idea, and one I didn't think about. I'll talk to Mom about it right away. Does anyone else in the family know about it yet?"

"No, and I'd like to keep it that way until your wedding is over. Ok?"

"Sure, if that's what you want. But if you decide to tell, it won't hurt my feelings. Do you know if it's a boy or a girl yet?"

"Not yet."

"Does Dane want a boy or a girl?"

"Well, we talked about that, but he said he doesn't really care. He just wants the baby to be healthy. But I think he really would love a son."

"What about you?"

"I'd love to give Dane a son, but I guess we'll have to just wait and see."

The wedding day arrived, and it had turned cold with a skiff of snow on the ground. The concierge had a fire roaring in the fireplace when everyone began arriving for the wedding. There were approximately sixty-five or seventy people waiting for the wedding to begin. Erin had wanted a smaller wedding than that, but because the Wilshire's were so well known and liked in the community, and Erin didn't want to hurt anyone's feelings by not inviting them, it grew larger than she had intended.

Aiden was standing just in front of the fireplace, nervous as a cat on a hot tin roof. He would shake his hands to try to calm himself down, but it wasn't working. He paced back and forth, glancing at the door every once-in-a-while in anticipation of Erin's entrance. He searched the faces in the audience, looking for a familiar one, but only recognized a few outside of the immediate family from the farm. Tom and Cody were busy seating everyone as ushers. Miriam and Lottie sat together on the front row. What was taking Erin so long, he wondered? He hoped she hadn't changed her mind. Did she really love him that much? His heart was about to break in two. He let out a sigh, took a deep breath, and slowly released it, hoping that would calm him down. Again, that didn't work. He could feel his heart pounding in his chest.

Miriam saw that he was in distress and rose to go to him. "Aiden, I know you're nervous, but take deep breaths and try to calm down."

"Why isn't she here? Did she change her mind?"

"No, no, nothing like that. This is a very special day for her, and I'm sure she is just taking her time to get ready. I know she loves you very much."

He looked down into her eyes, and prayed she was right.

About that time, the preacher announced, "Would all, please rise?"

The music began, Aiden adjusted his jacket, stood straight, and outwardly appeared calm, even though he was still a mess on the inside. Izzy began down the aisle, took her place across from Aiden, and soon Dane appeared with Erin on his arm. Aiden almost burst into tears. She was so beautiful. And soon she would be his, the little pesty girl he met the first time he came to Wilshire's farm to ask for a job. The girl that stole his heart that day. The girl he couldn't help but get a kick by her inquisitiveness. The long-awaited day had finally arrived. He took another deep breath to steady himself.

Erin kept her eyes on Aiden the entire way down the aisle, with the most beautiful smile he'd ever seen. He tried to smile back and hoped he didn't look like he felt on the inside. When she reached Aiden, he held out a hand to her, and Dane moved to take his place beside Aiden. Aiden and Erin stood looking into each other's eyes for a few moments before the ceremony began.

Soon they were repeating their vows, exchanged rings, kissed, and then the preacher was announcing them to the audience as Mr. and Mrs. Aiden Roberts. Everyone clapped.

The wall was then rolled back that separated the wedding from the reception, and everyone gathered around the tables that had been set up in the separate room. The food table had been set up already, the cake delivered, and the music began. Miriam had hired the same band that had played for Dane and Lottie at their wedding.

At the reception, Charles from the grocery store came up to Aiden, shook his hand, and said, "Well, son, it looks like you've done quite well since you moved here. And to marry into the Wilshire family is just about the best you could have done. I think you've got a very special girl there for a wife. I've known the Wilshire kids all their life, and I've always had a great admiration for Daniel and Miriam."

"Thank you, Mr. … Uh, do you realize I don't even know your last name? I've only known you as Charles."

"Charles Dawson."

"Thank you, Mr. Dawson. I appreciate that."

"Are your parents here? I'd like to congratulate them."

Aiden looked down. Maybe it was time to let the community know a little about him and his sisters. He took a deep breath. "No, sir. My parents are both deceased. Mr. and Mrs. Wilshire took me and my sisters into their family."

Mr. Dawson looked surprised at first, "Well, I shouldn't be surprised about that. The Wilshire family are very generous people, always ready to help ones in need."

"Yes, sir, I feel like we were blessed to have met them. They have certainly done more for me and my sisters than I could have imagined any stranger would do. Will you excuse me, I see my wife motioning to me?"

Charles laughed, "It won't be the last time. Women tend to wiggle their little finger and we men come running."

Aiden walked away, glad that conversation was over. He couldn't help but feel shame that he and his sisters had lived in the woods in the cabin across the road from the Wilshire farm. He didn't mind people knowing his parents were dead, but he'd keep the rest secret if he could.

Aiden led his wife onto the dance floor, took her into his arms, and began swaying to the music. He whispered in her ear, "How do you feel, Mrs. Roberts?"

"I'm still floating on air, not sure when my feet will touch the ground again."

Aiden chuckled. "I'm still a nervous wreck."

She looked up into his eyes, "Really? I wouldn't have known that. You seemed pretty calm during the ceremony."

"Didn't you hear my knees knocking?" She laughed and he added, "Don't believe me? Ask your mother. I was afraid you'd changed your mind."

"Oh, Aiden, I would never do that. I love you so much."

He squeezed her tightly, "I love you too, with every breath in my body. I want to do everything to keep you loving me. Promise me, that if I ever say or do anything to upset you, you'll come and talk to me about it. I want our marriage to be one made in heaven. Till death do us part. In sickness and in health, and all that stuff."

She smiled, "And I want the same from you. I feel like communication in a marriage is very important."

They continued dancing, and eventually she whispered in his ear, "I have a secret I just might let you in on, if you want."

He looked down at her, "What's your secret?"

She smiled, "Lottie is pregnant."

He gasped and just stared at her. "Are you kidding me?"

"Absolutely. She got pregnant on their honeymoon. She's been hiding it because of our wedding. She said she didn't want to detract from our day."

"Nothing doing!" He dropped his hands, walked to the band, and asked them to stop playing. Then he went to their microphone, and said, "Can I have everyone's attention." He looked down at Erin, who had her hand covering her mouth, she was so surprised at Aiden.

He took the microphone, "I know many, if not all of you, were at Dane and my sister, Lottie's, wedding. So, I'd like to take a moment to announce that my sister and brother-in-law are expecting their first child. Take a minute to congratulate them."

The clapping was thunderous, and hurrahs could be heard from the crowd. People made their way to Lottie and Dane's table.

Lottie's eyes threw daggers at her brother. He caught the look and laughed. Then he went to their table and asked her to dance. When he got her on the dance floor, he said, "Congratulations, little sister. Why didn't you tell me?"

"Why did you announce it to everyone? And who told you?"

He threw back his head and laughed. I'm happy for you and for Dane. Just think, I'm going to be an uncle."

"You're not getting off that easy. Dane and I should have been the ones to let others know about…?"

"Oh, get off your high horse. Everyone wants to know when a little one is coming into the world. They want to celebrate with you, and what better time to announce it than here with everyone to hear at the same time. Now I want you to take good care of yourself. Don't overdo it. I want this baby to be healthy."

"Yes, Dad." He laughed again, because every time he gave advice to her, she would call him dad.

Izzy came running onto the dance floor butting in between Aiden and Lottie. She grabbed both of Lottie's hands, and squealed with excitement, "You're pregnant? Really pregnant? I can't believe it. When are you due? Do you know if it's a boy or a girl? Have you thought of a name?"

"Whoa, slow down," Lottie said. "Let's talk about it after we get home. I'll answer all your questions then, right after I kill our brother."

54

After the wedding, Aiden and Erin left for Biloxi, Mississippi. He didn't go as extravagant as Dane had with his and Lottie's honeymoon, but he wasn't as wealthy as Dane. Still Erin was happy to go to the coast. They booked into a suite on the beach and spent the days lounging in the sun and sand, getting sunburned even though it was winter, and spending the evenings dining in restaurants. The water temperature in the Gulf was too chilly for swimming, but they didn't care. Just being together was enough to make them happy. Besides they had the hot tub by the pool that was heated. A couple of days they wandered through the historic district looking at the beautiful homes. They took in museums, caught a ferry to Deer Island to see the pelicans and turtles. But Aiden had to admit, the best part of their honeymoon was staying in their room, ordering breakfast in.

When they returned home, Aiden said to Erin, "What do you think about searching for a builder to talk to about building our home on our land?"

"That's a good idea. I really don't want to stay living with Mom. As much as I love her, I think we should have a place of our own."

Therefore, Aiden got busy contacting different builders to interview them. They began looking at floor plans. When they chose a builder, they met him on their property they had both inherited and showed him where they wanted the house built. However, the builder let them know that before he would start building, he wanted them to deed both properties into both of their names as one piece of land instead of two separate ones. He said if they didn't do that, it could cause problems down the road, should they ever decide to sell. They agreed to do that, even though they both knew they would probably never move.

Aiden contacted Daniel's attorney, Jake, and soon it was taken care of. Before Aiden and Erin left his office, he said, "You know Daniel said you two would be getting married someday. I don't think he suspected it would be as soon as this, though."

Aiden and Erin looked at each other and smiled. Erin spoke, "My dad was pretty shrewd. There wasn't much that got by him."

"How well I know. I still hate about that accident, and I'm sure you miss him very much."

"Yes, especially since he wasn't able to walk me down the aisle at my wedding."

"That must have been very hard. but Dane gave you away though."

"Yes."

"And speaking of Dane, how are Lottie and him doing?"

"She's pregnant, you know."

"So, I heard at your wedding. I thought that was very nice of you, Aiden, to announce that at your reception."

"Yeah, but I'm not so sure Lottie agreed with that. She didn't want to detract from our wedding she said. But I just couldn't let her keep that a secret from everyone."

"So, when is the baby due?"

"Around March sometime," Aiden said.

"March 9th," Erin corrected.

"Well, I hope all goes well for them and that baby."

"Thanks, Jake." Aiden shook his hand, ready to leave.

"Let me know if you have any other needs," Jake added.

Shortly afterward the builder began moving equipment onto the land to begin the building process. Aiden and Erin had chosen a one-story home that would have three bedrooms and two baths. It was not elaborate but would be a good starter home for them. Aiden didn't want to be in debt too much to start off their marriage because some day he wanted to build a barn, and he didn't want to put it off a long time in the future.

As the building progressed, Aiden would go regularly to see how it was coming along. It wasn't going up fast enough to his liking, but he knew these things took time. He was excited in wanting to see the finished product. And there were so many decisions to be made. They chose stone exterior on three sides, but Aiden wanted the back of the house to be wood siding in case they decided to enlarge the house in the future. If they needed to enlarge, it would be better not to have stone on all four sides. They had to choose the exterior colors to go with the stone, interior color scheme, flooring, cabinets, lighting, and more. Both Aiden and Erin were surprised at how many decisions they had to make. Some things they agreed on, but other things had to be discussed, and in some cases, at length before they came to an agreement. But after all the decisions had been made, they relaxed and waited for what seemed an eternity to them to see the finished product.

Lottie was due March 9th, and Erin wanted to have a baby shower for her. It was planned for February and Erin and Izzy invited several neighbors and a few girls Lottie had become friends with at school. Dane and Lottie knew they would have to share their bedroom with the baby until Aiden and Erin's house was completed, but it would only be for a few months, and Lottie wanted the baby close by at first anyway. They bought a crib but didn't put it together until Erin and Aiden moved into their new home and vacated the bedroom they were using. They bought a bassinet for the baby to sleep in while in their room, which was fine with Lottie.

At the shower, Lottie got a lot of boy's clothes since Lottie's sonogram showed they were having a boy. The girls found the clothing very cute and couldn't help but ooh and aah over them, especially the little cowboy boots someone gave them.

At the shower, Miriam's gift was the first one Lottie opened, and she couldn't believe her eyes. Miriam had finished the baby quilt she had been working on, and Lottie was ecstatic with it. Erin leaned over to her mother, "You know, Mom, you'll have to make another one for my baby when I have one. I'll keep telling you that until the day I deliver a baby of my own."

Miriam laughed, "I figured. Is this happening any time soon?"

"I hope not. We want to wait a while."

Miriam patted her arm, "Good girl. I think it's best to get used to each other first, used to being married."

Someone asked Lottie if they had chosen a name for the baby, and Lottie answered, "Yes, Daniel Aiden Wilshire."

Erin looked at her mother and noticed tears in her eyes. "Oh," Izzy said, "you're naming him after his grandpa Daniel, and his uncle Aiden. How sweet. That's some big shoes he's going to have to fill." Izzy continued, "Does Aiden know this?"

"Not yet."

"He'll be surprised, but I'm sure he'll like it."

Lottie smiled also, "I hope so."

It wasn't long after the shower that Lottie went into labor during the night. She poked Dane to wake him, "Dane, it's time."

"Um-hmm," he said.

"Dane, it's time. Come on wake up."

He finally came out of his grogginess. "Time. Time for what?" as he rolled over toward Lottie.

"Time to go to the hospital."

Dane jumped up then, "Holy crap, Lottie. Why didn't you tell me? Come on, get up."

"Relax, Dane. I've been timing my contractions, and I have a little bit of time."

"No, Lottie, we have to go now. Come on, hurry up."

"Dane," she said softly. "It's alright. We don't have to rush. I'm not that far along."

But Dane would have none of it. "If you don't get out of that bed right now, I'm going to drag you out." He was a nervous wreck, excited. Not knowing anything about childbirth, he needed to get her to the hospital right away, he was sure of it.

Lottie threw back the covers and stood up. Dane said, "Don't bother getting dressed, we need to go now."

"I'm not going to the hospital with my night clothes on, so you'll just have to wait a few minutes while I get dressed. Dane had been dressing the entire time he was prodding Lottie to get out of bed.

Lottie grabbed her overnight bag she'd packed ready for her delivery. On the way out the door, she looked at Dane and said, "Your shirt is buttoned up wrong."

He fumbled with his shirt, never getting it straightened out because he was intent on getting Lottie to the hospital as soon as possible.

While they were on the way to the hospital, Lottie's contractions stopped. She tried to get Dane to turn around and go back home, but he refused. He drove her to the emergency room door, unloaded her, and shuffled her inside. She was shown to a room, and one of the nurses told him he had to go move his car out of the driveway. He stated that he needed to stay with his wife.

"No," the nurse said, "you need to go park your car in the parking lot. We'll look after your wife."

When he got back from doing what he was told, he ran down the hall and into the room Lottie was in, and she was alone. "Where's the nurse? She said she would look after you while I was gone, but she left you alone?"

"Dane," Lottie said, "settle down. It's ok. I'm fine."

"But what if you weren't fine while I was gone?"

"Dane, settle down. Relax. Come here and hold my hand." She said this more to settle him down than her needing his help.

Eventually, which Dane was sure was almost a year later, the doctor entered the room to examine her. She let the doctor know that her contractions had stopped. Therefore, the doctor let her know she wasn't really in labor, it was just Braxston Hicks.

Dane said, "Braxston Hicks? What is that? Is it bad?"

The doctor answered him, "Nothing to worry about. It's just false labor. It's a way that her body is getting ready to go into real labor. Go home, get some sleep."

"But doctor, you don't understand. She was having contractions."

"Trust me, it was not real labor. Go home."

Dane helped her out of the hospital and to the car, thoroughly upset that they didn't take Lottie or him seriously. He knew he wouldn't get an ounce of sleep even if they did go home.

They got on the way, and Lottie said, "Do you feel like an ice cream sundae? I feel like an ice cream sundae."

He looked at her in disbelief. "In the middle of the night?"

"Yes, now."

After they had their ice cream, Dane seemed more relaxed. But on the way home he said, "I hope we don't get home only to have to rush back to the hospital, or worse, that you're having the baby at home. I've helped cows during birth, but this is different. This is MY baby. I've even reached up into a cow and pulled a baby out, but I won't do that to you."

Lottie laughed, "You couldn't do that even if you tried."

They had been at the hospital so long that the sun was beginning to peek up over the horizon.

Lottie said, "Oh, Dane. Let's pull over and watch the sun rise." He pulled over to the side of the road, and he took her hand in his. Rubbing his thumb over the back of her hand. "Lottie," he said, "I'm scared."

She turned to him. "Scared of what?"

"Scared to have this baby."

"But why?"

"I've seen cattle who have died during childbirth, and I know the same thing can happen in people. I want to protect you from any harm, but how can I do that during childbirth?"

She reached out and put a hand on his cheek. "Oh, Dane. Please don't worry. I've been going to the doctor regularly, doing just what he says. I've taken my prenatal vitamins right along. I'm healthy. I really can't imagine what could go wrong. And besides, if I'm in the hospital, if there's a problem, they have everything they need to take care of the situation."

Dane took a deep breath and ran his fingers through his hair.

A week later Lottie again woke Dane up at night and told him it was time to go.

Dane said, "Hmmm?"

"It's really time, Dane. Come on, get up," while she pushed at him to wake him.

Dane said still groggy, "Are you sure this time? I don't want a repeat of last week."

"I'm sure this time. I've been timing the contractions, and it's time."

"You said, you were timing the contractions last week too. Remember?"

"You know what, just stay here, Dane. I'll drive myself."

"No, I'll take you, if you're sure."

"I'm sure, now come on, if you're going."

Dane threw back the covers and sat on the edge of the bed, rubbing his eyes.

"I'm leaving without you, if you don't move now," she said urgently.

He finally rose, slid into his jeans, shirt, and shoes without socks.

Lottie had waited until her contractions were only two minutes apart. Then on the way to the hospital, she said, "Oh, hurry, Dane. Hurry!"

He looked at her with eyes wide, "Really? You're serious?"

Lottie screamed at him, "Hurry! The baby's coming!"

Dane took off like a bullet, slowing down for stop signs but not stopping. He drove up to the emergency room door, jumped out of the car, and ran inside calling for help. Soon people came running pushing a gurney. They loaded Lottie onto it and rushed her inside. Someone examined her, and told her she was eight centimeters dilated, and she wasn't far from the pushing stage of delivery. They put her into a birthing room, Dane walked behind the bed on his phone the entire way. He called Miriam and Aiden and told them the news. Soon everyone was loaded into vehicles and on the way to the hospital at three in the morning.

Little Daniel Aiden was born just before everyone arrived. The nurses were just cleaning him up. Everyone rushed into the birthing room and stopped. Lottie was still in stirrups. But shortly afterward, they had her covered up, and had laid Daniel on her chest wrapped up tightly in a blanket with a little cap on his head.

Dane was admiring his son when everyone cautiously crept to her bedside to get their first peek at the little guy. Miriam gasped when she saw him. "He resembles Daniel so much. Look, he has that same dimple in his chin, and I bet in his cheek as well, and he has his nose. It's so cute, just a little button. Oh, Dane and Lottie, you definitely chose the right name for him."

"Wait," Aiden said, "isn't there anything of me in there? He's also named after me, you know."

They chuckled. Lottie said, "I think you'll have to wait and see how much he changes before you'll see yourself in there."

"Well, he might look like his Grandpa Daniel, but maybe he will have my sterling personality."

They chuckled again. Izzy said, "I'd rather he have your looks and Daniel's personality." Aiden looked at her disapprovingly.

"Now listen, all of you," Dane put in, "let's just let him develop any way he wants. We won't try to mold him into one or the other."

Izzy added, "I don't care who he looks like, but he sure is cute. I'm your live in babysitter anytime you need one." That brought a chuckle from Dane and Lottie.

Erin said, "I don't know about that. We might just have to fight over him."

Once again, Dane said, "And no fighting over babysitting."

They all smiled before Miriam said, "Well, if push comes to shove, I just might have to pull rank and knock everyone else out of the running."

"Aw, mom," Erin said, "no fair."

Lottie said, "I believe with everyone who will volunteer to take care of him, he will be brought up by a very special family and couldn't be loved any more than he already is by you all."

Aiden said, "Do you care if I call him Aiden?"

Dane replied, "No, sir, buster. His first name is Daniel and that's what he will be called." Aiden just smiled. "Now Lottie and I have been up for a long time, and she's put in a lot of work, so I suggest you all get out of here so she can get some rest."

They all moved to leave, but not before congratulating Dane and Lottie, kisses and hugs for them and the baby as well.

On the way home, Erin said to Miriam, "Do you really think he looks like Dad?"

"Oh, yes. Didn't you see the dimple, and his nose?"

"Yes, but I guess I'm just used to seeing dad all grown up. Do you have any pictures of dad when he was a baby that I could compare them with?"

"Hmmm, I'm not sure, but we could go through our albums and see."

Aiden put in, "Well, he might not look like me, but I'm just happy they added my name to him along with Daniel. I feel privileged. Now I feel like I'm permanently attached to Daniel. I just hope he would have been as happy about that as I am."

Miriam replied, "Daniel loved you, Aiden, like you were his own son. I do believe he would be happy that little Daniel's middle name is Aiden."

"Thank you, Miriam. That means a lot to me."

Dane brought Lottie and little Daniel home the next day and settle them into their bedroom. Soon the family found out he had a great set of lungs when he wanted to be fed. Lottie spent the day resting in her bed, and Dane didn't want to leave her side in case she needed anything. As she dozed off, Dane held Daniel and rocked him while he slept. Eventually, he jerked his head up as he realized he too had nodded off. He chastised himself because he was fearful that he could have dropped Daniel while he was asleep. So, he rose from the rocker and paced around the room in order to keep awake. He didn't want to put Daniel down, but he needed sleep so badly he had no choice. He gently laid Daniel in his bassinet and crawled into bed beside Lottie.

He woke when Lottie got up from the bed to check on Daniel. Then since he was still asleep, she came back to bed. Dane reached for her, "Hey, Mrs. Wilshire, did you know we have a son?"

She smiled at him, "Yes, we do and what a fine son he is."

"You did really well. I felt so sorry for you. I know you were in a lot of pain."

"But it was worth it, don't you think?"

"Of course, now that it's over. I just wanted to do something to help you, something besides holding your hand and tell you to pant or to push."

"You did very well yourself. Thank you for being there."

He reached over to give her a kiss, "I'm so happy to have you, and I'm happy you gave me a son."

"Well, I gave you a baby, but you gave yourself a son."

"Oh, that's right. I forgot it's the guy who determines the gender."

"Right. And I'm very happy it was a boy. I know you didn't say it, but I was pretty sure you really wanted a boy."

"How did you know?"

"Just little things, like mentioning that *he* would be taught how to ride a horse, or *he* would need a little tractor of *his* own."

He chuckled. "But you know if we had a girl, I'd love her just as much."

"Probably spoil her terribly. I've heard girls have a way of wrapping their dads around their little finger."

"No, I don't think so. I'd have her out working in the barn just like us guys."

"Huh, I don't believe that for one minute." She turned on her side to look at him before going on, "I have a question. Do you really think he looks like your dad?"

"I don't know. He does have dad's dimple in his chin."

"But so do you. You know you take after your father a lot. I really think he looks like you. Maybe your mother just wants him to look like your father because of how much she misses him. Surely, she can see how much you also look like your father."

"Oh, she knows that. And I have to admit, I won't be upset either way, if he looks like me or my dad."

"I won't either. I'm just happy that he's a healthy little guy."

"Me too. Now can I get you anything? You haven't eaten any lunch."

"I guess I could nibble on a little something, but I really need something to drink."

Dane left to see what he could find for her. Soon he was back with a plate of food and glass of iced tea. He helped prop her up with pillows and after just a few bites little Daniel began to cry.

"Go ahead and finish eating, I'll get him."

"I suppose this is the way it's going to be from now on, every time I want to eat, he'll decide he needs to eat first."

"I'll change his diaper while you get a few more bites down."

Lottie agreed to that, but with Daniel crying louder and louder while getting his nappy changed, she found she was gulping things down as fast as possible. After Dane finished with Daniel and had him wrapped up tightly in his blanket again, he handed him off to Lottie to nurse. Dane watched in awe as Daniel greedily latched onto her breast and settled down totally content.

He laid down by Lottie again, rubbed Daniel's head, and said, "Eat hardy, son, so you will grow big and strong like your daddy."

Soon Dane was back asleep and when he woke, Lottie was rocking Daniel in the rocker. "Why didn't you wake me?" he asked. "I would have helped you out of bed."

"I'm not an invalid. I'm fine. You needed your sleep. But there's something you need to know. Daniel messed his pants after he finished eating, and when I went to change his diaper, you had put it on backwards. The tabs go in the front, not the back."

She laughed and Dane did too.

The next day Dane hated to leave Lottie to go to work, but he knew his mother and the girls would take good care of her and Daniel. He moved slower than normal because they had missed sleep during the night with Daniel's feeding schedule, but he figured this was all part of having a family and he was happy to lose a little sleep for his son, if he had to.

Aiden was in the office when Dane came out to the barn, "Hey, how's dad today."

Dane yawned and replied, "Sleepy. I just might have to throw Tom out of the loft tonight so I can get some sleep."

Aiden laughed. "I know what you mean. I remember when my sisters were born, the whole house was awake when they were. They made sure of that."

"How do people do it when they have several kids?"

"Don't ask me. So, are you here to just talk, or do you want to work today?"

"What needs to be done?"

"Well, I think there's something wrong with a cow, but I'm not sure. Would you want to take a look at her and tell me what you think?"

"Sure, but first I need to go over the books. I'm sure there's bills to be paid, and if you know of anything needing ordered, let me know."

Aiden left Dane alone but when he returned, he found Dane in the office with his head on the desk fast asleep. He smiled, went and shook

Dane and told him to go up to the loft bedroom and get some sleep. The rest could wait and working when he is sleepy would just cause him to make mistakes anyway.

Homecoming and the Senior Prom was the following weekend, and Aiden and Erin went to the game on Friday night. Tupelo won the game giving the seniors more reason to celebrate besides the prom. They also went to the prom. Tom wore his black suit he had bought to wear to Daniel's funeral. The memory brought sadness to him as he put it on. He supposed he would have these sad memories every time he wore the suit, and for that reason he decided that this would be the last time he would wear it. It wasn't the suit's fault, it was an expensive one and looked really sharp on, but the memory was just too painful to relive over and over.

Erin wore a pastel pink floor length gown. It was fitted down to the knees, but below the knees it was flared. The waist sported a chiffon cummerbund with long tails in the back. The low neckline showed just a little cleavage. Aiden felt sure he was going to the dance with the most beautiful girl in town.

They danced nearly every dance, and eventually a boy came up to them and tapped Aiden on the shoulder to cut in. Aiden turned around and stared at the boy.

"Excuse me," the boy said, "may I cut in?"

"Oh, hi, Jeff," Erin said. "Let me introduce you to my husband. Aiden, this is…"

"Your husband!" Jeff exclaimed. "You're married?" He turned and stalked off.

Aiden smiled at Erin. "Guess he changed his mind. Did you want to dance with him? Because if you did, I could…"

"Oh, stop it. You know I don't want to dance with anyone but you. Now are we going to finish this dance or just stand here talking?"

He chuckled, and swung her into his arms, holding her close to him, "Your wish is my command, Mrs. Roberts."

Sunday morning, when Dane came to the breakfast table, Aiden was already there. "I checked on that cow you thought had something wrong with it. I think we need to call the vet tomorrow and have him come out and take a look at her."

"What do you think is wrong?"

"Could be several things. She's not eating, just laying around. I've called the vet and he can't come till tomorrow."

Tom rushed into the room for breakfast and was happy to see Aiden was there. "Hey, I wanted to ask a favor."

"What is it?" Aiden asked.

"Well, I've ordered some vinyl plank flooring for my grandparent's house and wondered if you would help me put it down."

"Happy to. We can get a good start on it today if you'd like."

"Sure, after I get my chores done."

"I can help today," Dane added. "But tomorrow I have to be here when the vet comes."

"Why do we need a vet?" Tom asked.

"A cow's down. We need the vet to take a look at her."

After breakfast the guys all got busy with chores, and soon were loading the truck up with tools needed to work on Tom's grandparent's floors.

His grandparents were surprised to see Tom and bringing Aiden and Dane with him. "What's going on, Tom?" they asked. "Why are you all here?"

Tom explained what they planned on doing, but they complained that they didn't need any new floors.

"Yes, you do, grandpa," Tom answered. "That water that dripped onto your wooden floor has caused rot in that spot, and since it needs repaired, let's just do the entire floor. It's my gift to you." He went to his grandmother, put his arm around her waist, and said, "What do you say, grandma. You'd like a new floor, wouldn't you?"

"Oh, Tom, you're too good to us. You don't need to spoil us like that. You need to keep your money for yourself. We get by."

"But I don't want you to just get by, grandma."

His grandfather spoke up then, "You know what he's really doing, Mom. He's getting the house fixed up for himself because he doesn't think we're going to live much longer."

"Now, grandpa, you know that's not true. You two have given so much for me, I just want to give back. It's about time I took care of you like you did for me." He smiled at his grandfather who winked back at him.

His grandmother spoke up, "You're such a good boy, Tom. We are so proud of you."

"I know, grandma. That makes me happy."

"Ok," his grandfather said, "what do you want us to do?"

"Why not get a glass of iced tea and go sit on the porch," Aiden said.

"Come on, Mom," said his grandfather. His grandfather rose, headed to the kitchen and they were soon comfortably situated in their rockers on the front porch, while the three guys got busy moving furniture out of the living room into the dining room.

Dane cut out the rotting boards where the water had ruined the floor, measured the size of the opening, and Tom went outside to cut the plywood they'd brought to patch the spot. Soon they were tapping each vinyl plank into place, ending with quarter round around the edges, and were finished up before the girls arrived home from school.

As Izzy came out to the barn to see Tom, he was busy putting tools back into the tool room. "Hey, you," she said as she saw him. "What are you working on?"

"Nothing now. Just finishing up."

"What do you say about taking a horseback ride. The horses need to be ridden."

"Sure, go pull a couple of horses out, and I'll be out in a minute."

Soon they were on their way. Izzy decided to take Tom to the cabin in the woods. He had never seen it, and Izzy wanted to share that part of her life with him. He was taken aback when they arrived in the clearing and Tom got his first view of the cabin. He looked at Izzy, and stated, "This is quaint. How did you know this was here?"

She explained how she, Aiden and Lottie had lived in the cabin for several months before living with the Wilshire family. She didn't tell him the entire story, and he had questions, but he figured he would eventually learn more and more about Izzy's life. He loved her, and he could tell she was very interested in him.

He approached the cabin door, and when he turned the handle, was surprised that it opened. He turned to look at Izzy, and she said, "Go on in. It's Ok."

He entered and stopped just looking around at it all. "Who owns this?"

"The Wilshire's."

"So, they let you three kids live here? Why did you leave here and go live with them?"

"Well, we were young when we lived here, underage, and the Wilshire's became our foster parents."

"I see. This place is really neat. Can I go upstairs?"

"I don't care, help yourself."

He headed up with Izzy right behind him. He entered the only room upstairs, and asked, "There's only one bed, where did all three of you sleep?"

Izzy's eyes widened, there had never been a bed when they lived in the cabin. She had no idea why or how there was now a bed. "We slept on the floor in sleeping bags. There wasn't a bed here when we lived here."

He went to look out the window at the woods, catching a glimpse of a deer grazing just inside the tree line. "Well, someday," he continued, "you'll have to tell me the entire story."

"Someday."

They went downstairs and outside, where Tom spied the outhouse. He went to investigate and said he had never actually seen one before. Izzy said, "Aiden built it."

"Well, I could tell the wood wasn't that old, not graying like older wood. So, you used this when you lived here."

"Yeah, after he built it. Before that, we went behind a tree in the woods, dug a hole and covered it."

"Wow, you three were really roughing it. Were you living here just because you wanted to or what?"

"We lived here because we didn't have any other place to live."

"Oh, I'm sorry Izzy, I didn't mean to pry. Gee, and I thought I had it bad living at my grandparent's home." He took both her hands in his, looked deeply into her eyes, "Are you alright?"

"Yeah," she responded, even though he could clearly see the tears in her eyes. "Someday I'll tell you all about it."

"I'm sorry, Izzy, about your past, but I want you to know I think all three of you have come out of it really well. You're in a really good place now."

She turned from him, "I think we should be getting back. I'm sure it's getting close to time to bring in the animals for the night."

When Izzy saw Aiden alone, she went to him and said, "I took Tom to see the cabin today. Did you know there's a bed upstairs in the cabin now? I wonder how it got there."

Aiden looked both directions to make sure no one was around before answering, "I put the bed in the cabin. Don't tell anyone."

"What? Why?"

"It's a surprise for Erin. I want to take her there to spend the night soon, kind of a little get away."

"Aw, Aiden, that's nice. When do you plan to take her there?"

"Soon. But first we need to find out what's going on with this sick cow. Maybe this weekend if all goes well."

57

The next morning the vet showed up early and Dane and Aiden walked him out to where the sick cow was. She was laying down, even wallowing as if in severe pain. As they approached, she tried to get up but couldn't. She couldn't sit still, and worse, she couldn't stand.

The vet walked slowly toward the cow, talking in a soft low voice, so as not to scare her any more than she already was. The other cows in the pasture were far away from the sick cow, for which they were glad. The vet took the cows temperature, but said she had no fever which was a good sign. He asked if she was eating, and Dane answered that she hadn't eaten for at least three days that he knew. He asked a couple more questions about what they had tried or hadn't tried. He checked her eyes, pried her mouth open to look down her throat. When he was done examining the cow, he said there were a couple of things it could be. He asked what kind of food did all the cattle eat lately, and Aiden explained that it was mostly the grass that grew in the pasture, but they had supplemented it will bales of hay occasionally. The vet wanted to know what kind of plant the hay was made of, and Dane answered that it was bought from a neighbor down the road, and he'd have to ask him and let the vet know. The vet said it could be colic and he would give him some medicine for it and hope it would help. That was the only thing he could do for the cow today, but he'd come back tomorrow, and in the meantime could Dane please ask the neighbor what his bales of hay are from.

309

The boys shook his hand and thanked him for coming out. On the way back to the barnyard he told them it might be a good idea to move the other cows out of that pasture until they know for sure what is wrong with the cow.

Aiden asked the vet if he could vaccinate his and his sister's horses while he was there. Aiden let him know that he wasn't sure if his mother had ever vaccinated them before but just to be safe, he wanted them vaccinated, so the vet did that while he was there.

Then he looked at the llamas, and sheep and asked how they were doing. Dane assured him they were all just fine and didn't need anything. The veterinarian asked, "How has it been raising the llamas? You don't see much of them around here."

"It's good," Dane answered. "We always win ribbons each year because we only have the best quality llamas. And we get top dollar whenever we sell. It's worth it."

"That's good. If you have a problem with a llama, I'd have to do some research first because I don't get calls for them. Where do you sell them since we don't see them around here?"

"We have to leave the state. We've gone to Georgia, Kentucky, Tennessee, and once even to Florida."

"I had no idea there were that many people raising llamas. Interesting. Well, I'll see you boys tomorrow morning."

"Thanks again."

When Dane entered the office, he called his neighbor who had sold him the hay and found out it had been oats.

Therefore, when the vet came back the next morning and found out it had been oats the cattle were fed, he said, "I think it's colic then that the cow has. Let me go out and see her. Dane walked out to the pasture with him, and again the cow was laying down and definitely in distress. He said to Dane, "Well, I'd say it must not be colic then. The medicine should be working by now if it were." He examined the cow and said he felt the cow was worse than she had been yesterday.

He was perplexed. He stuck a needle into the cow's midriff in hopes if the cow was bloated it would release the pressure, in case that was the problem. He asked Dane if he was certain the cow was not pregnant because even though he listened to the cow's heart, he heard only one heartbeat. Dane was certain the cow was not pregnant.

Soon the vet and Dane were headed back to the barnyard and the vet said he would do more research to see if he could come up with another prognosis.

The next morning, Dane went to check on the cow only to find she had died. He called the vet to let him know and the vet asked if he could come out to see the cow. "Of course," Dane replied.

Soon the vet arrived, and Dane and Aiden both walked with him to the pasture. They rolled the cow onto her side, and the vet made an incision down the cow's breast, opened the slit only to find her insides had turned black.

"Come here," he said to both boys. He pulled the incision open for them to see what he had found. "This is what I was afraid of."

"What is it?" Dane asked.

"It's called Blackleg. It's a bacterial disease. It can be from the food she's eaten or in the ground. I'm surprised she didn't have a fever. Do you see how mottled the meat is? Her leg muscles in one or both legs will also show the same thing if we cut into them." He sighed. "You said the other cattle have eaten the same hay that this cow ate, right?"

"Yes, do you think they are sick also?"

"I want to take a look at each one of them. Is that possible?"

"Sure," Dane responded, "Aiden and I can get our horses and rope one cow at a time for you to inspect."

As the boys walked back to the barn for the horses, Aiden said, "You know I've never roped a cow before, right?"

Dane laughed, "And how often do you think I have? Guess we'll look like a couple of green horns out there. Cowboys we're not."

It became quite comical watching them attempt to rope a cow. They both tried to rope one cow at a time, one on each side of the cow they were trying to rope. They threw the ropes over and over, aiming for the head, but falling short or long. They both began to laugh, and when they looked at the vet, he was laughing too. He called to the boys, "Do you want some help?"

Dane answered, "I think we could use it. Go to the barn and choose any horse."

Soon three ropes were being thrown at one cow, and eventually one or the other of them would hit the target. Then as that cow struggled against the rope, Aiden would get down from his horse, and get close enough to throw another rope around his head, while the vet roped his leg or a couple of legs, depending on what he could catch.

This continued through the morning, and by noon they were tired, and needed a break. They rode their horses back to the barn, giving them a drink before tethering them to a hitching post. The boys invited the vet to eat lunch with them and he gladly accepted.

During lunch, they regaled the others with their hilarious antics trying to rope the cows and told everyone they had to do it all over tomorrow because they were too tired to continue today.

As they walked the vet to his vehicle, he admitted he hadn't been on a horse in years. "I feel a little bow legged and I'll bet I'm so sore tomorrow I won't want to get out of bed."

Dane and Aiden laughed, and Aiden said, "By the time we're done with this, if we get done tomorrow, we'll all probably have saddle sores."

The next day was a repeat of the previous day, but by noon they had finally finished with the last cow. Again, they invited the vet to lunch, and he gladly accepted. He let both Aiden and Dane know he didn't notice any problems with any of the other cows, to which they were very thankful.

"However," the vet said, "even though we don't see any problems, I'd keep the cattle away from the pasture where the first cow died." He explained that if the cow didn't get the bacteria from eating the bales of hay, maybe she got it from the ground. He recommended something they could spread in that pasture to kill any bacteria, but they'd have to leave the land alone for some time before allowing the cattle back in.

Aiden and Dane got busy herding the cattle into a different area, one now occupied by their black angus. But they had been able to erect a wire fence across the pastureland to keep them apart. They burned the dead cow where she lay in the pasture she died in. Aiden hated losing a cow and was certain he would never get used to that part of ranching. He stood watching the carcass burn long after Dane went back to the barn.

They were so happy they had Tom to take care of the sheep and llamas while they dealt with the cattle. They took the time to explain to Tom everything they had learned from the vet about the bacterial Blackleg disease. Tom felt he was learning so much by working on the ranch, something he knew would serve him well in the future because he wanted to remain in the employ of the Wilshire farm and hoped nothing would ever change that. He thought if he could convince Izzy to marry him eventually, he just might secure his future with the Wilshire's.

It wasn't long before it was shearing time once again, and this time they would have Tom and Cody to help, more hands to hold the animals still. Tom and Aiden were on horses to separate one sheep from the flock, while Dane and Cody roped him down. Then three guys would hold him down while one used the clippers. They loaded the wool into the wagon ready to go to market. They next day they would do the same with the llamas. Both Tom and Cody declared it was a messy job, and one they weren't very fond of.

Both Dane and Aiden laughed, and Dane said, "Better never raise sheep or llamas then when you have your own ranch."

Tom looked at Cody, elbowed him, and said, "Did you hear that? We're going to have our own ranch someday."

Cody just shrugged because he knew his mother had other plans for him once he was out of college. Still, spending the rest of this summer on the ranch would be good and he'd be able to save money before college next fall. Tom, on the other hand, fully believed in the dream of having his own ranch one day. He was saving as much money as possible so that when the time came, he'd be ready.

The next weekend, Aiden asked Erin to go horseback riding with him, he had something to show her. After they saddled their horses, she followed him to the cabin. She asked, "Why are we here, I've seen this before. Remember my parents own this cabin."

"Yes, but you haven't seen this." With that he picked her up and carried her to the cabin door.

"What are you doing?" she complained.

"I wasn't able to carry you across the threshold when we got married, so I'm doing it now."

"You are a nut. You could have carried me across the threshold at Mom's house."

After he entered the cabin, he set her down, and headed to the kitchen. She noticed sacks and went to look in them. "Food," she said. "We're eating here this evening?"

"Not only that," he replied. He took her hand and led her toward the stairway. When she stepped into the bedroom her eyes widened. She turned to Aiden, "What's this?"

"We are spending the night here. I thought it would be nice to have a little get away, just the two of us. We'll cook our food out over the campfire like I used to do, and we'll spend the night here tonight." He hesitated, "That is, if you want to."

She wrapper her arms around him, looked into his beautiful big eyes, and said, "Oh, yes, I want to. This is great. What made you think about this?"

"I want you to experience my life while I lived here. At least everything except sleeping on the floor like we did."

"This is so quaint, and romantic. I love you so much, Aiden."

He lowered his lips to hers, then to her cheek, neck, and back to her lips. "We'll have a good time tonight, I promise."

She replied, "I don't doubt that for one bit."

"Now I'd better go get the campfire going. It's getting close to supper time."

"And what are we eating for supper?"

"I brought something I could put on my homemade spit, chicken. And because we took our pots and pans with us when we left here, I brought a green salad, and potato salad and paper plates and plastic silverware."

"Sounds great, I'll get the paper products set out."

Aiden headed out to light the newspaper under the wood he'd previously set up. When Erin stepped out of the cabin, he said, "We could eat here by the fire sitting on this log, or inside at the table. Whichever you like."

"Well, I do want to see my food, and there's no electricity inside."

"No, but the lantern inside is filled with oil."

"Well, in that case, I'd rather eat in. No mosquitoes or other bugs, and it will be almost like eating by candlelight."

"I didn't think about getting candles. I'm sorry."

"No problem. Lantern light will work just fine."

Aiden had brought an extra blanket for the bed, but they both decided they didn't need it. It was warm enough. The next morning, Erin said, "This is a nice little love nest. I say we do this more often."

Aiden smiled and agreed wholeheartedly. They packed everything up and headed for the farm, getting there just in time to get in on the breakfast being served.

Dane said, as they entered, "There you are. We thought you'd died in your bed last night. Where have you been?"

Erin smiled, looked at Aiden, and replied, "Wouldn't you like to know?"

Aiden added, "Geez, can't anyone have a secret around here or are we supposed to be an open book to everyone?" He and Erin laughed, and Izzy joined in since she knew exactly where they'd been.

Soon it was graduation time for Erin. The family rented a room in town and invited all the graduating class and their dates for a party. Music was played, and everyone brought food to share. It wasn't over until Dane finally told everyone he had to shut it down at one am. Everyone didn't want to leave just yet, but Dane suggested everyone who wanted could go to Sonia's Cafe in town that served breakfast twenty-four hours a day. With that everyone began gathering up their things to leave, including Dane and Lottie, Aiden and Erin, and Izzy and Tom.

Aiden couldn't help but notice Tom and Izzy danced a lot during the evening, and as Izzy went out the door, Aiden caught up with her, and said, "It looks like you and Tom are getting pretty close. What are your plans for the future?"

She held up her left hand, wiggling her fingers, "My plan is to get a ring on my finger."

"That's what I figured. Just be careful. No hanky-panky."

"Don't worry, all's well. He hasn't said anything to me yet, but I'm keeping him on a leash."

Aiden laughed before strolling toward his car.

Miriam got a phone call one day, but it was for Tom. She asked Erin to run out to the barn and get him. When he came in, picked up the phone, Miriam was watching him because she knew who was on the other end of the line. He was somber, and after finishing the conversation, he slowly hung up the phone, and just stood there. Miriam went to him and put her arm around his waist, "Bad news?" she asked.

"My grandpa died last night."

"Oh, Tom, I'm so sorry."

"I didn't get to say goodbye to him. The last time I saw him was last month when we put a new floor down for them in their living room. I should have been there."

"Tom," Miriam began, "you couldn't have known. No one knows when they will die. I wouldn't have thought Daniel would have died as young as he was. You need to go see your grandmother, I'm sure she will need you now."

He wiped his eyes, turned and left. Miriam made her way to the barn to let both Dane and Aiden know about Tom's grandfather, then she went back into the house to prepare food to take to his grandparent's house.

It wasn't long before everyone made their way to Tom's grandparent's home, carrying food. Tom wasn't the only one there with his grandmother, there were neighbors and friends from their church as well. The small house felt crowded, and Tom was glad they had put a new floor down in the living room, even if it was so full of people that no one would be able to see it. Miriam made her way to the kitchen to set her dishes on the counter before going to find Tom and his grandmother.

Tom introduced his grandma to Miriam, and Miriam said, "We have so enjoyed having Tom work on our farm. He's such a good boy."

She smiled at Miriam before Miriam went on, "I'm so sorry about your husband. I've also lost my husband and I know the loss all too well. But just take it one day at a time, and you'll get through it. And, please, if you need anything at all, don't hesitate to call us. I'll be glad to come and sit with you. I'd love to get to know you better."

"Thank you. You're very kind, and you and your husband have been very kind to Tom. I know he loves working and living on your farm."

Tom was blushing. Miriam glanced at him, and leaning down, she whispered into his grandmother's ear, "I think he might have his eyes on one of our girls at the farm and wouldn't be surprised if there was a wedding down the road."

Tom heard what she said, and the blush became a crimson red reaching all the way to his hairline. But he said nothing. His grandmother looked at him and said, "Is that right Thomas? Do you have a girlfriend?"

Tom just looked at the floor still blushing. His grandmother went on, "Why didn't you tell me? I want to know all about her."

"Oh, grandma," Tom complained.

Miriam went on, "She's here. Let me go find her and introduce her to you." She went in search of Izzy and soon was back and introduced her to his grandmother.

"Why, Tom," she began, "she's beautiful. Hello, Izzy, I'm very glad to meet you. So, Tom is wanting to marry you, I hear."

Izzy's eyes widened as she looked at Tom. She couldn't believe Tom had already told him grandmother. His grandmother picked up on the communication going on between Tom and Izzy without words, and said, "Oh, don't be mad at Tom, honey. Love is a wonderful thing. I'd love for Tom to marry and settle down with someone like you. Now why don't you come to my house someday and let me get to know you better."

"Yes, ma'am."

Miriam entered the conversation with Tom's grandmother then, "Has any arrangements been made yet for your husband?"

"Tom called the funeral home, the one you used when your husband died. We were there at his funeral you know."

"No, I didn't know. Tom didn't say. I'm sorry I didn't meet you then. There were just so many people there I couldn't get around to everyone."

"My husband's funeral won't be anyways near as big as your husband's."

"Well, when someone dies by accident, it's such a shock I think it brings more people to the funeral."

"Yes, I suspect you're right. Clarence's funeral will be this Saturday. He'll be cremated and buried in the plots we bought years back."

"I'll be there," Miriam assured her, "along with the rest of my family." She looked at Tom them, "Izzy will be there too."

Tom looked like he was out of his element, which he certainly was. He wasn't used to being in a crowd and felt very uncomfortable. He stuck to his grandmother's side like glue and refused to leave her.

Soon a man came up to his grandmother and him. Tom's eyes widened in recognition. "Hello, Tom, Mrs. Tuttle. I'm just stopping by to give my condolences to you about Clarence's death. He was a good man. After all," he said, putting a hand on Tom's shoulder, "he took this renegade in and helped raise him." He chuckled. "Clarence will be missed. He was a pillar in this community, and I was always glad to call him a friend."

"Thank you, sheriff," she replied.

He turned to Tom then, "I'm hearing good things about you, Tom. I'm glad you've changed your ways."

His grandmother spoke up, "All boys have a few wild oats they sew when they're young, officer. Tom is doing quite well now."

"As I've been told. I'm sure he will be able to fit into his grandfather's shoes very well. Now I must get back to work. It was nice seeing you again, Mrs. Tuttle."

"Likewise, sheriff. Clarence always spoke highly of you. I want you to know that."

"Thank you for telling me." He turned and walked away.

Tom said to his grandmother then, "I don't like him."

She responded with, "You will when you need him and he's there for you." Tom thought about what she'd said. Perhaps he was too hasty in his judgement of the sheriff. After all, he was only doing his job when he hauled Tom and his friends in for the mischief they were into. He had to admit, his life was much better now. He figured he must be maturing, and inwardly smiled at the thought.

Izzy had watched the conversation between Tom and the sheriff, and she knew Tom was nervous being around him. Then after the sheriff left, she noticed a half smile on Tom's face and she realized Tom was alright, he had come to grips with his past, moved past it, and would be fine the rest of his life. She caught his eye and winked at him.

Soon it was time to head to the funeral. Tom had come back to the ranch, gathered some clothing, and headed back to his grandmother's house. He had decided to stay with her for a month to support her in her time of grief.

The funeral was larger than Mrs. Tuttle would have expected, and she knew it was because of her husband's stellar reputation in the community. She was so proud of her husband. He had been a good man, had lived a full life, and now he could rest. She would mourn his loss for sure, but she had known eventually one or the other would die first. She was just sorry it had to be Clarence instead of her. However, she knew if she'd been the first to go, Clarence would not have fared well and probably wouldn't have lived much longer. She wondered how long she would live without him. She was tired, tired of life, tired of not being able to do the things she used to do, tired of spending most of her time now just sitting at home, rocking, and wondering when it would all come to an end. She felt like she was just waiting for death to overtake her like Clarence. Well, it had begun, and she would be next, and Tom would inherit the house.

Oh, yes, she had a son, but where was he? He had left, left his wife, left his son with her and Clarence, and was never heard from again. She thought about him, Jason. Where was he? How would he ever find out his father was gone? Did he even care? She decided he probably didn't because after he left, he never looked back, never contacted them, never checked up on them to see how they were or if they needed anything. Tom had been a handful when he was younger in school, and she and Clarence understood why. They understood the anger at being left by his parents. They understood that he had to release that anger and didn't know how. Clarence had tried to help him, talk to him, but Tom didn't seem to want to open up and talk about his feelings with them. They understood that too. As things were now, Tom was a much better son than their son had been to them. She wondered why her own son had turned against them. Did they do something to make him hate them? She pondered that thought but couldn't think of anything. They had raised him the best way they knew how. They had been happy when he found a girl and married. They had envisioned that they would settle in Tupelo, have several kids, and would be there to take care of her and Clarence's needs as they grew old, but that didn't happen. Then as they grew old, too old to keep up their property, they had no help, except when Tom moved to the Wilshire's and began to see their needs and help to fill that need. She and Clarence had always wanted at least one more child, more if it happened, but it just never happened. Still, she was happy when she was able to give Clarence a son, even if she never got her girl she'd wanted. As she looked back on her life, she admitted she had had a good life with Clarence. Her only regret was how their son had turned out.

60

Mrs. Tuttle was shocked two days after the funeral when her son, Jason, walked into the house. "Jason!" she exclaimed. "What are you doing here?"

"I heard about Dad."

"Well, he's dead now. It would have been nice if you would have come to see him while he was still alive. I'm sure he would have enjoyed that." She was angry with him, at his insensitivity to other's feelings. "So why have you come now?"

Tom just stood staring at his father, saying nothing. His anger rose into his throat. It felt like bile, that he was going to be sick.

Jason looked at him, and said crossing the room to where Tom stood, "Is this Tom?"

As he reached out to Tom, Tom sidestepped him, and said, "Leave me alone. I don't want anything to do with you."

"I'm your father. Aren't you glad to see me?"

"After thirteen years? Why would I be glad to see you now?"

"Look, I'm sorry, Tom. I know you've missed me and your mother, but I'm here now."

"Well, I don't want you here, and I'm pretty sure grandma doesn't either, so just go away."

Jason turned to his mother, "I'm sorry, Mom, that I didn't come sooner. And I'm sorry that I've been a lousy son. I guess I'll stop by Dad's grave and pay my respects and be on my way then."

Mrs. Tuttle responded, "Take care of yourself, Jason."

He turned and left, knowing he was no longer wanted because he had abandoned his responsibility not only to his parents, but to his son as well. But the past could not be undone, and so he would move on, back to the life he had made elsewhere. He regretted not being able to reconnect with his son, but he could understand Tom's anger. He went to his father's grave, got on his knees, and wept.

After he left, Mrs. Tuttle said to Tom, "Tom, I know he has hurt you very badly. He hurt Clarence and I also. But we have each other, and that's all that matters. I don't know what I would have done if I didn't have you, you are such a Godsend."

Tom went to her, knelt in front of her, laid his head on her lap and cried. Her heart hurt for her grandson but there was nothing she could do except hold him and try to console him.

After Tom was all cried out, he rose and went outside. He needed to be alone, to think about things. He wanted to go back to the Wilshire ranch and forget about all of this. It was peaceful there, and Izzy was there. He could find comfort in her arms. But he knew his grandmother needed him now and he couldn't leave her alone.

He began to do some repairs that were needed around the house. Small one-man jobs, and it seemed to help. Then after he had been there for two weeks, his grandmother told him he needed to leave, go back to the Wilshire's.

"But grandmother, you need me."

"Come here, Tom." He went to her, sitting in his grandfather's chair. "I will be fine," she continued, "You need to get on with your life. I know you need to work, to keep busy, make some money for your future. And you've got that pretty little girl back there just waiting for you. Go home, Tom."

"Are you sure? I hate to leave you alone."

"I'll be fine, now pack your things and get out of here. You can always come and visit once in a while."

With that, he rose, packed his things, and headed back to his home in the loft at the Wilshire ranch. He was glad to be going back home, back to Izzy. Yes, he was still sad about his grandfather's death, and grandmother now being alone, sad about his father showing up, sad about his past, but he could find peace and happiness at the Wilshire home.

After putting his things in his room in the loft, he headed out to find Dane or Aiden. He went into the office and found Dane at the desk. "Tom," he said in surprise. "What are you doing here? I thought you were staying with your grandmother for a month."

"Well, I planned to, but she sent me packing, said she didn't need me there anymore, but I think she just said that for my sake, not for her own."

"I'll tell Mom so she can check on her soon. Now let's get you back to work." Dane looked at him closely and said, "Are you alright? You look kind of washed out."

"I'll be alright now that I'm back here. Being at grandma's house just brought back a lot of memories, painful ones."

Dane rose, came and put a hand on Tom's shoulder. "I'm sorry about that. If I'd known how hard it would have been for you to stay with her, we'd have brought her out here to stay for a while."

"She would never have done that. She wants to be home."

"Yeah, I guess that happens to a lot of older ones. Home is just more comforting to them."

"She has friends in town that will probably also look in on her, but I think she'd enjoy a visit from Miriam."

"And while we're talking about your grandmother, is there anything else we can do to help her?"

"Oh, there's a lot of things we could do, but I think I'd have to talk to her about it before we do anything. I think showing up without warning to do their living room floor was a little more than they expected, and maybe even wanted. But I'm glad we did it before grandpa died so the house looked good when everyone came to the house after the funeral."

Dane smiled then just as Aiden came in. He said, "Tom, what are you doing here? I thought you were staying with your grandmother for a month."

Dane and Tom looked at each other, and Dane said, "De ja vou."

Aiden said, "Oh, I see. You two have already had this conversation."

Dane said, "Mrs. Tuttle threw him out, and told him to get back here. So, let's put him to work. What needs to be done?"

Aiden and Tom left, and Aiden got him busy mowing. Then Dane came out and motioned for Aiden to come into the office.

Dane began, "I think Tom is still hurting from the death of his grandfather. He was saying how bad memories came back to him while he was there. Let's tread lightly on him for a while."

Aiden agreed before Dane went on, "I've been doing a little research on Black Angus cattle, and here's what I think we should do." He crossed to his desk and turned his laptop around to show Aiden what he had found, "According to the research I've found, you get a really nice calf if you cross them with either a Holstein or a Jersey. So, I propose we go to the auction and pick up a couple more cows to put in with the Black Angus'. It says here, the calves of the cross breeding will be worth more money when you sell them."

"That sounds like a good idea. Let's give it a try. When do you want to go to the auction?"

"How about next week. Now that Tom is back and Cody is here for the summer, they can take care of things while we're gone."

Izzy noticed Tom's truck in the barnyard and was soon in search of him. She found him in the Llama pen and when he saw her, he came out locking the gate behind him. He came to her, putting his arms around her and pulling her close to him.

She looked up into his eyes and saw the hurt, "Are you alright?"

"Not really. Can you just hold me for a while?"

She did and when he finally pulled away, she noticed the tears in his eyes. "My dad came back," he said.

She gasped, "Why? He missed the funeral. What happened?"

"Grandma and I threw him out, at least I did, but I don't think grandma was very happy to see him either."

"Is he staying here now?"

"I don't think so. He wasn't wanted and I made that clear, and I believe he got the point."

"I know how hard that must have been for you. It's been a long time since you've seen him, right?"

"Thirteen years. And I hope I don't see him for another thirteen or more."

"I'm so sorry, Tom."

"I was happy when grandma told me to come back here. This is where I belong. I wanted to help grandma for a while, but she said she didn't need me. I'm not certain of that, but I know she wants the best for me, and she told me you were waiting for me."

She winked at him, "She was right about that. I missed you. I'll go visit her tomorrow. Do you think that will be alright?"

"Let's give her a day or two to be alone with her grief, and then go visit her. I think she'd like that."

A couple of days later, Izzy packed a picnic basket of food, and headed to Mrs. Tuttle's house.

She was very happy to see Izzy and told her to take a seat. She asked Mrs. Tuttle if she could get her something to drink, and she agreed that a glass of sweet tea would be nice.

After Izzy got it, she sat beside Mrs. Tuttle, and Grandma Tuttle began the conversation. "So, tell me about you. Tell me everything. I want to know all about you."

Izzy began with her graduation party and went backward in time. She told Mrs. Tuttle everything, holding nothing back. When she was finished talking, she knew that Mrs. Tuttle knew more about her past than Tom even. And grandma Tuttle felt she would make a perfect mate for Tom, since they both had been through tough times in their life and had come through it doing well.

And by the time Izzy finished with her story, it was time for lunch, and she laid everything out on the dining room table. They enjoyed lunch, and afterward Izzy packed everything up, cleaned up the kitchen, washing the dishes, drying and putting them away. When she finished, and before she left, she told Mrs. Tuttle that on her next visit it was her turn to tell Izzy all about her life, to which Mrs. Tuttle agreed.

Tom was feeling much better after returning to the Wilshire ranch. He was ready to get back to work, eager to move on in life, trying to put his father's appearance behind him. He felt he had lived those thirteen years without his father in his life and he could continue without him. He had put his anger aside and made something of himself, and he wasn't about to let his father come along and spoil it for him. He was a different person now. He'd found peace and solace, was headed toward a bright future, one of hard work, but a loving wife by his side. He was determined that nothing was going to mess up his life anymore, not his father, not his mother, nor anyone else. He was learning the ropes of the business and wanted to learn more, and he didn't feel like any teacher could be better than Dane and Aiden. And he intended to start asking more questions about the business end of the farm.

Dane and Aiden headed to the auction to see about purchasing a couple of different breeds of cattle to add to the Black Angus herd, leaving Tom and Cody in charge of the farm.

The auction was busy by the time they arrived, people milling about, men announcing different things over the loudspeaker and smelling livestock everywhere you walked. It was a busy place full of seemingly disorganized structure. Men were inspecting the cows in the pens to be auctioned off. Dane showed Aiden how his father had taught him to spot a good one to bid on. They entered the different pens to look the cows over, chose a couple of Jerseys they planned on bidding on, and ended up going home with both of them in their trailer.

When they got home, Dane drove out to the gate to the Black Angus pasture, opened the back of the trailer, and the cows came out. At first, they just stood there looking around, not knowing where they were. Then when they spotted the other cows, they slowly ambled toward them. Aiden locked the trailer and gate back up, and that was another job completed. They hoped that they would soon have a couple of new calves to raise and then sell so they could add money to their till.

Dane knew how attached Aiden got to all the animals, so he said to him, "And we *will* sell them. Won't we, Aiden?"

Aiden knew immediately what Dane was getting at and laughed. "You might have to hog tie me when you want to drive them to the auction house."

Miriam went soon to visit Tom's grandmother. While she was there, she asked Mrs. Tuttle if others in the community had been stopping by to visit. Mrs. Tuttle assured her she had many friends that looked in on her. That put Miriam's mind at ease.

Mrs. Tuttle asked about Tom. She said, "Tom was pretty upset while he was here, I just need to know he's put all that behind him and is moving on with his life."

"He's doing fine. I'm sure it was very upsetting to him when Mr. Tuttle died. But I think he's put it behind him."

"Well, that wasn't what I was referring to."

"Oh?" Miriam responded, "Was he upset about something else then?"

"His father coming." Miriam looked surprised, so Mrs. Tuttle went on, "He didn't tell you?"

"No, not a word. But his father wasn't here for his funeral, was he?"

"He showed up two days later. Tom was very upset to see him. And when Jason acted like he wanted to maybe give Tom a hug, Tom pretty much told him to get lost."

"I don't know the particulars about Tom's relationship with his father. I know you and Mr. Tuttle helped raise him, but I'm afraid that's all I really know."

"I feel so sorry for Tom. His dad and mother both left him here with us and disappeared many years ago. Neither one ever called or came to see him. He was so lost. He felt they obviously didn't love him. I think that's why he was getting into trouble when he was younger. He was angry at the world."

"I can certainly see why. That explains a lot and helps me understand him so much better. I'm glad you told me."

Mrs. Tuttle asked, "What do you mean by 'it explains a lot'?"

"About how he came to work for us. I bet you don't know that story either, do you?"

"No, come to think of it. Tom never did say how he got the job on your farm."

"Well, we caught him and another boy trying to steal our horses one night."

Mrs. Tuttle stared at Miriam. Miriam went on, "But don't worry, my husband, Daniel, handled it just right. He didn't press charges but went to a judge and asked him to let the boys think they were being charged with a crime, and when they appeared before the judge, he sentenced them to work on our farm for a month as punishment. Then Daniel paid them a wage for the work they did."

Mrs. Tuttle laughed. "So that's it. Thank heaven for your husband."

"Yes, Daniel was good at trying to help others when he saw the need. He hoped it might turn the two boys around, and it worked that way. Tom and the other boy are still with us even though the month has long expired. Tom is a good worker, and we've all grown very fond of him, including Izzy."

"Yes, Izzy came to visit me a few days ago and she told me all about her past. I think she'll be a good fit for Tom. They both have had a rough life, and having come from that past, they know how to get through troubled times. That could make their marriage strong. At least, I hope so."

Miriam added, "I think you're right. And they seem very well suited to each other."

Miriam said she needed to be getting back to make supper for everyone, and asked Mrs. Tuttle if she'd like to come to Sunday dinner this weekend.

"Well, I don't drive anymore. But if Tom will agree to come and get me, I'd like that."

Tom was more than willing to go get his grandmother on Sunday. As they sat around the table, they began telling stories about life on the farm. Eventually, Lottie turned to Tom, and said, "You don't really know the whole story about Aiden, Izzy and me. I guess it's time you know the whole story."

She told him the story of how they came to live in the cabin across the road in the woods. He was amazed that they were capable of taking care of themselves since they were so young. He, at least, had his grandparents to take care of him, but they had nobody. His admiration for Aiden just increased about a hundredfold. He wanted to ask Aiden questions but would save them for later when others weren't around.

Taking his grandmother back home afterward, she said, "Izzy hadn't told you about that before, right?"

"I knew a little. I knew their mother had left their father. I guess he was abusive, and their mother moved them as far away from him as she could. Then she died of COVID. I can see why they would run away in order to stay together. I think Aiden probably made that decision. And I can't believe he was able to take care of the girls for the months they lived in the cabin in the woods. Izzy took me to show me the cabin. She said they lived there but didn't really say why. If it had been me, I doubt if I would have even thought about Child Family Services possibly splitting them apart to go to different homes. Aiden's very smart. I admire him a lot."

"But Tom, can you see how you aren't the only one with a hard life? Think about what those kids have been through. They had no one to take care of them. Yet, I believe the Lord directed them to the right place, and I know he has guided you to the right place as well. Now that you know everything about the Roberts kids, I hope it will help you be able to get over the hurt from your own past."

"I've already put that behind me, grandma. But I still don't want to have anything to do with my dad. There's just no feeling left for him. He's made his decision perfectly clear to me about how he feels about me by his actions. And like they say, "actions speak louder than words," and his actions were screaming at me."

"I know how you feel, Tom. And Jason has hurt your grandfather and me as well. But I don't want you to harbor a grudge against him. I don't know why he left, and why he left you, but maybe he had a good reason. I just don't know."

"Well, if he had a good reason, he's had plenty of time to tell us what that reason is. But he hasn't, so let him live his life without me. I'm really happy now. I'm happy living and working at the Wilshire's and with Izzy. I believe she will be my wife someday. And some day I want to have my own ranch. I have it all planned out."

"And I hope you can realize all your dreams. I really do. Now I'm so tired and glad I'm going home to my bed."

"I love you, grandma," he said as he looked at her.

"I know you do, Tom. I love you too."

The next day, Tom asked Aiden if he had some time to go with him to his grandmother's house to do a little more work on her home.

"Sure, what did you have in mind to do?"

"Well, this will be the biggest job on the house so far, but I'd like to update her kitchen for her. New cabinets, paint, and new flooring."

"Wow, that will be a big job. Let's see about getting Dane and Cody involved. That will help it go faster. Are you sure your grandmother is up for that?"

"Well, I haven't asked her yet, but I feel so sorry for her, living in that old house that needs so much work. I'll call her and see what she says."

"While you're doing that, I'll go see what Dane says about helping out."

Mrs. Tuttle didn't answer the phone when Tom tried calling, so he decided he'd try her again later. Dane told Aiden he would be more than happy to help out on the remodel.

They got busy with work, Aiden had Tom saddle a horse and ride the fence lines to check for breaks in it. The milk truck pulled into the barnyard to siphon the milk from the Wilshire's tank into the truck. Dane went to purchase more hay for the cattle and horses, and soon he and Aiden were storing it up into the loft.

As they were working, Aiden's phone rang, and when he answered it, found it was the contractor building his house. He begged off helping Dane with the hay, grabbed Erin, and they headed to their house. When they arrived, they were told the house was completed, and the contractor needed them to do a final walk through and sign off on the project.

They walked slowly through the home, but only found a few places that needed touched up with paint. Other than that, it was fine, and they both were so pleased with the outcome. The contractor left and Aiden wrapped his wife in his arms, "Are you going to be happy living here?" he asked.

"Oh, Aiden, this is so beautiful. Of course, I'll be happy here. But I admit, I will be sad to leave Mom's home."

"Well, I'll still be working there, at least until I can build a barn and get some cattle of my own, but you can always come to their house with me."

"Yeah, I guess I could. It's just kind of sad to be leaving Mom so soon after Dad's death. I hope she'll be alright."

"Are you kidding? She's got a grandson to help raise. She'll be fine."

Erin chuckled, "Yeah, I guess you're right. I might feel a little separated from everyone for a while, but I can see how if I go with you when you go to work, it will be a slower transition to my own home." She thought for a minute, pulling away from Aiden's embrace, and asked, "Now what will we use for furniture? It's a beautiful home, but I'd really like it better if it had some furniture."

Aiden laughed, "Well, I guess we'll just have to do something about that. But I'd like to take our time to furnish it. I want quality furniture that will last our lifetime, not cheap stuff. It might take a little time to build up more reserves for that. Why don't we start with our bedroom so we'll have a bed, at least?"

"I can buy some small things though, can't I? Like bathroom things, towels, and other toiletries."

"Sure. That way we could come back here at night to clean up and sleep right away. Then we can slowly add another room and another room until we finally get it just like we want."

"Sounds like a plan, Mr. Roberts."

"What's with the Mr. Roberts?" He asked with a gleam in his eye. He began walking slowly toward her, but she took off running through the house, dodging his arms as he'd get close, squealing in delight the entire time. When he finally caught her, he leaned down and kissed her tenderly. "I wish we had a bed here right now."

"Then let's go shopping," was her reply.

"Now? You want to go right now?"

"Why not?"

He took a deep breath, and relented, heading to the truck after locking the house.

After they got back home to the Wilshire's, having picked out a nice bedroom outfit, Miriam looked worried. Aiden asked, "What's wrong?"

"Tom's been trying to reach his grandmother about remodeling her kitchen, but she's not answering the phone, so he and Dane left to go check on her. I hope she's alright. She could have fallen or something, and without Mr. Tuttle there to call for help, well, I just hope she's ok."

Aiden poured a glass of iced tea and sat down at the kitchen table. He didn't feel like going back to work until he found out if Mrs. Tuttle was alright. After what seemed like an eternity, he couldn't stand the waiting any longer and decided to give Dane a call.

When Dane answered, Aiden could tell right away that something was wrong. "What is it, Dane? What's wrong?"

"She's dead. Evidently died in her bed. Tom's pretty torn up about it. He said that she told him on the way home yesterday that she was very tired, but he didn't give it a thought that there could be something wrong."

"I'm so sorry to hear that. Is there anything Tom wants us to do?"

"I don't know yet. We've called for an ambulance, and they just now took her away. I'm just glad she went to bed and died in her sleep. I think that's the best way to go if you die."

"I agree. So let us know what you or Tom want us to do. We're here and ready to help."

"I know. I will. I'll take Tom by the funeral home to make arrangements before I bring him back home."

The next day, Aiden and Erin went to their new house when the bedroom furniture was delivered. Erin told the delivery guys just where she wanted the bed and vanity, side tables, and side chair. While they were setting up the bed, Erin unpacked and set up some bathroom things she had bought. Then after the delivery guys left, she and Aiden made up their bed, complete with pillows, and topped it off with a white quilt, and added a few throw pillows on the bed, adding color to the all-white room.

They stood back to admire it. Erin smiled at Tom, "So what do you think?"

"I love it. Let's come back here tonight and spend our first night in our own home."

She agreed on one condition, that tomorrow he would hang the white curtains in the bedroom for her. "Do I have a choice?" he asked.

"Hmm," she thought, "not really."

Mrs. Tuttle's funeral was held that weekend. Tom seemed lost, so hurt. Dan and Aiden stuck by his side the entire time. After the funeral, they headed back to the farm, Tom had told them he didn't want any after funeral meal. He felt it was one thing that was just too hard to go through.

He said, "That's the last of my family. Now I have no family left."

Dane replied, "You have us. Let us be your family."

"Thanks. I already do feel like you're my family. Better than any family I ever had. I'm just glad my dad didn't show up at the funeral. But he probably won't know about grandma's death until he reads it in the paper, and by then it will be too late to come anyway. There won't be anyone to come back to see anyway, and he won't know where I live."

He seemed to be talking more to himself than to Dane or Aiden. "Anyway," he went on, "the house will be empty. And I guess it's my house now. At least, I think it is. I'll have to figure out if she had a Will or not."

"We'll help you look for one. She probably has a copy at her house, or maybe a bank safety deposit box. We can go look whenever you're ready."

"Thanks, I'd like that."

Izzy was sad that she would never get to hear the story about Mrs. Tuttle's life. She had been looking forward to finding out about her past. She felt it might help her know Tom better if she knew more about his family's past.

Tom had decided to stay away from his grandmother's house for at least a week, just in case his father did show up. But the following week, he asked Aiden to go with him to his grandmother's house to see if they could find a Will and try to decide what to do with everything in the home. He let Dane and Aiden know the remodel planned for the kitchen of his grandmother's house was cancelled. There didn't seem to be any reason to do any more work on the home.

When they arrived, Tom unlocked the door, but when he entered, he gasped. Everything was in disarray, trashed really. Tom just stood there staring at the mess. Aiden was the first to speak, "What in the world happened here?" He began to walk through the house slowly, checking each room to make certain no one was inside. When he came back into the living room, Tom was still standing where he was when he first entered.

"Tom, are you alright?" Aiden asked. "Who do you think did this?"

Tom seemed to come out of his stupor then, "There's only one person I can think of; my dad."

"But why?"

"Can't you guess? He was looking for a Will."

"To see if he inherited anything?"

"Right. I wonder if he found it?"

"Well, even if he did, the attorney who drew it up would have a copy. So, we need to figure out who her attorney was."

"Well, I'm sure there's no point looking here. If she had a copy, I'm sure it's long gone. And I'd be surprised if grandma left anything to my dad after the way he treated her and grandpa. That might be why he trashed the place, because he wasn't in the Will."

"That would be really stupid."

"Maybe he found the Will and grandma left everything to me. If that's the case, he might have trashed the house to get at me."

"That would be truly sad. I can't imagine any father feeling that way about his own son."

"You don't know my dad."

"But if your grandmother did leave everything to you, what would trashing the house help. It's not your fault if you inherit and he doesn't. Why take it out of you?"

"He probably needs money. I'm afraid I haven't seen the last of him. I could imagine him trying to get money from me, if that's what he needs."

Tom looked at Aiden, and continued, "Let's get out of here. No need to stay. But I'm going to be looking over my shoulder for my dad. He could be out there sitting in some vehicle waiting for me to show up so he can follow me to your house to pay me a visit in the middle of the night. I don't want that to happen."

"I don't either. We'll be careful going home. Make sure we're not being followed. But while we're in town, let's contact Jake and see if he can figure out who your grandmother used as an attorney. Then we'll stop at Home Depot and get a new doorknob for your room in the loft, and even a dead bolt, just to make sure you're safe."

Tom took one more look at the house, locked the door, and walked slowly back to the truck. This was something totally unexpected, and he didn't like the thought of having to deal with his father again. He had hoped his dad was out of his life for good. He was also frightened to think his father might turn violent toward him, if he wouldn't share the inheritance with him. He didn't trust his father and didn't feel like he really even knew him. Thirteen years can change someone a lot, and Tom was only seven years old when his father left. Did he really know his father at seven years of age? Maybe he never really knew his father at all. And if his father had always been violent, or screwed up mentally, he was glad he'd been out of Tom's life all those years. So instead of feeling angry about being left at his grandparent's home, now he was feeling glad that he had been left with them, without his father in his life. He could now view it as a good thing instead of being resentful toward his parents.

Then he began to wonder about his mother. Where was she? Was she still with his father? She hadn't come back with him when his grandfather had died. Had they split up? He pondered the possibilities but figured he would never know the truth anyway so why waste time trying to figure it all out.

They went to Jake's office and waited until he was free to see them for a couple of minutes. The secretary told them Jake wouldn't have time to see them, but since they only wanted to ask him a question, she figured it wouldn't hurt to let them sit and wait.

Eventually, when Jake walked his client out into the front office, he was surprised to see Aiden and Tom. "Hey boys, what brings you here?" he asked after shutting his outer door when his client left.

Tom looked at Aiden in hopes he would take the lead, so Aiden began, "We're sorry for barging in on you. We know you're busy, but we just wanted to ask you a question."

"Sure, come on in."

The boys didn't even want to sit down because they weren't planning on staying but just a few minutes. Tom said, "We just wanted to ask you if you could find out who my grandparents might have used to draw up a Will. They have both died recently, and we don't even know if they had a Will."

"What are your grandparents names?"

"Clarence and Wilma Tuttle."

"Well, I can tell you that they were my clients, and that yes they both had a Will."

Tom's eyes lit up. "That's great."

"Tell you what," Jake went on. "Set up an appointment with my secretary and we'll get together and go over it. And I'm really sorry to hear about your grandparents. They were nice people."

"Thank you. I think so."

The boys turned to leave, but not before Jake asked Aiden, "I know you and Erin got married and you had me put yours and her acreage together into one parcel. Have you made any plans for using it?"

"Our house was just completed, and we're in the process of furnishing it so we can move in. Next, I want to build a barn, and fence off the pastureland."

"That's wonderful. I'm sure you'll do quite well out there. Sounds like you're going to be a rancher, like Daniel."

"That's the plan. He taught me so much and ranching now seems to be in my blood."

"Well, good for you." He slapped Aiden on the back as he walked them to his door. The boys made the appointment to meet with Jake in a few days, and Tom left his phone number with the secretary before they left.

Next the boys made their way to Home Depot, careful to spot a car that might be following them but were relieved that they didn't pick up on anything unusual. They got new locks for Tom's room, and headed home. They purposely used the backroads to get there since they were pretty much deserted of traffic and could easily spot someone following them.

As soon as they got home, Tom installed the new locks and felt much better having done it. He knew the barn would be locked up each night, but asked Aiden to make sure of that before retiring. Aiden could tell he was concerned and assured him he would be safe, especially with all the locks someone would have to get through to get to Tom.

64

Dane let Tom know that Aiden had brought him up to speed on the situation, and that he and Aiden would be happy to go with him to his grandparent's house to take care of the mess.

Tom thanked him, and the next day, Tom, Dane, Aiden, Erin, and even Izzy, headed to his grandparents in order to get everything taken care of in one day. They didn't want to draw it out any longer than necessary just in case Tom's father was lurking around the neighborhood.

While they were working, putting things into contractor trash bags Tom had gotten at Home Depot, Izzy came into the bedroom where Tom was working. "Look what I found," she said.

Tom stopped working to see what she had. It was a small envelope. As he reached for it, he asked, "Where did you find this?"

In the kitchen. I was pulling things out of one of the bottom cabinets and noticed that the floor of the cabinet wasn't fastened down. So, I took a knife and pried it up, and found this."

Tom opened the envelope to find a lot of paper money. He looked at Izzy with wide eyes, "Wow. This must be their savings." As he flipped through the bills, he could see they were all one-hundred-dollar bills. His eyes got even wider. He was shocked.

"I can't believe this. They had all this money but didn't spend any of it on fixing up their house. They must have thought they would need it in their old age, funeral costs, or maybe to send me to college or something. Do you suppose they hid it there and forgot about it?"

"Who knows. But it's yours now."

"Only if the Will says it's mine. But I think I'll hold onto it until we know what's in the Will."

Izzy turned to go back into the kitchen, but Tom stopped her when he said, "Thanks, Izzy. Keep an eye out for other hiding places they might have stashed more money. I've heard old people do that sometimes."

Tom told the others what Izzy had found and alerted them to keep an eye out for money stashed other places. Dane agreed and added, "Let's riffle through pages of books and magazines, check the couch and chair cushions down in the cracks. Check in pill bottles you think might have medicine in them, or other jars and cans. And Tom, what about the garage? Could they hide money out there, you think?"

"Who knows. I haven't been in that garage for years. Let's go look."

Dane and Tom headed to the garage while the others were still busy inside. When Tom opened the door, Dane let out a whistle. "Wow, look at that car. It's a classic."

"Grandpa was proud of his old car. I wonder where the keys are. If dad is the one who trashed the house, I wonder why he didn't take the car. It should be worth some money, I'd think."

Dane walked to the car and tried to open a door, but found it locked. "Locked," he said. "Let's go look for the keys."

Tom found his grandmother's purse where he thought the keys might be but didn't find them. However, he did notice her wallet was in it, so he took it out and found there was not even a dime in it. Whoever had trashed the house had obviously taken what money she had in it. He was certain his grandmother would have had a little spending money to carry. He didn't remember her ever having a credit card and hoped she didn't have any because there weren't any in her wallet. He would have to get to the bank and put a stop payment on anything coming in, just in case someone took a credit card to use.

When he brought this up to Dane, Dane insisted they leave everyone to work on the house, while they went to get the death certificate from the county records, and head to the bank to take care of any bank accounts she had. He didn't want Tom to find out too late that a credit card was being used, racking up a large bill that he might have to pay off. As it was the only thing Tom could do at the bank until the Will w read, was to put a stop payment on her grandparent's checking and savings accounts.

When they came back to the house, the girls said they had opened all the towels, sheets, and other linens, shook them all out, and found more money.

Tom said shaking his head, "Grandma, grandma. What were you thinking stashing money all over the place like that?"

Aiden let him know he also had found money hidden inside some socks that looked like they had been his grandfather's. Dane added, "I have an idea, Tom, do you know if your grandfather had a ladder?"

"Sure, it's in the garage."

Dane headed to the garage and found it along with a flashlight, brought them inside, and set the ladder up at the opening in one of the bedroom ceilings to access the attic. He pushed up on the drywall used to close the attic opening and shone the light into the attic. It was partially floored, and there was a cardboard box that Dane could just barely reach. He dragged it over to the opening and handed it down to Tom.

He took it to the couch and began sorting through it. There were old pictures, of his grandparents when they were young standing beside an old black car, several of people he didn't know, and when he came to ones of his parents, he stopped and stared at them. He saw pictures of himself when he was little, of his parents holding him when he was just a baby. He needed to stop looking at them or he would become too sad, and he didn't want to cry in the presence of everyone. He sat them aside, lifted out a locked metal box. He looked at it and knew there had to be a key around somewhere to unlock it.

"Has anyone found any keys?" he asked.

"Well, we weren't really looking for any. Where might your grandmother keep them?" asked Erin.

"Check her purse. I just put it on her dresser in her bedroom."

Erin went to look but found no keys.

"Izzy, check the kitchen drawers? Maybe she kept them in one of those."

Izzy was soon back with a ring of keys. Tom was able to locate a key for the lock on the box easily since he could tell it would be a small key. When he inserted the key, turned the lock, and opened the lid, he gasped. The box was full of cash, all in wrapped bundles of a thousand dollars all in one-hundred-dollar bills. "There must be thousands of dollars in here." He looked up at everyone gathered around to see what he discovered. They began cheering for Tom, so happy to think it would all be his.

"Not so fast," Tom said, "we haven't seen the Will yet. This could all belong to my father."

"No way," Aiden said. "Surely your grandparents would leave everything to you. You're the one who stayed with them, took care of them."

"Yeah, but I know how much grandma still loved my dad. She felt sorry for him, she said so. So, I could see her leaving him an inheritance. Wow, I wonder why they would put money in a box in the attic. If Dane hadn't thought to look up there, it might never have been found."

Dane said, "Well, now that we've found their stashes, I wouldn't leave any of it here in the house in case whoever trashed things comes back."

"Right, it goes with me, at least until I know what's in the Will."

"Did she have a Will?" Izzy asked.

"Yes, Dane and I found out from Jake that he wrote their Wills, and we've made an appointment to get with Jake in three days. Guess I'll find out then if this money is mine or not."

They all got busy again, and soon had everything in the house either in bags, or boxes ready to be either disposed of or taken to Goodwill.

Dane asked Tom if he could have the keys to the car, he wanted to see if it would start. Soon Dane, Aiden, and Tom were all three in the garage. Dane slid into the driver's seat and smiled when the car started right up. "Anyone want to go for a ride?" he asked. The car was a 1957 Chevrolet Impala four door hard top, red and white in color, with red interior. Automatic transmission.

Tom opened the garage door, jumped in beside Dane, and with Aiden in the back seat, they backed out of the garage. But before they could drive away, Erin and Izzy came running out the front door to stop them.

"Hey, wait!" they yelled waving their hands. "We want to go too."

Soon Erin and Izzy were in the backseat with Aiden and Dane took off. The car purred right along. No blue smoke coming out of the exhaust. It was in mint condition.

Aiden said, "Tom, your grandfather took really good care of this."

"He always said it was his pride and joy. It used to tick me off when he'd say that, because I wanted to be his pride and joy. I guess I was jealous."

They laughed before Aiden asked, "How many miles are on it, Dane."

"28,957 miles. It's barely broke in. Tom, this is great. I hope you keep it. You could drive it in parades. Show it off."

"Grandpa and grandma didn't drive much. They didn't see the need to go anywhere other than to the grocery store. Most of the time Grandpa said he wanted to walk wherever he was going. He said it was healthier, kept him young."

Dane added, "He might be right about that. Look. Do you see how people are staring at us?"

"Not us," Izzy corrected, "the car."

Soon they were back to the Tuttle house. They threw the things into the back of the truck they brought, and Aiden drove to the Goodwill and dropped everything off. Next, they loaded things into the bed of the truck to take to the farm to burn. The only thing left in the house was a few pieces of furniture, furniture that had been searched for money.

They locked everything up, the house and the garage. But Tom said he wanted to drive the car out to the Wilshire's farm for safe keeping, in case someone broke in again and decided they wanted it. Izzy declared she wanted to ride back to the farm with Tom, and they all headed home.

After they got home, Tom told the others how Izzy had rolled her window down and when anyone stared at them, Izzy would ask, 'Do you have any Grey Poupon?"

They all laughed about that, and Aiden said, "Leave it to Izzy."

Dane told Lottie to come and see the car. She was impressed and asked if it was Tom's to keep, but he let her know that wouldn't be determined until Jake read the Will. Everyone was standing around admiring it. The car looked very flashy. Lottie got in, looking it over carefully. She ran her hand over the seat, smiling. She said to Dane, "I wish cars today had a bench seat like this instead of two bucket seats. That way a girl could sit by her boyfriend on dates. Dane smiled at the thought. He agreed he would like that too. It would have been nice to have Lottie snuggle up to him when they were dating. He could imagine dropping his hand to her knee while he drove or wrapping his arm around her shoulders.

Miriam came outside to see the car also. "My, my," she said. "What have we here?"

She went to look it over, "I remember a guy I went to school with had one of these back in the day. His was copper and white colored. He used it to attract the girls." Everyone laughed and agreed it would probably have gotten a guy a date if he drove one of these. Miriam said to Tom, "Someday you'll have to give me a ride in that thing. I never dated the boy in school who had one." That brought another chuckle and Tom promised he would do that.

When everyone finally got tired of looking at the car, Tom drove the car to the barn and pulled it inside, just to keep it safe, he said. That way it would be locked up at night so no one could get to it.

Three days later, Tom asked Aiden to go with him to Jakes office for the reading of his grandparent's Will. Jake said he would read the Will of Clarence Tuttle first since he had died first. They found that the Will stated that if he would die before Wilma, then everything would go to her. But in the case of her already being deceased when he died, everything was to go to Tom.

The same applied to Wilma's Will. Clarence would be the sole heir if she died first, but if he was already deceased, then everything was to go to Tom.

Tom was smiling when they left the attorney's office. He had it all. It was really all his. He decided he would sell the house. Even though he had no idea what the value of it was, it would be several thousand dollars he could put toward a place of his own. And now he felt he could count the money in the metal box, and all the other money found stashed in different places around the house. He could go to the bank with the death certificates and clean out their checking and savings accounts there, and deposit everything in his own account. He said a silent prayer of thanks for loving grandparents who wanted him to have everything they owned when they were gone. He felt blessed and just a couple of years ago he had felt his life was worthless. Now he felt like it had meaning. He was sorry that his grandparents had died, something he never wished to happen, but he was also thankful they had thought of him instead of his father.

That night, he opened the box in his room that contained the money and began to count it. He found that it had two-hundred-eight-thousand dollars in it. Then he counted the rest of the loose money that had been found, and there was another seven thousand.

The next day he drove to the bank and was in for another surprise. He found that his grandparents not only had over nine-hundred-thousand-dollars in a savings account, nine-hundred-fifteen-thousand-dollars, to be exact, along with another fifty-three-thousand-dollars in checking, but also owned CD's worth two-million dollars. They also owned bonds worth five-hundred-thousand-dollars. He was in shock to find out how much money they actually had, and he thought they were poor people. How could his grandparents live in such a rundown house, pretending they had no money, when they had plenty? He had heard that there were people in this world who had no money but acted like they were rich, and people who were rich but acted like they had nothing. Was it a mental sickness? Were people who lived like his grandparents afraid of something? Maybe afraid if people knew they actually had money, they might be robbed? It looked to him like they were hiding from something or someone. He knew that people who had lived through the Great Depression tried to save everything they could after it was over, in case it ever happened again. And even though both of his grandparents had been born after the Great Depression, had they learned to be frugal from their parents who had lived through the Depression? Or did they feel that they had everything they needed, and because they weren't materialistic, they didn't see a need to spend money needlessly, so they just socked it away? These were questions he knew he would never find the answers to.

He deposited the money found in the house into his own savings account and changed the name on their CD's and bonds into his name, closed out all their checking and savings accounts and deposited it all into his own account. He felt he still had too much money in his own savings now and thought he needed to invest some of the money in order to grow it. Perhaps a financial planner would be a good idea. He definitely didn't want to start spending any of it. Not just yet. He was doing fine as he currently was, and would use his finances to become even more wealthy, if that were possible. Even though he was still staggering from the knowledge of his sudden wealth, he wanted to act wisely with it.

As he came out of the bank, he stopped and gasped. The realization hit him like a ton of bricks. He was now a millionaire! Wait, not a millionaire, a multi-millionaire! He wanted to scream it to the world that he was now a millionaire. He was barely able to keep his mouth shut, but his insides were jumping all over the place, he was so excited. Life was now so good to him, too good, he felt, and he didn't think he deserved any of it. He couldn't get to sleep that night he was so excited. He lay awake a long time trying to make sense of life. There was so much to consider.

The next day, he told Dane he needed to go to town and talk to a REALTOR about selling his grandparent's home. He didn't want it to set empty for very long in case of vandalism. So, by the end of the day, the house had been listed at a price of one-hundred-seventy-eight-thousand-dollars. He was told by the Realtor, it wouldn't sell for that price, but he had room to negotiate. He left the keys with her, and mentally figured approximately how much he might have after the sale of the home.

His mind was reeling. He could purchase his own ranch now, if he found one he liked. But he decided he was too young to strike out on his own. He wanted to wait until he learned even more about the ranching business. He needed to learn about animals, horses, and cattle. But he wasn't sure he would raise sheep, although he wasn't ruling anything out. But he didn't think he would raise llamas. But again… maybe he would. He just didn't know. It was shocking to him to realize he might even be wealthier than Dane now. But he wouldn't say anything to him or Aiden about how much he had. It was his secret and he wanted it to stay that way.

He knew the first thing he wanted to do was propose to Izzy. He would propose to her soon and try to get her to set a date if she said yes. But after they were married, where would they live? Would she even want to live with him in his loft bedroom? And if she said no to that idea, where would they live? No, he decided that bringing her to his loft bedroom was unacceptable. Maybe they could rent something in Tupelo, but would she be happy with that being so far from Lottie and Aiden? He knew there was a lot of communication needed between them, *if* she said yes. He was nervous and wasn't sure when he would propose. He wanted to but was still hesitant. What if she said she liked him but only as a friend? His pride would be so hurt, he'd never want to see her again, he would be too embarrassed. But here was his job. If she said no to his proposal, would he even want to continue working for the Wilshire's? He had a lot to think about and wasn't sure about any of it. He wished his grandmother was still alive to talk to. She always was the wise one, the one who could help him figure things out. She had a way of asking questions until you came up with the solution to a problem without her outright telling you what to do, or what the answer was. He felt the hole in his heart, the place she had always occupied. He missed her even more than his grandfather. He supposed that was because his grandfather was quiet, not being very talkative, whereas his grandmother was always there to help, talk to him about his problems, soothe his troubled soul. He felt so alone.

It seemed to Tom that Izzy was showing up wherever he was more often than she used to. He took that as a good sign. She surely wouldn't seek him out unless she was interested in him. He knew Aiden said to keep his distance from her because she was still in school, but hadn't Aiden married Erin while she was still in her senior year of high school? Why should he wait for Izzy to finish school, when Dane didn't wait for Erin to graduate either? Why would there be different rules for different people?

He had tried staying on 'friend only' bases with Izzy, but he found it hard to do. He hadn't kissed her yet, but he wanted to. One day she asked him if he wanted to take a couple of horses out for a ride or take the four wheelers out for a spin. He chose the horses since they needed to be ridden regularly, or they'd get cantankerous and not want to be ridden at all. Of course, they rotated which horses to use each day to work with the animals, but that wasn't a long enough ride.

They rode all over the property of the Wilshire's. Eventually, they found a large tree limb that had fallen to the ground, and they decided to stop and sit on the log for a few minutes to rest. The horses contented themselves by eating grass while Tom and Izzy perched on the log. After they were seated, Izzy said, "This land is so beautiful. Don't you think?"

He agreed and she went on, "It has nice open pastureland to ride on, but it also has woods. Someday I'd love to go exploring some of the woods. They just seem to be calling me."

"Then let's set a date to do that."

"I'd love that, but we'll have to be careful."

"Why?"

"Because when we were living across the road in the cabin, we saw a wolf once and bear once."

"A bear? That's hard to believe. I didn't think there were bears around here."

"Well, I know what I saw. And he stole all our fish we'd caught and ate them."

Tom was shocked about that and decided he didn't think he wanted to go exploring the woods after all. If they should happen upon a bear, how could he protect Izzy? What could he do to get out of exploring the woods with her? Would she think he was a coward if he begged off? If she knew there could be danger, why would she want to go into the woods at all?

He was quiet as he pondered this. Izzy looked at him, and asked, "Are you alright? You're awfully quiet."

He sighed and said, "I'm fine. Just thinking."

"What are you thinking about?"

"Nothing really. Just how peaceful it is here." He lied. He couldn't tell her the truth for fear she might make fun of his cowardice. He continued, "Do you think you'd like to live here, close to Aiden and Lottie?"

"Of course, I would. Where else would I live?"

"Well, there's a whole world out there. You could live anywhere?"

"I would never want to live far from Aiden or Lottie. Aiden risked everything to keep us together and I'm very grateful for what he did for us. I'd never break our promise we made to each other to always stick together no matter what. But why do you want to know about where I'd like to live?"

"I don't know. Just a thought."

"Do you want to move away from here? Go live somewhere else?"

"No, I love it here too. I was just thinking about the future." He had a burning desire deep within him to ask her to marry him, but he couldn't find the right words to say what he felt. He opened his mouth to let her know his feelings for her, but no words would come out. So, he just sat, staring out across the field.

"You're a strange dude, you know that, Tom Tuttle?"

"Strange? What do you mean?"

"You say you love it here, but you ask me if I'd like to live somewhere else."

"Yeah, I guess you're right. I am strange." He thought a minute and added, "Can I ask you another question?"

"Sure," she replied.

He looked at her, "Would you…I mean. Oh, never mind."

"Like I said, you're a strange dude."

He laughed, rose, and said, "Shouldn't we be getting back?"

As they rode back to the barn, she was truly perplexed about her conversation with Tom. Why was he asking such a question about where she wanted to live? And why would he start to ask her a question, but change his mind and not ask?

She turned to him as they rode, and said, "I'll race you back to the barn."

"No, don't." He sounded alarmed.

"Why not?"

"Because I'm not a good rider. I'll probably fall off my horse and injure myself."

"Oh, then I think you need to go riding more often. That's the only way to get good at it."

"You're probably right, but I don't have a lot of time with all the work to be done every day."

"Have you ever heard the saying, 'All work and no play makes Jack a dull boy'?"

"Who is Jack?"

"Nobody. It's just a saying. The point is, you need to make time for leisure. Don't just work away your life."

"I'll keep that in mind. Izzy, I want to ask you something."

"Yeah, you already said that, but you didn't ask."

"Can we stop a minute?"

She stopped her horse. He dismounted. She just sat on her horse looking down at him. He said, "Can you get down?"

When she did, he took her hands, looked into her eyes, and asked, "May I kiss you?"

She stood staring at him. She said nothing, but slowly closed the gap between them and kissed him, just a fleeting little kiss.

He smiled, and wrapped her into his arms, and kissed her in return. more ardently than her kiss.

"Why, Tom, I had no idea you felt that way about me."

"I wanted to tell you, but I just couldn't find the right time and now that the right time was here, I couldn't find the words."

"I thought you just wanted to be friends."

"I've wanted to be more than friends for a long time. But…"

"But what?"

"Your brother."

"What about Aiden?"

"He warned me to stay away from you until you're out of school."

"Oh, he did, did he? Just wait till I get my hands on him. Why would he do that?"

"Aw, don't be mad at him. I know he was just looking out for his little sister."

"But I'm not little anymore, and I don't want to be treated like I'm too young to date."

Now Tom was sorry he had told her about what Aiden had said to him. If he got Aiden mad at him, it could ruin the good relationship he had with him. He didn't want that. He said, "Please don't say anything to him. Let me talk to him." He had decided he would ask Aiden if he could date Izzy. By asking permission, he hoped he could avoid a rift between them. And besides, if he began dating Izzy, it could then lead to a proposal after some time passed. After all, didn't every couple spend time dating to get to know one another better before marriage?

He felt he had another advantage now when it came to Izzy. If Aiden had any doubts about Tom being a good provider for his sister, he could let him know that he was well set financially after the death of his grandparents. He had plenty of money in his savings, had hired a financial planner and now owned some stock in an electric company, and owned some bonds. He could buy land, and do like Aiden and Erin, and build his own house and start ranching. He would also have more money after his grandparent's home sold. Financially he was ready to get married, he just had to make sure Izzy was old enough and ready as well.

And the more he thought about it, the more he thought he should begin looking for land soon. He didn't want to marry Izzy and bring her into his loft bedroom. That was no way to start off a marriage. He needed a home ready for her as soon as they married.

He was very happy to find that Izzy was obviously interested in him. He hoped Aiden would allow him to begin dating her. A warm feeling came over him at the thought of their kiss and he couldn't help but smile. Yes, life was good.

67

One evening as they were all gathered around the dining room table in the Wilshire home, Erin said, "Do you all remember when we would go up into the loft in the evening, listen to music on the radio, and dance?"

They all agreed except Tom. He said, "I didn't get in on any of that." "That was before you came here," Aiden said.

"So, you quit doing it because I came?"

"No," continued Aiden. "I don't know why we stopped doing that. I guess life just got busy, and eventually we just forgot about it."

Izzy put in, "Well, I think we should do it again. What do you all say, after dinner tonight?"

Everyone thought it sounded like a great idea, so they all convened in the loft later. The space for dancing was smaller than it used to be, both because Tom's bedroom had been built in the loft, and there was more hay in the loft now. But they didn't feel that they needed a lot of room. Soon the music began, and the girls formed a circle and began dancing to fast music. The guys watched with pleasure as the girls moved every part of their bodies in tune with the music.

As Izzy took a peek at Tom while she was dancing, she couldn't help but notice that all three guys had smiles on their faces. She leaned over to Lottie and whispered for her to take a look at the guys faces. Lottie did so and got the point. She leaned back to Izzy and said, "I think we'd better get the guys out here on the dance floor too. They're enjoying watching us too much."

As it worked out, the next song that came on the radio was a slow song. It didn't take long for the guys to all rise and ask the girls to dance. The guys held them close, including Tom. He whispered in Izzy's ear, "I love you, you know?"

"I know. But did you talk to Aiden about that yet?"

"Uh… no," he admitted.

"Why not? Don't you want to date me?"

"I do, and I will soon. I promise."

"Don't wait too long, if you're serious, or I just might not be available when you finally get up the nerve."

Tom laughed, but it was a nervous laugh. She had figured out correctly that he was nervous about talking to Aiden. He felt sure Aiden was a reasonable person, but still Izzy was his baby sister and still finishing up her last year in school. Would Aiden use that as a reason why Izzy couldn't get married? Tom was afraid that he would.

Lottie stated shortly before ten o'clock that she needed to get back to the house to check on little Daniel. That broke up the party. They all decided it was time to turn in as well.

The next day Tom met with a REALTOR he had hired to look for land. She had called him about a piece of property she wanted to show him. Therefore, in the afternoon he met her at the address she gave him. It was a farm in the country. He was surprised that it wasn't just land, rather it had a Victorian style home on the property that Tom fell in love with at first sight. It sat on 200 acres, and had a barn, and other out-buildings. The Realtor explained that the farmer had died recently, and the home needed to be sold to pay for the farmer's wife's expenses for her care in a nursing home. The couple had purchased the home back in the 1950's, farmed the land, raised the children who had grown and moved on to other locations. She handed Tom a paper from the MLS which explained that the home had five bedrooms, four upstairs, one down, and three and a half baths.

Tom looked up at the house as they walked toward the front door. He was in awe. Three stories tall and four sides stone. They walked to the steps leading to the front door, and while the Realtor unlocked the door, Tom walked around the large porch which spanned across the front of the home and wrapped around the corner then continued along the side of the house to another door. He looked the porch over carefully looking for any repairs needing to be done and determined that it was in good condition. The left side of the porch ended at the three-story turret at that corner.

The Realtor had the door open by then, and she stood back to allow Tom to enter ahead of her. He passed through the entry room and into a wide hallway. He just stood looking at everything. The wood was exquisite, in beautiful condition. The stairway leading to the second level was on the left in the hall. The wood railing with carved spindles were beautiful. The living room ceiling was at least twelve feet tall and sported a picture rail two feet below the ceiling all around the room. There was a large fireplace with a beautifully carved mantel with two long windows on each side. He was glad none of the woodwork had been painted. Large columns separated the living room from the dining room, and the fireplace had small columns to match the larger ones. The floors were wooden with different types and colors of wood in a border around the room. Tom figured with a little sanding and refinishing they could sparkle.

On the left, just inside hallway was a five paneled door. He slid the door back into the wall and found a room that was inside the turret he'd seen on the left side of the home. Rounded walls full of long windows. The REALTOR explained this was a sitting room, or parlor as they used to be called. It was where the Victorians received guests that came calling.

Back into the living room he noticed a five paneled door on the left side, and he went to open it. He found it was an antique half bath tucked underneath the stairway. The toilet bowl's water tank was mounted high on the wall, and the sink was a pedestal type that was quite old. He thought the half bath had probably been added after the house was built. He was pretty sure it had originally been a closet.

Tom closed the door and turned toward the dining room, which had a curved set of windows along the outside wall with a curved seat built of wood under them. Again, there was the picture rail two feel below the twelve-foot ceiling. One wall had a lower single shelf on it, the height of the doors. The Realtor explained it was to display plates along that wall. The floor matched the living room floor with the unique border around the edges.

He saw another five paneled double-door on the left side of the dining room that he went to open. He found they were pocket doors that slid into the walls on each side matching the parlor pocket door. When he entered the room, he saw that he was facing a wall with a row of four long windows, and a door with a long window that exited to the outside. The two walls to the right and left had built-in beautiful wooden shelving. This was the library. He crossed to the door which had a key in the lock. He turned the lock and pulled the door open. It led onto another covered porch, large enough to hold either a table and four chairs, or several chairs for lounging.

He went back inside, turned left and opened another five-paneled door to his right. He was now in a very large bedroom, which the Realtor explained was the master bedroom, as they were called back in the day. There were several long windows, and at the far end of the bedroom was a door on the right that led to a full bathroom. It had a tub, and one pedestal sink. Again, it seemed antique but quaint.

Tom was taking mental notes of things he'd want to change in the home, if he were to purchase it.

He left those rooms and headed back into the dining room and on into the kitchen, where he stopped dead in his tracks. It was a huge kitchen, but archaic. He knew this would definitely have to be ripped apart and completely brought up to date. There was plenty of room for cabinets, and he'd have to hire a contractor to redesign it. He was glad to see it had wooden floors that were still in good shape. He went to the door at the back of the house and walked out onto another porch. A large porch with plenty of room for outdoor furniture. He could look at the land from here, at least, some of the two hundred acres.

The Realtor led him back into the house and to the stairway. He rubbed his hand along the banister on his way upstairs, thinking of all the others in times past who had done the same thing. He wondered how many children had slid down the banister and wondered if he would ever have children that would do the same in this house. If only a house could talk.

At the top of the stairs, the railing turned and ran along the floor and curved again to head up to another level above the second level.

He inspected the four bedrooms on that level, all with wooden floors, as well as the two bathrooms on this level. Again, the bathrooms needed to be updated. One of the bedrooms included the turret which made it larger than the others and had more windows than the other three. He could imagine having a little sitting area back in the circular area.

His mind was reeling. Could he handle such a large home? What could the utilities run to cool and heat the home? What would it cost to remodel what needed to be redone?

The Relator encouraged him to go up to the next level. He thought it probably went to an attic and was surprised to see it was finished out as one large room. It also had nicely finished wood floors with the same unique border that the living room and dining room had.

"What would this room be used for?" he asked.

"This would be the ball room."

"The ball room," he repeated. "Did they really have balls up here?"

"Oh, yes, when this house was built in the 1800's, the wealthy people entertained lavishly. They'd have tables of food, and an orchestra, and invite all their friends in for a lavish evening."

Tom was stunned. Was this more than he could take care of? Would Izzy even want to live in something like this? Maybe she'd want something more modern. What should he do? He'd thought he'd purchase land and build something, but he had to admit, he was in love with this house. He thought of all the memories others had made in the home, and he knew he'd love to make his and Izzy's own memories here as well. He'd love to raise children here, to see them slide down the banister, run around the yard, play in the barn. The barn? He wanted to see the barn.

He told the Realtor, but she told him first he should see the basement. "It has a basement?" he asked.

"That's where the furnaces are and hot water heaters."

"Furnaces, as in more than one?"

"Yes, there are two. One is for the main level, and the other is for the upper levels. There are also two large hot water heaters. There are three and a half baths you know, and with kids, the homeowner needed enough hot water for laundry and baths."

"Laundry. Where's the laundry room?"

"It's in the basement."

"Then by all means, let's see the basement."

The door leading to the basement was in the kitchen, and Tom was disappointed to see that the furnaces were old and probably needed to be replaced. Although the hot water heaters seemed pretty new. He took a look at the electric panel, which was also in the basement, and felt it was also pretty new.

Soon she led him to the barn, which he was happy with. It was large with stalls, and still smelled of animals. He went up the ladder built on one wall to the loft, and found it still had hay stored there. The barn was in good condition which surprised him because he figured when the owner had gotten old, he might have quit farming, allowing the barn to run down. However, when he asked the Realtor about that, she informed him, that even though the owner had quit farming, he had rented his land out to another farmer who also used the barn and kept it up.

He thanked the REALTOR and let her know he had a lot to think about before he could make a decision. She understood.

Tom didn't sleep well that night. He had so much on his mind. He tried to weigh the pros and the cons of the property he had seen. Yes, he could purchase a home with land and a barn, ready to farm. But was it the home that Izzy and he could live in the rest of their lives? If he purchased a home already built, he wouldn't have to build one. He knew all the decisions Aiden and Erin had to make, and agree on, in building their home. Could he and Izzy agree on what they wanted in a home? Could they even find land in the country to build on? This home wasn't far from the Wilshire's which he was sure she would like. However, they had never discussed together what they wanted as far as living quarters. And of course, they hadn't. He hadn't proposed yet, hadn't even begun dating yet. Would Izzy want to keep up a big house or would she rather have a small home?

The next day, he made a trip to town, went to a jewelry store, and bought an engagement ring for Izzy. Having decided that, he needed to ask her for a date, which meant having a talk with Aiden.

He made another couple of stops in town before heading home. One was to see his financial planner. He wanted to discuss with him the idea of purchasing the home, versus building a home.

Later he saw Aiden in the office in the barn. Tom went in and shut the door. "Have you got a minute," he said.

"Sure. This must be serious, you shut the door. You're not quitting, are you?"

"No, nothing like that. It's just that, uh, well, it's just that…"

"Just say it, Tom."

"Well, I love Izzy," he blurted out. "I want to marry her, and I want your permission to date her."

Then something happened that Tom wasn't expecting. Aiden laughed.

"Well, it's about time. I've been waiting for you to talk to me about her," Aiden said.

"But you said …"

"I know what I said, for you to stay away from her, but I'm not stupid. I've known how you feel about her for a long time. And I know how she feels about you too. So what took you so long to talk to me about her?"

Tom looked at his feet, shuffled around a little before answering, "I was scared."

"Too scared to talk to me?" Aiden was surprised at that.

"Well, I thought I was to stay away from her till she graduated, so I figured you'd tell me to stay away from her."

"Did I stay away from Erin until she was graduated? No. I know what I said, but I also know love comes when it happens no matter the age or circumstances. And I understand hormones and how trying to wait to marry can cause real turmoil in both the man and the woman. So, if Izzy is agreeable to date and marry, I say go for it. You have my blessing."

Tom didn't realize he'd been holding his breath until he let it out. He took a deep breath, "Boy I'm glad that's over. You have no idea how hard it was for me to come to talk to you about this."

Aiden laughed, "So that's what took you so long."

"I was afraid you might fire me if I wanted to date her before she was out of school."

"And fire my best worker? Not on your life."

Tom turned to go, saying, "I've got to go find Izzy. She threatened me that she might not wait on me if I didn't talk to you soon."

Again, Aiden chuckled. "Now get out of here, I have work to do."

Tom found Izzy and asked if he could have a date with her that evening. She looked at him, smiled, and said, "You talked to Aiden, didn't you?"

He smiled back and she was ecstatic.

That evening, Tom took Izzy out to dinner at an upscaled restaurant, then told her he wanted to show her something. He drove to the Victorian farmhouse to show it to her. He had stopped in town to see if the REALTOR would give him the key to show Izzy. When they pulled up to the house, Izzy's eyes lit up. "What a beautiful house. Is this what you wanted to show me?"

"Yes, come on. I've got the key." They wandered through the house, Izzy pointing out things she loved.

As they finally reached the third floor, and they were standing at the windows in the turret viewing the sunset together. Izzy with Tom's arm around her waist. Tom reached into his pocket and pulled the ring out of his pocket, got down on his knee and proposed to her. Izzy was stunned. "Tom, I didn't think…I mean…I thought…"

Tom began to think he had misread her feelings for him. Had he rushed things too fast? He stood, "I'm sorry, Izzy. If you're not ready, I will wait. I'll wait for as long as you want me to."

"No, I didn't mean…I mean, yes, I'll marry you."

Tom threw his arms around her, pulling her close, kissing her with all the passion he felt deep in his heart. When he let her go, he took the ring out of the box, and put it on her finger. He kissed her again then.

"You scared me. I thought you were going to say no."

"You shocked me. I mean, this is our first date and all. I figured we'd date a while and then you'd propose. That's all."

He pulled her to him, leaned down to put his forehead together with hers, and whispered, "But you said yes."

"Yes, I did. I love you, Tom Tuttle."

"And I love you with all my heart, Izzy Roberts."

She pulled away but looked deeply into his eyes. "So why did you bring me to see this house."

"Do you like it?"

"I love it. I've always loved the Victorian Era."

"What would you say if I told you I bought the house?"

She was shocked, "What?!"

"No, I didn't. But I'm thinking about it. But I decided I needed to know what you thought before I did anything. Do you think you'd be happy living here?"

"But how could we ever afford something like this?"

"I spoke with my financial planner today, and he assured me I can do it. I won't offer full price. They need to sell, and it's been sitting empty for six months already. I'd think they would consider coming down on the price. And I'll get a loan. It will work, you'll see. But only if you really want to live here."

"It's so grand, so rich. Do I fit here?"

"You deserve the best, Izzy. And I want to give you the best."

"It's only three miles from the Wilshire place, so you could go visit anytime you like."

"How could I keep this place up? It's so big."

"I can hire someone to clean for you if you need help."

"What about that kitchen? It's awful."

"Yes, I know. I figured we'd hire a contractor to tear it apart and design a new modern one for you. And redo the bathrooms as well, and we could refinish all the floors."

"No, I love the old-fashioned bathrooms. I wouldn't want to change anything there. I think the antique look is perfect. But how could we afford to buy it plus do the remodeling as well? And then buy a lot of furniture for it?"

"Not to worry. I can afford it. Trust me. And guess what? It has a barn, and two hundred acres of land. I haven't figured out where the land lays yet, but I can bring one of the horses and ride it to find the survey markers. What do you say? Do we buy it, or do we look for land to build a new house on?" Tom was talking so fast; he was so excited.

For Izzy there seemed to be so much to take in all at once, her head was spinning. "Build a house on land?"

"Well, that's what I figured we would do, like Aiden and Erin. But where would I find two hundred acres to build on? Where would I find *any* acreage to build on? Just think, this is already here, with the acreage and ready to begin farming."

"This is all so overwhelming, Tom. Yes, I love the house. And yes, I would love to live here. And yes, I'm glad it's not far from the Wilshire's. But I'm scared."

"Scared? Scared of what?"

"We are still so young, and to begin a marriage with all this," she said sweeping her arms wide. "It's just more than I could ever have hoped for. I figured this is the kind of home with all that land, that people can only afford as they get older. Are you sure you can do it? I mean, afford the house, and do the farming by yourself?"

"I've been working for the Wilshire's and Daniel, Dane, and Aiden have taught me quite a bit, and if there's anything I don't know how to do, they'd just live three miles away. I can always call them for help. And I know without a doubt I can afford it.

"The Realtor said the man who lived here rented the land out to another farmer. We could continue to let him rent the farmland until we're married and move in.

"I know this is a big step for you, for us. But it would be a great start. And I want to see my kids grow up in a home like this. I want to see them slide down that banister. I want to see them playing in the yard and in the barn and swing on a tire swing tied up under that big tree out front. I want to teach my son or sons how to run a ranch like Daniel, Dane and Aiden taught me. I want a life like the Wilshire's had when they raised their two kids on their farm."

She slid her arm around his neck, kissed him tenderly, and said, "Alright. If that's what you want, let's do it. But before you buy the place, would you do me a favor?"

"Sure."

"Would you get a quote from a contractor on the work you want to do to the kitchen and the floors? And would you get someone to go through the house with a fine-tooth comb to make sure everything works? And ride your horse around the grounds to make sure you like what you see before we make it ours?"

"You know I will."

"Are you sure there's no one else interested in the property?"

"There's not. It's unique. It would take someone looking for that many acres and a house like this. I doubt if there's very many interested in this size of farmland."

"It's unique alright. I really do love the house. Now before it gets any darker, can I go down and look at that kitchen again.

As they passed through the living room, Tom caught her hand and stopped her. She turned to him, and he said, "Can you picture us here in the living room in the winter with a roaring fire in the fireplace? We'd have candles lit around the room, and wine to drink."

"Why, Tom. I believe you're a romantic. And I'd love to snuggle up on a couch right here in front of the fire with you."

They went into the kitchen and Izzy stood looking around with a different eye, no longer just an interested party, but as her own home. She was planning on how her kitchen could look when it was finished. The entire project frightened her, but she trusted that Tom knew what he could do and afford. She had so much to think about.

69

When Tom and Izzy got back to the Wilshire's home, they announced their engagement. Aiden was shocked, as was Erin and Lottie. Miriam wasn't shocked at all. Aiden said, "Geez, you just asked if you could date her today. You didn't ask if you could marry her."

Tom looked sheepishly, and replied, "The time just felt right."

"You already had the ring bought even before you spoke to me today, didn't you?"

"Yeah."

"If I'd known you were planning on proposing on your first date, I would have made you wait longer to date."

Lottie spoke up then, "Oh, stop it Aiden. We've known for a while that they were in love. Don't act like this is all of a sudden." She turned to Izzy and said, "I'm very happy for you and Tom."

Miriam asked, "Have you set a date?"

Izzy replied, "Not yet. But we did discuss my schooling and I think I will finish up school at home here. That way I will have more time to plan and prepare my wedding."

Aiden said, "Well, you know I'm very happy for you both. I just had to play the father roll, you know, put the boy through the wringer. And speaking of father roll, are you going to live in the loft bedroom after you're married?"

"No," Tom answered, "I'll get us a place." He didn't want them to know about the house they were going to buy just yet. He told Izzy not

369

to say anything about it either, not yet anyway. He wanted to surprise everyone after it had the renovations competed on it. And it wasn't their home just yet anyway. Why tell everyone in case they backed out of purchasing it?

Miriam said, "Things just keep changing around here. I can hardly keep up. We have a wedding, then another, then a baby, now another wedding. And shortly after that, we'll probably have another baby."

Everyone laughed, and Lottie said, "Erin's turn."

Erin shot back, "Not yet. I haven't even been married a year yet."

Miriam said she was tired and going to bed, and so did Dane and Lottie. On the way to their bedroom, Dane stopped by Tom and lowered his voice, "Good for you, Tom. You're getting a great wife. I hope you two will be happy."

"Thanks, Dane," Tom replied. "We will."

Aiden, Erin, Tom, and Izzy decided to pour themselves glasses of lemonade and head to the patio. Izzy declared she was too excited to sleep. The air was warm, and the sky was cloudless. Without streetlights the stars were shining in abundance, and Izzy commented on how beautiful the night was. The others agreed and they lapsed into silence for a while. Finally, Tom asked Aiden if he could use the truck and trailer to take a horse for a while.

Aiden looked at him, curious about what Tom was up to. "What are you planning on doing, Tom?"

"Well, I've found some acreage for sale, and I'd like to ride a horse over it to get a good look at it."

"So, you're planning on doing what Erin and I did and build a house?"

Tom just looked at him, and finally said, "Maybe."

Aiden agreed that he could do that, then added, "Where is this land you want to see?"

"I'd rather not say until I've looked at it. I might decide I don't want it after all. No need to get anyone's hopes up just yet. But I've got to find a place we can live in, so I'm beginning to look around now to see what I can find."

Aiden looked at Izzy then, "So you don't want to live in the loft, huh?"

Izzy looked at him with disdain, "Not really. But if that's all we can afford, I'd do it."

"I can't see you being happy with that."

Tom spoke up then, "She's not going to live in the loft. I can promise you that."

"Well, if you need any help finding a place to live, just let me know," Aiden put in.

"I've got a REALTOR to help me."

"Wow, you've been busy."

"I don't want to let the grass grow under my feet," he replied before taking another swig of his drink.

The next day, as Aiden was passing the office door, Dane called him in. He had been doing some research on raising cattle and wanted to share what he'd found. "I found out about this study that was done in another country. And it's pretty interesting. They've found that cattle tend to slow down on their eating in the summer, and if you give the cows beer they tend to eat more."

"What? You're kidding? Beer?"

"That's what it said. And if they eat more, they grow larger, and you make more money when you sell them."

"And what? You want to try this?"

"Why not. If it doesn't work, all we would be out is the cost of the beer, but if it works, we'll make more money."

"You're insane, you know that?"

"Maybe, but I say why not?"

"It's your cows. Do what you want with them, but the neighbors might wonder why your cows are staggering out in the field when they're drunk."

"I don't believe you need to give them that much."

"Well, you figure it out. How will you get the beer down their throats?"

"I haven't figured that part out yet. And I've got to figure out how much to give them."

Aiden took off his hat, scratched his head, and as he turned to leave, he said, "What a waste of good beer. I've heard of everything now."

Dane just laughed and turned back to the research on his computer.

Izzy seemed to be in a daze for several days. She was ecstatic at the prospect of marriage to Tom, but still fearful that his plans might not work out as he wanted. He seemed so sure of himself, and he mentioned that he had a financial planner, so he must have gotten quite an inheritance from his grandparents after all. Of course, she knew he'd found several thousand stashed in different places in their home, and he'd gotten money from the sale of their home, but she didn't figure that was much from the condition of the home. She just couldn't figure out how he could afford that home and two hundred acres. Was he just not thinking straight? Was he being impulsive? In such a hurry to find a place for them to live, that he was making rash decisions? Yet, he assured her that his financial planner agreed that he could afford it. So where did the money come from? Was he taking out a large loan to do the deal? Perhaps getting them into too much debt to start their marriage with hanging over their heads? Thinking about that frightened her. Was he involved in something he shouldn't be involved with? Perhaps something illegal? She knew he'd been in trouble with the law before, and hoped he wasn't reverting to his bad ways. She thought he had put all that behind him, but now she had questions. Had she agreed to marry him too hastily? She decided she had to confront him about it.

Later in the afternoon, when he brought the horse back, she went out to him. She waited until he had the horse in the barn and was brushing him down before saying anything.

She began with, "Would you like a cold glass of something to drink?"

"Yeah, just water, please."

She went to the house and brought him a large bottle of cold water, handed it to him, and said, "Can we talk?"

"Sure, do you want to talk about that land I just went to see? It's a great piece of land. The farmer's been plowing and planting quite a bit of it, and he's got a good-looking crop to harvest this fall. If I buy the property, I'd get a cut of the proceeds."

"That's nice, but that's not what I wanted to talk to you about."

Tom could tell by her voice that she was bothered about something. He stopped brushing the horse and looked at her.

She hesitated to say what was on her mind. He walked over to her, took her hand in his, and asked, "What is it, Izzy? I can tell something's bothering you."

She looked up at him and said, "I need to know how you can afford that house and that land. I know you found some money in your grandparent's home, and that you got the money from the sale of their home, but I know that's not enough to buy that property."

He looked around before answering her. He didn't want anyone to know how much he had really inherited from his grandparents. He lowered his voice and answered, "Izzy, I'm a multi-millionaire."

"What?!" she said very loudly. She was in shock.

"Shhh. I don't want others to know."

"But how?" She was frightened at his answer. How could that be?

"My inheritance from my grandparents."

"But they didn't have much, right? I mean, look at their house, the condition it was in. Surely, they didn't have much."

"But they did. I've heard of people who are rich, but they don't want people to know they're rich, so they live like they're poor. Then there's people who are poor but want people to think they're rich. My grandparents were rich, but no one knew it. All their money was in

CD's, stocks, and bonds. Plus, they had a nice wad in their saving and checking accounts."

"Are you sure that's where the money came from?"

Tom stepped back, dropped her hand, and said, "You don't believe me, do you?"

"I do. I want to. It's just a lot to wrap my head around. I worried about..." she stopped afraid to go on.

"You thought I had gone bad again, doing things like I used to. Do you believe I'm into illegal things? If that's what you think of me, maybe we shouldn't get married."

She could feel his anger way down to her bones. She was so sorry she had doubted him. "Tom," she began, "I'm so sorry. Please forgive me. I shouldn't have doubted you. I trust you. Really, I do. I just had a thought that maybe... well, it doesn't matter now what I thought."

"Look, I know I've done some bad things in the past, but that's behind me now. I suppose I'll still have to live down my reputation I had back then. But believe me, I'll never be like that again. Izzy, I need for you to believe in me, to trust me."

He was holding both her arms, looking into her eyes. Searching them to see how she really felt about him. She teared up and soon tears were sliding down her cheeks. He put a hand under her hair, wrapping his fingers around her head and wiped a tear away with his thumb, then he lowered his lips to hers. He could taste the salt from her tears in the kiss. He was sorry he had hurt her. She moved closer to him, and his arms held her tight. She wanted to stay like this forever. He hadn't meant to be so gruff. She vowed in her heart she would never mistrust him again. She wanted their marriage to be strong, right from the start, and she felt that as long as they were both honest with each other, and really trusted each other, they would be happy. She would support Tom in whatever endeavor he undertook, she could help to make it work.

"I'm sorry, Izzy. I didn't mean to hurt you."

"No, I'm sorry that I doubted you. I'm the one at fault." She wiped her tears away, and asked, "May I ask you a question?"

He answered, "You know you can ask me anything."

"You said there was a farmer who farmed quite a bit of the land. Do you plan to keep the land as farmland, or ranching?"

"Well, I don't really know that much about farming, so I was thinking about letting that farmer continue to farm what he's farming now, but there's still enough land for a herd of cattle. I could always start with that and see how it goes. Then eventually, I might turn some of those other fields into cattle pastures as my herd grows. That way I'd still be making money from the crops while my herd grows. But who knows, maybe I'd want to just continue renting out the farmland to the farmer. That is, if he wants to continue farming it."

"It sounds like you've given this a lot of thought."

"I think I have. Now I've got to call a contractor to come and look at the kitchen and get his bid, and the REALTOR has an inspector I am going to meet with tomorrow to go through the house with a fine-tooth comb."

"Boy, when you decide to do something, you move awfully fast."

"Except on proposing to my girl." He smiled at her and went back to brushing down the horse.

70

om asked Dane if he could have a couple of days off, which was granted. He then met with the contractor and an inspector at the house. The contractor said he would draw up some plans for the kitchen and get back with Tom. The inspector took several hours, so Tom left and went back to the Wilshire's with the understanding that the inspector would contact him when he was finishing up and Tom could come by and go over what he found.

The inspector had stated that because it was an old home, Tom could expect him to find quite a few things needing repaired. Tom was reasonably sure of that already, and in fact, he let the inspector know he didn't have to inspect the furnaces or the air conditioners, because he had already decided to replace them.

"She is a real beauty though, isn't she." the inspector said admiring the woodwork.

"That she is," agreed Tom. "Oh, and don't bother inspecting anything in the kitchen because I've already decided to rip it apart and install a modern kitchen."

"That's fine. Say, can I ask you a question?"

"Sure," Tom answered with curiosity.

"Are your parents planning on purchasing this house?"

"No, I am."

The inspector seemed very surprised that someone so young had the financial ability to purchase an old treasure like this one. "You're a very fortunate young man then, I must say."

"That I am," Tom answered with a smile.

"I'd hate to see this beautiful house run down if it sat for a long time."

"Me too."

Later he met with the inspector again and he told Tom that usually he found problems with plumbing, electrical, heating and air. But he was surprised at how well the house had been kept up. He said, "I expected to find old knob and tube wiring, but the whole house has been rewired. The electric panel is in great shape, and so is the plumbing. Most of it has been replaced, even though the older fixtures have been left. All the windows open and close properly, even though they do allow air around them. They don't seal tight like the new ones."

"That's ok, I want to keep the old ones. The more of the old we can keep, the happier we'll be."

"The only thing I found was a couple of termite tunnels up the back foundation. But I didn't find any damage in any wood. I'd encourage you to have the house treated."

Tom thanked him, wrote him a check, and locked up the house and headed home. He was excited and could hardly wait to get the estimate on the kitchen remodel.

He decided on the way back to the Wilshire's to take a detour to see the REALTOR. He was ready to put in an offer even before he got the estimate on the kitchen. When he walked in, he handed the keys of the house to the REALTOR and said, he wanted to make an offer on the home.

She led him into a conference room and began to gather papers to write up the offer. "I want to offer $300,000 cash," he told her.

"But it's listed at $499,000. That's quite a drop. I don't think that will be acceptable to the sellers."

"Who are the sellers anyway, if the lady of the home is in a nursing home?"

"The kids. There are three of them, and they will all three have to agree on the offer. It could take a while to get a reply from them."

"Well, let them know I will be glad to close within two weeks, and I'll pay all their closing costs."

She didn't look too pleased but agreed to write it up. He signed it and said he'd be waiting for her to get back with him about it. And he let her know he didn't want to go back and forth in negotiations. Either they accept his offer, or he'll look elsewhere. She figured she just wasted her time writing up such a low offer.

That evening at the dinner table, Aiden asked Tom what he was busy doing that he needed two days off from work. "I'm trying to find a place where Izzy and I can live after we're married."

"Any success?"

"Maybe. We'll see." He stole a glance at Izzy and winked.

Izzy soon had her books she had ordered for her schooling. She wanted to get busy on it right away so she could graduate faster. Tom hardly saw her after that since she had locked herself away in her room, hitting the books hard.

Dane and Aiden took a ride on the four wheelers to check on the field of oats to see how it was coming along. They were happy with what they saw, and decided it would be ready to cut soon, or so they believed.

Tom got the name of the farmer who was renting the farmland on the house he wanted to purchase, a Mr. Crawford, and met with him to make plans with him for when he owned the home. "I want you to continue to farm the land, if you're agreeable."

"That would be great. I figured once it sold, I'd have to lose the income I made by farming that property."

"Well, I'm not a farmer, I only know ranching, and planned on finding a place I could raise cattle. And it's going to take a while before I can move into the house. There's some work I want to do on the house first. And I want to thank you for taking such good care of the barn. It's in great shape."

"Felt I needed to if I was to use it."

"Well, thanks again."

They agreed to terms for the rental of the land, and what Tom's percentage would be on the sale of the crops. Tom had noticed that a lot of the fields had been planted in cotton, and even though he knew it was a good cash crop from what Mr. Crawford said, still Tom asked him if his crop next year in one of the fields could be oats for his cattle he planned to put on the property. Mr. Crawford agreed and said he also had planned to plant field corn next year that his cows would also like. That pleased Tom also. They shook hands and Tom let him know he would have his attorney draw up the papers on their agreed deal.

A couple of days later, he got a call from the REALTOR asking him to come to her office. Soon he headed into Tupelo. She let him know that his offer had been accepted. Tom let out a sigh. He had been worried that he'd have a problem trying to convince the sellers to accept the offer. He's heard how often the children would argue and fight over their parent's property.

"Why did they accept so readily? You didn't think they would."

"Well, they needed the house to sell, and they knew it might be a hard property to sell because of the price, as well as the type of property it was. They knew it would take someone who would want to farm the land, and there aren't many around wanting to begin farming, and especially at such a high price. Besides they needed the money to pay what is needed to the nursing home. They wanted it to be over. They made a nice chunk of money from the sale of the contents of the home, and they said that was enough."

"Well, I'm glad it all worked out that way. So did they sign the offer?"

"I've got it right here. I'll take it to the title company as soon as you leave."

Tom wrote out the checks she needed to take to the title company, and when he left her office, he was feeling mighty happy. He could close on the property as soon as the paperwork was completed and get the contractor in there to begin on the kitchen as soon as possible. He made a trip to his bank to transfer funds into his checking account for the closing.

Soon the contractor called him and wanted to go over what he'd come up with a design for the kitchen. Tom and Izzy met him at his office. Tom wanted Izzy there because if it was to be her kitchen, he wanted her approval on it.

When they sat down, the contractor unrolled the blueprints that had been drawn up. He explained what they were looking at. Where the cabinets were to be placed, the range, refrigerator, and sink. He put the sink under the short window of the house, where it was currently, with the dishwasher beside it. The stovetop, complete with a downdraft, was on the island, The double wall ovens would be to one side of the Island, along with the built-in four-door, double drawer, see through large refrigerator. The island would be large enough for six bar chairs around it. The cabinets would be custom made, thirty-six inches tall, and finished to match the other wood in the house. There would be a built-in wine rack at one end of the Island. The counters would be granite, and Izzy could pick out which color she wanted. The kitchen would be large enough for either a breakfast area at the other end of the kitchen or could have a small couch or overstuffed chairs for company to sit on while Izzy worked in the kitchen. The contractor would install wanes coating and chair rail around the walls in harmony with the age of the house. The wood would be finished to match the flooring. There would be cam lights around the outer walls of the kitchen and drop lights over the eat-on bar. He recommended putting long windows on the end wall of the kitchen opposite from the seating area, where a breakfast table could be situated with a great view of the outside. Izzy clapped her hands, and said, "Oh, yes. I love that idea." Tom agreed even though some of the stone exterior would have to be removed to allow for two long windows.

Izzy was excited and couldn't wait to see the finished room. The contractor let Tom know it would be an expensive kitchen, but Tom didn't care. Only the best for Izzy. They signed the contract hiring the contractor, and he let them know he could put his guys to work on it as soon as Tom owned the home.

Izzy squeezed Tom's arm as they left his office. "I'm so excited. I can't wait to be able to cook a meal for you in a kitchen like that. And in the area where he said could be a breakfast area, I want to put a couple of overstuffed chairs like he said instead of a breakfast area. We won't need a breakfast area with bar chairs around the island. Do you agree?"

Of course, Tom didn't care what they did as long as Izzy was happy. "I've been thinking about our wedding too," she went on. "I don't want a large wedding. I haven't been here long enough to have friends from school, and I'm pretty sure you don't mind not inviting your old friends. Right?"

"Right."

"So, what do you think about getting married on the Wilshire's patio with just all of us. No one else. And afterward we can have a meal at their house. What do you think?"

"Sounds good except for one thing. I want our house to be finished by the time we get married. I want it all furnished, and ready for us to move in. Why don't we have a meal catered and we can then invite everyone to our house, and we can have tables in the third-floor ball room. That is, if we can keep the house a secret till then."

"Oh, that sounds wonderful. I like that idea. The others might not like us getting married at the house, but when I give them the reason for that, surely, they'll understand. What do we tell them if they want to fix a meal afterward?"

"We'll tell them we don't want that, but that we want to do it our way. Then afterward, we'll ask them to get in their cars and follow us, and I want to have Miriam ride with us in my '57 Chevy."

"Can you imagine their faces when we pull up to our house and they see it for the first time.?"

"Won't they be shocked? But I do want to have it be a surprise for them. It would mean a lot to me."

"To me too."

losing day came soon for the purchase of Tom and Izzy's house. Tom had included Izzy on the Deed, and they celebrated after receiving the keys to their home. Izzy wanted to go back to the house and walk through it again. Tom would change the deed after they were married so it would have her married name on it.

As she walked through the home, she envisioned how it would look after it was finished. "Oh, Tom, can we refinish the floors downstairs right away so I can begin furnishing it?"

"Absolutely, the contractor and his workers can come and go through the back door. And we'll put something across the butler's door to the kitchen so they can't go into the dining room. I'll speak to the contractor about getting one of his workers on that right away. And I'll also tell him to put a coat of polyurethane on the baseboards, windows, and fireplace and mantel. But it will need a good cleaning first, so do you think you could do that?"

"Absolutely, but I'll need a ladder to reach the tops of the windows."

"I'll bring one over for you."

"What do you think about the upstairs?"

"Let's let that go. We'll mostly use the downstairs until…until you know, we have children."

"But you know I have enough money to at least get the floors and woodwork done. Then we can finish the rest later if you want. But I'm of the opinion that we need to finish it soon. You know if you should get pregnant, we'll need a nursery, and I doubt if you'll want to use our bedroom downstairs with a baby upstairs, so we could use the large bedroom that includes the turret and make the closest bedroom a nursery."

"Oh, that's a great idea. I like that. Yes, let's do it. Whatever you want to do."

With that concluded, they headed back to the Wilshire's. Tom took the ladder to the house, while Izzy followed with her car loaded with cleaning supplies. She worked the rest of the day on cleaning and knew there would probably be questions that evening from others, and she'd have to be ready with answers.

There was a wedding coming up, so she would use that as the excuse for why she had been gone all day.

Sure enough, Erin asked that evening where Izzy had gone all day. "I was shopping, getting ideas for my wedding."

"But you didn't buy anything evidently. I didn't see any packages when you came home."

"No, but I'll go looking again tomorrow."

Lottie piped up with, "I can go with you if you'd like."

"No," Izzy wanted the conversation to end. She had to think fast for a reason she didn't want Lottie to go. "I'd like to make my own decisions without any input from anyone else trying to persuade me otherwise."

Lottie added, "You've always been so different from Aiden and me. Have it your way."

"Speaking of being different," Izzy continued. "Miriam, Tom and I have thought we'd like to get married on your patio if that's alright with you. We don't want to invite anyone else but you guys."

"That's fine with me, if that's what you really want."

"But why?" Erin asked. "Why not invite others."

Izzy stole a glance at Tom before answering. "Well, I haven't gone to school and gotten close to anyone really, and Tom doesn't want to invite any of his old friends from his teenage days. And I think you know why. And since his grandparents are no longer alive, well, there's just no one else we want to share that day with."

Everyone could understand their decision and that ended the conversation.

Miriam said, "If that's the case, I can make a nice meal for us for after the wedding."

Tom answered, "Izzy and I will talk about that."

Tom walked Izzy to the car and after making sure no one was around, said, "So what do we do to stop Miriam from cooking a meal after our wedding?"

"I don't know. Let me think about that. I'll see you later, I'm on my way to *our* house."

"I like the sound of that, *our* house." He then pulled her into his embrace, he ran a thumb across her lips, so soft, so inviting. He lowered his lips to hers, "I can't wait to marry you," he said. "I hope the contractor works at lightning speed, because as soon as he's finished, we're getting married."

She smiled up at him then, got in the car and left, with everyone thinking she was going shopping.

She made a trip to the store to purchase their own cleaning supplies so she wouldn't have to sneak them out of the house in the future. As she worked inside the home, her mind was ablaze with ideas for this or that. She decided on floor length drapes and wondered if they'd have to be custom made or if she could find the right length online. She imagined the furniture she wanted and where each piece should be placed. She thought about a large area rug, and smaller rugs to match. She thought about where they might put a TV. She wanted it to be mounted on the wall and decided she would talk to Tom about that. Her idea was to mount it in the sitting room, or rather the parlor. She could turn it into their TV room, with a cozy couch with plenty of throw pillows. She cleaned until she finished the entry room, living room and dining room. Next, she wanted to tackle the parlor, library, and master bedroom. Lastly, she would clean the bedroom up the stairs that had the turret. Then she changed her mind, wanting to clean it all.

When she returned home, she found Tom and let him know how much she had accomplished. The also let him know she wanted to clean the other rooms while she was at it, and he told her he would take a couple of days off to help her. She smiled at that and thanked him. After a couple of hugs and kisses, he told her to get lost because he would need to get more done today if he planned to take tomorrow off.

The next day they both headed out together. It seemed things were completed much faster. Izzy was amazed at how fast Tom could clean. She decided to tease him a little. She said, "You know, Tom, as fast as you can clean, I think I'll just turn that job over to you after we're married." She had a smile on her face.

He came down off his ladder where he'd been cleaning the carvings on the header over the archway between the living room and dining room, and said, "Not on your life, little girl." He then chased her around until he caught her upstairs in one of the bedrooms. He grabbed her and pulled her to him, holding her tightly. He looked deeply into her eyes, and she into his. They held the gaze for a while, just relishing the moments together. He kissed her lips over and over, then her cheek, and lowered to her neck.

She pushed him away, "We can't do that. Not yet. Let's get back to work. There's too much to still do."

"You take away all the fun," he said as he lowered his arms in defeat.

They went back downstairs, and before the day was through, they had completed the remainder of the rooms downstairs, and the banister all the way to the third floor.

72

The next day, they completed the entire second level, and Izzy and Tom went downstairs and admired their work. He left the ladder inside the upstairs so it would be handy for whatever next project they needed it for. He was happy that he'd kept his grandfather's ladders. He decided he needed to bring the remainder of the tools he had kept in store into one of the sheds on the property. And he purchased a padlock to lock the shed up.

It was soon that the contractor got two guys busy adding polyurethane to all the woodwork downstairs. There were three guys who got busy ripping out the old kitchen. They piled the old cabinets where Tom indicated so they could be burned. Then after Tom thought about it, he changed his mind, and decided to put the cabinets in the shed with his tools so he'd have a workbench and someplace to store tools. But he let the workers know he would take care of that himself.

After two days all the woodwork was finished, and dried. Tom marveled at how fast they worked and how polished everything looked. He brought Izzy one evening to look at it all. She went directly into the parlor, and asked Tom what he thought about making this room their TV room. He thought about it a few minutes, walked back into the living room and looked around the walls there. Then he went back into the sitting room.

"I think you're right. There are way too many windows in the living room."

"Plus, I was thinking about turning the living room into a receiving room for guests. I know the sitting room was used for that in times gone by, but I believe when we have our family all over, that room would be too small. But we have plenty of room for everyone in the living room. Plus, you could have a booze cabinet in it so you could serve drinks."

"Yes, I like that idea."

"Question: When can I begin ordering furniture for the downstairs?"

"You want to order furniture? You mean online or from stores?"

"Well, I was thinking about furnishing the living room with time period furniture."

"Time period?"

"Yes, like the time period that the house was built. Victorian style."

He put his arm around her waist, pulled her close and looked down at her, "Whatever you want, my dear."

She smiled up at him and couldn't wait to get busy. "I want you to also let me know what you want, you know. This isn't just my home."

"I trust you'll do a fantastic job, and I know I'll be happy with whatever you decide. So, here's my credit card. Order away."

She let him know she needed to take a few measurements first. Therefore, Tom went to the shed to get a tape measure, brought the stepladder downstairs, and began measuring the windows. She also had him measure the length and depth of each room downstairs.

When she got home that evening, with pencil and paper, she began to sketch the first floor out, then she went online to search for just the right furniture. She ordered several things to be delivered to the house and tracked the shipping so she would be at the house when things began to arrive.

One morning, at the breakfast table, Lottie said, "You sure are busy. What have you been up to?"

Erin quit eating to look at Izzy for the answer. She decided to just tell them the truth. "Tom and I have found a place to live, and we've been busy cleaning it. He doesn't want me to live in the loft bedroom."

"Why didn't you say anything," Lottie said, "we would have helped you?"

"No, we want it to be a surprise for you all. We don't want to show it to you until after we're married."

"Ok, if you insist. I know this is a big deal for you two," Lottie replied. "Still if you need help, just let us know."

"I sure will, and thanks." She had no intention of asking them for help.

"And just so you know," Erin put in. "We know Tom doesn't have much money, so we're all pooling our money to give you and Tom a nice wedding present of a honeymoon."

Izzy had to hide her smile with her napkin, pretending to wipe her mouth. "Thank you all. I'm sure Tom will appreciate that."

Tom laughed out loud when she told him about their wedding present from the family. "And now that I know," he said, "I want to go ahead and furnish the rest of the house now, complete with nursery and child rooms complete with furniture and everything. Let's even get some toys to make one of the rooms a playroom."

She giggled. "Let's do it. Won't they be surprised."

Tom let the contractor know the upstairs rooms were also ready to have polyurethane on all the floors and woodwork. It was completed within a week, and Tom went to inspect everything after it was dried. He went inside the back door to see how the kitchen was coming along. He was surprised to see all the cabinets had been installed, new lights installed, and the island built. The counter tops needed to be installed yet, along with the stovetop, wall ovens, and refrigerator. They had been ordered, he was told, and as soon as they were delivered, they'd be installed. In the meantime, the long windows were in the process of being installed, the chair rail and wanes coating were in the process of being added. Then the cabinets and chair rail and wanes coating would be stained and finished. Tom asked them to clean the window frames and put a coat of polyurethane on them as well, and after everything was installed could they also put a coat on the wood flooring.

The workers let Tom know that they expected the appliances to all be delivered in a week or two. Tom gave that information to Izzy.

"I'd better get really busy ordering furniture then." Izzy had searched and found a website called EverythingVictorian.com. Things began to be delivered to the house, and Izzy was busy telling the delivery guys where she wanted everything placed in the home. She had even been able to find draperies in a beautiful gold color that were long enough to more than reach the floor. They had a gathered valance to match, and she hired the workers to install them. Things were coming together soon and with each thing accomplished, Izzy would stand back to admire it. She took Tom regularly in the evenings to take a look also.

Within six weeks everything was completed at the house, even furniture on the front porch. She bought a round table and four chairs for the rounded corner, and wicker chairs scattered along the remainder of the porch.

Izzy had ordered her wedding dress. She had chosen a knee length white spaghetti strap dress, with another lace dress to wear over it. She chose a small round white pillbox with a short veil to wear. She ordered flowers and chose the menu for the caterers Miriam had used for the previous weddings. Tom had long tables brought in and placed on the third floor, hired a band to play, and soon it was time for the wedding. Tom and Izzy decided to go ahead and allow Miriam to cook a meal, they would simply load the food into their cars and take it to their house to add to what the caterer's had brought.

The wedding turned out beautifully, lights strung and lit all around the patio. Extra chairs were set up for everyone. Even though Cody was back in school, he was invited to the wedding as well since he seemed to be part of the family now.

Aiden waited in the living room, and Izzy surprised him that she was not wearing a floor length dress. "You look lovely and so practical. I didn't think you'd choose that kind of dress though."

"I wanted a dress I could wear more than once, without the veil, of course."

Aiden smiled, held his elbow out for Izzy to take, and they headed to the patio.

The music began, and Aiden led Izzy to the preacher who had been hired and handed her off to Tom who was beaming like the cat that just caught the mouse. Everyone was smiling. How wonderful Izzy looked, and Tom in his tux. The ceremony was soon over. Tom kissed his bride, and Mr. and Mrs. Tuttle were introduced to everyone. Everyone clapped and Miriam rose to go inside.

Tom caught her before she left the patio and asked her to stay. "I have an announcement everyone. I'd like everyone to follow us to Izzy and my new house we've bought."

"But the food will be cold by the time we get back," Miriam complained.

"Let's load it up and take it with us. We can eat it there," Tom replied.

"Are you sure?" she asked."

"Positively. It will be fine. Trust me."

Aiden and Dane loaded all the food into the back seat of a truck, then everyone piled into different vehicles and Tom instructed them to follow him. He made sure Miriam got into the 1967 Chevy he had inherited, to which she was excited about. Soon there was a line of vehicles headed down the road, farther away from Tupelo, but just three miles away from the Wilshire home.

When Tom pulled into the drive of their home, others pulled in behind him, and as everyone got out, their faces were astonished, shocked. Everyone just stood staring at the beautiful stone three story Victorian home with the turret on the left and large wrap around porch on the right.

Dane was the first to speak, "Tom, how could you do this?"

Miriam replied, "This is the Watson home. Are you two renting this?"

Everyone advanced to where Tom was standing, "No, we bought it."

Aiden replied, "You what?!" he gasped.

"We bought it. Won't you all come in?" Tom held out his arm to direct them toward the freshly stained and finished front door.

They left the food where it was in the truck, too shocked to even consider it, and followed Tom and Izzy into the home. The girls, all three, Miriam, Lottie, and Erin, gasped. Everyone advanced slowly through the entry room and into the hallway, looking around at the beautifully decorated home in Victorian style. Izzy couldn't help but smile. She thought her face would crack, she was so happy and excited.

She led them into the living room. The drapes were so long they puddled onto the floor. There was a gold and red Victorian couch between the windows with marble top end tables and coffee table. There were two gold chairs on either side of the end tables. There were also two red chairs with wooden backs, arms, and legs on either side of the fireplace angled toward the middle of the room. The large rug was red with splashes of gold and black in a pleasing Victorian pattern. Everyone oohed and ahead at the carvings of wood on the archway separating the living room and dining room, as well as the pillars on each side of the archway.

There was a bar at one corner of the living room, and Tom advanced to it to fix drinks for everyone. After everyone had drinks in their hand, Tom continued to lead everyone through to the dining room, but realized Miriam was left standing in the living room. She stood staring at everything, unbelieving this was at all possible. How could Tom have this much money? Tom noticed Miriam was lagging behind, so he stopped to wait for her to catch up.

"Miriam, are you coming?" he asked.

"Oh, uh…yes. Sorry."

She entered the dining room and again was shocked. Here was a large table with twelve chairs around it. The curved outer wall with the bench built under the windows sported padded cushions to match the gold silk drapes in both the living room and dining room. The chandelier over the table was lit, like all the other lights though out the house, spread dazzling multi-colored spots on the walls because of the prisms.

Tom continued to the Kitchen, and not only did Miriam stare she gasped. She went around the Island looking at everything. She ran her fingers over the granite counters. Her eyes met Izzy's and she noticed the smile on Miriam's face. "Can I come and cook in your kitchen?" Miriam asked.

Izzy laughed and said, "I knew you'd like the kitchen."

"Like it? I love it. I'm just speechless."

"Come on, I'll show you the rest of the house." She led Miriam back to the dining room, opened the door to the library. Although they didn't have books on the shelves yet, there was a desk and desk chair in the room. She explained that eventually she planned to add two overstuffed chairs for reading in the room. She opened the door on the right side of the room and led them all into the master suite.

Lottie spoke up, "Izzy, this is gorgeous. Absolutely gorgeous." The white curtains were tied back, and the bedspread was white with little touches of pastel pink. Two pink throw pillows were added to the bed. A large pink and white throw rug by the bed, and pink side chairs at one side of the room with a Victorian looking side table between them. A large chest of drawers with a marble top was in one corner.

They were led out a second door leading to the dining room, and through to the parlor room in the turret at the front of the house. The room Izzy and Tom turned into the TV room. They loved the Cobalt blue and cream couch with all the throw pillows on it, and side chairs that matched. There was a large round rug in the middle of the room. And Tom had hung the TV on the wall, just like Izzy wanted.

Then they headed upstairs, and everyone loved the first two rooms they saw. One decorated as a child's room, another was the toy room. The third they came to was to be the nursery. Lottie looked at Izzy and said, "You're planning on a baby soon?"

"No," Izzy replied. "But we have it ready for whenever. And when we have one, we'll use this bedroom," she stated as she led them into the bedroom that sported the turret at the corner.

"It looks like you've thought of everything," Dane said.

"We tried."

Tom broke in, "Now let's go upstairs. They headed up to the third level, and there was the band and caterers, ready to show everyone a good time. Once more, everyone just stared at the tables, band, and food along one side of the room. Tom got Aiden to help him bring in the food Miriam had prepared, and Dane offered to also help.

As the guys headed down the stairs, Dane couldn't help but ask, "Tom, how can you afford all of this?"

"Trust me, I can."

Dane was so curious about that and wanted to ask how much he actually inherited, but he knew that would be inappropriate to ask. But he and Aiden looked at each other with eyebrows arched in shock.

Aiden said, "And I think I saw a barn out back as well."

Tom replied, "Along with two-hundred acres." Again, Dane and Aiden turned to look at each other. Tom couldn't help but laugh. "But," he added, "I didn't just buy this property, I stole it."

"What do you mean, you stole it?" Aiden asked.

"I offered such a low price, I just knew it wouldn't be accepted, but it was. Of course, there was a few things needing to be updated, but it all came together just as Izzy and I planned. And because I wasn't sure Izzy would want a house like this, I brought her to see it before we were married, and she fell in love with it immediately, as I did.

"And since the property already had a home, barn, and plenty of property, I didn't have to try to find land to build on. It just all seemed to fall into place. And now that I have this house with a party room upstairs, we'll have plenty of room for our parties besides Miriam's patio. So, boys, let's go party."

Soon everyone was seated at small tables dotted around the ballroom, plates full with plenty of food, and drinks. "Wait," declared Tom. "I think this calls for more than iced tea and lemonade. I see you've all finished your drinks." He then went to the service table, reached under the tablecloth and came out with some champaign he'd brought. He popped the corks on several bottles, and brought a glass to everyone in the room, including the band and two women at the serving table.

Everyone was so happy. And eventually Dane was able to get Tom off to the side of the room where he lowered his voice and asked, "Tom, how in the world? I just have to ask because I thought your grandparents were poor."

Tom laughed and said, "Grandma and grandpa. Seems they saved every dime they made. I thought they were poor too, but they weren't. Believe me I was as shocked as you all when I found out how much they had."

Tom went on, "And there's a farmer who rents some of the land and has planted cotton on it right now. But there's still plenty of land for cattle. I've got a contract with him to continue to farm the land for me until I decide I no longer need him."

Dane put a hand on Tom's shoulder and said, "Tom, you have no idea how happy I am for you and for Izzy. I'm so proud of you. You've really made something of yourself."

"Thanks, Dane. That means a lot to me. No, that means everything to me. But I don't think I did anything to make something of myself, I think my grandparents set me up for a wonderful life, and I'm just so happy Izzy has agreed to share it with me."

"To tell you the truth, when I first met you, I wouldn't have bet that you'd end up this successful."

"Back then, even I wouldn't have bet that I would have ended up being this successful. And Dane, I want all of you to keep your money for our honeymoon. I really don't need it."

"Uh, that's something I'll have to discuss with the others. We want to give you two a wedding present and we all agreed that was going to be our gift. So, I'll have to let you know about that, but for now, please take this and hold onto it until I let you know what we decide." With that he withdrew an envelope from his jacket pocket and handed it to Tom. "Guess I'll have to find someone else now to move into the loft bedroom. You got married and Cody's off to college."

Tom laughed, he felt so happy, and was about to burst with pride. To have Dane say he was proud of him was about the best thing he'd heard anyone say to him, about him, except his grandmother. She obviously saw Tom's heart was good after all. Something he didn't think anyone else really saw, except maybe the Wilshire family and Roberts family.

Izzy came up to Tom, and his arm slid around her waist. Dane said to her, "Izzy, I'd say you've done well. I'm glad I won't have to worry about you two. But if I should ever need any money, I'll come looking for you."

Tom and Izzy laughed.

The band had been playing soft dinner music while they ate, but afterward they struck up dance music, and soon all the tables were moved to the sides of the room and everyone took to the floor. Tom was dancing with Izzy of course, but Lottie told Dane to go dance with his mother while she watched little Daniel. She smiled at how everything had turned out for her, Aiden and Izzy. She contemplated how it seemed so long ago now that they'd lived in the cabin. Their life had been hard then, and very sad, but God had been good to them. He took care of them better than she could ever have imagined.

She began to ponder over the house Tom and Izzy had purchased and wondered how long it would be before little Daniel would have a playmate. Evidently, Tom and Izzy had both agreed that they wanted children. They seemed well prepared ahead of time for one. She hoped it wouldn't be too far down the road. She wanted Daniel to have cousins to grow up with.

Aiden eventually asked Izzy to dance, and he looked down at her as he moved her around the floor. "Izzy, what can I say? I'm so very proud of you. It seems you've come out on top of all three of us." She was blushing. He went on, "I remember when we said Erin could have Dane, and I could marry Erin, and you'd be the odd man out, and we'd have to find someone for you. Well, you found your someone."

"Oh, Aiden, I think it's all wonderful now. I'm happier than I ever thought I could be."

"I'm very happy for you. But tell me, how is it you and Tom were able to financially afford this place?"

"His inheritance from his grandparents."

"But I thought they were poor people."

"So did Tom, until they died. He was shocked that they had so much financially. It seems they had a lot in the bank, and in investments as well. I'll tell you a secret if you don't tell Tom I told you."

Aiden leaned down to hear her. She went on in a whisper, "He's a multi-millionaire."

Aiden's eyes widened in shock and a gasp escaped his lips before he even realized it. Questions ran through his mind about Tom's grandparents about why they would have a lot of cash but live in such a rundown house needing so many repairs. And here he'd helped repair their roof for them, put a new floor down in their living room, and was ready to remodel their kitchen. For millionaires! Even multi-millionaires! And they had allowed Tom to foot the bill for the repairs they had done to the home. Life was perplexing. How could you understand that kind of thinking? Why? Perhaps Tom's grandparents allowed him to do those repairs because they knew it was important to Tom and it could show them that he had changed. So maybe it was a good thing for Tom to do, not just for them but for himself. He was so happy at the way Tom and turned out. He was very happy for Izzy *and* for Tom. He said, "Well, it looks like I'll never have to worry about you and Tom. That's a relief. I doubt I'll have to worry about Lottie either. Looks like I'm the only one to worry about. Guess I won't grow old fast after all, like I thought if you or Lottie didn't marry well."

Izzy laughed. "You just take care of that lovely wife, and don't worry about the rest of us. We'll all be fine, even you. Haven't we turned out alright?"

"That we have, little sister."

"But tell me, what are your plans for the future, Aiden? Do you plan to eventually get cattle of your own, or stay working for the Wilshire's?"

"Honestly, I haven't thought that far ahead. I admit I am very happy at the Wilshire's. Dane is great to work for as his right arm man. And he treats me more like a brother than just a righthand man. We make decisions together, except for feeding the cattle beer."

Izzy laughed. "That really sounds ludicrous, doesn't it? Tell me, is it working?"

"No idea. That's his project, so he's tracking the results. Guess time will tell. But I'll tell you one thing, I would never leave Dane in the lurch with no hands to help him run his place." Izzy smiled, because she knew Aiden well enough to know he'd never do that.

Miriam sat on the sidelines, holding little Daniel. As she looked down into his eyes, she saw her husband looking back at her. She was sad that he wasn't here to see how wonderful their family had turned out, all of them, even their foster children and Tom. She would have loved to sit back with him in their old age and watch the grandchildren grow up and just relax after a life of hard work. Yet, she was so happy. She felt she'd had a good life, and was looking forward to watching her family grow, and just enjoy them.

Soon Lottie came to Miriam with Erin at her side. She said, "We want to go through the house again, do you want to come with us?"

She agreed, and Lottie took little Daniel from Miriam, and put him in Dane's arms. She smiled as she saw Dane dancing with Daniel in his arms as she headed to the stairs.

Miriam said as they descended the stairway, "I want to have another look at that kitchen." The girls laughed and weren't surprised at all about that.

When they came to the bedroom with the turret on the second floor, Erin said to Lottie, "If you and Dane have a squabble, you could always come and stay here for a while."

Lottie laughed, "And I could say the same for you if Aiden ever makes you mad as a hornet."

"Come on girls," Miriam said, "let's go downstairs."

Erin said, "She's about to bust a gut before getting to that kitchen."

Miriam continued, "I want ideas for the new kitchen Dane's going to do for me." They all laughed at that, not at all surprised that Miriam would want a new kitchen.

The girls eventually came back upstairs, and as they did, Miriam said, "I'm glad they're young. Very much of these stairs would do me in, I think."

When they got to the third floor, the guys were back picking and munching on things on the buffet table. Dane was spooning mashed potatoes into Daniel's mouth. "Glad you're back," he said, Daniel needs changing, and he's rubbing his eyes. I think he's partied enough. We should probably head home."

Izzy overheard their conversation, and let Lottie know she could use the changing table in the nursery to change Daniel, and if they wanted to stay a while longer, they could put Daniel in the crib in the nursery. They took her up on that and stayed to dance longer. No one wanted to leave, even though Tom was anxious to get Izzy alone.

Eventually everyone began to head to the stairs. The band had just left. The caterers had cleaned up everything, leaving Miriam's dishes on the serving table for her before they left, and Dane gathered the empty dishes.

Everyone thanked Tom and Izzy for a wonderful evening at the front door, and especially for the surprise of having their reception at their own lovely home that everyone had fallen in love with, and Tom and Izzy thanked all of them for a beautiful wedding and for sharing it with them.

Before leaving, Lottie stopped took Izzy's arm, and said, "From now on, all of our family gatherings will be at your house, so prepare yourself."

"That's why I have such a large table in the dining room. I had hoped to entertain all of you for as long as we live. And we can always party on the third floor. Oh, Lottie, I'm so happy, and to think I can finally stop worrying about all of us."

Lottie hugged her tightly and held her for a long time. When they pulled apart, Lottie had tears in her eyes, and Izzy couldn't help but notice. She felt tears sting her eyes also, and she blinked them back. Aiden was next in line to give her a tight squeeze. He hugged Tom as well and told him how proud he was of him and happy for them both. Tom tucked his reply deep within his heart to cherish forever along with Dane's praise. Cody gave Tom a hug before leaving, saying, "Hey, man, I'm happy for you. Really happy. I only hope to be able to do what you've done. And to think. I was sure I'd marry Izzy, but she's much better off with you." He turned to smile at Izzy.

Tom replied, "Yeah, who knew back in the day things would turn out like this?"

"But I have to tell you, if you ever get tired of Izzy, just let me know. I wouldn't mind marrying a wealthy woman who could take care of me for the rest of my life."

Tom chuckled before Cody went on, "But I'm putting you on notice that if you ever hurt her, I will be waiting in the wings." Tom just smiled at him as his gaze wandered to Izzy. Her gaze was on him as well wondering what the two guys were talking about. He winked at her.

When the last of their family had finally left, Tom and Izzy stood on the porch waving until they were all out of sight. He then turned to Izzy, putting his arms around her, he looked into her eyes, reached up and played with a curl that had come down, and whispered, "Mrs. Tuttle, would you like me to show you my bedroom?"

"I'd love to see your bedroom," she whispered back.

AUTHOR'S NOTES

Even though the story begins in 2019 when COVID-19 was raging, I took the liberty of extending the end of the story to several years later into the future. Please forgive me for that, but as a writer, I figured it was allowable. I just couldn't see having the young people struggle with their lives through two years of Covid, trying to survive in the cabin in the woods. And would they be any better off at the end of just 2022?

However, I believe you will enjoy following their lives through living in the woods and coming to a better place in the end. So rejoice with each of them. And I hope you grow to love them as I have.

I'd like to thank my husband for being so patient with me while I read the entire book to him so I could repair and mend the story.

I'd also like to thank my publishers. I know they work very hard to make each publication the best it can be.

9 798890 313003